THE BRONX BOY
No More Awnings In The Bronx

by

Gerard Flynn

Any resemblance to actual persons
living or dead is purely coincidental.

FIRST EDITION

Copyright 1993, by Gerard Flynn
Library of Congress Catalog Card No: 92-91076
ISBN: 1-56002-246-9

UNIVERSITY EDITIONS, Inc.
59 Oak Lane, Spring Valley
Huntington, West Virginia 25704

Cover by Bob Burchett

This book is dedicated
to the memory of
Emma and Wilkins Micawber.

I dedicate my autobiography to Geraldine Veronica Monahan and her family

With love,

James Ignatius Murphy
JIMS

About the Character

The character of James Ignatius Murphy is best revealed in his own words of modesty: "Although I am no Keats, no Byron, no Shakespeare, my sentiment surpasses theirs and I have more to say. I know that. I take no personal credit for my superiority, after all, my vision was higher than Shakespeare's. I am one of the Gnostics. I saw the Bronx." (Chapter 6, *The Bronx Boy*.)

TABLE OF CONTENTS

1. A Prologue Explaining the Unusual Circumstances Surrounding This Autobiography With An Apology From Its Editor

In the summer of 1984 James Ignatius Murphy took a cruise with the United States Navy to South America to work in the College Afloat Program. The third week of June he traveled to Roosevelt Roads in Puerto Rico, 'Rosie Roads' he called it in one of his letters, where he stayed for a week accompanying the officers and men on maneuvers. Early July found him in Puerto La Cruz, Venezuela:

> July 5th: The bus didn't come on time so five of us took a cab to Barcelona at five dollars apiece. Peter Bruhl and I stayed together. I bought writing paper and post cards in various stationery stores, which seem to be the principal industry here. The lady at the museum was very nice and gave us the grand tour, showing us statues of saints, vestments, trunks, swords, stone grinders, books and other accoutrements of a great collection. Some of the statues were clothed. We had a good time and then more fish and beer back in Puerto La Cruz. When I went to buy ceramic tile I learned they are scarce in these parts but even so I managed to purchase four. I noticed the port was heavily guarded with barbed wire, especially the oil.

A week later he got to Cartagena, "a beautiful city" he wrote, that reminded him of Miami in 1939 when he visited his Uncle Billy. The admiral denied the ships liberty for fear of terrorism but Murphy could go ashore because he was a civilian:

> July 13th: A chief, Manuel Calomarde of the Colombian Navy, drove me to the Hotel Hilton where we had beer and ate American food. Then he took me to several places in Old Cartagena and I bought Anna a shawl; I also bought the *Odyssey* in Spanish in a stationery store. Then I returned to the base. Coming aboard ship I translated the conversation of some jewel merchants who had arrived to sell their wares to the officers and men. I taught my classes and went to bed early because we were to leave in the morning. While in port I couldn't help but notice the guards with submachine guns.

The classes he refers to were Elementary Spanish, taught to the crew by civilian instructors.

His next stop was Rodman Base in Panama, where he bought

all sorts of gifts for his family and a Panamanian souvenir made in Taiwan for me, a beautiful plaque of redwood. He really enjoyed Panama although he had an unusual experience:

> July 17th: Today Peter Bruhl and I went to Panama City, the Plaza de Francia, the church with the gold altar, the Presidencia and that area. We made a friend of Licenciado Joaquín López Alarcón who took us to his house where his mother served us a delicious cold papaya drink. Peter bought some samplers called *molas* and other handiwork from her and Alarcón's father gave me a sampler as a gift. After we left I had my pocket picked of my Venezuelan and Colombian money, right out on the street, a broad daylight, desperate stealing by a little middle-aged man who ran off; curiously Peter felt worse about it than I did. Later we went in a cab to the posher part of town. Again I noticed the barbed wire.

At the end of July he was in Esmeraldas, Ecuador, a small city he immediately took a liking to because a man gave him and five companions a lift in a pickup truck and drove them around town; he bought two more books in a stationery store and sat in the open air drinking beer. He fondly called this episode The Battle of Esmeraldas, "which we won," he said. As he returned to the dock to take a small boat out to his ship, the *USS Dempsey* FFG 982, he was struck by the heavy security around the wharves; indeed the six letters he wrote me that summer comment on the abundance of barbed wire, soldiers and submachine guns held at the hip in South America. He noticed similar precautions at the airports, which he enjoyed visiting.

The last letter I received from Jim Murphy is dated August 1st, 1984:

> 9:10 a.m. We are cruising now up the river to Guayaquil on a misty cold morning, one degree from the Equator and it is cold. Seamen McRay, Berryman and Walters have this area of the ship pretty well taped off since they are cleaning and painting in preparation for the admiral's visit, and there is to be a press conference at 10, the hour of our arrival. The river here is impressive; it seems wider than the Mississippi and I imagine it is deeper . . .

He finished his letter that same evening:

> I went into Guayaquil at 11:30 or so. At the Hotel Continental next to Bolivar Park I had baked mackerel, excellent bread and butter, two beers and the rest was good too. Later I bought watermelon three times from street vendors and still later I tried *humitas*, similar to Mexican tamales, and *maracullá*, a delicious tropical

8

drink. I went to the National Library to take a look at *Those Who Are Gone* by Enrique Gil Gilbert and those other two Ecuadorians, which includes the story of Chanchorengo the Miserable and his only friend the vulture, who protects him. I took a bus out to the airport and made a reservation for Quito, 3000 sucres round trip, that's about thirty dollars. I couldn't believe the price. I returned at 6 or so, taught a class to Tim Biddle singing Spanish songs, and at 8:30 I saw *The Flamingo Kid*, a good story about a boy and his father. Tomorrow I think I'll go in again, the next day I leave for Quito.

On August 8th Anna Murphy received a telegram from the U.S. State Department saying that her husband was missing and needless to say she was shattered. It has since been presumed he was the victim of foul play. No one has heard from Jim Murphy since, neither the government, his family nor close friends like me. He seems to have disappeared. I have checked with Peter Bruhl of the University of South Carolina, who had one or two ideas on the subject though no specific clues; he said there are two principal types of terrorists in Ecuador, the revolutionaries, and the drug dealers who have promised to take vengeance on American citizens for the interruption of their trade. He also told me that Bolivar Park in the plaza near the Continental would be a dangerous place to go after dark. His letter reads in part:

October 12, 1984: As you know, Mr. Lynch, Jim could be quite a loner. We had been advised not to enter any city by ourselves and to go in in groups of four or five, always, but at Puerto La Cruz, Rodman and Guayaquil he went in several times all alone. As a civilian he even went to Cartagena in spite of the warnings; the military of course could not go. I myself thought that Guayaquil and the airport there were dangerous and particularly dangerous the park near the Continental Hotel where I saw several men in their late twenties I didn't like the looks of (one even had a hate stare), and although it may have been safe enough during daylight hours, at dusk, well, who knows?
      It's been more than two months now. I hope that Jim is all right . . .

II.

      Just before Jim Murphy left for Roosevelt Roads he came to visit me in Brooklyn where we had taught together in the 1950's. I hadn't seen him in more than ten years so it was good to see my old friend, still his old self, effervescent, optimistic, literal and yet inclined to hyperbole, which may be the specific character of literalness, a tendency to exaggerate the particular. Jim said he was leaving a manuscript with me about himself and his native Bronx. "Will you edit it?", he asked me; he planned to pick it up on his return. He said he was satisfied with the Bronx scenes and most of the personal history but he was afraid the ensemble might read like one of those eighteenth century novels with all their digressions, inaction, didacticism and stories poorly told from over-explanation. "What do you think?", he wanted to know. He said perhaps he'd take the James Ignatius Murphy part and publish it as an autobiography and then put either a glossary of Bronx Institutions at the end, encyclopedic A to Z entries (from *Association* to *Zoo*), or publish the Institutions separately as a local color dictionary with a small firm he knew out in Colorado. Again he wanted my opinion. Now of course with Jim's disappearance I have the task of being ultimate editor for he won't be here to reflect on what I say and correct me: I shall have to make a decision and stick to it even though the original inspiration was not mine, an exceptionally difficult choice for several reasons.

First comes the problem of moderation. Jim mentions me in the text when he comes to his Brooklyn days teaching at the College of Seamus Orsini and his judgment of me is most kind. What does an ultimate editor do in such a case, omit it entirely out of alleged modesty, remove the adjectives, leave it as it is, or what? After much deliberation I have chosen *not* to alter the text on the argument that what is subjectively true for James Ignatius Murphy may or may not conform to external reality and that it is best to conserve the original idiom wherever possible; thus my editorial decision has been literary rather than ethical. Readers may call me smug for keeping allusions favorable to the editor but they cannot accuse me of poor redaction. Nor can I be accused of censorship.

The second problem arises from Jim's categorical opinions (at Seamus Orsini he was never known to sit on a fence), an example being his derogatory remarks concerning Harvard. I myself attended the Ivy League and know from experience that conditions there cannot be as bad as he says. Oh, there are lacunae to be sure but total condemnation is unthinkable: How about the collection of Serbian ballads at the Harry Elkins Widener Memorial Library? Consequently I have left only one Harvard epithet in the present pages to reveal Jim's true feelings and have omitted the others as of questionable taste. I have also reduced my friend's anaphoral references to "fatuous deans" and "braying chancellors" to one entry since in my judgment their constant repetition is detractive; the reader need only augment this one entry in his mind to receive the adequate impression.

The third problem arises from Jim's zealous reading of Kierkegaard, who always cropped up in our daily conversations thirty years ago at Seamus. He idolized that gloomy Dane, and I gather that his harsh opinion of certain clergymen is not so much his own as an imitation of his Danish paradigm; once again I have molested the text as little as possible although I have seen fit to eliminate two passages of excessive individualization. The original Murphy manuscript has been deposited at Widener Memorial should future scholars wish to check my editorial judgment. This cannot be done until thirty years after my demise.

The fourth difficulty would tax the genius of a Max Perkins: I refer to my friend's constant adulation of the Bronx, which he seems to prefer to Athens and ancient Rome. In the original manuscript he wanders back and forth telling of his days at P.S. 11, then description after description of what he calls Bronx Institutions, Candy Store, Sun Pictures, Cheesebox; then his days at All Saints High School; then more Institutions like Chewing Gum Cards, Stickball, Diamond Ball, Box Ball; then his days at the University of Rosadabrigid; then Institutions again, Tin Foil Balls, Baseball-Against-The-Wall, Anything-For-Thanksgiving; and so on and so on, alternating the Second World War with Kick-The-Can, Graduate School with Roast Mickies, his various teaching jobs with the O car trolley tracks on Ogden Avenue. Jim Murphy was my good friend, I loved the man, but I find his Bronx bias incorrigible. Consequently, in fairness to him and to those who might want to read his text I have decided on the following pattern: As ultimate editor I shall have Jim tell his life's story and allow him to interrupt himself twice in short spurts called Bronx Institutions (see Chapters 6 and 20); I shall also include a few of his expository drawings. This will leave some eighty Bronx Institutions omitted from the autobiography, for which I have made a provision; they will appear in a glossary at the end of the book in addition to the scholarly note to Chapter 4 that Jim insisted I retain the last day I spoke to him prior to his departure for Roosevelt Roads. I have also included in Chapter 24 his additional sentimental verses dedicated to Joey Bacigalupi, Halvah and Ringalevio; the first twenty-four verses appear in Chapter 6, where I suspect that the aposiopesis in the last line is not so much aesthetic as an inability on Jim's part to write any more stanzas with spontaneity, for although Jim was exceptionally articulate he was not celebrated for his versification. (I must say parenthetically that his acute stress on *maltèd* is questionable although his Bronx friends Segal, Bacigalupi and Kelly may have spoken that way. He also writes *Spaulding* whereas the famous sports concern of that appellation has always stressed the penult.)

The fifth difficulty concerns Jim's peculiar use of *you*, which lies somewhere between the French *on*, Spanish reflexive, English impersonal *you* and simply a speaking out loud as if he were addressing either someone who is not there or a personalized manuscript. I know that at Seamus Jim used to speak to himself all the time and on the El train one day I saw him stage a veritable one man dialogue; this *you* of the manuscript is rather like that. Wherever possible I have changed this pronoun to an I, and *your* to *my* in order to objectify his conjectures but sometimes I couldn't manage this transposition and have simply left the *you*. In other words I have done my best to make the text as uniform as possible so it will sound the same throughout; occasionally, however, the monologuist James Ignatius Murphy will peep through.

My final problem: I have reservations about Chapter 22, which strikes me as neurasthenic rather than joyous, not the work of the happy and jocular J.I.M. I used to know. I see it as far too kinetic. I said before that when Jim came to visit me he was his old self, effervescent, optimistic, literal, which is true, but I neglected to say there was also an I-don't-know-what about him, a certain nostalgia, a flight of memory, a hint of gloom. Perhaps he was suffering some crisis as he faced old age, one symptom being his manuscript's comparison of Bronx boys skating in echelon down Plimpton Avenue with Napoleon's legions. I find this image excessive, an adumbration perhaps of senility. One can never be sure of these things, and who knows, it may have had something to do with his disappearance. Be that as it may I am leaving this chapter intact since it is vitally accurate, an authentic account of my friend's state of mind in 1984, before he visited the Navy.

De mortuis nil nisi bonum. But then we are not sure that Jim is dead. I myself prefer not to think so. I doubt it; some of his optimism has rubbed off. Whatever his fate I do not mean to speak ill of my friend though at times I appear to do so; I only want to do the editing that he himself requested. The James Ignatius Murphy I knew was honest, loyal, bright, courageous, kind; he could also be abrasive, imprudent, and as I recall him at Seamus in the fifties a loner who joked about things not jokeable. I didn't always take these jokes at face value since I sensed beneath them the *gravitas* of an authentic human being. Jim's actions required a higher criticism. Here in his own words is his story.

—Arturo Lynch
Department of English
Seamus Orsini College
Brooklyn, New York
December 1, 1986

12

2. Lauds

I think of the Bronx, I think of golden days of yore, of
Kelly, Bacigalupi and Segal, Denny, Big Phelan and Billy who
died in the war; of the O and U and Z, swaying cars moving in
rhythm; of P.S. 11, Mrs. Kavidson, Adrienne; Vannie, Macombs
and the Harlem; the El, Menasha Skulnik signs; the Sacred Heart
Bazaar; Mary Janes, Loosies, Gowdy Gum cards; sun pictures,
cheesebox and orange crate; tin foil balls, tops, horse manure
balls; "the parkie's coming," "cheese it, the cops"; Sedgwick and
Unie, Undy and Concourse; anything-for-Thanksgiving and
baseball-against-the-wall. I think of the Bronx and I say: I have
seen the Elysian Fields, more than that, I have lived there. I
know. Mount Parnassus, Arcadia, Plato's sun, they are real. I
have been there. Bacigalupi never lied to me nor I to him, how
could we? What would we lie for? Kelly never stole from me nor
I from him, what would we steal? You won immies, you didn't
steal them. And Segal never gossiped about me nor I about him,
what would we gossip about? His sun pictures were as good as
mine. The only talk I ever heard was of Jackie Smealy, the time
he threw manure at Phelan, but that wasn't gossip, that was fear.
Real fear. Everyone's afraid of horse manure balls. No, I have
been there. I don't believe. I know. Saint Paul says that hope and
faith will pass away but never love, that love will always be
there and he's right because he must have seen it too, in a vision,
the Bronx, Paul of Tarsus he saw the Bronx. You didn't have to
believe, you saw it with your own eyes, Candy Store. You didn't
have to hope, you knew the orange crates would be there,
diamond ball, lots and mickies. They always were, you could take
them for granted. Love was everywhere, we all loved cheesebox,
stickball and P.S. 11, we all did, yes I have seen the Elysian
Fields, I have lived there, the Bronx 1930 when I was a boy, the
Vanished Arcadia, you can take my word for it, we never lied in
the Bronx.

3. Matins

Where does the Bronx Boy start? I am tempted to start with
Candy Store, the most important institution, but I shall resist and
cite the earliest thing I remember. And what is that? Have you
ever tried to recall your oldest memory? It isn't all that easy. Oh
there was a little boy and his name was tiny tucoo.
I myself have three early memories vying for first in the
mnemonic race but I believe this is the absolute first: I am lying
in a room on a warm, light evening, looking out at the
whitewashed wall of the courtyard. All is silent. I am crying.
Don't they know I want them? Can't they hear me? Why don't
they come? They never come. From this I gather I was a one
year old narcissus feeling sorry for himself or that my mother
was one of those Victorian ladies who believed man was made
for the law not the other way around. I suspect that both answers
are correct; my mother was a great law-giver even in the face of
tears and I have always been very fond of myself. This was the
year 1925 at 1245 University Avenue, The Bronx, New York, or
perhaps it was over in 1200, where my family lived briefly. The
important thing to remember in the Bronx was that you were
1225 (Denny); 1245, 1239 and later 1235 (me); 1257 (Big Phelan
and Smealy); 1220, which we called The House of All Nations
(Segal and Bacigalupi), and so forth. And you said you lived at
1235 Unie, the diminutive for University. As I lay there crying
they didn't come, and I haven't forgotten.
The second event, going way back, is my father, my mother,
my brother and I in the back room, the living room of our
apartment, which faced on the roofs of the apartment buildings
below on Undy. The West Bronx in Highbridge is a cliff carved
out of rock by the mighty Harlem millions of years ago and you
descend from Unie to Undercliff to Sedgwick Avenue, the park,
railroad tracks and river; and so we looked down on the
apartments below. The man in the room, my father, is frustrated,
not angry, but absolutely frustrated, anguished, and he has struck
either my brother or me, I am not sure, and one of us is under
the table. I have a feeling it must be me for the bottom of the
table top looms like a roof over my head, but it may have been
my brother, ten years, one month and twenty-one days older
than I, who had been asked to take me out and didn't do so. I
gather this was the cause of the commotion but whatever the
cause I know I was crying again with no apparent sympathy. This
must be 1926 and though I'm not certain of the metaphysics I
remember the phenomenon clearly. As I say I didn't sense anger
only deep-seated anguish. I must have inherited some of this
distress because I remember a few years later making balsa wood
fighter planes and I'd smash them in despair if the wings didn't
glue on just right. I can still smell the banana glue.
The third event is about as old as the second and it has to do

with rickets, alleged rickets or fear of rickets, I'm not certain. I remember someone forcing my legs into metal braces with leather straps on them and I was resisting with all my strength and again I was crying and screaming. I lost the battle so I assume my mother was doing the forcing for had it been my father I am sure he would have desisted, at least the father I later remembered would have done so. I believe my rickets interpretation is correct because all my early life my mother was always feeding me nutritious foods especially bonebuilders. I must have had scrambled eggs every day for lunch until the third or fourth grade at P.S. 11 when one day I got sick and threw them up I just couldn't take them any more. But I always had lettuce, tomatoes, carrots, potatoes, red meat, chicken, fish; hot cereal for breakfast; heavy cream—a quart bottle of Bordens was always in the ice box—butter, custard, rice pudding, tapioca, apple pie, home cooked fruits like prunes and apricots, and vegetable soup when I was a child, and never starchy, fancy foods or what they call junk food today and idle calories. I never ate between meals and I never had anything like pretzels, potato chips, oreos, nabiscos, marshmallows and other tasty, valueless items, never, ever. I even remember taking half a head of lettuce and a tomato to high school in my lunch bag and eating them as others would an apple. And no money for Plantation Pies either!

My mother's counter-rickets campaign has had three effects on my life: (1) I grew to be six feet two inches, the maximum for someone with my genes. (2) I occasionally get a severe cramp in my right foot, which I attribute to the brace-forcing episode sixty years ago. I remember in my high school days when I used to go ice skating in Van Cortlandt and all of a sudden my foot would twitch and I'd have to throw myself on the ice to remove the shoe and massage the foot. I still get the cramp twice a year or so usually in the middle of the night when I'm dreaming and I have to get up quickly and walk about the floor to get rid of it. I don't know where the braces are now but I recall seeing them after the war in the closet; my war is World War II so I am talking of 1225 Unie as late as 1950, but I haven't seen them since. (3) I am still very conscious of food and eat very little junk food although I do eat some and whenever I go out to eat I usually have beer and a pizza, the pablum of fat Sicilians. Perhaps we can call this comestible adventure the Victorian Compromise.

The mind is a well that once you start to tap it keeps sending up water. Someone told me that a long time ago, my friend Bobbie O'Brien from All Saints, and it's so very true because other events come to mind now. I recall one trip on my tricycle, maroon it was, from Unie down to Undy on the hill past the two small oval parks on Boscobel Place. It was quite steep and when I took my feet off the pedals to see what would happen the wheels took off making the pedals fly and I couldn't get my feet back on to slow them so I went right past the red iron fire box on the corner of Boscobel and Undy into the cobblestone street and as you might expect I was crying again, head over heels in the gutter, all shaken up and scared beyond imagination. I have since been very careful about two and three-wheeled vehicles although in the four-wheeled kind I have been known to glide through STOP. I must have been three or four when I took off on this tricycle flight to Undy.

The next experience served up by my bottomless well took place in November 1928 and if I got out an old calendar I could pin it to one of two days, a Tuesday or a Wednesday. I heard my father say: "A Catholic can't be president." I think my father's statement may have been wrong or both right and wrong depending on how you look at it. A Catholic couldn't be president in 1928 on the Democratic ticket but he might have made it in 1932 though not by President Roosevelt's margin. In any case my father's words throw a great deal of light on American politics; he always told me to say *a great deal of*, Jims, and not *a lot of*, it is not good English he said.

Al Smith didn't even carry his own state. The wonder man of the Lower East Side, the dese, dose and dem boy, Manhattan Prince, Mr. New York, East Side West Side all around the town, when Irish eyes are smiling, didn't carry his own state. He must have had a great deal of the ethnic vote in Buffalo, Rochester, Syracuse, Binghamton, and New York so where were the others? Smith's politics were correct and had they delivered the vote he would have carried New York so where were the others? . . . I have written extensively about this in my original draft but I think I'll just plain scotch it now. What's the sense of going over it? What's the use? I think Bobbie O'Brien had the best thing to say I ever heard; he said it's a good thing Al Smith wasn't elected or we would have had a Catholic Depression. So where were the others?

What next? Oh yes, three more buckets from the well and then I'll close this chapter of my life, proceeding to other subjects such as family, Bronx Institutions, church, P.S. 11 and high school until the war. For someone my age there is only one war, after 1941, The Watershed of History.

I look at a scar halfway down my shin and remember 1225 on Unie, Denny's house, with the long green awning over the iron pipe to the curb (there are no more awnings in the Bronx). The landlord's name was Mr. Dexter and we used to yell "Mr. Dexter, Belly Bexter" and run, and this tall, thin, stern-faced, unhappy looking human being with the red complexion and brown eyes used to get angry or feign anger and . . . well he never chased us very far so he must have been too old or too decent to do so, probably the latter. But he did not radiate joy. Well one day I went to the back of 1225, to the lots above Undy and the long stone staircase leading down there, and in the backyard over the cement walk was a chain, put there either to prevent passage or to invite little boys to jump over. I accepted

16

the invitation and ended up crying again; to this day I have 1225's response, the scar on my left shin, six inches below the knee. I loved 1225 and Aunt Cora and Uncle Don, who were not my real aunt and uncle but close friends of the family, and Denny. 1225 Unie was the only house on our block with an awning and elevator, and years later when Kelly, Botchie, Big Phelan, Sammy and I rode it to the fifth floor to call on Denny we used to douse the lights and have a free-for-all. Someone would yell: "Reach for your balls!" Then we'd all laugh. It was very funny. And one day Denny and I were swinging on the awning's bars when the whole apparatus collapsed on us but this time I didn't cry; ten years had passed from chain to awning so I didn't cry.

Two more buckets and we change the venue which is all a chapter in a book really means, a change of venue. One day a girl named Joan and I went into the cellar at 1239 and performed an action corroborating Freud's thesis of erotic dawn, Freud's or someone else's, I am hardly a psychoanalyst. We went into the cellar, giggled, pulled down our pants and looked at each other's go-go, which some people call wee-wees. After that the curtain is drawn for another ten years. This must have been 1930. I believe that all love should be like that, two innocent people, a boy and a girl, in complete privacy, a shaded wood, an oasis, a quiet barn, a New York cellar, all by themselves, enjoying each other's naked presence, looking at each other's go-go and giggling. It must have been like that before Adam and Eve had to go and spoil everything. Adam and Eve in the garden require an extraordinary act of faith, but my faith in wee-wees is absolute especially when I see the openness and cynicism so prevalent today. I believe in haystack marriages providing they are just that, marriages, not mere adventures in which one partner takes advantage of the other. They should be closed and discerning.

Joan moved from the Bronx to Manhattan when we were both very young but I heard about her from time to time since her family was fairly well known. Ten years later she heard I was a senior in high school and wrote to me but I was a smart alec and sent her a brusque supposedly humorous teen-age letter. I have never heard from her since nor do I know where she is now. A small paragraph in History but reams of pages to me.

I never saw sordidness as a child, not even in the movies, and for any youngster this is a blessing. I remember a man who must have known sordidness although my awareness of his wretched state comes only now after fifty years as I reflect on things past and write these pages. And I remember him as a sweet, kind, gentle person, a soul of goodness. He was a hopeless alcoholic.

His name was Joe Gaspel. He would show up at our house every six months or so neatly though poorly attired, clean, his hair combed back and very respectful in his manner. Although he'd address my mother as Kate and was not much younger than she, he'd always show her a certain respect like a, I have to search for the simile, like an older son to a mother. My own mother was one of twelve children by two marriages and apparently Joe's mother had served in their house in some capacity, as maid or cook. Joe had known my mother since boyhood and whenever he came she would prepare him a nice meal and give him clothing and money; this was the Depression so the money was probably a few dollars, a not untidy sum in those days. Joe would stay for an hour after his meal and go off. I gathered he would be all right for some time holding down a job and then he'd end up on a binge and drying session at one of those East River island hospitals; after being released he would come back to see us. The thought has just occurred to me, it has never occurred to me before but only as I write these lines, that Joe was like the whiskey priest in that Mexican novel. In the face of terrible adversity—imagine having no family and being enslaved to alcohol, with evenings in a vestibule or gutter—he held on to fortitude, faith, hope and charity. A saint. I could see the courage and love. He was such a kind, lovely man. He must have had great faith. I have seen a saint. In the Bronx I have seen a saint.

4. My Father

Let us get to the heart of the matter, my father. I could say ladies first my mother but that wouldn't be authentic because in my case my father belongs there; besides that's where I have always put the males. You must remember that after P.S. 11, which I loved, I went to a boys' high school, boys' college and boys' military service and when I went to the 9 o'clock Mass on Sunday the boys sat on the right of the church and the girls sat on the left. I grew up under segregation so that I was a child segregationist or better said a little boy who sat on the right side every Sunday and went to boys' school after puberty because of segregationists. I have had a hard time shaking off this tradition although I am gradually managing to do so; for forty years now I automatically sit in the back row *on the left* when I go to the movies, a subconscious attempt at integration, and I also prefer the left side of a church. You might say I am a leftist. I wish all my experience were like P.S. 11 where I was a leftist with Phyllis, Elaine, Sylvia, Doris, Cynthia and Adrienne. I haven't forgotten any of them. I could mention their last names if I had to.

When you get to your father you draw a curtain over some remembrances of times past; you are not going to tell everything down to the last detail and how it affected you because some things should not be divulged. I agree with Bonhoeffer that some knowledge should be kept secret and that the cynic is a liar; he may appear to be truthful and likeable and humorous because he says so much but his words do not conform to the way things are, which is after all the definition of a lie. So I am drawing a curtain . . .

I have heard many people say: "Your father was the kindest man I have ever met," and he was. I never heard him speak ill of anyone although I do remember his saying once, just once, in extreme nervousness and despair, "the fakers", to describe the lawyers who didn't pay him his accumulated fifty cent fees for answering the calendar at the Bronx County Court House. And I only remember his uttering an oath once, on an extremely hot, humid June Friday night in 1941, when he was tying on my bow tie for high school graduation ceremonies at Town Hall; the tie kept falling apart in his hands and after several minutes of nervousness and frustration, the sweat rolling down his face, his eyes gleamed as he thought he had it all put together properly when it fell apart again and I heard him whisper through his gritted teeth: "Holy Shit!" I only remember his being drunk once, after a Christmas party at the Court House although perhaps "having imbibed too much" is a better expression than "drunk" because there was no boisterousness, no flailing of arms, not even the utterance of one word, just a gentle weaving down the apartment hallway at 1235 that I sensed not saw; and I remember

19

my bedroom door being discreetly closed and I imagine my father was discreetly helped to bed for I didn't see him anymore that evening, and the next day he was his kind self again: "Hello, Jims, have some turkey." I knew him for seventeen years, ten months and two days and in that time on the negative side I only heard one vague reference to swindling lawyers who surely deserved a sterner dictum, one hushed protest of sanctified excrement over a collapsing bow tie and one three second soundless navigational weaving after a Christmas office party. There were many plusses. When I was very young, this could almost go back to Chapter 3, he always took me to the zoo. We'd have our lamb dinner with my mother at 12 on Sunday, with apple pie and cheese, and then we'd say "Goodbye, House" as we went out the door and headed for the Z trolley on the other side of Washington Bridge, not the one over the Hudson, the newcomer, but the real Washington Bridge over the Harlem which was always there before I was born. We'd go over to McBride's Diner, wait for the car, get on it and I'd head down the aisle for the idle conductor's seat at the back where I'd sit on the stool and grab the handles and operate them as if I were running the trolley. People today will not remember that trolley cars have two trolleys or poles which can be released by a rope to the live wire above and that when a conductor gets to the end of the line he lowers the one pole and raises the other; paradoxically the back pole feeds electricity to the forward seat enabling the conductor there to start the car. So I sat in the idle back seat and pretended to drive the Z.

My father had a way of picking at his teeth with his tongue especially the gap between his molars where the false teeth would have gone if he hadn't carried them in his breast pocket. He always wore a homburg, white shirt, dark blue suit, black shoes, dark tie and overcoat; somehow I associate the zoo with brisk days in autumn, and sometimes he smoked a cigar. Later in life he tried cigarettes and a pipe but he always apologized to me when he smoked: "Pardon me, Jims," he used to say as he lit up because he felt guilty about it. Why he apologized I am not certain; perhaps his motivation was subconsciously religious: "Thou shall not destroy the temple of the Holy Ghost," the temple being the body destroyed by tobacco's legions of evil, or perhaps it was physical, for he had heart trouble. I may not be certain of the cause but I do know he always said: "Pardon me, Jims," or "I'm sorry, Jims," and because of this I found it comparatively easy to give up smoking in 1956. I have never smoked since.

At the zoo we bought peanuts from the Greek's, maybe he was an Italian, bright copper, good-smelling, steam-emitting peanut stand and then went through the huge eight foot turnstile gate. I recall standing on a bar of the gate and having him push me through. Memories like this are extremely important because they save a boy in his teens or twenties and beyond, when he needs foundation stones and supporting walls to lean on, like the buttresses on old cathedrals; I don't mean he's aware of the zoo experiences at all times, I mean the memories are there below the surface, his vinculum with his father shoring him up. It may sound strange but a few trips to the zoo, which cost five cents on the trolley, a five cent bag of peanuts and two hours that seem delightfully forever may be the most significant experiences of a man's life. In my case I will assent to this thesis and that's more than fifty years ago.

"Your father was the kindest man I've ever met"; that's true and yet there's more to being a father than kindness and that something more my father did not have. Although this lack of the more wasn't his fault it was an omission I have lived with all my life. Put it this way: when you're a father you should take your son to the zoo every day of his life so to speak until he is eighteen and then teach him to break away, but my father only took me zooing the first few years and then only on Sundays, and he knew nothing about breaking away. He never did so himself. In later years I made sort of half-zoo trips with him to the annual track meets at the Madison Square Garden—Glen Cunningham, Venske, Chuck Fenske, John Borican, Ben Johnson, John Woodruff, Al Blozis, Cornelius Warmerdam, Leslie MacMitchell, Greg Rice, I can still see them all, they meant so much to me almost as much as the peanuts at the zoo and the empty conductor's seat.

The most important event in my father's life and probably in mine occurred when he was a baby, more than forty years before I was born. His father, Patrick Joseph Murphy, a fireman, was killed on the job in New York; I had heard he was killed in a fire but my brother thought it may have been in the firehouse so I can't say precisely. But the effect was the same; this left my father and his two older brothers in the hands of their mother whose name I believe was Annie Brown. Doesn't that tell you a great deal about Americans? The Bronx Boy believes his grandmother's name was Annie Brown, he doesn't know for sure and has taken no onomastic pains to find out. Perhaps the Bronx Boy is a peasant or perhaps an American or both, or perhaps Americans are peasants without financial problems, like the druggist in Harry Pulham's memoirs. Can you imagine a European not knowing about his family tree?

Annie Brown, daughter of an English Methodist minister, fell in love with the Irishman Patrick Joseph Murphy sometime in the 1870's. They were either married over there and then fled over here, or fled over here and then married, but in either case I understand her Reverend father did not attend the wedding ceremonies. I have sometimes wondered what he must have been like, in 1870, an English Methodist minister. Patrick and Annie Murphy settled in Washington Heights near 155th Street, the place they called Irish Row, where they had six children, three girls who all died young, and three boys, my Uncle Billy

(William J.), my Uncle Joe (probably Patrick Joseph, he may have dropped the Pat, again my onomastics are vague) and John Francis, my father, born in 1881. Annie Brown became a Catholic convert and I understand she knew a great deal of theology which she gave lessons in to my father, theology from the Baltimore Catechism and doctrines of John Wesley both of them revealing an uncommon knowledge of Original Sin. Thus my father knew more about this ancient creed than most people although he never preached it, not once, I don't believe he ever mentioned the word sin or evil to me once in my whole life with him nor did he ever point a finger at a public sinner and say look at the devil's work except perhaps the one time he called swindling lawyers fakers, in a whisper. John Francis Murphy never spoke of evil or practiced it but he bore its theology on his shoulders all his life; I believe this burden is called Jansenism in the one ball park and Calvinism in the other and he had to play in both of them. No one should ever have his father die when he is a baby, especially in 1881.

My father after the zoo years, this kindly man, was not there when I needed him, I was going over to say *never* there, but that's not quite true, he was and he wasn't, more wasn't than was. On Sundays he was off to Van Cortlandt Park, Vannie he called it, roaming around by himself, to get the fresh air he so deeply cherished. My brother once told me my father once said he wished he had a bedroom where he could cut a hole in the wall so that he could sleep at night with his head outside to get the fresh air, his body warmly enclosed in the bed within, and I know that in my Bronx bedroom I always slept with the windows wide open in winter even at ten below zero; all that steam heat and fresh air. When I was eleven, twelve, thirteen and fourteen I spent my summers at my Aunt May's in Ohio—surely I was the only Bronx Boy with a relative way out West, quite a distinction!—Boy Scout Camp, Cardinal Hayes' Camp and my Uncle Billy's apartment on the beach in Florida. These were great adventures to me and worthy episodes in themselves but now I realize I was being gotten rid of, removed from the scene so my father could have peace and quiet. He always wanted peace, quiet, fresh air and cleanliness, he made a great fuss about excrement, calling it "grunt mud" and about cleaning up after it, and he spent a full hour every morning with his ablutions; and to get peace and quiet he had to be alone. No noisome lawyers. No neighbors, no children. Just wander about the hills of Van Cortlandt on a nice brisk autumn afternoon, away from it all, with only a nickel in your pocket, and the one Sunday you forgot the nickel you could give the conductor two three cent stamps as carfare, which John Francis Murphy did one sabbath afternoon in the 1930's. And the cigar. I forgot about the cigar, which I used to get the gold paper ring of from my father but more from my Uncle Joe than from my father.

One Sunday afternoon when I was eleven my father and I

had the roast lamb, mashed potatoes, string beans, gravy, apple pie with cheese and coffee for him, milk for me, said "Goodbye, House" and went to Van Cortlandt Park on the U car, not the Z car which left Unie at Tremont for the zoo, but the U car, the Unie itself. The Z cars had more a box car appearance whereas the Unies were rounded; the latter I found out in my teens were harder to hitch on. It was winter and I was going ice skating. We went into the club house at Vannie and spoke to Joe Bogan, who ran the operation there, and then I put on my skates and tip-toed down the wooden ramp leading to the ice. I skated for quite a while when my father came out to the edge of the lake, where the snow was; I could tell it was him from his big frame, homburg hat, white shirt and dark overcoat. He was smoking a cigar and the end was fairly well chewed. "Well, Jims," he said, "it's about time to go home." Saying this, he threw the cigar on a small snowbank. Then he straightened it out so its side was parallel to the lake shore, went back to look at it, went off again, and back again, several times, until he finally said firmly, with decision; "No, I'm going to bury it!" He lined it up for the last time, making sure it was perfectly parallel to the shore, took its last measure and kicked snow over it. We walked off but a few seconds later he said "I'm going back," and went back to look for the cigar. He couldn't find it. He turned the snow over with his foot but the snow was everywhere the same. He kept turning the snow over, anxiously, over and over. An hour later, when we got off the U car at the Washington Bridge, walked across the cobblestones past the Veteran's Statue and came to the sidewalk on the corner of Ogden and Unie, I heard him say between his teeth: "I wish I hadn't buried that cigar." He was desperate.

His whole life was like that. Gentle, kind, honest . . . and scrupulous. My brother once told me (I was never told anything by my mother who was always sparing me, I was always being spared) that on April 17, 1942, just before he died, my father said to my mother: "I'm so glad, Kate. I couldn't take any more." He was sixty years, eight months and twenty-three days old. Sixty years of desperation removing grunt mud from a sin-laden catechism, seeking fresh air. *Requiescat in pace.*

Imagine his life, symbolized by a buried cigar perfectly parallel to the shores of a Van Cortlandt pond. It had to be that way, perfect. I remember his handwriting, it was perfect; without training, without knowledge of calligraphy his letter was perfect. Letter perfect as they say. On his desk the pens, the pencils, the paper knife, all lined up in a row next to a large blotter, as clean as the day he bought it. His work was that way too, neat, tidy, punctual, and for a reward he had scheming quevedesque lawyers teasing him to save the two percent interest on a fifty cent piece. There could never be repose. Unlike a compleat artist or cabinetmaker exhibiting his portrait or Shaker's table he could never boast: "This is mine. I made it. It is a thing of beauty. I am content. Amen."; there was always imperfection if only in the form of a mutilated cigar.

I believe I know the origin of this kindly man's trouble. Imagine a Female Theologian in 1881 and a little baby, a manchild, with no other god to turn to. Everything he does is stamped with the sign of the Fall. Sin. Evil. No matter what he does, no matter how he tries, he always falls short of the mark, which was erased that dim distant day in a garden when our first parents did the undoable and spoke the unspokable. Everything became polluted, you, I, a little manchild, your excrement, the air, even a toothmark on a cigar. And no other god to turn to . . .: "I'm so glad, Kate, I couldn't take any more."[1]

I was the product of segregation. Boys' schools, girls' schools. Nine o'clock Mass: boys on the right, girls on the left. Boys' colleges, girls' colleges. Boys' army, girls' army. At a party, boys in the kitchen with the beer, the jokes, the card game; girls in the living room with a hot drink and discreet, informative conversation, or sometimes the setting was reversed with the girls in the kitchen, which after all affords greater privacy for even more discreet conversation. Sometimes my daughters have complained of this—"he's always praising the boys or helping the boys or taking them on trips; no matter what I do I can't please him, or he doesn't seem to care." They may be right, and as time goes on I try to make amends. But one does as one is trained, and somewhere deep down within is interred the image of the snowbank cigar. I cannot forget. There is so much to be done. I must teach my children a new theology and although like my father I come under the old I do everything I can to remove the chaff, to get at the grain, which consists of joy and redemption. If you are going to stress something then let it be hope hallelujah so that one day we shall all sing and dance at the beautiful heavenly fish fry, Hallelujah Brother, Amen.

5. My Mother

It is difficult for me to write with equanimity. To be fair. To be just. I was never comfortable in her presence. Never. And yet I know she loved me. I know that now but I did not know it then, when I was young. As I say, I was never comfortable in her presence. Never.

I can prove she loved me. You can prove very little about love but I can prove she loved me. One day during the New York World's Fair of 1941, my guess is it was April, I went with the All Saints High School Fife, Drum and Bugle Corps to Flushing, Long Island to play at the fair grounds. I played the fife: D-G-A-G-G-B-D-D-E-D-D-B-G-A-G-A-B-A-G-E-F-E-E; I still remember the notes of this lively jig though I haven't touched a fife in forty-five years; and my friend Bobbie O'Brien played the bugle. We wore blue uniforms, light blue trousers with a thin white stripe, dark blue jackets with brass buttons, a Sam Browne white cloth belt and shoulder strap, white shirt, blue tie and a garrison hat to match jacket and trousers. I remember nothing of the Fair except for the funny mirrors and one freak side show, I believe it was Strange As It Seems; I recall Siamese twins and a woman's saying she had led a life of perdition and had taken the long road back, from drugs she meant, which was unusual in those days. I only once heard my Uncle Billy say: "If anyone offers you a funny looking cigarette, don't smoke it." This was the extent of Drug Education in 1941.

When the bus returned to the Bronx in the evening Bob and I were not on it for we were sixteen going on seventeen and decided to stay for awhile. But when you are sixteen you still have no conception of time, everything is still a vast IS, as it must have been in the garden before Adam and Eve spoiled everything. So we stayed until two in the morning and then took the subway home. I got off near the Yankee Stadium, which was near Bob's house, and I distinctly remember walking up that steep, steep hill on Ogden Avenue from 161st Street to 163rd Street, then north on Ogden all the way to 171st Street, left to Merriam, down the short hill to Unie, a door or two from my house, 1225. At last! I went into the vestibule, opened the brass-knobbed door and walked up the three flights to Apartment 32. I let myself in. My father said, very softly (he was incapable of an outburst): "Look what you have done to your mother." Those were real tears, that was real agony, and as I think back I know she loved me. And yet I was never comfortable in her presence. Never.

The next morning it was business as usual. I washed, had my home-cooked prunes, hot oat meal from the double boiler, heavy cream and milk, all from a neat tablecloth. I put my napkin in its ring, picked up my brown bag with the tongue sandwich on protein bread, fruit, half head of lettuce and tomato, my nickel, my stack of books and looseleaf bound by a belt, and headed downstairs to Unie. From there I walked to Merriam, to Ogden, to 169th St. at P.S. 11, east to Woodycrest, down Woodycrest to 168th Street and the Noonan Plaza, east to the public library and Judge Smith's hill, down the hill to the park and then the rest of the two mile trip to All Saints on Concourse. I could have used the nickel for the X trolley on 167th Street, as Denny did, but I preferred to keep it for two loosies, a seltzer and 2¢ Nestles at Mr. D's candy store.

I was not comfortable in her presence. Catherine Mahoney was born in Washington Heights in 1885 of Matthew Mahoney, an engineer I am told from Dublin, and his wife, of whom I know nothing except that he had two wives and this may have been the second, my mother probably being the oldest girl of the second family of Mahoneys. Apparently her own mother died when she was fifteen so at that age she became the mother of a large household, head cook, shopper, house cleaner, bill payer, administrator, bottle washer as they say, a job requiring great skill and leadership, and imperiousness. She was always the captain, there could be no doubt about it.

My knowledge of my mother's family is scant except for three aunts and the uncle I knew. I have a vague impression of serious problems with alcohol and of a brother who long before I was born was ejected from the house and never returned, which would leave a terrible scar and yet I never remember my father or mother inveighing against the evils of alcohol. She had a bottle of Burke's Ale before going to bed every night that I distinctly remember buying in Otto's delicatessen, with the green bottle and 2¢ bottle deposit, and I never recall my father's drinking at all, perhaps a glass of elderberry at Thanksgiving. When I was in my teens I must have had a glass or two of beer too many and she may have been apprehensive, but I was never dragged to the church and made to take the pledge as a friend of Bobbie's, name of Danny Murphy was. He was no relation of mine; in the Bronx Murphy was a very common name, like Moscowitz and Caruso.

My mother had a distinct sense of class, so much so that when I saw the English television series *Upstairs Downstairs* in the late 70's I understood everything perfectly. I could have gone Downstairs with Mr. 'Udson, Mrs. Bridges, Ruby, Rose and Edward—Rose and Edward are more my type—and been perfectly at home, or Upstairs with Captain James, Mr. Bellamy and Lady Marjorie although I would have been a weaker Captain James since Mr. Bellamy was more assertive than my father. Put it this way: I prefer Downstairs, I always have and I always will and I wouldn't know what to say to Georgina.

My mother didn't think Italians conformed to her sense of class and never encouraged my associating with them, which is remarkable, because I have always liked Italians and consider Joey Bacigalupi my best friend. And when I went to Naples in

26

1982 I fell in love with that city, where no one stops for a traffic light, no one pays their fare on buses, jogs, watches their weight, refrains from smoking or from swimming in the bay whose creamy brown sewerage surpasses the Harlem's. And they all stay up till midnight in the park. *Dolce far niente.* No yesterday, no tomorrow, only today, live in the present. I love Naples. It's for children, like me. Mind you, my mother's sense of class was never stated in a syllogism, no overt remarks, no crudeness, no talk of race, never that, you only had to live in her presence to sense it; you sensed a sense of class. And people from Southern Italy did not conform to that sense.

I must be accurate. My mother was always charitable and kind in speaking to people of other backgrounds. She had very cordial relations with John and Tony, who owned the vegetable store and saved their very best produce for us; with Pete, who owned the fish store and set aside his best swordfish and halibut; and with Tony the barber. And accuracy further demands that I record her admiration for John De Sanctis, our family doctor, a fine gentleman and physician. He would have been all right, an acceptable candidate for marriage if she had had a daughter; as I look back, Dr. De Sanctis's family must have come from Tuscany.

As for the Irish there were two types, trolley car conductors and white collar civil service workers and up. Again, you sensed a disapproval of trolley conductors although I myself liked a conductor named O'Malley very much; he was a humorous man and I used to stand in the front of the car and joke with him on my way to college. Her favorite Irishmen were judges, especially Supreme Court judges.

As everyone knows, in New York City in the '30's there were only three groups of people, the Irish, Italians and Jews, and I should say my mother placed the Jews somewhere between the Irish and Italians although she placed some Jews, the owners of the *New York Times* for example, even above the Irish. The Jews fell into two categories: on the one hand, the owners of the *New York Times*, distinguished doctors and attorneys though certainly not the vulgar kind, a bank president she knew of through my aunt, and certain philanthropists and patricians she had heard or read about: "Isn't it nice, Jims, how kind those people are?" The other category was the Jews we lived next door to in the Bronx, like the laundryman who had his shop around the corner, at 1260 Ogden. He was a little guy with a grin on his face and he always had a big sack of laundry on his back. He spoke English with a Yiddish accent and always had something nice to say. We were friends. I liked him very much. My mother ignored him.

As with Italians, there were exceptions. My mother liked Simey the Jewish tailor very much. Simey was always punctual, respectful and polite. He seemed to know he was Downstairs.

It is strange. Although my life was narrowly circumscribed

27

by the Bronx institutions of the Roman Catholic Church I don't ever recall my mother's discussing religion or the clergy. Neither did my father. I have a feeling she didn't like the nuns, which is why she sent me to P.S. 11. Thank God! The best school I ever went to, better than the Ivy League, State universities or sectarian colleges, I've been to them all.

Either from my mother or my cousin Neenie, who like most women knew more about the family than the men, I gather the nuns ran an orphanage in Washington Heights that was a bit of a hell hole and that my mother and her brothers and sisters hid two of the orphans one night when they escaped. This will sound like something out of Huckleberry Finn but I distinctly remember that story. An orphanage would attract a few sadists and perhaps that's what happened in Washington Heights in the late 1800's, and then again it may be the nuns didn't have class. Daughters of trolley car conductors. Downstairs.

Certain priests, however, were of blessed memory. Monsignor Dumpher in our parish was a convert from Protestantism, an Upstater, a well-spoken gentleman with a resonant voice, an incipient Cardinal Newman. Protestants by and large were wonderful people; well bred; there were still a few left in the Bronx although after the new George Washington Bridge went up in 1932 most of them emigrated to New Jersey. (I remember the fine Protestant church opposite P.S. 11 on Ogden, it was never open. That was why the Bronx Boy believed until 1961, when he moved out west, that Protestants never went to church; only Catholics did and Orthodox Jews, who were better than the others.) There was also a Father Donovan, whom we used to meet summers up in the Catskills, at Hattie Brown's place. He was a gentleman. Pius XII was a fine man who knew five languages, but I don't recall any talk of other hierarchy or clergy. Time of course creates difficulties when you're trying to remember but even so I have the impression my mother really didn't care for the clergy, certain ones were all right but not as a class. She must have thought well of the brothers from Ireland for that's where I was sent to high school, All Saints, but neither religion nor the clergy were mentioned much at home. Perhaps my father felt the same way; having had his mother's homiletics, he stood in need of no additional Theology.

I have two very pleasant memories of my mother, both of them from grammar school and earlier days. She was an excellent cook and to this day I can see her rice puddings, bread pudding, tapioca, custards, apple pies, lemon meringues, chicken fricassee, boiled tongue, roast lamb and on Sunday nights the huge pot of vegetable soup she left on the stove. Sunday nights you were on your own, not a bad custom; you heated the soup, which was the best I have ever tasted (in 1955 I liked Shirley Courts in Mexico City because the soup reminded me of my mother's), served yourself and ate it with several pieces of rye bread and a great deal of butter. It was delicious. The best of all these cookeries were the days I got to bake the tarts, once a week in winter. When she cooked her pies she always had dough left over and I'd get to roll it and fill it with strawberry jam and put it in the oven. The tarts you make yourself when you're eight years old are the best ever. The other pleasant memories are my trips down to Gimbels with her on the 6th and 9th Avenue El, when we went to the elevated station at 170th Street and Jerome Avenue three short blocks west of the Concourse and took the train south, but just before it went into the tunnel at the Yankee Stadium it turned west, over towards the Polo Grounds on the other side of the river, then south I don't know on what avenue for I had only been to Harlem once, and past St. John the Divine's cathedral. From here on I am hazy although I do remember the upper floor windows of those apartment houses facing on the El; but if you were on the 9th Avenue El train you had to change somewhere for the 6th Avenue El because that's the one that took you down to Herald Square, 34th Street, Gimbel's and Macy's. We got off the train and station and went right into Gimbel's on the second floor without going into the street. We always shopped at Sak's and Gimbel's, which were owned by the same company, because that's where my mother had her charge card; Macy's wasn't quite the same caliber. I loved to go on these expeditions, you saw the world, and I think if my mother and father had taken me on more of them I would have been a better person. I am not the best person. Some people don't like me. As a matter of fact, a great deal of people don't like me.

I have some other memories. I'll serve them up just as they came to me a few minutes ago, when I scribbled out a list of them on my yellow note pad.

With my mother there was a fifth cardinal virtue, punctuality. Prudence, justice, fortitude, temperance and punctuality. Supper at six meant supper at six, not one minute before or one minute after. I remember when I was very young, five or six, and I stayed playing on the street until after six one evening, she met me on the first floor of the staircase at 1225 where the brass rail was and slapped the back of my hand all the way up to the second landing where the brown wooden rails were, telling me that on time meant on time and didn't mean after six. That slapping really hurt. I was crying again. She was a stickler for time. As I will explain later on, my Uncle Joe lived with us for many years at 1245 and 1239, where he had the back room and I used to hear him read the *Adventures of Mario* and play Russian Bank. At meals Joe would chew his meat and because of his poor false teeth discreetly hide the chewed substance in little balls within his baked potato skin, which my mother didn't like and although she didn't say anything I sensed her attitude. Joe would also come in at seven or eight o'clock many nights and my mother would have to keep his food and dishes warm and then wash his dishes later on and I know she

29

really didn't like that although she never made an overt statement. My mother was not one to make overt statements against another human being, only discreet actions, and I noticed she didn't slap the back of Joe's hands, not literally, but after a few years we moved from the six room apartment in 1239 to the five room apartment in 1235 which meant we had one room less, Joe's room, so he had to move to bachelor quarters across the river in Washington Heights whereas we lived in Highbridge. Joe seemed to resent this very much and ten years later at my father's funeral I noticed he didn't speak to my mother. All I remember is I used to love to play Russian Bank with him and listen to him tell *The Adventures of Mario*. I think perhaps that's what might have saved me, firing the .22 rifle with my Uncle Billy and *The Adventures of Mario*. I can't remember a line from that book but that's not the point; it's just that everyone should have two bachelor uncles to play with. But more of this later.

I shall describe the movies of the 1930's further on but here I just want to bring up one movie, which I went to with my mother. One afternoon we went to the RKO Coliseum, the motion picture palace at 181st Street and Broadway, at the bottom of the east-west hill and top of the north-south hill. First we went to Horn and Hardart's Automat for lunch, next door to Wertheimer's, then over to the Collie for the movies; it was diagonally across from Nedick's where you got the five cent hot dog and orange drink. We did not eat at Nedick's. I remember we were up in the balcony of the Collie, it was very dark and the shaft of light coming from behind us spread out and illuminated the screen, you could see specks of dust in the rays, and I got sick, it all came up, every bit of it. I was cold and in pain and crying again and my mother took me home. We took the Unie over the bridge to the Comfort Station and then a short turn left to McBride's. We got off, walked past the War Memorial of the 1918 doughboy hurling the grenade with one hand, his rifle in the other, past Irving's drug store and then to our house. I fell asleep immediately. When I woke up it was twilight and I thought it was the next morning but my father was bending over the bed reassuring me and asking me "Are you all right, Jim?" and I said yes. This happens every once in awhile. You're dead tired and fall asleep and when you wake up you think it's the next morning only it's the same evening and the world is funny and when I do that I think of the day fifty-five years ago when I went with my mother to the Collie diagonally across from Nedick's where the hot dogs were a nickel.

I shall never forget the CHEAP sign written over our name on the dumbwaiter button. They don't have dumbwaiters anymore so I ought to explain what a dumbwaiter is although strictly speaking it belongs under Bronx Institutions, indeed it was one of the more important social structures of the Bronx as I remember it.

Inside a five storey apartment house (Bronx apartment houses

30

had five storeys except for the swells on the Concourse who had seven and even more) there was a shaft, like a small elevator shaft, four feet across and four feet deep. Inside the shaft was a large wooden box, open in the front, that could be pulled from the ground floor up to the fifth and down again by ropes, and if you opened the small door in your kitchen you could see the two ropes and shaft and by looking up and down you could ascertain where the dumbwaiter was and bring it to your floor by pulling one of the ropes. The dumbwaiter was great. I loved the dumbwaiter. The milkman rang the buzzer and sent the milk and heavy cream up on it and you sent him down the empty bottles. The janitor called for the garbage on it and you sent him down the brown paper bags of garbage, not plastic. I loved the dumbwaiter. You could send a friend a message on it if he lived on the same shaft or he could come and ring the buzzer in the basement and you could send him down anything you wanted. I never realized how much I have missed the dumbwaiter until I started to write these lines; every child should have a dumbwaiter and experience the joy it provided. There could be a tragic side, however; I knew a fellow with a glass eye who lost the real one the day he asked his mother to throw down a stick for a stick ball game and he looked up the shaft just as the stick was coming down and it struck him in the eye. I almost forgot; if the dumbwaiter was above your apartment you could throw things down the shaft to a friend, a pack of baseball cards, candy, a baseball mitt or maybe a Spaulding, anything that wouldn't squash.

To get back to the CHEAP sign. The delivery boys used to bring boxes of food to the dumbwaiters to send them up to the customers. Well one day I was in the cellar and looked at the nameplate next to our buzzer, MURPHY, and over it was written CHEAP, put there I am sure by a delivery boy. She never tipped delivery boys, who belonged to the third estate and contributed to society with their labor. The first estate prayed for society, the second estate, which we belonged to, protected it, and the delivery boys worked for the first two estates. That nameplate has affected me to this day. How shall I put it? I am less zealous about money than most. Of the seven capital sins, pride, avarice, lust, envy, gluttony, anger, and sloth, pride and lust run high with me as do all of them but ordinarily I should put avarice in seventh place. Sure, I like money, who doesn't, but I have always been careful about my nameplate.

I remember once I wanted a bike. I was fourteen years old. Everyone in the gang had a bike, big balloon tires mostly, but I remember a fellow named Columbia had a slick sleek European bike for sale and that's the one I wanted. The gang would go riding around in a squadron, up Merriam, down Ogden to the steep Plimpton hill, down the hill—you had to watch out at the corners—all the way to Boscobel and down Boscobel to 167th Street coasting with their hands off the bars. When they came back they had to walk their bikes part way up Judge Smith's hill to the library and Sacred Heart and then they could ride back up to Unie. And I couldn't go. I asked her if I could have a bike and she said *no*. I knew she meant it and I wasn't one to insist with her and I must have said to Denny that I was going to run away from home it meant so much to me and Denny must have relayed this information to his mother because one day out of a clear blue sky my mother said to me "You can have the bike" and that's how I got my European bike with the generator running off the front wheel and a powerful light. I loved that bike. When I was in the service my mother sold the bike and the .22 rifle I had and I knew nothing about it until I came home after the war. I wish I had the .22 rifle now that my Uncle Billy who used to teach me to fire it is dead.

My theme is memory, *memoria bronxoniensis*, and I could go on and on drawing thoughts from the bottomless well but I want to save some of them for Bronx Institutions, the most important chapter of this book. People will surely forget James Ignatius Murphy, J.I.M., Jims, but if I do my job correctly they will never forget the Bronx. Some will call my Bronx scenes local color or *costumbrismo* but they are hardly so parochial; they are a key, I myself should say *the key*, to the meaning of America. America is stamped in the image of the Bronx. Peter Stuyvesant's Manhattan Island is but a stone's throw from the Bronx and may be more cosmopolitan but being so it has less American character. When I walk the streets of the Bronx I have the definite feeling of being in the United States of America; when I go to Manhattan I find I have reservations.

Did you know that the Bronx is the only one of the five boroughs on the mainland? *Tierra firme*, the most substantial. There is a more philosophical way of saying all this: You cannot be absent from a Platonic Idea, you cannot miss it, so people will always remember the Bronx. St. Paul saw it. Plato too. The Bronx, a Platonic Idea, you cannot be absent.

One last memory then. I remember our gang, Denny, Botchie, Sammy, Big Phelan, Segal and Kelly, and occasionally we'd be joined by someone from down around 165th and Nelson. I remember hitching on a trolley once with a boy from there, Wiggie, who rode *on top of* the car rather than the back and later pulled the trolley off the wire. We were on our way to Tuckahoe to swim in one of the lakes there.

Well, some of the gang used to call for me every Sunday around 12:30 to go to the movies, and then we'd walk over the bridge to the Gem, Lane, Collie or Loew's 175th, or around the corner to the Ogden Theater, or down Ogden Avenue to the Crest or maybe over to the 167th or 170th Street Loews over near the Concourse. After a while my mother decided to have Sunday dinner at one o'clock sharp and you had to be punctual and the meal took a long time. Denny and Botchie and the others would wait in the back room till 2:00 or so, when we finally got to go to the movies. After a while they didn't come any more because the second feature started at 1:30 and if you got in in the middle of the picture it wasn't the same. They finally got tired of waiting. I didn't see most of them for years, what with the war, although one morning in 1947 I saw Kelly and his father from the Ogden trolley. They were walking east on 167th Street and I distinctly remember they were carrying their metal lunch boxes with them. So that was it. Downstairs. I might have known. She did it deliberately. She broke me off from my gang. As I say, I was never comfortable in her presence. Never.

6. Instituta Bronxoniensa

According to scholars an institution is anything giving form to society. When we speak of institutions we usually think of church, state, family, and large banks and industries although many lesser entities are also institutions and every bit as profound. Think of the wheel, how that has changed society. The printing press. Automobile. Cigarettes. The ball point pen. All have wrought changes on society. And think of games. The effect they have on life. That's it, life! Games! Life! When I think of the Bronx I think of games and their vitality so when I write of Bronx institutions I am writing a philosophy of life, the only worthwhile kind. Life, The Bronx, America. They are synonymous.

CANDY STORE

The most important institution in the Bronx beyond peradventure of a doubt was Schapiro's Candy Store, between 172nd and Merriam on Unie. Any reputable historian will affirm that; and the most important hours of the day there were the early morning, 12:40 noon and night time around 8:30, the last hour being variable. Of course when I was a little boy I didn't know about 8:30 p.m. but when I got to high school I came to appreciate the gravity of that hour when the news trucks came.

Schapiro opened at 5:30 a.m. He put the newspapers on the stand, the *New York Times, News, Mirror, American, Herald Tribune* on the surface piled in rows with the four foot long two-by-four covering them to protect them against the breeze, and the other papers, the ones in foreign languages, *Erin Go Bragh, Il Progresso Italiano* and *Forward* against the vertical surfaces, behind the thin railings. The stand was colored red, faded, and had some lettering *New York Journal* in white, also faded. Shapiro stood there most of the time till 7:30, depending on the weather and the customers entering his store. The *Times* and *Tribune* were three cents, the others two cents, and I don't know what the foreigners were because I never read them; there were only a few of them anyway. I ought to have mentioned that propped up with the foreigners were *G-8 And His Battle Aces, The Shadow, The Lone Eagle* and other magazines commonly called *pulp*, but I can't for the life of me see why. I frequently read these journals especially *G-8* and *Lone Eagle* and attribute my dexterity in English to their example. They were finely written novels with exemplary plots; I remember one in which a friend of G-8 with a mathematical flair had calculated that a Fokker could not shoot him down in his Spad if he maintained a certain angle, 150° off his starboard, which he did, with impunity. He was invulnerable. He found, however, that he couldn't shoot a Fokker down from that position either so in the end he threw mathematics and caution to the wind and in one reckless afternoon of derring-do destroyed five Fokkers, making himself an ace for the day. He had flown all over the sky; a very fine story and well told, as the priest says in *Don Quixote*. G-8 and his peers have served as my vital as well as my literary model, for owing to their sterling example in the First World War I joined the Navy V-5 aviation program in the Second. I am certain that thousands of others did the same.

Schapiro's newspapers and magazines accounted for half the life of the Bronx. In the mornings millions of New Yorkers clung to their subway straps, read the columns of the *Times* and looked at the pictures of the *News* on their way to work; and in the evenings they read the Shadow and Lone Eagle. These customs preceded the enervating era of television. I imagine that before the advent of radio Schapiro's influence was even greater but that was before my time; I was born in 1924 and am relating only the Golden Years of 1924-1942, before I entered the service.

12:40, the most important hour of the day! I got out of P.S. 11 at noon, walked up the Ogden Hill to 170th Street, along Ogden past the vegetable store, German deli, the candy store I never went to except once to look up Lou Gehrig's batting average, the laundry, Cushman's bakery, fish store, grocery store, to 171st Street and Merriam, and down the hill to Unie. 1235. I went up to my house, ate my scrambled eggs, Thomas's protein bread, butter, tomatoes and lettuce, and then, at twelve-thirty my mother gave me the nickel. I went downstairs, out the door and across the street to Schapiro. 12:40!

"How much is that, Mr. Schapiro? I want a Mary Jane. A licorice twist. And two Gowdy Gum Company Indian cards. How much is that now? And I'll have one of those bananas."

On the way back to school I ate the banana first. That was the easiest. I never knew what the candy was made of, I still don't, but it was a pale orange marshmallow substance and delicious and tasted much better than scrambled eggs or real bananas. Then I ate the Mary Jane, which was difficult because the paper wrapping stuck to the taffy, but it was delicious with the peanut butter inside. Then the licorice twist, a foot long, a very wholesome candy for a penny. Last came the Gowdy Gum Company Indian cards. Those two slabs of gum, the same size as the cards, were of the highest quality; to this day I have never chewed gum that tasted so good, it was better than Wrigley's, Beechnut or any brand you can name and any flavor you can name, and infinitely better than the sugarless phantoms vended today. The Gowdy Gum Company of Boston knew how to make gum. Equally good were the cards, Sitting Bull, Crazy Horse, Geronimo, and the other chiefs, all portrayed in fine colors with their feathers on. I even kept the wax wrappers in a pile at home because there was something substantial about them, not like the gossamered paper and plastic leaf you see today. The wax felt good too. Of all the good things in Schapiro's store, the Gowdy Gum Company was my favorite. Some days I'd buy five of them, five cards, five gums and five wrappers, all for a nickel. Today you spend a half a dollar and get five insipid cards in much less vivid colors, and the wrapper so thin as to symbolize our current inferiority.

After I opened the Gowdy Gum I went into the school yard to show my cards to my friends. We played for a while throwing the ball against the red brick wall. Then the bell rang.

I wish I were a lyrical poet, I would write immortal lines in praise of the candy store. Unfortunately I am not so these sentimental verses, composed by a Bronx boy who will always remember, will have to do:

EULOGIUM CANDYSTORI

I've wandered to the West Bronx, Jim,
I went to see the store
Where Botchie bought the Halvah,
the store is there no more
nor Liebowitz who captained it
in the golden days ago
when a boy got two for lyin'
playing Ringalevio.
I went to buy a loosie, Jim,
to have an old time puff,
there aren't any loosies now
and if that weren't enough
Segal's gone and Kelly too,
on the Bronx Boy it's been hard,
the tears fell fast upon my face,
that's why I'm playing bard.
The Ogden car is altered now,
it's gone the way of horses
so I strolled down to Eleven
P.S. where we took courses,
ovals, straights and penmanship,
spelling bees, subtraction,
where I sat next to Adrienne,
whose beauty was my faction . . .

I should explain that Botchie is Joey Bacigalupi, my best friend, and that I've written more verses about High Cash Clothes and the others but I'm painfully aware they don't measure up to the song I really want to sing. So I don't know, I'll keep them *in petto* for a while and maybe one day . . . Although I am no Keats, no Byron, no Shakespeare, my sentiment surpasses theirs and I have more to say. I know that. I take no personal credit for my superiority, after all, my vision was higher than Shakespeare's. I am one of the Gnostics. I saw the Bronx.

I associate the night hours in the candy store with single men, the age as I recall them between thirty and sixty; there were some married men too. They went over to Schapiro's after supper, at 7, 8, or 9, getting dark in the summer, very dark in the winter, to get their cigarettes and newspaper and also *The Lone Eagle, Shadow* and *G-8 And His Battle Aces.* The next day's newspapers put out an early edition the night before, so some of them would wait until the news trucks came to go down and get their papers. 8:30 P.M. Vespers. In my mind I see the news trucks as being dark green with big tires and billboards on either side; it was said that the drivers had a good job and were very well paid. That was the 1930's. In this final era before television the only alternative to Newspaper Vespers was a trip around the corner to the Ogden Theater to see two major films, the Pathé News with Lowell Thomas, selected short subjects, play SCREENO and get a dish as you entered; under SCREENO, which was more imposing than five lettered BINGO, you received a card whose numbers were spun on the screen instead of being drawn from a cage filled with wooden balls.

Schapiro stayed up past midnight before closing his store, which meant a nineteen hour day. He didn't do it all by himself because his wife took stints of duty and also his daughter Beverly. I have tried to keep sensationalism out of this true autobiography for I am not so anxious to sell my book as to record my life's history, my quest being immortality, but a friend told me something about Beverly. She was ten years older than I so it didn't mean anything to me at the time, but Beverly had beautiful hips and an extremely attractive figure; "she was well stacked," he said. The older boys used to order their malteds from her because she had to lean way over the ice box to dig out the ice cream, revealing her beauty. The ice cream was very hard so she had to do a great deal of digging . . .

I am convinced that every candy store owner in the Bronx had just one child, usually a girl named Beverly, Joanie, Shirley, although I remember one boy, Sam, over near the Concourse. I don't think Liebowitz down on Ogden had any children, I don't know, but I never saw them. It must have been an ascetic life. After the war I heard one ice cream shop keeper make a remark about candy store owners, "all muscle and no brains," he said, pointing to his temple, "I close at seven." Maybe so but I would never make such a derogatory remark about these ascetics because they made me very happy. I have never been so happy as I was in Schapiro's candy store. Never.

What comes next after CANDY STORE? What is the second Bronx institution? It would have to be the games. Our lives were formed by games, the candy store and games, and we had so many of them, so imaginative, so beautiful, so intelligently

37

devised that I find children nowadays dull and boring. Kids today have everything spelled out for them and everything is made of plastic, nothing is natural anymore. Nature was so abundant and the children were so natural and unspoiled in the Bronx that it would take me several tomes to tell about Bronx Games 1930. So I shall stick to only ten or twenty of them to give an idea of the delightful variety of the Bronx. In his *Art of Writing Plays* Lope de Vega describes good theater, saying that on the stage variety is the source of beauty. And so it is with life. I must say the Bronx was very beautiful, there was so much variety.

RINGALEVIO CAW CAW CAW

Ringalevio caw caw caw. The name was onomatopoeic but only the meaning of caw caw caw comes clearly through. Caw must have meant *caught*; Ringalevio caught caught caught, which sounded like the call of a crow and also the act of claw, claw, claw, and you had to say it three times quickly before the rascal escaped your clutches. I can still see Robbie Raughtigan grabbing Phelan in the lots and hanging on: "Ringalevio caw caw caw, Ringalevio caw caw caw, Ringalevio caw caw caw, I gotcha Phelan!" Then Big Phelan had to go to prison and wait until someone freed him or until Raughtigan caught all the others, and then someone else was it. Apparently other countries have similar ideas though less profound than the Bronx's; the Spanish for example say *Tú las traes* but *las* hardly contains the depth of *it*, as in "You're *it*."

Ringalevio was a sophisticated form of hide 'n seek, much like Bridge is to Whist and Sheepshead, and in the Bronx lots we developed it into an art. I never knew what Ringalevio meant and I still don't never having steeped myself in the science of etymology, but perhaps a popular etymology will be helpful. I have two theories. Either there was a ring around the prisoners and someone tried to *lift* it, as in *levity*, *levantar* (Spanish), *lever* (French), or else it was invented by an old Bronxite name of Levy. Ringo Levy.

We had other hide 'n seeks. Much as French, Spanish, Italian, Catalan, and Portuguese belong to the Romance family of languages, so we had hide 'n seek, Ringalevio, kick-the-can and cops-and-robbers. The last of these is easy to explain. There were cops and there were robbers and the latter hid themselves, in the cellars, in the doorways, in the lots, behind a lamp post, and the cops went out looking for them. After they caught them all, the robbers were *it* and now became cops looking for the new robbers. Come to think of it, it was better to be a robber because they got to hide and the cops were *it*.

But kick-the-can had a finesse shared only by Ringalevio. All the games of this family had a mode of freeing the prisoners, the caught ones (caw caw caw), but kick-the-can's was the best.

I remember one day Smealy was it. He had to catch the prisoners and guard the can as well, to keep them in confinement. He set the empty tomato soup can upside down on the sidewalk, hid his face in his arms, turned and leaned against the point on 1232, the House of All Nations. He counted out loud to a hundred as fast as he could while everybody ducked for cover. Reaching a hundred he shouted: "Anyone around my base is it, ready or not here I come." Then he wheeled around and started looking for the hiders. "I see you, Kelly, behind the newsstand, one, two, three." He tapped the can on the ground, one, two, three. "Come on in . . . You too, Botchie, I see you. One, two, three." Kelly and Botchie came in, caught in the den. Smealy turned his back and a specter appeared out of nowhere, from the doorway of the House of All Nations; he came running in at full speed and kicked the can as far as he could yelling "Allee—allee—in free, allee—allee—in—free," three times, the magic rite freeing the prisoners. It was the great liberator, Segal! They all took off for the cellars again and Smealy had to restore the can to its original position and start searching again. Still *it*.

COURTYARD SINGER

I have seen them! I have seen the bards of yore, *jongleurs*, *juglares*, *Meistersingers*, minstrels, the singers of tales, the oral tradition! They came to 1235 Unie in the Bronx in 1930, they came and they have gone, like the brave nomads who sang the Song of Roland and My Cid the Campeador.

One day I was in the kitchen with my mother, eating my scrambled eggs so I could get over to Schapiro's and back to school. It was just after noon and the sun came streaming into the upper part of the courtyard, illuminating the whitewashed walls of 1235 and the house opposite, 1239. The walls were so steep and high and narrow that the sun came only for an hour and couldn't get down below the third floor, but even so it was magnificent when it came. Our windows gleamed, and the snake plants on the sill, green spears with gold borders, reached up toward the sun, soaking it in. I had just finished my tomato and protein bread and was reaching for my milk when I heard a man say: "Ladies and Gennulmen . . ." The husky throat of the Meistersinger!

When he came he always came that time of day. I ran to the dining room to get a better look. He was standing by the courtyard entrance, hat in hand, his brow raised reverently to the sky; he always looked like that when he gave his preliminary speech. The husky words came forth:

Ladies and Gennulmen! I'm a poor man, down on my luck, can't get a job. I've tried everything, scrubbing floors, washing windows, selling apples, but of employment I am de-prived . . . Out of work, Ladies and

Gennulmen! I have a wife and five children and I can't
make a go. My wife takes in washing but it's hard to
make a dollar a day and the little ones come to me
hungry. They want a good meal. I look at their little
innocent eyes and say Daddy will get you something, and
that's why I'm here, asking for your help, begging your
so-li-ci-tude, will you help a poor man down on his luck,
can't get a job, I've tried everything. Thank you, thank
you, Ladies and Gennulmen and God bless you, God
bless you all. Go-o-od bless you. And now I'll sing you a
little song.

Then he walked to the middle of the courtyard, his hat left on
the back wooden outside stairs so he could gesture. He was
preparing for his art.
    "Ladies and Gennulmen, I shall now sing *The Rose of
Tralee*:

Oh the pale moon was shi-i-ning
Across the green mountains
The sun was decli-i-ning
Beneath the blue sea
When I strolled with my love
To the clear crystal fou-oun-tain
That lies in the beau-eau-tiful
Vale of Tralee

The other words still come through to me:

. . . But twas not her beauty
Alone that won me
Oh no-o-o, twas the truth
In her eyes ever dawning

And then the finale:

That made me love Ma-a-ary
The Ro-ose of Tra-a-leeeee!

"Thank you, Ladies and Gennulmen, thank you and God bless
you, God bless you all. A wife and five children. Can't get a job.
Go-o-od bless you!!"
    There was a pause, and then I heard something clink on the
pavement. He looked around when he heard the noise, saw the
paper, picked it up, unwrapped it, put the coin in one pocket
and the paper in the other and said: "Thank you. Tha-ank you!"
I heard another clink. I ran into the kitchen and asked my
mother if I could throw him a nickel. She was going to say no
again but she changed her mind, went into her room and brought
me back, not a nickel, but five pennies. That was even better, it

would make more noise when it landed. So I tore off a piece of newspaper, wrapped the coins in it, opened the kitchen window and threw it out. It made a fine clink, louder than the others. I ran around to the dining room window again, to watch him. A couple of the coins had popped out of my packet, so he had to walk a couple of paces to pick them up. Then he went over to the stairs to get his hat; he waved it kind of, towards the four walls. He saw me in the window; I think he kind of nodded his head. "Thank you, thank you, Ladies and Gennulmen. I'm a poor man, out of work and Go-o-od bless you!" He left. Sometimes if I stuck my head out the window I could hear him a few minutes later, faintly, in the courtyard between 1239 and 1245.

Oh Meistersinger of yore, jongleur, Bronx minstrel, I salute you! I have read the words of other rhetors, Quintilian, Augustine, Erasmus, and listened to the rhetoricians of our day, politicians, priests, professors, but never have I encountered anyone to match your homily! In your exordium you showed humility—"Ladies and Gennulmen, I'm a poor man . . . a wife and five children . . ."—not the specious self-effacement of rhetorical device but that existential nothingness of man before God, whose name you invoked. In your oration you presented your story, honestly told—"out of work . . . a good meal . . . little innocent eyes . . . Daddy . . ." And in your peroration you summed up your argument, concisely, simply, and displayed your heartfelt gratitude. You respected your audience and showed your respect with your song, the beautiful Mary, Rose of Tralee. Thank you, oh Meistersinger, bard of 1235. I in the autumn of my life salute you. I want to keep your memory alive, for knowing you I have known blind Homer.

Recently I read a book called *The Singer of Tales*, about the oral tradition. Some future candidate for the Ph. D. will want to study the bards of my youth, of the Bronx 1930, and add their opera to *The Singer of Tales*. In this fine scholarly tome they are the only poets lacking.

7. The Autobiography

I have been meaning to write this book for a long time but I wasn't sure if I ought to write it as a novel or autobiography. A novel has much to recommend it; when an author comes to intimate scenes he can write pretty much as he pleases; he has all the freedom in the world and would have to be very deliberate and malicious, emphasizing certain actions and features, before people could say: "Oh yes, that's his next door neighbor, John Smith, the rake! the miser! the thief!" In a novel, the statement "Any resemblance to actual persons living or dead is purely coincidental" will get the author off the hook; it may not be true—how could it be? Of course the characters resemble persons living or dead or they wouldn't have any literary value—but even so it gets the author off the hook.

An autobiography isn't like that. People can be identified right away. Take me for example; I have attended several universities and seen mass reprehensible action and if in my autobiography I say "this fatuous policy is Dean Burdock's doing" then it is indeed Dean Burdock's doing, it can't be anyone else's. The result is apt to be that in my autobiography I will hold back out of charity for the dean or fear of his reprisal, more likely the latter, and finally omit the episode entirely, destroying the veracity of my story. Of course I could attach a clause to my autobiography stating that "these papers are not to be published until fifty years after my death," but who wants to do that; who wants to wait until he's in his grave for half a century, no, everyone wants the glory here and now, including me. I want my book published.

On the other hand, a novel has certain drawbacks for ordinary people like me, James Ignatius Murphy, who am no Dickens; a novel may be more difficult to write. I am not sure, but I think it is. I have written a few novels and had three of them rejected outright, absolutely, with the kind words: "You can write, but . . .", meaning I can write but I haven't written anything they can publish, meaning probably I can't write a novel. So a novel may be more difficult to write than an autobiography. I am not speaking of course of St. Augustine's *Confessions* opposite *David Copperfield*, both of which require genius.

Whatever the case, the author of these lines, who seems unable to publish novels, will choose the path of autobiography. This, however, creates another problem. What kind of autobiography shall I write, or which kind, for as I see it there are basically two. One I perceive to be Serious Autobiography, the paradigm being the *Confessions*. The man Augustine steals pears from a neighbor, joins a gang called the Wreckers, is a rhetor, a Manichaean for nine years, fathers an illegitimate child, has a mother pursuing him down the nights and down the days, wrestles with the problem of evil, meets Ambrose, who introduces him to a new faith, becomes bishop at a time when bishop meant Prime Minister, molds western thought for centuries to come and finally is canonized Father of the Church and First Autobiographer. I cannot match that example nor can I follow it. I simply cannot follow it, I cannot compete. Rousseau did, Kierkegaard did, and the young American Merton did as late as 1948 but I can't, I'm the Bronx Boy. To be totally serious for three hundred pages and maintain some criterion of art, however minimal? Impossible! I am not the great God-seeker or man of passion or harbinger of an age. I am James Ignatius Murphy, J-I-M, Jims of the Bronx, with all that implies, Highbridge, P.S. 11, heggies, mickies, anything-for-Thanksgiving, stink bombs, Botchie and Segal, hitching rides on the Z, Halvah Mr. Schapiro, scumbags, Allee-Allee-Infree and the rest of it. How can I compete? I daresay my experiences are serious enough, everybody's are, but after all I never met Ambrose or studied at Columbia University and I've never been to France. I've been to the Bijou off the Concourse all right but I've never been to France.

The other kind of autobiography may not be fitting either. I am thinking of Graham Greene's *A Sort of Life* and Somerset Maugham's *Summing Up*, where you sort of poo poo your sort of life but this requires a sort of Summit Position of sorts that you can poo poo. You are an accomplished raconteur, an eminent novelist, peer of the Realm, in good form; you have been to an English public school, to Oxford, to Cambridge, you have holidayed on the continent for a fortnight, you know Latin, French, the flora and fauna (the heather and gilly flowers, the tawny pippet), the Mediterranean is *mare tuum*, so you sum up, casually, off-handedly, cursorily, your sort of life which really wasn't much old boy, a sort of fillip of the fingers. And you do so *sans* emotion. You can write about playing Russian roulette as a young chap or say you would never play golf for your liver only for fun, but when you go to speak about your Mumsie and your Popsie, old Governor, you are strangely silent. *Why* did you play Russian roulette? What really happened at public school? This is reserved for the backshop. Don't rock the boat. Chuckle at yourself old boy.

In the Bronx? Is this the style for the Bronx Boy?: "Up yours, Bacigalupi, bofangoo.". . ."A celery seltzer, Mr. Schapiro, and a malted and don't use the frozen milk, it puffs up too much, I'm on to you, Schapiro. And gimme two loosies." It just wasn't a sort of life; it had a very definite configuration. (Even so, we didn't say *ain't* in the Bronx.)

Augustine and Merton, the Godseekers, they stand on some Parnassus. Although I share many of their thoughts I cannot write as they wrote, I am not the Serious Autobiographer. Greene and Maugham, Tellers of Tales, my love of a story resembles theirs but my patience does not, I do not have their aplomb. Why

43

come Halloween I used to chalk on the sidewalk: KICK ME HARD! There was nothing sort of about it.
So I shall have to compromise. I shall have to be both Augustinian and Maughamian, serious and jocular, if the latter is the word for a sort of life, a sort of juggler of Notre Dame as in the Christmas story, a merry-Andrew, a zany rolling on the carpet before the altar of the Lord. I wish I could write a novel. I can't. I wish I could write classical autobiography. I can't. So I am settling for egg cream teleology, that's it, I have very fond memories of the Bronx, I loved the Bronx, with the awnings at 1225 and 2301, the maple trees and sycamores, Loring and Andrews, the cobblestones going down to Undy, P.S. 11, stick ball and egg creams and scumbags in the Harlem. Love they say will cover all sins, I pray it will cover my deficiency.

8. My Father's Brothers

My father had two brothers, Billy and Joe, and in keeping with the principles of segregation I always associated the masculine with this side of the family, cigar smoke, football games and rowing on the Harlem; and the feminine with my mother's, cigarette smoke, bridge parties and baked pies. The difference between the sexes can be seen in the two smokes, cigars, augmentative and come to think of it a phallic symbol; cigarettes, diminutive and petite; the smoke of cigarettes is gossamery. Only Uncle Joe smoked a great deal on my father's side but that was enough for me; in the archaic imagery going back, back, back, the proverb about swallows is wrong, for when you go deep into memory the appearance of one swallow does indeed make a summer.

Billy was different from my father and Joe; as the oldest boy he had probably known his father until he was five or so, so he had seen the Male Spouse of the Female Theologian. Perhaps the Spouse had played ball with him or gone fishing with him in the North River, or taken him to the zoo, whatever it was Billy had a spirit in him the others were lacking, call it a spunk of sorts that liberated this orphan from the maternal womb. He did not always use that freedom wisely.

It is a pleasure for me to talk about Billy. When I won the .22 rifle at the high school bazaar he taught me to load it, fire it, clean it and take care of it. On Saturdays he took me to the clubhouse of the 77th Division, where he had served in the 305th Machine Gun Battalion in 1917, and we'd go into the basement to the shooting range and fire. I'd take the El down to his hotel on 46th Street off 6th and then go up to his room. He slept with a pillow under one end of his mattress so his head was lower than his feet, "which is good for the heart," he told me, and when I got there he'd get up, go into the bathroom, fill the tub with ice cold water, open the window to let in the winter air, and get into the tub. After washing he dried himself briskly, got dressed and combed his hair, which was thinning now since he was turning sixty. He'd finger the gold pinky ring the police had given him when he retired as a lieutenant back in 1928 and we'd take the elevator down, walk along one of the avenues and go to a health food restaurant, the kind they made hamburgers at without meat. Then we'd walk, always at a brisk pace, heads high, until we got to the 77th Division; down at the shooting range he'd say: "Look for two parallel lines of light along the barrel and let the target sit on the bead, then slowly squeeze the trigger, never pull it, until you fire. And never point a gun at anyone, see! Even though the metal clip is out there's still a bullet in the chamber," a bullet he had placed there to teach me safety.

Billy was a friend of Bernar MacFadden or at least he

45

admired MacFadden and knew him well enough to go up with him in his plane over the Seminole swamps of Florida. Every year he went up to MacFadden's place in Danville, New York, and every year I'd get a huge box of McIntosh apples delivered to me at 1235. They were the most delicious fruit I've ever eaten. Billy ate everything MacFadden ate, shredded carrots, raw cabbage, vegetables, juices, fruits and when his ulcer permitted it, nuts, nature's food, unspoiled by cooking and meatless. I believe MacFadden introduced him to Dr. Jackson's meal, which Billy cooked and ate with heavy cream. "You should never use milk with grains," he told me, "it creates acids in the stomach, always use cream." I have seen him drink milk with lemon juice, which apparently does not create acids, but I have never seen him use it with cereal. Another favorite of his was brown rice, raisins and bananas all cooked together in boiling water, the bananas disappearing into the rice, their flavor not disappearing, and all of it topped with brown sugar or honey and of course cream. "Do not use polished white sugar, which is bad for you," he used to say. Billy had a bad ulcer and had to be careful of what he ate.

In the summer of 1939 I spent six weeks at Miami Beach with Billy, and I was there when England declared war on Germany again. I was fifteen. My brother and I had traveled down to Florida on a coastal liner and I can still remember the waiters rubbing and polishing the table glasses until they shone like jewelry. And I remember the small swimming pool, filled with salt water. I remember two other things, the flying fish, which I had never seen before, and my own happiness; I was with my brother on an ocean liner going down to see my Uncle Bill.

If you lived with Billy in the summer of 1939 you got up early in the morning, six o'clock, put on your shorts and a Frank Buck helmet and went for a hike. This was at 77th Street on Miami Beach, a block from the shore. You walked to the beach, thirty feet from the water line; and then in the loose sand, which builds up the arches Billy said, unlike the firm sand formed by the pounding waves, which makes walking too easy, you headed out at a brisk pace for Baker's Haulover at 125th Street up north. After a city block's distance Billy saw a large empty bottle, which he handed to you, and then a club, which was for you too, and then two similar objects for himself, and then the exercises began. Walking as fast as you can you hold your head erect, shoulders back, chin in and start swinging the arms until they come to a point high out in front, and then back; back, back, back until they reach the level of your shoulder blades and beyond. Head up, chin in, shoulders back, brisk walk, swing arms forward, swing arms back, toes dug in the sand and you walked up to Baker's Haulover where you placed your feet in the soothing, swirling liquid of nature's waters, to refresh them and maybe pick up a souvenir. Then you headed back to 77th Street, only this time perhaps you varied your course a little, up to the high beach's edge, then down to the water and back again, a zig-zag path enabling you to increase the distance from Baker's Haulover to 77th Street and home and so augment the exercise. This made for variety of expression and since as I have said variety is the source of beauty this is what my dear Uncle Bill must have had in mind. As I made my peregrinations from the Haulover home, bottles and clubs acquired additional weight, making for an increase of intestinal fortitude. Billy never mentioned the four cardinal virtues to me, prudence, justice, fortitude, and temperance, but I gather now that justice and fortitude were especially close to his heart. It seems odd now although it didn't then that after our hike Billy always had his pockets full of string, buttons, cord, colored glass, a cap, a bathing slipper, a pencil, a pen and all those things that wend their way somehow to the beach. How he did that I never knew for as far as I could see he was always swinging his clubs briskly over the sand. After we lay down our clubs and Frank Buck helmets, we went swimming for an hour, "letting nature's soothing swirling waters restore our tired bodies," Billy said. I loved my Uncle Bill and although forty-seven years have passed I have never forgotten those walks up to Baker's Haulover.

I remember similar experiences with Bill. Once in New York, right in the middle of the Depression, he took me to Chinatown and bought me anything I wanted, jade rings, back scratchers, lychee nuts, chow mein, souvenirs, all of this on his $145.00 a month police pension or the fifteen dollars he used to get for his gold police ring at the pawn shop, just before he went somewhere. When our day together was almost over, up around Times Square, he said: "Wait a minute, Jims," and then he bent over to pick up a safety pin. "Here. Keep this. You never know when you may need it," he said. "It could be valuable."

After the war when I was married Billy came to see me in the Bronx. My father had died and my wife, baby and I were using my mother's apartment until I graduated from college. I never knew it at the time but this was the last time I was to see him. He had a few dollars so he went to Roger Peets to buy two suits and his eyes lit up as he whistled in his peculiar way and unpacked the suits from their Roger Peet cardboard boxes. A great consumer, he loved clothing and jewelry and fine things and that's why he had no money, he a bachelor who could have amassed a fortune. A year later I received a telegram from him in Florida describing all sorts of illnesses, blood pressure, blood count, pulse, temperature, heart beat, kidneys, liver and other viscera, which was his way of telling me "I am dying. Fast. Not much time.", but the Bronx Boy was so stupid, dumb, naive that he didn't get the message. The Bronx Boy could have flown down there to see him or at least call or send a God Bless telegram. Something. Anything. But no, a few days later I got a call from an Army chaplain, a Protestant with a southern drawl,

47

saying Billy died that day and had received the last rites of the Church. I cried. Billy hadn't been to church in forty years I guess or more and he told me more than once that you didn't have to be a Catholic or anything to be a good person and that some of the best people he knew were Protestants and unbelievers and you had to judge every man by himself. So when I heard he had died well shriven it came as a big surprise. So that's partially why I cried though it wasn't the only reason or even the main reason, which I came to know in 1956, seven years later, when I went to see the doctor. But more of that later.

Perhaps Billy's relations with his brother Joe, my uncle, is why he never stressed the Catholic religion, or, if anything, said he liked Protestants and unbelievers as well as Catholics (I even got the hint he *preferred* the others.) Billy never spoke to Joe. I think it had to do with money. So now I had better talk about Joe.

Joseph Murphy, my Uncle Joe, orphan, tall, thin, bald, clear of eye and skin, vacationer in Lake Placid, New Yorker, austere, methodical, collector of Horn and Hardart napkins, insurance calendars, insurance pens, letter openers, golf tees, paper clips, erasers, cigar bands, golf balls, toothpicks and all the *objets d'art* Washington Heights bachelors gather and stuff in their large, inherited-from-their-mother bureau drawers and leave there for forty years until their loving nephew Jims comes to their Washington Heights rented room to dispose of them in late December 1945. The end of the War. The end of an era. The end of Uncle Joe. Two watersheds in History; The War and Uncle Joe. I forgot to say that Uncle Joe was worth a fortune in 1929; a man of little formal education, clean, neat, intelligent, well-spoken, and written, an orphan child and immigrant's son and worth a fortune. This could only happen in the United States of America.

Joe and Billy were opposites, not like night and day exactly but more like an afternoon in November and an afternoon in July. Joe was never the sport Billy was but then I wouldn't call him a winter's afternoon either because he wasn't as dead as all that and had a sparkle in him reminding you of something like plum pudding. When I think of Joe I immediately smell elderberry wine at Thanksgiving, peanuts at the football game and those cigars he always carried around in his pocket. When I think of Uncle Billy I see a white house in Florida on the shore with the waves breaking and pink flamingos standing out in front eating ovaltine and lychee nuts.

One Sunday afternoon my father and I took the O trolley down to the Polo Grounds to see the New York football Giants play Sammy Baugh and the Redskins. We got off the car on the Bronx side of the river, walked through the park, down the stairs and across the bridge to the turnstiles on the Manhattan side. Joe had told us to be at the Press Gate so that's where we went; it was one of those deep dark places, down in the recesses of the

El.

The afternoon was beautiful and even down there we could appreciate the sun, which was so bright it pierced through the railway ties forming irregular squares of light on the ground. From time to time a train passed bowling the light away, but the rays returned as soon as the last car was gone. The crowds were coming in packs and I was happy because we were going to see the game. Five minutes passed . . . ten. No Joe.

My father pushed his Homburg a little way back on his head and looked up at the rafters. It was very dusty up there. Then he looked at the peanut vendor's stand, which was whistling near the ticket windows. They all said $2.75. Most of the people were going in that direction because that's where the elevated train had a stairway coming down, and the subway had an exit only a block away; there weren't as many people going in now as before when we first got there but still there were more than you ever saw at the Ogden Avenue movie, even on Saturday afternoon.

My father put his hands in his pockets, stretched his neck and walked up and down. Then he went over to the grilled fence that was guarded with the heavy padlock and looked in; the crowds in the underground walks had all gone in to the playing field and the food counters weren't doing any business any more; the boys with the white uniforms, frank baskets and coffee tanks were leaving for the stands. My father asked a man for the time. No Joe.

My father's tongue went up to the space between his left canine and nearby molar and tugged a little; then it went down to the place where his wisdom tooth used to be. He held his hand about a foot before him and cupped the fingers so they were perpendicular to his thumb and all the fingernails were visible; he looked at each fingernail. They were pure white and the ends all matched. He put this thumbnail under the pinky-nail and clicked it once or twice but I couldn't hear the sound. Suddenly there was a roar inside the stadium and my father went over to the grilled fence to look in. Then he went over to the press gate window that said PASS TICKETS 37¢ TAX. He walked out a little and looked at the window where the sign said $2.75. IMMEDIATE SEATING. He looked up at the ties in the El tracks.

I was standing maybe fifteen feet away from my father and I looked across the street towards the dark stairs leading up to the bridge over the Harlem River. They were empty but then a foot came off the bridge on to the top stair and then another foot; it was hard to see who it was but after it came off the stairs it walked over to one of the patches of light and stood there thinly surveying the scene. Joe.

After a minute he saw us and slowly walked up to the press gate.

"Hello, Jack, beautiful day for a game, have a cigar. Hello,

Jimsie, hope the home team wins, bet you five cents they do."

This wasn't the end of the story at the ball game for Joe didn't have any press tickets, all he had was six cigars. I don't know what kind they were because they didn't have any bands on them and although I spent many's the weekend with Joe I never saw him buy one. He always gave me bands though. I guess he must have had friends who liked him so much they just gave them to him.

My father suggested we go over to the $2.75 window and get a couple of tickets and me a 40¢ student's ticket and go in and see the game but Joe told him we didn't have to do that, we were going to see the game and all he had to do was speak to the captain of police in charge of the press gate. This police captain was a big man, six feet four and three hundred pounds, and my Uncle Joe was six one but I don't think he weighed a hundred-and-fifty. While my father and I waited a few feet back, Joe went over and stood before the captain.

"Captain, how are you today?"

The captain looked at Joe and I must say I've never seen a man with less expression in his eyes, he seemed bored for some reason or other and I know my Uncle Joe wasn't boring because I knew him better than anybody else except perhaps my father. Joe was a great deal of fun.

After Joe greeted the captain I never got to hear the rest of their conversation because he put the back of his right hand to the left side of his mouth, tiptoed up a little and whispered something into the captain's left ear. I never saw the captain's face change and he didn't say anything but he nodded his head yes. Then my Uncle Joe turned and said:

"Come on Jack. Jims!"

He stuffed five cigars into the captain's hand and went to the 37¢ tax window. My father offered to pay but Joe wouldn't think of it, he was very generous that way.

It was fun. I loved my father and uncle very dearly; we never failed to have a good time and to this day I can still remember Tuffie Lehmans, Ward Cuff, Ed Danowski, Johnnie Dell Isola, Mel Hein, Ken Strong, Jim Lee Howells and all the rest knocking over the Chicago Bears and Washington Redskins. I know more about the ball of those days than I do about today's. I don't remember Ken Strong on kickoffs however.

As I said before my Uncle Joe lived with us at 1239 just before we moved to 1235 and he used to read to me every night when I was a little boy, the *Adventures of Mario* and *Pinnochio*. We had some good games of Russian Bank too that lasted all night, and I yelled STOP at him much more than he ever did at me. And after supper we balanced our napkin rings on the lace tablecloth my mother put over the white one; I had the purple ring and he had the white. My father had the silver ring but that was no good because it had bumpy edges and couldn't be balanced. This balancing was the only thing Joe could beat me at, to this day I don't see how he could crumble up the lace tablecloth like that, set the napkin ring on its edge and leave it there in equilibrium, at a forty-five degree angle. He could do it twenty times to my one and what's more he did it quickly, without stopping.

Sometimes we had a good hour's fun after the custard and rice pudding dessert my mother used to make. A couple of times though I couldn't find the rings, I looked high and low for them but no dice; it's funny how something as large as a whole set of napkin rings can get lost like that but that's apartment living for you.

I'd like to say one more thing about my Uncle Joe. When he was twelve years old he had the bicycle parking business and candy-gum business at the old Polo Grounds up on Coogan's Bluff, before they moved it down to the river and took the concession out of his hands and gave it to Stevens. Joe was a born director. It wasn't that he had more talent than Billy and my father, but he had something else besides, he had all the get up and go, the drive you need that takes you where you're going. Joe was a great success.

As a young man Joe got into the stock market, which he really liked, something like Billy and the horses. As a matter of fact, I made this comparison to him once but he got angry and told me it was the most far-fetched thing he ever heard of and how could anybody think like that; the market, he always called it the market in the same way I talk about my wife, and how could the market be mentioned in the same breath as anything like the horses, which are out and out gambling where you don't stand a chance, he said. The market was business, he said, the most marvelous business in all the world where if you put a thousand dollars down on the right stock you might come up with fifteen hundred and long term growth, and how was that like the horses where you go with a bunch of gamblers who slap two dollars down on an animal in hopes of getting three. One was a profession and the other was a waste of time he said. I also spoke to Uncle Billy about this but he said all he knew was he was cleaned out in 1929 and that's all the horses did, they couldn't do any more. So I guess Joe was right after all if Billy couldn't put up a better argument than that.

For Joe, who had a grade school education, the market was his Ph. D. He was a scholar of utilities and always put his money there. I remember once I was in his furnished room over at 168th Street and the Medical Center and he had several documents, business letters and other papers in Economics he was studying; one of them was a big folder with kilowatt hour consumption graphs on it, which he had spent months examining. This night he pointed at the burning bulb in the lamp and said:

"Jims, if you ever invest in the market, always buy utilities. Remember that. No matter what happens they won't let you down. People have to have lights, they have to use electricity, they have no other choice. You've got them coming and going."

I know that Joe knew the market because after he died I had to go to his room to clean out his papers and possessions, and in one of his drawers, underneath the golf tees, insurance calendars and Lake Placid napkins, was a balance book which showed he had a million dollars in 1929. Just think of it, a million dollars and I had it down in black and white to prove it. Once I heard someone say he knew how to buy stock better than anyone else—he certainly must have.

It was fun going through the old balance book like that, looking up the names and the numbers of the shares. The balances were all in the six figures too; a hundred thousand dollars was a day's work to my Uncle Joe. Well, I thought it'd be fun to read the stocks that he sold, that would give the whole thing a more dramatic air; you know a thousand shares of United Gas, up five, sell. But I hadn't any experience in bookkeeping so I couldn't find the sell columns. One of those trained accounting people could have put his finger on them in a minute, but I couldn't, and it took away some of the fun.

Joe wasn't the kind to take it on the chin and let it go at that when the Depression came; he lost somewhere near a million but he started his comeback right away. Once I heard him say he had a friend in the market and this man, whoever he was (I haven't been able to find out), got him to place his money on Electric Bond and Share and Florida Power and Light. As a matter of fact, Joe was about to go whole hog on the Florida utilities but he never made it. In December 1945 he bought a ticket on a Monday morning train for Jacksonville, where he was going to inspect the power plants, but that Sunday night a few hours before he was to leave he died in his sleep. It was not unlike the football games you know his not making it like that, you'd almost think he planned it that way.

Joe left a bunch of stocks in his will which I got about twelve thousand dollars of. I used this money to subsidize the GI Bill and the New York State War Veterans Scholarship I had, bought a home in Long Island, had my summers off, went to Mexico for a year and got married. And what's more I still had 61 shares of Long Island Lighting, 23 1/4, that's $1418.25. Not bad when you come to think of it. I'm sure Joe would approve.

9. My Mother's Family

As little as I know about my father's family tree I know less about my mother's. As I said before I have reason to believe that my grandfather, Matthew Mahoney, was an engineer who came here from Ireland. My mother told me this, but as for her mother, I'm not sure, I think she was born here; it just strikes a note, that's all. I'm not sure of my grandmother's maiden name either although it may have been McGuiness, because my cousin Neenie had a sampler that used to be in our house with the name *Catherine McGuiness, January 1837* on it, and she would have been my mother's grandmother if she's any relation at all. I don't know.

My grandfather must have been a bibliophile because we had a big bookcase when I was a boy filled with volumes over fifty years old; they're all a hundred years old now. These books had some gold on the cover and the names Chaucer, Milton, Shakespeare, Edgeworth, Ignatius Donnelly were either tooled in gold or to be seen in the color of the cover itself, generally maroon or green, with a gold patch as background; and at the bottom of the spine of the books was inscribed the name Matthew Mahoney, in gold. I guess bibliophiles were rare in the Bronx and Washington Heights, where my grandfather lived, because I never saw anyone open one of these books, not once, and all I ever read was *Robin Hood*, a blue book with black letters and lines on the cover. I read it so often I really got to hate the Sheriff of Nottingham.

My mother had an old Aunt Kate Kate, her half-aunt, who was way up in her eighties; in 1942 she thought the search lights on the George Washington Bridge over the Hudson were enemy bombers. When she died during the war, I didn't go to her funeral because I was in Texas taking my advanced training in SNJ's. My one real memory of Kate Kate is she was a little shriveled up old lady who looked perfectly Chinese, which is the way all little old ladies looked to me at the time.

The only Mahoneys who are a vivid part of my recollection are my aunts Mary, Grace and Ann, my Uncle Mal and my mother. It seems to me a child will be close to his aunts and uncles in one of two conditions, if they are unmarried and have lots of time to take him out and buy him things, or if they are married and have a child the same age as he. A lot too depends on the wives, how they get along with the in-laws because people will be people, but a boy with a good aunt or uncle can't ask for any more and if he has a cousin his own age he won't find a better friend; he eats at her house, stays overnight, can borrow things and maybe even goes away with her for a summer though I'd say the best of all is eating because your aunt really puts the dog on for you. My aunt Mary died when I was twelve, which puts the memory to a test, but I can say this, when I went to her house at 1261 Unie I had the best time ever and that's what counts after all. It's fifty years since I've been in that apartment but I know it better than the apartment I'm living in now.

You went up to the fifth floor and entered the door on a small foyer, then a large living room lit up by the windows facing the front, and after that was the bedroom; it was separated from the living room by two French doors; at the far end left of the living room was another little foyer, which Neenie's room ran off of and also the bath and kitchen. One day I went there to stay overnight. I was going for supper too, which suited me just fine, because Aunt Mary always let me have things I wasn't used to; this night Neenie and I had waffles with butter and syrup, oreos and two glasses of hot toddy. Uncle Martin drank five cups of coffee and Aunt Mary ate white toast as she always did; the kitchen had a nice golden warm smell.

After we ate Neenie and I went into her bedroom. She turned the slate over on its stand, rolled up the top of her desk and said; "Jimsie, let's play school. You be the boy and I'll be the teacher." I said: "All right." Neenie gave me two pieces of yellow paper and she told me to write my name on them and I did. She came over to the flat desk I was sitting at and picked up the paper:

"Your penmanship is very poor, Jimsie, your first lesson tonight will be ovals and straights. If you do them well then you may start on the rainbows. You have five minutes. Pay attention to what you are doing and don't disturb the other children. I'll be up at my desk. I have some papers to correct. Ready? Time!"

Neenie adjusted the watch she had on her wrist. Sometimes she let me have it and I found it very hard to set; when I turned the little knob both hands moved as if they were glued together and I could never get the time I wanted. But Neenie told me it was seven o'clock and I had till seven o' five; if I didn't have my lesson finished by then I would be kept in after school and punished.

When she said *Time*! I started in with the ovals, just as I did in P.S. 11, where Miss Greenberg said that for a second grader my penmanship stood in need of improvement; I erased too much, she said, and didn't always stay within the lines, not even when we double spaced.

My first line of ovals was very good; they all stayed within the lines and they were well knit without the usual defect of well knit ovals, the smudging of the centers. I looked up at Neenie; she was sitting at the roll-top sideways to me looking down her nose at a bunch of yellow papers; she held her pencil halfway down the shaft and gave the top paper a couple of flourishing strokes, which I knew were checkmarks. Her eyes went down the page until they darkened; she shook her head and made four quick movements with the pencil. These were two X marks; somebody hadn't stayed between the lines. Neenie put down her yellow pencil with the black lead and picked up the red one; at the top of the page she made a stroke and a curve. This was the red D, the worst of all. Whoever it was had really done badly and Neenie was giving him what he deserved.

After marking this one of the many papers she had to correct, Neenie looked up before I could get back to my ovals. When she saw that I was watching her, she arched her eyebrows and said; "You had better do your lesson. This last batch of papers is very bad and I'm furious with all of you. Now do your lesson or stay in after school." She looked at her watch. "You have three minutes till I pick up all papers."

I put my eyes back on my yellow paper. I skipped a line and started my second row of ovals; as I got near the end of the line I smudged some ovals and went over into the space I had just skipped. Neenie didn't leave me an eraser on the desk so I reached into my pocket for one, which was a little black but all right since it was the soft kind that does a good job. I quickly went at the smudged ovals.

When the last part of the second row of ovals was erased, I looked up at Neenie. She must have been watching me because as I looked up her head was turning and she spun around in her chair so her back was facing me. She crouched over her papers. I got up to see what she was doing, but her back blocked my line of sight and even though I didn't make any noise she said: "Sit down and behave yourself. You have one minute." That isn't much time when you only have two lines of ovals done and the second line is all smudged.

How did she know what was going on behind her back? She always caught me when I got up like that to see what she was doing. Once I tried to take an old assignment from the leather schoolbag on the chair near my desk but she only said, bent over her papers and all: "Children are not allowed to receive unauthorized help." I told her I wasn't trying to get help, I only wanted to see if there was a ruler in the bag so I could draw a line under my name. She said: "It won't do you any good to take an old paper and try to use it on your test. Even if I haven't corrected it I've put a dot on it somewhere and I know where that dot is and whether you've been cheating or not. Sit down and do your test and leave the bag alone." That was one night a long time ago but this was tonight and I only had one minute to go with two lines of ovals done, the first one very perfect but the second one erased at the end. Neenie was furious with me when I erased and she always found me out even if I used the five cent gum kind that rubbed out clean because the corners fell off in little balls with the dirt on them. The black never got on the gum kind.

"TIME! Stop whatever you are doing immediately! Drop all pencils, eyes to the front of the class!" Neenie never turned around when she said this and I began to do the ovals as fast as I knew how; I finished the third line and started the straights; up and down my pencil went like a piston and pretty soon I had three spaces of straights all shaded in without using the eraser once, not even once. Best of all, I stayed within the lines.

I put my pencil down and waited. Neenie got up from her chair and came down to my desk; she didn't look at me. She held her head very high as she looked down at my desk and the leather bag, then she picked up my paper with two fingers and walked back to the roll-top. Since I wanted to know if my penmanship was improving, I was anxious to find out how I made out on the test but Neenie never said anything. She sat there with her back between me and the paper, and no matter how I tried I couldn't see if the pencil was making the long flourishing strokes or the short quick ones. Once her arm moved in such a way I thought she was putting down one pencil and picking up another; but I couldn't be sure. I wanted to tip-toe up behind her and look over her shoulder but I was afraid, because she always found me out, and every time I tried that she never gave me my paper back. That was the worst of all. I'd sooner be kept in than not get my paper back. I'd even write silence is golden.

After Neenie did her correcting she folded up my paper so only the blank side showed and put it on top of her desk. Then she took the ruler with the red lines on it and laid it on the writing surface, half in the desk, half out, and then she lowered the roller. "I have to leave the room, James, to see the principal. Here is your test. While I am gone you must not under any condition look into my desk; if you do, I shall know. And you will be punished, I can promise you that." She said no more but left the room.

I opened up my paper. At the top was a big red double D. Under the D it said: *This paper is a disgrace. Have your mother come to see me.* In the margin by the first line of ovals was *Fair.* By the second line, *Erased, when this is absolutely forbidden. Can't stay between lines.* There was a big red bracket by my last line of ovals and my three lines of straights, and next to the bracket was written, in red pencil: *Worked after Time. Such disobedience can no longer be tolerated.*

Another red D. I folded up the paper and I put it in my back pocket, next to the Indian cards. Then I looked at the ruler.

A little while later Neenie returned. She had a tray with two hot toddies and toast and jam on it. She gave me my drink and my plate and put the tray with hers over on the chair by her bed; the toast was very good and the chocolate in the toddy nice and strong but she didn't eat any of hers; instead, she went up to her desk, examined it for a minute, and said: "Someone has been in my desk. Now I wonder who it could be."

I bit a big hole in my second piece of toast; it wasn't even, it was down in the left hand corner too much. I bit up in the right hand corner and then in the upper left and bottom right corners; the hole was really big now and except for a few teeth marks it was pretty even. If a slice of bread was only a little bigger than it is you could frame your face with it.

"James, you were the only person in the room when I went to see the principal. You must know who did it."

I said I didn't know who did it, nobody did it because it wasn't done in the first place, that I was going over my paper, which didn't deserve a red D because I wasn't disobedient and I didn't erase on the second line.

"One thing at a time, James, first things first. We will discuss your paper when the time comes. Why did you open my desk?"

I said I didn't and prove it anyway, you can't prove it and I'm not going to take the blame for something I didn't do; you always blame me for everything that happens around here even when it doesn't happen. I didn't open your old desk and you can't prove it.

After I said this the hot toddy tasted very good. I dipped the last piece of crust in it and drank it down to where the thick chocolate had settled at the bottom, then I shook the glass in a circular fashion to mix up the rest of the contents and make them flow better, and I raised the glass vertically above my lips until no more came out. After that I put my tongue in the glass as far as it would go and licked the glass half clean.

"But I can prove it. Come here, James."

I put my glass on the desk and went up to the roller top where she was standing.

"When I went out to see the principal, the ruler was under the top where it says eight. Now it says seven."

I looked at the ruler and I looked at her and I was going to say oh no it wasn't, but I put my hands in my pocket and I didn't say anything.

"Your punishment is to write twenty-five times *I must not lie to my teacher*. And bring your mother to school next Monday. We must do something about you."

I don't see why she made all that fuss about her old desk, there wasn't anything in it but some pencils and crayons and a lot of old junk. And a mirror.

I feel I am off on a tangent. I wanted to talk about my Aunt Mary and it looks as though the only things I've talked about are 1261 and my cousin Nancy. But as I say, I was only twelve when Aunt Mary died and what I most remember is a nice lady gliding about the house, 1261 and my cousin Neenie. But come to think of it, all of that is my Aunt Mary to me. I recall one last thing. On New Year's Eve 1936-1937 my brother was having a big dancing party at our house, just three doors down from 1261. He had the dining room rug removed, there were paper streamers on all the walls running out to the chandelier, and the table was off in the corner with a big roast turkey on it. All of a sudden the phone rang. My brother answered. He told me it was Aunt Mary and she heard he was throwing a shindig with a big turkey and would he mind sending her over a nice sandwich. He said he would. I was the one who brought the sandwich and I didn't know it but this was the last time I ever saw the inside of 1261; it was twilight, there was just enough light coming through the window facing on Unie to give the apartment a very nice soft appearance. A lady, dressed in a maroon gown, come out of the gray and said: "How have you been, Jimsie? Thank you so much for bringing the sandwich. You were very kind." My last look. It was sort of like the indelible pencil my father always used. Two months later she died of cancer.

My Aunt Grace lived up at 1560 Unie, on the north side of the Washington Bridge over the Harlem. The fourteen hundreds ran up to the bridge and the fifteen hundreds picked up on the other side right where we caught the Z trolley for the zoo and the U car for Van Cortlandt. Aunt Grace lived on the east side of the street, where the even numbers were, and we lived lower down in the 1200 block on the west side with the odd numbers. There weren't any odd numbers opposite Aunt Grace's because two whole blocks were taken up by the old Ogden estate, which was sold to the French nuns who had their Elmtree school there. Neenie went to Elmtree and once I got to hear Midnight Mass at the chapel. I don't know why but for some reason I tie up that Midnight Mass with the famous story by Alphonse Daudet, not that the priest butchered his Latin or anything or that I sensed the smell of roast meats and truffles, it must have been the sense of mystery, the late hour and twelve manorial undisturbed acres on this estate in the Bronx.

I didn't spend much time up at Aunt Grace's house on the second floor of 1560 and I never did stay there overnight. This wasn't because I didn't like it, it's just that my cousins there were ten years older than I, and when you're a boy, ten years older is like your father almost. I remember once when I was seven Aunt Grace was standing in front of Barone's apartment house at 1245, which was one of the doors between 1235 and 1261; October it was because the sun had that pale color that looks so nice and puts a glow on New York. Aunt Grace was there and I brought home a D in conduct from P.S. 104. My mother had promised me ten cents if I brought home a good report card but for some reason I had a D again; she wouldn't give me the dime so I set up a wail you could hear as far down as the steps to the river at 1225. I was hoping my Aunt Grace would help me but she didn't. All she did was stand there.

Writing these pages has wrought many changes in me. I myself have only a vague idea of what these changes are although last week I took a walk with my old friend Bobbie O'Brien, who put me wise to a few things. We met at the London Shoe Store on the northeast corner of Fordham Road and the Concourse, and from there we walked down the hill east, across Webster, past Roosevelt High School to the zoo where we looked at the Japanese deer, the seals and the new outdoor bird cages; since it was late we didn't have time to feed the squirrels and see

58

the birdhouse so we left and came back to Arthur Avenue, down Arthur Avenue to Mario's for veal cutlet parmigiana, which happens to be my favorite, spaghetti marinara and beer. While we were walking like that Bobbie and I had a good long talk. He's the only one I know who has a memory like mine; perhaps we don't hang on to everything that's happened but once something sticks we've got it for good, not for a year, not for ten years but for good. I was telling Bobbie about my writing, how before I sit down I have a plan in mind but when I start to write the plan gets twisted around and people and places come back to me I haven't thought of in twenty-five years, like the ovals at 1261. Bobbie said that writing a book is like tapping a well because you have a pretty good idea of what you're doing but you don't know what the results will be, especially since the well is your mind. And he is right. The changes are going on, that's for sure.

Where was I? Oh yes. I was talking about 1560 and the convent on Unie. 1560, 1261 and 1245 are gone now; they were torn down after the war to make room for the cloverleaf of the new superhighway from the Washington Bridge to Throg's Neck, which we are told will make the Bronx a better place to live in. The convent is gone and so are the trees; there's a new housing project with odd numbers where the convent used to be . . . James Ignatius Murphy, J.I.M. *Laudator temporis acti.*

10. P.S. 11

I have a yellow paper with a hundred topics scratched on it, ranging from Association, Deli and Egg Cream to Skate Boxes, Wooden Clappers and the Zoo. These are my Bronx institutions and I am wondering how to weave them into this narrative. If I merely list them here and describe them I shall be writing a local color lexicon, a kind of *Angels' Dictionary*, which will interrupt the thread of my life's story; my book will be ponderous with digression like those eighteenth century novels; on the other hand I don't want to omit them they mean so much to me. So perhaps I can place a couple of them at the end of each chapter and put the leftovers at the end of the book in a glossary. I would like to immortalize Egg Cream, Skate Box and Tin Foil Balls they are so beautiful, and what is more posterity has a right to know them.

After Schapiro's candy store the most important building in the Bronx was P.S. 11, Public School Number Eleven, 169th Street and Ogden Avenue, one mile from the Polo Grounds, one mile from the Yankee Stadium, a quarter of a mile from High Bridge and the Harlem River. This scholastic citadel of the western borough had sister establishments throughout that fair land, like P.S. 70 at Unie and Tremont, next to the Park Plaza Theater where I went to the movies every Saturday morning, and P.S. 104, over across Boscobel near Shakespeare Avenue. I went to P.S. 104 for first grade.

I have read of Oxford and Cambridge and once, in 1962, I slept on the Tom Quad where I was even assigned a scout. I have read of Harvard. I have seen Princeton, Madison, Stanford and Berkeley but no matter how far I travel I have never seen a citadel of learning to compare with P.S. 11, the Bronx.

For one thing, the women were more beautiful. I remember in the 4th grade, my teacher was Miss Riley. I had a crush on Miss Riley whose cheeks were always pink, not sallow like the pasty-faced teachers you see today. And in the 8th grade it was Mrs. Kavidson; she was gorgeous, she was full of life; I was eleven. And then there was Adrienne Kalm; I loved Adrienne, she didn't know it but I loved her and after we graduated in 1936 I only saw her once, in 1947, after the war. She lived down near P.S. 11 in Coonan Towers whereas I lived up at the bridge, but one day I was standing on Ogden and she came walking by, that gentle smile, that lovely countenance, that carriage, I shall say no more. "Hello, Jims, how are you?" "Hello, Adrienne, fine thanks and you?" Then a few words more and she was gone. I have never forgotten. Have you, Adrienne? Are you reading these lines or have you gone to that Platonic Bronx where we shall relive the past forever? I am looking forward to seeing you. Goodbye, Adrienne.

The girls were very nice at P.S. 11—Concetta, Sylvia, Phyllis, Doris, Elaine, Adrienne, Henrietta, and the boys too—Lester,

Leon, Mortie, Daniel, I liked them all. I never met one I didn't like. One boy's name was Philomeno something or other and he joined us around the sixth grade.

I only remember three men at P.S. 11, Mr. Dawkins the principal, a nice old man, who was replaced by Mr. Holson, the next principal. There was some talk about his being mean but I never saw he was mean, and the 7th grade teacher, Mr. ------, I never learned his name so I can't write it here, tall, ruddy cheeked, hoarse, balding, was supposed to be mean too, but he was never mean to me. I was in the other 7th grade from his, 7R, R standing for Rapid. Mayor LaGuardia wanted to cut down on the budget in the 1930's so he had all these Rapid classes, meaning you skipped a half year at a time, with the result that I graduated from grammar school when I was eleven years old. Sometimes I have wished I was older. I might have made all the teams in high school instead of none and who knows I might have seen Adrienne.

P.S. 11 was heaven to me. I learned to read and write there and I must have learned grammar very well for I never learned anything at Mecca, Ivy or graduate school that I hadn't learned at P.S. 11. Nominative clause, adjectival clause, adverbial, parse the sentence, prepositional object, just name it and I learned it at P.S. 11 with two possible exceptions. I didn't really learn the subjunctive until years later when I had sentences of fear and apprehension in Spanish, but then as Fowler says the subjunctive has had it exequies in English. The other exception came at State U., when a learned colleague casually remarked on the accusative genitive, for example, "the attack of John" being susceptible of two interpretations. Outside of that I learned everything at P.S. 11.

As for Math, I remember the times tables up to 144, 12 times 12, and I can readily improvise after that, 13 times 13—169; 15 times 15—225. I am quick on the trigger at Math. I myself take no credit for this, P.S. 11 did it for me; as a matter of fact, all Bronx citizens were accomplished grammarians and mathematicians. I would like to go back to those days, to see all those intelligent faces. Everything today looks like Appalachia.

"This is the forest primeval, the murmuring pines and the hemlock . . ." "Speak for yourself, John . . ." "Don't fire till you see the whites of their eyes . . ." "I regret that I have but one life to give for my country . . ." Literature, History, Geography, again, just name it and we learned it at P.S. 11. Phyllis, Elaine, Concetta, Daniel, Morty, Jims, peripatetics of Highbridge, the Bronx, New York.

My theme is memory. I remember the assembly. I always liked them. We marched in the hallways with our class, along the walls down the corridors to the back and into the auditorium: "I pledge allegiance to the flag of the United States of America and to the republic for which it stands. One nation, indivisible, with liberty and justice for all." When I said this in the Boy Scouts I raised my right hand, held my pinky down with my thumb and held the three middle fingers vertical in the air. But at P.S. 11, it's over fifty years now, I placed my right hand on my heart. I loved saying the pledge of allegiance, with the flag and dignitaries—I didn't know they were dignitaries then—on the platform, the monitors in the aisles with the metal badge and white elastic band on their arms and everything so clean and tidy. I have never known such peace and contentment.

Everything was so peaceful. I remember one day I went home for lunch and decided to buy my candy in the candy store around the corner, on the corner of Merriam and Ogden, instead of Schapiro's. I can't remember the man's name although Mr. Barshak strikes a note and I'd recognize him to this day if I saw him. He was a tired looking man in his fifties. I went there because I was saving the Presidential card series and had all the cards I needed for the prize except one. I can still rattle off all the presidents: Washington, Adams, Jefferson, Madison, Monroe, John Quincy Adams . . . all the way to Roosevelt, and I must have had fifty Martin Van Buren's but not one James Madison. This was the company that gave you a big slab of caramel instead of gum with your cards so it wasn't the Gowdy Gum Company of Boston, Massachusetts. This day I bought five cards hoping to get a James Madison. I broke one of the slabs and put it in my mouth and was going out the door when I heard a voice say: "Hello dollink." It was Mrs. Silver next door, who had one of those specialized tailor shops you don't see any more with ladies furs in the window, and I recall her sitting with a fur around her neck with some silver in it and somehow I associated her name Silver with the fur and I gather it must have been the fall, sunny but cool and so it was the fall. I don't know why but she seemed to want to talk to me; she asked me my name and where I lived and went to school and then she told me about her life, how she had lived in Austria as a little girl but her sister lived in Russia and how she wanted to go to see her sister but she didn't have the money. I guess Mrs. Silver was sixty years old the day she spoke to me, so this must have happened forty-five years before, maybe more. She told me how she went to see the Emperor and how he gave her her railroad ticket, and then she looked out across Ogden Avenue and sighed. She was very sad. Then she said something I didn't understand: "Ay! Franz Josef, he wass an angel!" I can still see her sitting in her chair, in front of her shop as I left for P.S. 11. There was so much peace and contentment. This was 1935.

One day not long ago I was up in the Thruway Diner in New Rochelle and I thought I saw Mrs. Silver. I could have sworn it was she silver fur and all but no I was mistaken. She couldn't have been sixty in 1935 and sixty in 1984. Impossible. She was very beautiful whoever she was. She reminded me of Mrs. Silver.

Memories, memories, dreams of long ago. There is a song with these words, and as I write about the Bronx I find I am light of heart and singing. Memories, memories . . . I never did get all the presidential cards, so I couldn't send them away for the free box of candy.

What else do I remember about P.S. 11? It's hard to say, all those grammar school years rolled into a moment. I remember I was reading *Penrod and Sam* or *Peck's Bad Boy* or had seen one of them in the movies and I thought it was funny to dip a girl's long hair in the inkwell. I wouldn't do that now but I did then; her name was Annette and she had long black hair neatly braided. The inkwell. If I were one of those poets who writes Odes to an Onion, Odes to an Artichoke and so forth I would write Ode to an Inkwell. What fond recollections I have of it, the wooden pen, the new pen point, the small glass vial, the ink pot kept in a closet. The paper was handed out and we were ready to write or do the penmanship exercises. Circles: ⠀⠀⠀⠀⠀⠀⠀⠀⠀⠀⠀⠀⠀⠀⠀⠀ ; Straights: ⠀⠀⠀⠀⠀⠀⠀⠀⠀⠀ ; Rainbows: ⠀⠀⠀⠀⠀ , page after page of them for calligraphic improvement. I loved penmanship and worked hard at it but I don't recall ever getting a good grade. My failure in penmanship is one of the great disappointments of my academic career, which began in 1929 and remains unfinished.

One year at P.S. 11 they changed the dollar bill, I remember that; the new one was smaller and had different printing on it so with a little research I could verify the year. It was about this time that I smelt something I had never smelt before for I was walking along Ogden Avenue one Sunday morning to go to the nine o'clock Mass and at the corner of 170th Street top of the hill was a candy store I never went into and next to it a new store. As I went by I smelt . . . the smell of stale beer though I couldn't have named it at the time. Prohibition was over and the country was emerging from its strait jacket so it must have been the spring of 1933. That author was right about the odor of small pastries; olfactory recollections like my stale beer are the strongest. In 1955 I went to Mexico City when my daughter was three years old, and again in 1968, and the second time the only thing she remembered was the distinctive odors of Mexican cooking, tortillas, beans, tacos al pastor.

I haven't done P.S. 11 justice, so I ask the reader to take it on authority: the most profound institutions of the Bronx, giving that society its distinguishing form, were the candy store and P.S. 11. Everything else is ancillary. I have sometimes wondered why Henry Adams went to Europe for his *Wanderjahr* when he could have gone to the Bronx.

As I recall my young days I think of P.S. 11, Schapiro, Mrs. Silver, Bacigalupi, Kelly, stick ball, the U car, the Z and the streets but especially the streets where all these people and institutions and events congregated, University Avenue, Undercliff, Sedgwick, Boscobel, Nelson, Shakespeare, Plimpton, Anderson . . . This reminds me of a poem someone wrote using only names for aesthetic effect, and when I lived in Long Island after the war I thought of writing a poem like that using the place names there: Shelter Rock Road, Oyster Bay, Syosset, Mineola, Jericho . . . Could a poet express the joy of the Bronx and its invisible reality listing only the names? Should he write his poem in consonant or assonant rhyme? English does not lend itself to assonance the way other languages do, but it would be a marvelous feat if he could execute it and the Bronx deserves only marvels. I might try it but if I fail I ask the reader's indulgence and hope he will attribute the imperfections to the pen rather than the heart or reality, for my intentions and the reality are perfect. There can be no intentional fallacy in these verses:

Oh Grand, Nelson, Woodycrest,
Ship Canal, Loring, Highbridge,
Walton, One O Four, Concourse,
Andrews, Van Cortlandt, Sedgwick,
Ogden, Mount Eden, Jerome,
River, Mannion's, Undercliff,
P.S. 11, Burnside,
Concourse, Featherbed, Judge Smith,
Fordham, Tremont, City Island,
Harlem, Orchard Beach, Shakespeare,
Crotona, Deegan, Aqueduct,
The East-West's One Forty-Ninth,
Merriam, One Seventieth, Highbridge,
We who are about to leave
Salute you.

The assonance breaks down and the syllabification but not the admiration. This is a West Bronx poem, Crotona, City Island and Orchard Beach being the only toponymy from other regions. Although Judge Smith's is a hill and Mannion's a bar, Mannion's #1 and #2 on Ogden Avenue, I felt the Bronx would be incomplete without them. I repeat the name *Highbridge* since I was running out of an *i* sound and also wanted to emphasize that neighborhood, which happened to be my own. One O Four is P.S. 104, my preparatory school for P.S. 11. I realize that lyrical poets like me don't usually explain their art but in this case I was anxious to do so. I shall risk the accusation of hubris for the sake of the Bronx.

One could write another type of onomastic poem, Bacigalupi, Shea, Schapiro, Montefiore, Kelly, Schwarz, Civita Vecchia, O' Shaughnessy, Liebowitz, Caruso, Kennedy, Wiseman, with a few Kowalskis and Kochenmeisters thrown in, as accurate a portrayal as Unie and Undie. With Caruso the poet can stress the penult, with O'Shaughnessy, the antepenult and with Schwarz the ult. And there are all sorts of onomatopoeia, Bacigalupi, Kowalski, and even synecdoche, Wiseman. The possibilities are unlimited. But I must forgo the pleasure of writing this sonnet for rather than joy I should express stumbling, bumbling ineptitude, so

uncharacteristic of the Bronx.
After the war I met a fellow from the Bronx, one of the new
Highbridgers, who enrolled in a graduate school with me. He was
as enthusiastic about his homeland as I was and wrote me the
following verses:

ROMANCE DEL BELLO BRONX

Andando por calle Woodycrest
saudade, morriña tengo
por una nación tan bella
que el cielo tiene recelos
puesto que los mismos ángeles
no ven lugar tan ameno.
Yo don Jaime Ignacio Murphy
las memorias guardo en pecho
de Loring, Unie, y Shakespeare
que reñidas con lo feo
me ensalzan el corazón
me enseñan lo verdadero
me dicen que eres tú Adrienne
me hacen contemplar lo bello.

My new friend told me he could go on and on and add *lo bueno*
after *lo bello*, giving the Greek trinity of the good, the true and
the beautiful, which is the Bronx all right.
     Well, I myself am gone from the Bronx thirty-five years
now, I am a DP, and consequently my English has suffered. Ex-
patriates lose their touch. It is time to move on, to return to
other institutions.

11. All Saints

In 1936 I became a confirmed segregationist. I enrolled in All Saints High School, a second kind of confirmation.

A three mile walk from my house each day, each way, with an eight by eleven inch hard-covered looseleaf notebook; six books strapped in pairs of three to the notebook with my brother's belt since it was unmanly to use a briefcase, a small homework pad in my back pocket and a brown paper lunch bag, I made my trek south and east to the Concourse. What does the Post Office say: "Neither rain nor storm, snow nor sleet shall detain these couriers from their course." That was me all right, every day, rain or shine, five below or ninety above, the courier, making his rounds, delivering his books to All Saints outside Highbridge. At the time it seemed all right and I was happy in a way but as I look back I think it might have been a good idea to go to Evander Childs. Yes, I should have gone to Evander.

This reminds me of an author I once read who ontologizes everything and for whom every deed is a metaphysical problem, down to the existential anguish of shining your shoes. I have always admired his prose and wish these Bronx recollections were written with half his power, but as a philosopher he seems to me a bit pompous. Still, he has some good things to say. "I can imagine," he says, "wanting to have what someone else has but I can't imagine wanting to be someone else." In other words, I want what Rockefeller has but I don't want to be Rockefeller, only myself; which makes sense for after all our being is our first possession. And so I don't wish I was someone else but I wish I had gone to Evander Childs.

This is the hardest chapter to write, the hardest of all, not because I am reluctant to say what I have to say but for reasons of possible misinterpretation, and I especially don't want to be misunderstood here. I hope I can get my message across when I say I am a confirmed segregationist, which has something to do with boys apart from girls of course, but something else also.

The name of Anthony Burgess comes to mind, an outstanding novelist who seems very likeable on Dick Cavett's television show. He says his ancestors were Catholic, and in criticizing Evelyn Waugh's *Brideshead Revisited* he says the book is illusory, that Catholicism in England meant poverty, wretched poverty; the Catholics paid a price for their faith, even if they were upper class they still paid a price for what they believed. Mr. Burgess then says that he himself is no longer a Catholic, and here is where he and I part ways. Were I to lose my faith in such circumstances I believe I would keep it to myself; yes I, James Ignatius Murphy of the Bronx would keep it to myself or tell it privately to someone very close to me, my wife. But air it publicly, I don't think so. I wouldn't give them the satisfaction. As a professor in a university I have seen too much fence-sitting, too much insincerity, too much avarice, too much pusillanimity in the chancellors, deans and faculty to make such an admission. Even were I to abandon their beliefs I would stand by the credo of my ancestors; though they were misers in a peat bog (and probably were) I would stand by them for I feel they were more honest and courageous than the people I see today. This is not a criticism of Mr. Burgess, I don't know the man except through a hazy film, it is only a statement of what James Ignatius Murphy would do or thinks he would do in similar circumstances. I wouldn't give them the satisfaction.

I don't want the reader to get me wrong, I have not lost my faith. Creation, Trinity, Incarnation, Resurrection, especially the person of Jesus, who brings everything together, matter and spirit, visible and invisible, phenomena and noumena, are still very real to me. It all comes together in Him and without Him I should find the universe unbearable. If others don't share my belief I don't feel sorry for them because I don't feel superior to them, I have my father to thank for that, but I do sense a kind of compassion when I see them agonize excessively over evil—pollution, war, starvation, injustice, hatred, even the threat to the snail darter alarms them—particularly evil in the abstract, over which they have no power. The best thing to do is to follow His example, which is not easy to do, I don't do it myself, but if everyone acted like Him for just one day there'd be no turning back; it's as simple as that and as difficult. Metaphysicians say that the higher the being the more simple, until one arrives at Pure Act. So be it. Let us try to be simple.

I haven't lost the faith but I must say I no longer admire the accoutrements. I still prefer the Latin Mass, a missa cantata with the *Panis angelicus, Praeceptis salutaribus moniti, Gloria, Ave Maria,* and I like candles, incense, the monstrance, benediction, rosary, stations, *Tantum ergo,* which is another way of saying I am sixty years old. These things are a matter of taste rather than faith and my taste is ancient; I do not like the new style, bland English, unmusical lyrics, unspontaneous spontaneity, but again this is a question of taste; were a Shakespeare to come along and firm up the English, tuning the lyre and wedding art with spontaneity, there is no reason the new style might not surpass the old. But taste is not the issue as far as I'm concerned, for Jesus was not a snob. His church is for everyone, Latins and Unlatins, lyrical and unlyrical, bright, stupid, educated, uneducated, rich, poor, fat, thin, tall, short, people of good taste and bad taste, everyone. Heaven is not a place where artists go and socialites, only saints, and although it is good to have a Ph.D. in one's dossier it is not a celestial union card and besides Ph.D.'s are frequently boring.

I speak of other accoutrements which I hope will make themselves clear as I write about my schooling at All Saints.

All Saints High School, 1936-1941, five years, where I did eighth grade over because Mayor LaGuardia had skipped me so much I was still a little boy when I went there.

I have many fond recollections of the school; after all, who doesn't recall his halcyon days with some tenderness unless he be an English boy at the flogging block? And All Saints was no lonely boarding school with a fagging system; we all went home at night, dayhops as they called us in New York City.

I remember the handball games in the west yard, which was bounded at one end by an apartment building, then by a red brick wall facing on the sidewalk, and a wall of the school itself, so we could play a three wall game. The rubber ball came at you and you could hit it directly, play it off the back wall without a bounce or off the side wall; the fourth side was open, a painted line in the middle of the school yard, but this cement patch was not built as a handball court and you could hardly ask for more. The only court I ever saw better than All Saints' was that huge red rising wall at P.S. 11, off the auditorium.

I remember the lunch room, tables and food line; I don't think I ever stood on that line where the hot meals were served for twenty-five cents; chicken croquettes, mashed potatoes and gravy, corn and other delicacies. They looked so good and smelled even better but I never ate them because I had my tongue sandwiches on whole wheat bread, my half head of lettuce, tomato and apple. Sometimes I had cheese. I had a nickel on me but I used to save that for after school when I went to Mr. Dee's candy store for an egg cream and two loosies, or an egg cream, pretzel and loosie, or halvah, seltzer and two loosies, or a 2¢ Nestles, whatever the traffic would bear. I used to stay and watch the big guys, the football team mainly, play pin ball in the back of the store, and to tell the truth I don't think Mr. Dee and his son Seymour really liked them. They always had to prove they were better than everybody else, they were always showing off, tilting the machine, shoving it this way and that and they made an awful lot of noise. One day one of them asked Mr. Dee if his father was a B, and Seymour being there had to take an awful lot of guff. The worst of all though was Big Tim Taafe, who later became a college star and played in the pros. One day at school he held little McManus out the window with one arm, three stories up, and although McManus was a game kid who went out for the JV's, that was too much for him, he was trembling all over and crying. Imagine the problems Big Tim caused the Dees.

Come to think of it, All Saints was an awfully noisy school, which is what happens when you practice segregation and stick four hundred boys in school with no girls around. They get noisy. When I think of All Saints I think of two experiences, the movie Mr. Roberts with Henry Fonda, where the young timid boy hit the teasing bully with a wrench, opening a twenty-five stitch wound, and the school Fray Juan de Zumárraga, the Mexico City All Saints, where I sent my own boys in 1968 and the segregationists tore the sole off one of their shoes. When it comes to boys, segregation leads to violence, which is why I'm an anti-segregationist. Girls present problems, they can be malicious too, but they are the lesser of two evils, yes, the more I think of it I realize that girls are the lesser of two evils.

But All Saints was segregationist in another way and this is not so easy to explain. I don't think the school meant to be that way, I honestly don't, I think the separation was an unintended result rather than a cause, an effect growing out of ignorance and misguidance.

I don't recall any of the Brothers there singling out Protestants or Jews for honorable or dishonorable mention, or atheists for that matter. As far as atheism was concerned it was never alluded to; I guess it was simply assumed that religion was here to stay like the sun and the rain, a natural phenomenon. Just as Americans take democracy for granted, or the Yankees and Giants for granted, Joe DiMaggio and Carl Hubbell, so All Saints Brothers and boys took religion for granted. It was there, it was simply there, in the air, in the walls, in the ceiling and plants and trees, atheism didn't exist there was no such thing as an atheist and so contrary to what outsiders might think there were no harangues against atheism.

Protestants appeared occasionally in Religion classes, which met twice a week. There was always Religion. Each class started with a Hail Mary and Glory Be, and the last class ended with a long litany: House of Gold, Pray for us, Ark of the Covenant, Pray for us, Tower of Ivory, Pray for us, Star of the Sea, Pray for us . . . all in honor of the Virgin Mary, the sorrowful one and the Glorious Mother of God. I remember these prayers with fondness. And on First Fridays we went to school early for Mass and Communion, and I went too for those delicious sugar crumb buns and coffee, which I never had at home. After Mass they said Benediction . . . Tantum ergo, sacramentum, veneremur cernui . . . I still remember the Latin words though I don't know all their meaning, *cernui* for example with the Italian pronunciation on the *ce*. I liked those hymns, I still do though you don't hear them any more, and I sometimes hum them to myself. This removal of beautiful songs goes under the rubric of Second Vatican Progress.

Protestants appeared only in Religion classes, not in Religion, and then only occasionally under casuistry. The Brothers never called their ethical studies casuistry and wouldn't have known the meaning of the word, but that's what it was, casuistry. I don't use the term as a pejorative, for willy nilly we are all casuists making decisions concerning right and wrong. About Protestantism we learned the following rules:

1. Can you go to a Protestant church?	1. No.
2. Can you ever go to a Protestant church?	2. On rare occasions. Very rare.

3. When can you go to a Protestant church?
(a) If your best friend is a Protestant and invites you to his wedding. Try not to be the best man.
(b) If a close Protestant friend of the family dies and has a service. (He must be very close).
(c) If your mother is a Protestant and asks you to go to a baptism. Protestant baptisms are valid, and marriages are valid between two Protestants, but not between a Catholic and a Protestant if performed in a Protestant church. Remember the Pauline privilege.
(d) In an emergency. If a Protestant church is burning down you can help put out the fire. Leave as soon as it's over.

This was all we learned about Protestantism. We learned nothing about Luther or Calvin and most of the boys, perhaps all of them, had never heard their names. Melancthon and Knox would have been as unknown as Mithras and Osiris, both to the Brothers and their students.

The Jews were never discussed at all, not once, at least I don't recall their getting the same generous mention as the Protestants. Perhaps there are several reasons for this. I suppose it was assumed that your father might have married a Protestant but not a Jewess; ergo, you had to discuss the possibility of going to Protestant churches, which looked a little like Catholic churches in their feeble, drab, mimetic way, and were empty inside, whereas going to a synagogue would not occur to anyone, at least not in All Saints in the 1930's. One boy had a Jewish father but he was brought up a Catholic, *naturally*, and that's why he was at All Saints and the Brothers seemed to like him even cotton up to him two of them. Casuistry did not concern itself with the Jews for they were they and you were you and ne'er the twain shall meet and if you never meet someone how can you and they have ethical problems?

The Jews unlike the Protestants were ubiquitous. The Protestants had all left New York, everyone knew that, all the Protestant churches were empty, like that stark fortress facing P.S. 11, the Methodist structure on Featherbed Lane and Unie, and the other vacant building on 183rd and Unie up by NYU. There were only Italians, Irish and Jews. All Saints was ninety per cent Irish, ten per cent Italian, and the Jews lived up and down the block, in the apartment house forming the back of our handball court, and they had a small synagogue on the next street. So Protestants were dying, decadent, gone, heretics, on the wane, unsubstantial, whereas Jews were not dying and would never die; they were here, around you, substantial, they even had the true religion but didn't know what to do with it. They were right but they were stupid; in any case, they weren't heretics. This was never said explicitly and I doubt that Brother O'Strich would have formulated such thoughts but he and everyone else at

All Saints assumed it. That's the word, assumed, segregationists make assumptions. They are not evil as some people might think, they make assumptions without realizing what they are doing. Boys go to All Saints. That is good. Girls go to St. Margaret Mary's. Protestants are wrong. That is bad. Stay away from their churches, besides, they are dying out, let them die. Jews are right but they're also wrong and not too intelligent. Ignore them if you can, it may be hard, but ignore them; unlike the Protestants they are always around and always will be since Himself has ordained it so be nice to them but keep your distance. You can shun them if you have to because you must flee the proximate occasion of sin. Again, these premises were never formulated into words, they were never written or spelled out, they were just there, in the air, like the trees and grass and church, sparrows and El train. Like bees and pollen, floating from one vine to another.

The Jews did appear in one course, Bible History, which was a simple prose recasting of biblical episodes on the order of Lamb's tales from Shakespeare. This course was really worthwhile, far and away the best of the Religion classes, and what little Old Testament I know, what very little, I know from Bible History. It goes without saying that the Jews appeared here, after all if they don't appear who else is going to? I don't recall their being portrayed malevolently as eager participants in the deicide business although there was the fact of rejection; Christ appeared to them, they did not accept Him, He turned to all nations. Later I learned that St. Paul preached the doctrine of the Uncircumcision—"I withstood Cephas to his face"—and that he answered the call of the Macedonians but I didn't learn this at All Saints and feel certain that the brothers there were not familiar with it.

Still, it was segregation. No girls. No Jews. No Protestants. Also no Economics, no Philosophy, no Sociology, no Anthropology, no History really, not the tinned History we learned, and nothing resembling Utility. Historians have called this a ghetto mentality and I guess when you come right down to it that's what All Saints was, a ghetto; though I didn't know it at the time that three-walled handball court was a symbol of All Saints and the Catholic Church in New York City, an American ghetto, not a Pale of Settlement ghetto, which had four walls in Europe, but an American ghetto, three walls. There is always an opening in America where ghettos are wont to break down or are broken down, by the War, the automobile, intermarriage, by the Economy I suppose. The blacks and Indians might like to hear this; blacks and Indians didn't exist at All Saints in the 1930's since the janitors there were Pat and Jim, immigrants from Downstairs Ireland.

All Saints had a great effect on me and still does. I am still a separatist and it's funny because I don't remember my father's mentioning sex or religion to me in all his life except the day Al

Smith was defeated. One of my uncles made a derogatory remark about the Jews once and my other uncle said he knew lots of Protestants and unbelievers who were better than Catholics, he even seemed to prefer them. As for my mother, she didn't like the nuns and yet she seemed to have the greatest admiration for the brothers who she seemed to think were fine dedicated men. But she never mentioned religion either. I gather that I am what I am, narrow, parochial, and stubborn for two reasons, the pollen in the air at All Saints and the noumenal legacy of my grandmother's Theology. Parochialism may not be the intent but it is the effect, which is what I meant before when I said 'the accoutrements." I don't consider them to be articles of faith since they don't appear in the Nicene Creed and I don't like them.

I arrive now at the two master keys of my life's story, something like the O and U trolley cars were to the Bronx since you could travel nowhere without them. Neither is easy to explain so I shall seek outside help from literature and history.

First I want to mention a little known Spanish novel, Padre Luis Coloma's *Boy*, which might have been a masterpiece had its author not suffered the censorship of his own religious order. Count Xavier de Baza, nickname of Boy, as in English, is a fine young gentleman who is accused of murdering a loanshark. Though innocent he refuses to defend himself in order to protect the honor of a married woman he was visiting the night of the crime. He finally goes off to die in the Carlist wars but before departing he takes leave of his friend Paco Burunda, also a nobleman. Paco is narrating:

We arrived at the crossroads where the two highways parted . . . and on reaching the mile post I stopped my horse and prepared to dismount. Boy quickly detained me. "Where are you going?" he asked me. "What's the hurry?"
"You said we should say goodbye here, and I . . ."
"No matter. Keep on a little . . . stay with me as far as there," he added, indicating with his finger a bend in the road not far away, where he had to turn.
In this brief space Boy asked me insistently to write him, and I promised I would . . . At the bend in the road I dismounted, biting my lips so as not to show my anguish, and I said, apparently calm:
"Goodbye, Boy. Adiós."
"Goodbye, lad," he said, stretching his hand out to me from the horse.
And quickly rearing around, he went on his way. But he had scarcely gone six paces when he quickly turned around again . . . He jumped from his horse, leaving it free, and impetuously ran up to me and embraced me, putting his cheek next to mine. I could feel the moisture on my own face, and when Boy let go his face was full

of tears . . . Then in a natural voice, but heartrending in its very naturalness, as the sorrow of strong men always is, he said:
"Now, lad, you must be satisfied!. . . You have seen me cry! The glory is all yours!. . . Why now we are Romeo and Juliet!"

Earlier in the novel Paco Burunda had spoken of his friend's 'stoical pruritus,' his inability to show emotion, which Boy overcomes just once in his life, as he goes to his death.

That's the phrase, that's the key, that's what I'm trying to say, stoical pruritus. I am James Ignatius Murphy, J.I.M., Jim or Jims, my other name is Boy. Bronx Boy. I have a stoical pruritus. No matter how happy I am inside, I do not show it. The English schoolboys may do the same and say it's bad form to make a show but that has nothing to do with me, I don't care about form, or good show as they say. I would say that All Saints, my father and mother and my grandmother's Theology taught me that, not to show it. You just don't. The same goes if you are bleeding inside, you don't show it. You can't. A professor does you a great favor, you thank him but not too warmly, you express a limited gratitude; you are indeed most grateful, you are overjoyed, but you make no display; "thank you," that's all. Another professor is a cad, a bounder, a trickster, you don't complain, you keep it to yourself. "Stay away from people like him," my father said. That's all. No remonstrance, no complaint, no surface agitation. Gratitude or disgust, the countenance is the same. I wonder what the source is. Not English public school form, which is meaningless for the Bronx Boy, James Ignatius Murphy. A charity of sorts, misdirected, but still a charity? Perhaps. Shyness? Perhaps. Irish Jansenism? That's likely. I knew an Irish nun once who was amused by an Italian wake where emotion ran wild and they had a flower display indicating the time of Mama's death. Jansenism. A likely source. Luis Coloma, S.J., who wrote *Boy*, was educated in French seminaries after the Revolution of 1868. Irish Jansenism, the hedgemaster educated in France, Maynooth, Coloma, James Ignatius Murphy, French Jansenism, Xavier de Baza, Boy: perhaps All Saints should have been called All Boys, more Jansenist than Catholic, perhaps that's what I meant by the atmosphere when I said "what was in the air," the pollen everywhere. The accoutrements.

I must tell an acecdote about an Irish family in the Bronx, which is apropos of what I am trying to say. I heard that three brothers were playing in the lots one day when one of them fractured his skull; he was dizzy and nauseous but at table that night they wouldn't tell their father. Perhaps the man was an unreasonable brute and they were trembling with fear, which would make this an isolated case, or then again they might have had the same moral fiber as Boy, he of stoical pruritus. They just wouldn't speak up, they couldn't, they didn't know how. That's what people don't understand, Boy and Murphy, you keep it in; good or bad you keep it in. I know that if I had spoken up in my sophomore year at All Saints, if I could have spoken then, my mother would have taken me out and sent me to another school, where I had won a scholarship. I would have left All Saints for sure because that's where I met Brother Solomon.

Most of the brothers were nice enough fellows. I remember O'Malley with his red hair, blue eyes and smile. He pretended to be severe with the boys, tough even, but it was all a pretense; he was a good man and we were all with him. He was a good teacher too. O'Malley came from the Midwest rather than New York, for the brothers had orders just like the military each year and were sent about the United States. And Brother Monahan in the grammar school was liked by all, tall, curly hair, brown eyes, gentle, patient, kind, a perfect grammar school teacher. The boys loved him. The principal, Brother McGuire, was a nice man, Mickey we called him, much older than the others, and he commanded everyone's respect. Nickle and Lenihan I'd rather not talk about. Nickle was all right until he lost his temper and bit savagely at his nails like the time we booed his refereeing in the gym and I had to hide in the third floor toilet booth so he wouldn't punch me with that frenzied fist. As for Lenihan there was something inadequate about him; he later left the order but not before slapping the boys in moments of hysteria.

Solomon was another cup of tea. Thin, tall, handsome (more handsome than Tyrone Power), neat, clean, soft spoken, he went about quietly on tiptoes. I can see him now, black soutane, black hair, black eyebrows, a study in blackness. One day Bob O'Brien and I were playing practical jokes when we did something to his dislike. I was the class exhibitionist, I know that now but I didn't know it then, because if you don't get attention at home you'll seek it elsewhere when you're fourteen years old, stand on your head, laugh out loud, make shadows on the blackboard in class, like a donkey's nibbling on a teacher's nose. He never raised his voice, not once. An angel of death, a drawn sword, a ray from the firmament, he simply raised his eyes and whispered, "See me after school," then tiptoed out of the room. This was ten in the morning and meant you had to live with it all day.

At three o'clock Bob and I showed up at his room on the second floor. He closed the door. He drew the shade. "Assume the angle." I bent over the desk and he hit me with the strap four times, a thick heavy rubber strap four times, as hard as he could, four calculated times and not on the fat but on the bone where the buttocks meets the spine. The pain was excruciating and forty-five years later I still remember it; why I remember it better than the plane crash I had in 1944. I still remember it. It was deliberate, calculated, cold, cruel. He did it on purpose. Not like the other brothers. Solomon knew what he was doing. Strapping was part of the system but even so most of the brothers didn't use it; O'Malley did once but it was a make-

74

believe, gently on the hands, and he was practically laughing as he did it, a joke for everyone's amusement; why then you could go and brag to everyone about your battle scars, like those band aids for children you see with purple hearts on them. Nickle was usually all right, Lenihan wasn't, but those two neurotics didn't have "full consent of the will," as they say . . . "A deliberate bad action with full consent of the will," that's the definition of an evil act. Solomon was different. He had five hours to give "full consent of the will" to his bad action; he was deliberate. He wanted to inflict pain the kind of pain you'd remember a half century later. And he was successful. I hope he reads these lines and repents before he meets his Creator.

The bad thing about all this was I didn't tell my parents. I couldn't. I didn't know how. I never discussed anything with my father, who taught me not to by his example; he never discussed anything, politics, religion, money, nothing. And had my mother ever known she would have yanked me out of All Saints on the spot and sent me to another school, I know she would have. But no, I didn't tell her either because I didn't like to talk to her and wouldn't know what to say if I did. So I kept it to myself. So did Bob O'Brien.

I can't say I hated Solomon, I never did nor do I today although I didn't like him that's for sure and when I later learned he had spent several years in French Canada I could understand part of his problem, more Jansenism, a double dose. He has affected me to this day and whenever I see people abuse authority like him I take it really hard, haughty deans and chancellors (are there any other kind?) phony chairmen, teachers, police, government agents, I don't like it. And I do something about it, I send off letters denouncing these tyrants. Solomon did that to me. I would never send my children to a school run by his religious order lest they meet an avenging angel like him, and to think that if things had been different I might have gone to Evander Childs.

There was no politics, history or philosophy at All Saints, none whatsoever, I don't recall any comments favorable or unfavorable about England, France, Germany, Italy, Spain, Russia or any other country, not even Ireland and our own country, and we never heard the names of Mussolini, Stalin, Hitler, Franco, Dollfuss or the other leaders of that era. I learned my anti-Communism from my Uncle Joe's Hearst newspaper, *The New York Journal*, and my pro-Franco sympathies from some other part of the Church, which they said was being persecuted. I never heard about the New Deal one way or the other or about the saint or traitor, depending on your point of view, in the White House. The brothers, the other students and I lived the way children do, in the present, no future and no past, and we lived this side of the horizon, which was etched for us by a three-walled court of handball. The order of the day was counsels of perfection, Mass on First Fridays and salvation of the immortal soul; flee the proximate occasion of sin. We were innocent of what was going on around us. Children.

A professor once asked me why Catholics always have to have their own outfits, Catholic Boy Scouts, Catholic Sea Scouts, Catholic Schools, Catholic Parades, Catholic Knights of Columbus, Catholic Bingo, even Catholic Insurance. He was visibly annoyed by their separatism. Although he was a fine scientist rigorously trained in Mathematics he resembled the brothers at All Saints; he was not conversant with history.

English-speaking nations are hostile to Catholicism, they don't like it. You might put it this way: at my first university convocation in a State University a New Zealand lady asked me what I taught and when I replied "Spanish", she said: "You don't look as though you have a knife in your teeth." Or then again you might put it another way: in the movies it's a question of Errol Flynn playing the noble, dashing, lovable Jeffrey Hawkins in Rafael Sabatini's *The Sea Hawk* against Jack La Rue, the foul, greasy, scheming, black-bearded, sweaty, gold-helmeted and gold-hearted malevolent Spaniard. Catholics are ultimately a bunch of Spanish cutthroats and if they are going to call Elizabeth Monarch of England and Head of the Church the harlot queen, a whore, and Protestants heretics and left-footers, then the Pope by God is the Antichrist. And the Irish are the worst of all; austere, ascetic, stubborn, ungrateful, dumb, they have been the despair of all who have tried to help them and they are so damned clannish, unlike the English. They remained neutral during the war the same as the fascist Franco and wouldn't let crippled ships fighting for liberty, democracy and the dignity of man into port but permitted courageous English sailors to die in the frigid sea. They are fascists by God, look at Senator McCarthy and Father Coughlin and besides they broke up birth control meetings in New York. Contumacious. Intransigent. They even want their own Boy Scouts, Holy sweet Jesus they can't even share a pot of baked beans with the kid next door and then there's the frogs up in Canada, RC's, Papists, who want out from a good government. This is the English heritage.

I have thought for many years now that Catholic Sea Scouts and Catholic Life Insurance are a phenomenon of the second generation. You get off the boat and are told you can't be a good American and that No Irish Need Apply and you have stones thrown at your stained-glass windows so you answer by being more American than the Americans. You have more Purple Hearts than the others, more Congressional Medals of Honor, more anti-Communism, more jingoism, more All Saints, more and better Boy Scouts until one day, seventy-five or a hundred years pass and you start to feel at home; it all starts to fade away except for McCarthyism, which doesn't really mean "the systematic methods of McCarthy" or "actions like those of McCarthy," as it's supposed to mean, but the "systematic methods of the Papists"; after all, how many Lutherans do you know name of McCarthy? And the Eastern liberals who coined this *ism* in the 1950's knew that; they knew what they were doing; they acted deliberately.

By the way, I forgot to mention the Polish jokes, which I find interesting because they're really the old moron jokes we used to tell in the 1930's. They serve to illustrate my point about McCarthy for let me simply ask: How many Baptists do you know name of Kowalski? I must discuss a paradox here. The Jesuits have alluded to McCarthyism in their magazine *America* and some distinguished Jesuit educators have been known to tell jokes about our Polish pope; on top of that, Senator Eugene McCarthy of Minnesota has himself mentioned McCarthyism when speaking of Senator Joe, whose actions he opposed. How is this possible if my thesis holds water? The answer is obvious to the student of history. The Jesuits have fallen a long way from their eminence of centuries gone by and are much more dim-witted than they imagine; as for Senator Eugene, he is a midwesterner and consequently naive. The most humble New Yorker will tell you you don't take an identifiable name like McCarthy, Mancini and Liebowitz and put an *ism* on the end of it unless you have something else in mind, an attack on a nation or religion. It's as simple as that.

Things seem to be clearing up now, *ecumenicism* they call it, and a great deal of people are feeling rosy but then I don't know there's all them Jack La Rues sneaking up from Mexico.

12. Rosadabrigid

When I graduated from All Saints my father helped me on with my bow tie and we had the ceremonies on a very hot June evening. All Saints' graduations were always like that, suffocating, so we dated our summers by them even though they came two or three weeks before June 21st.

June 5th that year my parents and I left as usual for the Catskills. I say *as usual*; this was a point of pride at the time, it meant you were somebody if you could get away for the summer and I remember that every August when I came back to the city my friends had grown two inches. I find this same bias exists in other countries; it's a phenomenon out of the nineteenth century, which was so obsessed with phenomena, railroads, steamboats, rising towers, bridges . . . and vacations. Vacations are palpable, a proof of excellence and of class for after all servants do not leave the city on holiday. I have read many Spanish novels and you'll find that anybody who was somebody vacated Madrid in the summer, Madrid, 'nine months of winter and three of hell.' I even went to Madrid in 1982 to the Aguilar bookstore on Goya Street to buy some volumes (I had been purchasing by mail for years) and was greeted with this sign in large block letters:

THIS STORE IS CLOSED FOR THE MONTH OF AUGUST
SO THAT OUR PERSONNEL MAY REST

A memento out of the nineteenth century: Aguilar is clearly a superior emporium.

Civil Service Bronxites were no different and my mother got us out of the city for ten weeks every summer SO THAT OUR PERSONNEL MAY REST. Segal didn't go, Botchie didn't, or Kelly, but James Ignatius Murphy, J.I.M., went every summer to enjoy the mountain air with his peers, to recoup his forces for the vital struggle of the year ahead. That was the spirit of the annual affair, blue collars and shop keepers remaining behind.

We went to the slips of the Hudson River Day Line at 125th Street and boarded our vessel, which left the pier at 8 a.m. its flags waving in the breeze. We headed out into the river and up north under the girders of the new Washington Bridge, past the palisades, Yonkers, Nyack, Tarrytown, Tappan Zee, Bear Mountain, Indian Point, West Point, Poughkeepsie to the town of Hudson, where Alley's Bus Service awaited us. Our luggage was transported from water to wheels and we were under way, Alley himself doing the driving, up, up, up, into the mountains twisting and turning to Delhi and Stamford, New York, where we stayed at Hattie Brown's, a lovely lady whose food was incomparable. My father rested for the summer and I swam, bought candy, saw Hoot Gibson, Buck Jones and Ken Maynard in person, climbed mountains, walked through buckwheat fields and went to Jackie Ott's pool Sundays to watch the diving and greasepole walk, where the contestants tried to grab the small flags for a dollar, while my mother ran the show. This went on from 1933 to 1941, with a trip to Bantam Lake, Connecticut in between, but 1941 was to be the last journey. The next year would be different. And in late September of '41 I went to Rosadabrigid College.

Rosadabrigid was a boys' school, Irish, Italians, an occasional Pole or German, more segregation. I am loathe to engage in reckless abandon as I write about Rosadabrigid: I am not anxious to cause damage nor am I attacking anybody or defending them for that matter. I am merely here to narrate the life of James Ignatius Murphy, Jims, myself and what I saw; I only want to be fair. If I can enthuse and delight the reader, fine, so much the better, I will have done my job well. That is my intention and contrary to what literary critics may think the author's intention in my book can never be fallacious for I am consciously, deliberately setting down what I want to say. I may have insights I am unaware of at first, but on inspection they will prove to be logical corollaries of my intention. I want to show Rosadabrigid as it really was not as it appeared to be. I loved many people there, one of whom is my best friend; nevertheless I will not sweep the ashes under the rug.

The College of Rosadabrigid was an extension of All Saints and could itself be called an All Saints; from all the high schools they came, from St. Thomas', St. Peter's, St. Francis, St. John's, St. Aloysius, St. Michael's, St. Cyprianus, St. Athanasius, from Queens, Brooklyn, Manhattan, The Bronx, Staten Island, from New Jersey and even from Connecticut and Poughkeepsie. And of course from my own high school, All Saints, eight of whom enrolled there, including James Ignatius Murphy.

The campus was beautiful, the most beautiful in New York, and when you consider its position in the middle of a large commercial setting, the most beautiful of its kind anywhere. The long circular drive lined with elms, the nineteenth century buildings, the new Medieval Tower, the athletic fields, the back field, the gardens, the cemetery, it was beautiful, especially in May. Tulips, forsythia, azalea, all the flowers were there, the air bore the smell of honeysuckle and the sweeping lawns extended on all sides. Rosadabrigid wanted nothing physically.

May was the month of the Virgin and every noon the students gathered near the quadrangle before her statue to recite the rosary. "Hail Holy Queen, Mother of Mercy, Our Life, Our Sweetness and Our Hope . . ." The scores of students gathered there were unquestionably devout since attendance was not compulsory, and as I look back I can see them on the cobblestones, heads bowed or looking up at the Mother of God, her statue, the grass island around her, the walk, the railing, the posts, the May day, blue her color and golden her radiance. The students were of college age now and didn't have to attend so this was the very best a religious school had to offer, without the ruckus and clamor of high school. Religion was lived by many students at Rosadabrigid, religion was authentic. The classes known as Religion, Religion 101 and 102, were flour from another sack as they say; they were nothing really, nothing at all so you might say they were unauthentic. The Administration casually looked around and got some old priest put out to pasture to teach them; the truth is my first year at Rosa the octogenarian who taught the class did a pretty good job because he was earnest and humble and everybody liked him, but that was mere accident. Or the Administration got a novice in the order who might or might not be good just like the old man and gave the course to him; they didn't bother to get a theologian who specialized in the subject because they really didn't care. The book we used was a catechism of the glorified variety repeating everything we had learned in Sunday school and all it had additional was a hard cover; I never heard Luther mentioned or Calvin, Donatus, Irenaeus, Augustine, Gregory, Jerome, Basil, Origen, Tertullian, I don't even think St. Thomas Aquinas came into the picture, at least he was never referred to by name. Merely the old Baltimore catechism with some perfunctory flesh thrown on to stretch it out to three hundred pages to make it appear good, a college text with a hard cover.

This was the peculiar thing about Rosadabrigid and very few people understood it inside or outside the Church: A major religious order created this college so young Catholic men could have something called a Catholic Education and study the Catholic Religion, yet of all the courses on campus Religion commanded the least respect, or more accurately, it was the most disrespected. Religion itself was respected by the students, as the May devotions to the Virgin will testify, but Religion as a subject of study, Theology, was a gawk, a boob, a zany, a merry andrew, Ray Bolger playing the straw man in the Wizard of Oz without the straw man's dignity. The clergy took it for granted and the students merely crammed it the evening before a brief rote final examination. It was ridiculous. The psychology seemed to be that you don't have to convince your friends, they already know, so make believe and go through the paces. Now if only the students had been atheists, the clergy would have been on their mettle and made to produce exciting courses. Only atheists should go to Catholic schools. It would be better for both sides.

The rest of the classes were somewhat better than Religion though not by much, although there were always individual exceptions. Except for one professor, history was a joke. One priest laughed and joshed with the students in order to kill time and asked them to read from the textbook, with no comment whatsoever: "O'Shaughnessy, read!. . . Hennessey, read!. . . Caruso, read!. . ." and so on until the hour was expended. His examinations were also a farce. Hennessey, a socially perceptive student, simply filled up two blue books with tall tales and jargon and got an A; he told me so privately one day. It's true they also taught History by reading out of the book at All Saints but there at least the brother was not a clown. Why do they teach History that way? Why do they abuse her? I think one reason is that many high school teachers don't know much history and are often Math teachers or athletic coaches stuck with an assignment. They don't like History and may even despise it, at least the History teachers I knew. And think what they do to a whole generation of students when they do this, Catholic students, their own crowd, or *Our Crowd* as they say in New York; they fashion them into dullards at least and even fools and some poor devil of a lawyer will get up and make an ass of himself in public some day because a priestly professor joked about History in college, a Catholic college, bastion of Ultimate Truth! The priest did not do his job or fulfill the obligations of his state in life, a doctrine the Church teaches over and over again to its disciples. Can we say such a priest is a public sinner? I will not cast the first stone.

I think there's another reason for this abuse of History before the Second World War. It's a question of eschatology. If the only thing that really matters is the salvation of your immortal soul, if everything on this planet is temporary, ephemeral, straw in the wind, dust, nothing, then History is a bagatelle and the clowning priest logical. If something is virtually nothing then treat it as nothing if you want to be real about it. This may explain why Rosadabrigid had unlearned priests teaching History.

Religion? Why you already have them in the fold! History? Who cares? That was the college I went to.

Public institutions had similar problems but I like to think they were not as bad. Just as Catholic high schools were always filling their history books with French and Spanish missionaries, who to hear them tell it created America, so public school textbooks were patriotic until the 40's ("I regret I have but one life to give for my country"), international and idolatrous of the United Nations in the 50's, and full of unspontaneous good will in the 70's, preaching civil rights. Some of these doctrines are good, just as religious doctrine is good, but when school systems preach them they are spreading propaganda and attitudes, they are not teaching History. Still, I doubt that any public university had any History teacher more unlearned, foolish and disrespectful than my professor at Rosadabrigid.

History should be taught with joy and delight by a professor of complete dedication. The Greek city, *mare nostrum*, Mohammed and Charlemagne, Cisneros, Richelieu, Louis XIV, French Revolution, British Empire, Cavour, Bismarck, The Great War, the American Revolution and Civil War, everyone should study these subjects with joy and attention. When you study History you acquire a certain judgment you will never acquire studying current events, which are filled with passion; History is a clothes tree that once in your possession provides a place to accommodate everything. A liberal can study Edmund Burke and learn from him with enjoyment, a conservative, the revolutionaries of 1789 and do the same. An Italian boy can study Austria and an Irish boy Cromwell and learn if he wants to rather than plunge into diatribe. But we never had this at Rosadabrigid, none of us did. Rosa was offensive to the intellect.

But as I say, there was an exception, a true historian, scholar, gentleman and layman, a professor under whom serious students could study and go on to graduate school. But he was not the rule; the rule was: "O'Shaughnessy, read!. . ."

Religion. History. What was Philosophy like at Rosadabrigid, which prided itself on its Scholasticism; indeed, every student who went there had to take Philosophy courses every semester of Junior and Senior year. To graduate schools and industry Rosadabrigiders must have looked like sages on paper, well-rounded Renaissance men leading contemplative lives midst which they found time for their daily duties. Giant Plato wrestling an opponent or saintly More conducting a case in chancery.

The curriculum was impressive. Logic, Ontology, Epistemology, Cosmology, Natural Theology, Ethics. The Logic was well taught by an old priest who once said to me: "Go down to Mecca and get the other man's point of view." He spoke with a brogue and was not a native American, as we used to call persons born this side of the pond; perhaps he had gone to Trinity College instead of native American seminaries and so acquired some expansion. The other courses were an extension of Religion, perhaps a tiny, barely perceptible cut above that discipline though I don't think so. One clergyman with a round, ruddy, European face and a gentle warming smile was a very good person who read from his own book and commented on the passages there. We all liked him and respected him although he was not an inspiring teacher; I don't remember anything he said in class or any books he suggested for reading. Another clergyman (only priests taught Philosophy) also read from his own textbook but unlike the European he was self-centered and intolerant, not in a boisterous, violent way, but intellectually if one may predicate that term of him. He seemed to personify Rosadabrigid; he was intolerant of ideas and of people who delighted in them; he was an anti-humanist teaching the pride of the Humanities, who closed young minds rather than open them. I remember his saying once that educated people, meaning himself, should have more votes to cast than the masses because they know more, so he must have looked upon Philosophy as a forty shilling freehold and expected a metaphysical pocket borough. Lord save us from such Philosophy.

Another priest was a man of sweet disposition who talked for an hour every day about things I don't remember and was a good person like the European but not a philosopher, at least he didn't come across that way. You knew he was trustworthy and couldn't help but like him but that was the size of it.

Another clergyman I shall have to call the Jester, not a jester with oversized feet, bulbous nose and giant maw but a square-jawed allegedly down-to-earth type who feigned a toughness he was totally wanting. He was a good-to-the-guys guy, one of the boys, a model Christian who talked about law courts, sports, politics, a wee bit of mountain dew don't you know and very rarely about Philosophy. Once in a while he made remarks about people like my friend Segal from Highbridge (he was the only one I knew who did that at Rosadabrigid) and he thought that a woman's dying in pregnancy wasn't so bad, "one more saint in heaven" he used to say. You might call this attitude Baroque disillusion, doctrine of Ash Wednesday, life is a dream, otherworldliness . . . in caricature. Although he was the worst of the Philosophy teachers, and one ought to judge all institutions by their best representatives rather than their worst, he somehow typifies Rosadabrigid as I knew it; Rosa was an academic distortion.

As I write these lines I am tempted to imitate Pío Baroja's *Tree of Knowledge*, where the narrator calls all the professorial humbugs eunuchs, cretins, idiots and ridiculous old fools, deforming them aesthetically through metaphorical zoology, a most effective remedy for academic buffoonery, but if I did that it wouldn't be me, James Ignatius Murphy, Jims, he of stoical pruritus. Baroja and his idol, Schopenhauer, yes; James Ignatius Murphy the Bronx Boy, no. It wouldn't be me. Even so I am determined to write the truth and nothing but the truth in these pages, which is all that appears here, otherwise I wouldn't write it down in the first place.

I know of only one student who went on in Philosophy, to the University of Toronto, where I am sure he learned a different Scholasticism from the one we were taught. As for me, I have done some additional reading and personally accept the *philosophia perenne*, which is what they disfigured at Rosa. I arrived at this destination by an unusual itinerary. In 1948 I was reading Thomas Merton's autobiography, which swept like brushfire that year, and came across the name of his professor, Daniel Walsh, so when I went to Mecca for graduate school I dropped over to Columbia to hear him. What I saw there was so different from Rosa, the exact opposite, reading, learning, tolerance, the intellect; Professor Walsh spoke of Etienne Gilson and other critics and of hylomorphism as something philosophical rather than dogmatic. He patiently listened to all questions and tried to answer them; believe it or not, I had never heard of Gilson at Rosa. It's curious, just the other day, forty years after witnessing Rosa's caricature, a colleague told me that the seminaries have changed and that Rosadabrigid arguments are now answered with the acidulous formula: *Tu es Suarezianus.*

Religion, History, Philosophy. How about the other subjects?

One Latin class was a farce where the fat clergyman who taught it kept a trot on his lap beneath the desk and liked to talk about football. Another Latin class was not a farce but the saintly gentleman in charge got very little across although he had obviously mastered his subject; he was an exemplary Latinist but not a Latin teacher. French? Not well taught. English? Not well taught either though I only took a couple of classes. Mathematics? Extremely well taught by a layman and here arises a question that a Rosadabrigider could get very bitter about; I haven't because I have fallen into something good, I was merely lucky that's all. I want to explain what I mean.

I liked Mathematics and did well in it and I liked the professor and he liked me, one of the few people who do. He was an exceptionally nice person, clear, patient and gentle in his teaching, but in spite of all his knowledge and human worth it never occurred to hm to say to me: "Murphy, why don't you major in Math?", or, "Why don't you go to graduate school?", or even, "Why don't you take Math 201, you might enjoy it?" No, he didn't do that because he had no idea that professors do things like that. Everyone was on his own. It was in the air. You went to Rosadabrigid and then happened to go to law school or med school or the civil service or a job or push a broom, led a good Christian life and went to heaven. That was the atmosphere. If you took a subject because you loved it or it loved you, that was sheer accident, a falling into, a casual flopping. A few drops of rain fell from the sky and hit an occasional blade of grass, the blade greens and ripens, the rest of the lawn is drought. That was Rosadabrigid all right, a few green blades the rest was drought.

13. The Second World War

I was going to slip more Bronx institutions in here but have decided against it. My hunch is that more digressions will interrupt the flow of the narrative and destroy the curiosity of anyone desiring to read on so I shall change course and observe the following itinerary: I shall simply tell the story of James Ignatius Murphy, me, and then put the hundred and ninety-seven Bronx Institutions I still have on my list into an appendix in alphabetical order. Thus the reader in the first part of this narrative can go Murphy-Bronx-Murphy-Bronx-Murphy, and then pure Murphy from now on until he arrives at the Appendix where he can delight in the local customs of the Bronx as I knew it, Association, Bakery, Cheesebox, Cuban Cigar Rollers all the way to Van Cortlandt Park, Wagons (Delivery), Wagons (Con Ed) and Yo Yo. There is so much talk of the hellish today, pollution, famine, terrorism, racism, nuclear war, disappearing species, that we all need some sort of relief, a song, a poem, a dance, and perhaps I can provide something like that with my memories of the Bronx. That's it! Do you remember the trick question in school, "What is poetry?", and everyone including the poets themselves had a different answer and couldn't be too specific about it? Elusive stuff. Well, I have the answer, the Bronx is poetry. My memories of the Bronx will save you if you're worried about nuclear war.

I always remember the sayings of an ancient seer who when asked about evil made two observations. First he said that the man who constantly thinks of evil himself becomes evil, and then he said it is better to light one candle than to keep cursing the darkness. That's what this book is all about, that's what I mean when I say the Bronx is Poetry, I am lighting a candle. Anyone who gets to know Botchie, Segal and Kelly, egg creams and tin foil balls won't worry about nuclear war. They're kind of like the beatific vision.

Speaking of war, my days at Rosadabrigid were interrupted by the events of 1941, The Watershed of History. Every generation has its war, Korea, Vietnam, and for the really old, 1914, these veterans are almost all gone now, but if you say *the* war it can only mean one thing, 1941.

Before the war I remember inkwells, peas in the pod, wrapping paper and long walks; after the war it was ball point pens, Birdseye, plastics and "Can I have the keys to the Volks?" Before the war, wool and moth balls, six months pneumonia, thirty-three cents an hour; after, polyester, penicillin and ten bucks an hour and perks. Before the war, lending libraries, after, paperbacks; before, marriage; after, —————————what we have today. I could go on and on, I haven't even mentioned the snail darter's disappearing, but I want to talk about other things, 1940 as I remember it, the 1940's, The Bronx . . . but don't get me started on that.

First I recall Richard McGuire, who lived with his mother and sister in 1239, where we used to have our apartment . He was very tall for those days, six foot six, and he always dressed with a coat, tie and fedora. I'm not sure I ever really knew him for he was much older than I, I probably said hello to him a few times I guess. I never saw him smile and I can still see his lean figure go quickly down the street or take the apartment house stairs three at a time. McGuire was one of the first to go. He had been in the Naval Reserve, was called up, and his ship went down so early in the war they named a destroyer after him; his monument became the USS McGuire. It's funny. I haven't thought of him for years but as I write these memoirs his mother and sister and he, 1239, 1235 Unie and his thin rapid quick frame come back, clearer than the events of yesterday. Lt. Richard McGuire, USNR. Deceased.

I also think of Clancy O'Dwyer, who sat next to me at All Saints. Fat Clancy, always jolly, a fine citizen, good at handball, I never saw him after our graduation at Town Hall in June of 1941 and I never heard any more of him except that he was killed in action somewhere in France. I can still see him in the yard, picking the rubber ball off the red brick wall and hitting a killer at All Saints. When Clancy did that he always won the point, no one could hit it back.

There was one other, Billy Smalling, who was one of our gang on Unie. You might say he was never my cup of tea, which is why I haven't mentioned him with Botchie and the others, but I would be remiss not to mention him here. I was told by his cousin Mackie who lived over near P.S. 104 across Boscobel that he was killed in a very quiet sector, near the end of the war. "Nothing was going on there," Mackie said. Billy was very courageous, to a fault you might say, and my guess is he volunteered for something. After the war, his mother kept claiming he wasn't dead, she kept hearing news that someone saw him, but he never did come home.

Before I get to myself, there's one other name I ought to include here. The West Bronx had a hero, actually it was filled with heroes, but there was one who got the Oscar. Down around 167th and Boscobel, two thirds of the way to the Yankee Stadium, lived a skinny boy named Reddie O'Day. I didn't know him very well and still don't know his real first name because he went to parochial school instead of P.S. 11, I only remember his red hair, blue eyes, pale complexion and lack of flesh and wraith-like way of walking. I never saw him after 1940 but I heard he was commissioned in the field with the Congressional Medal of Honor. Imagine that, our own Commando Kelly! And he lived! As I recall the Marine Corps, someone by the name of Napoles or Amoroso was always getting the Medal posthumously for smothering a hand grenade with his body. But Reddie survived the war.

My own family came through unscathed, no wounds, no fatalities, although my cousin James had a ship sunk from under him and James' best friend Moscowitz died at Anzio.
"Damn the torpedoes, Gridley, full speed ahead!" I never heard anyone speak like that who saw action, not if they saw action; some of us statesiders did, and the movies and newspapers did, but not those who had been there, especially to places like Guadalcanal. They say it was awful. And one veteran of the Bulge told me he was so scared, "the shit was flying," he said, he was crawling around on his belly for three whole days; everyone did. Once it began, he said, nobody knew what was going on, where the front lines were, the rear, or who was off on the flanks. In a battle like this people often shoot at their own men, like the time we shot down our own C 47's in Italy. War is bad news.

But at eighteen I didn't know that. I was the White Knight. I went to Hickory, North Carolina for Pre-Pre-Flight Training. The expression Pre-Pre will sound foolish, but it makes sense if you remember that the Navy had a program with Pre-Flight (Athens, Georgia and Chapel Hill, North Carolina), Primary Flight Training (Peru, Indiana; Glenville, Illinois; and the air station with the Indian name in Rhode Island, I forget it now), and Advanced Flight Training (Pensacola, Florida and Corpus Christi, Texas). Pre-Flight, Primary and Advanced, it makes sense, but as the war went on and they had more pilots than they needed they added Pre-Pre-Flight, a limbo to give you some sort of military training and keep you on the back burner until Pre-Flight had enough room to take you.

They dressed us in old green coarse wool CCC uniforms and shipped us off to Hickory from New York City via Atlanta, Georgia, a waste of five hundred miles. We traveled in an old nineteenth century train recommissioned for the war; I remember all that tobacco smoke, the dice, the little sleep and one of our leaders, an older cadet nicknamed Broadway Brown teasing an unusually effeminate homosexual who had taken to him; he promised to write him, to meet him after the war and to keep undying friendship. I must confess the Bronx Boy didn't understand what was going on until someone told him later.

I don't recall eating on this train or other trains later but we must have eaten for we were on it more than twenty-four hours. It seems every time we traveled we had a dice game with twenty dollar bills in it and I was never winning; I always ended up at a new place without a dime in my pocket and several debts to pay. We finally got to Hickory, my introduction to North Carolina the state where I spent two years of my three years service, so I have no battle ribbons or other decorations on my tunic, but people like me used to say: "I fought the Battle of North Carolina."

North Carolina is one of the most beautiful states in the Union. Imagine going inland about two hundred and fifty miles up five thousand feet and having the terrain slope gradually to the sea, that's North Carolina; mountains, piedmont, tidewater; Hickory, Chapel Hill, Cherry Point; Pre-Pre-Flight, Pre-Flight and Operational, which came after commission.

Joke about Pre-Pre but at Hickory I met the finest flight instructor I ever knew, Mr. Charles Peabody, a soft spoken, refined Southern gentleman; I say *Southern* because they have a special way about them that has something to do with the family. Since 1970 I have been going to the Keeneland Races every year with my son and grandson and when we approach the entrance gate the man is apt to say: "How old are you, son? Eleven? Now suppose you just duck under that turnstile and I won't see you. How's that?" Then he laughs, takes my ticket and nods to me. Some people find this patronizing, I don't. Surely he knows I'm a Northerner, a damnyankee, "Why ah was twelve years old before ah knew damnyankee was more than one word", one of them tourist fellows, yet he sees a child and family and puts that first; he knows that a family is pre-1865, pre-1789, pre-A.D., pre-B.C., pre-Pre-Pre-Flight, pre-everything; a family is the real pre-pre, the one and the only pre-pre, it always comes first. The family! That's the ticket taker's philosophy and it's mine and my hat's off to him. I wish some of these deans and social engineers in the universities today had that philosophy, why I'll take a Southern gentleman to those bozos any day of the week and you can tell them I said so. Health, Education and Welfare versus the South? Long live the South!

Mr. Peabody knew he had an eighteen year old immature cadet who was not a man but a child on his hands, a six foot two, one hundred and ninety pound attention-seeking child. I can still see him, soft, patient, modest, sun glasses, cigarette, brown light leather jacket: "Now, Murphy, why don't we try landings today?" And up we went. I'll never forget the day he flew pylons, six hundred feet up in a Cub, tracing eights above the river; when he had the stick the ball never left center, as if we were flying straight and level. Those pylons were Mr. Peabody all right; when you were with him, twists, turns, complications, problems seemed straight and level. I didn't realize it at the time but I know it now; I would like to meet him again and some day I will.

One Sunday the Catholic boys wanted to go to Mass from the flight line; it was a holy day of obligation. A couple of the Southern instructors found this amusing but Mr. Peabody didn't, he understood; he may not have agreed but he understood. Then the boys abused the privilege and went horseback riding instead of attending religious services, with Broadway Brown in the lead. I went with them.

After Pre-Pre-Flight we returned to New York for a week, and Broadway arranged a party for our last night there at the Pennsylvania Hotel, just the fellows. We had drinks, listened to the music and then Broadway said: "Let's beat the check." he had cased all the exits and assigned them to us two by twos, each pair to leave separately, so one by one we got up to go to the bathroom and then out the exits. Our shepherd had us meet him at a designated spot, where he dismissed us. Next morning we took the train for Glenview, Illinois. Chicago!

My entrance to Glenview might have been a disaster and had this been Berlin or Moscow I would have been court martialled and sent to a camp in Siberia; we all got to Chicago all right, eight hundred and fifty miles, but I missed the final twenty minute ride to Glenview. Since we had an hour to kill before the Glenview run I went off by myself, and as I returned to the track I could see the last car with the grate across the back pulling out of the station. As I look back I know I deliberately missed that train if you can call subconscious actions deliberate; I have told myself I didn't want to miss the train and was upset over seeing it leave but deep down within that was what I really wanted. I was always seeking attention. At Rosadabrigid I would arrive at a class late balancing a cup of coffee in my hand to attract the eyes of others, and after the war in my first days of teaching I'd stand on a desk to give my oration. I wanted someone to notice me. So here in Chicago it was the train. The root cause was always the same, only the manifestations were different: inflict pain, and one person will laugh while another will cry but it is pain nevertheless. And so it was with me.

I don't recall the details of that night. The others had arrived at six and were all assigned bunks and squads whereas I got there at ten and was given a vacant assignment. No harsh words, no reprimand. This was the United States of America and more than that the Midwest, where you call everyone by his first name, more so than in the East.

I loved Glenview. I loved every new experience, it is only when experiences cease to be new that ennui sets in and life becomes a heroic struggle and search for salvation. At the time, however, I didn't appreciate eschatology. First of all, I loved the food. Rumor had it that our cook was the chef from the Drake Hotel drafted for the purpose right out of Chicago and I can believe it; to this day I can still see those breakfasts, crumb cakes, sweet buns, eggs, bacon, ham, sausage, cocoa, coffee, milk, fruit, the kind you buy now at expensive Sunday brunches in the Hyatt Regency, ten dollar brunches and more only we had them every day for four eternal months in the summer of 1943. My family had always stressed the importance of food by their example and here it was laid out before me in regal splendor. You woke every day starved to find it set before you like a king. I was a king.

The flying at Glenview was the best I have ever known. Instead of conventional runways there was a broad cement circle they called the apron, adequate for our N3N's and N2S's, Stearmans, so when the wind changed all the pilots had to do was observe the sleeve and take off or land directly into the wind; the sleeve was never a degree off so they never had to lower a wing for a side wind. After a few introductory hours the fun began, but most of all I loved shooting circles thirty miles out from Chicago where they had painted huge white zeros in green fields and the object was to land the plane in them with no power. I used to skirt one of the fields at five hundred feet, ease back the throttle and glide the plane in a large U turn towards my goal, using my stick and rudder to hold off or accelerate my approach, and if I was on target at circle's edge, three feet in the air, I let her stall in; the plane's three wheels touched ground within the circle and then I revved her up again and took off to five hundred feet and another try. By the time the flight tests arrived a pilot was supposed to hit three circles out of six or more, which came easy after a while. One day I even hit all six.

In the flying program we had A stage, B stage, C stage and D stage, each of them progressively more difficult. I remember the slip: you lowered your wing with aileron and rudder to lose altitude in a controlled fashion, something a pilot had to know when simulating forced landings or in the advent of a real emergency. At the end of D stage the testing instructor would cut the gun and say in the tube, "Forced Landing," and when you heard this bad omen you had to pick out a good field nearby, glide to it, holding off a little perhaps, and then come in just as you did when shooting circles. Usually you were fine when you did this, you could always slip it. Nothing was done without reason. In 1978 I showed my old flight book to a pilot in Waukesha, Wisconsin and he said: "That was some program!" The Navy always prided itself on having better pilots than the Army because of its carrier landings. The Army boys could fly a plane to the ground coming in hot because they had mile long runways to work with but the Navy had to bring it in almost at stalling speed to a foot or so above the ground, cut gun and drop it on the carrier deck. It was the old question of human pride. Hubris. We were better than the Army.

I myself had two instructors. The first was a very short man who liked to act gruff and when you made a mistake compare the plane's stick to your phallus. "What are you doing back there?", he liked to bellow, and then follow this suggestion with some obscenity. I suppose this was his version of the strap at All Saints, spare the rod and spoil the child. Real tough. It was also his confession of personal inadequacy. After B stage I was given another instructor, a thin red-headed man who reminded me of Mr. Peabody; he was very patient and that's what I needed. We flew upside down. We flew the falling leaf, which I found so fascinating that I failed to notice the loss of altitude and would have taken it in had he not warned me. I imagine something like this happens to scuba divers who become so entranced by their surroundings they forget the supply of oxygen. We did snap rolls, slow rolls, Immelmans, spins, and one day we took two planes up, flew formation and made a short navigational hop. I shall never forget those days, I especially liked those puffy clouds of

90

summer and the high majestic ones too; it was fun to fly around the puffs or pop through them or fly down the canyons of the big ones. You weren't really supposed to do this, five hundred feet from a cloud being the base line, OFF LIMITS, but I imagine everyone did it if they had any poetry in their blood, any poetry at all. Sky, sun, clouds, eighteen years of age, everything blended for the White Knight; the clouds were a target put there by Nature to play with and it would have been unnatural to stay away from them, a deviation, only a pervert would do that. The clouds were a toy, the war was a toy, my toy, for Murphy was at play.

We had night flying too. I remember when you first started it how confusing it could be, especially near Chicago; you took off in the blackness and that was all right since everything was dark except the air base and an occasional farm house to show you the ground, but if you flew toward Chicago there were so many lights they were positively bewildering. You'd see a red light in the distance and think it was the port wing of another airplane, with a white light near it to indicate the tail, and it was really an automobile just below the horizon. Or you'd see a whole series of lights like those streamer bombs they shoot on the 4th of July and that could be confusing too. I never liked night flights over settled areas. Later on I even liked formations at night better than night solos over cities, although the fire of the exhaust from the plane ahead of you could be mesmerizing.

I have a couple of anecdotes related to night flying. Two of the cadets I had known back in Pre-Pre-Flight, my CCC days as it were, had gone to St. Louis for Primary Training and word got back they were on a night hop and decided to dive bomb the St. Louis Cardinals during a ball game so they came in, flat hatted across the field and swept out again. It must have been fun and I can still envisage the picaresque face of McKane, who led the raid. The trouble is someone caught their numbers. If thousands of candlelight power can illuminate a baseball field they can also light up the distinct black numbers on a yellow bi-plane, the Navy's chromatic scheme for N2N's. Both of them, McKane and Nielsen, were thrown out of the V-5 program and spent the rest of the war as seamen. What price glory?

The other anecdote is more somber. One night a plane went in at Glenview with student and instructor and the next morning it was on the flight line where it didn't look too bad really; there was some broken windshield and a little blood and scrap of flesh around the cockpit. This sight didn't affect me, I never gave it a thought, and no one did I think until they had an accident of their own; later on at the big bases you'd see a Navy Lieutenant or Marine Captain with grafted skin on his face from a fire he had been in and I'm sure they were impressed by accidents; but eighteen years of age, summer, Chicago, blue sky, clouds, a two hundred and twenty-five horsepower winged toy, Pegasus, you never gave it a thought.

Every eight days we had a night off and all went on liberty
to Chicago. At that time the Bronx Boy had never heard of
Milwaukee, which was only seventy miles to the north and a
great town for servicemen so he went to Chicago every time he
was able. Come to think of it, eight goes into a hundred and
twenty days, four months, fifteen times, so I must have gone
there fifteen evenings. All those evenings with nothing to do; I
didn't know enough to go to the theater, concerts, museums,
exhibitions, fine hotels, so I did what everyone else did, drink.
My father had never said anything to me about drink one way or
the other and although I sensed that my mother didn't like it in
spite of her nightly bottle of Burke's ale she had never said
anything either. Certain things were not mentioned in the house
of John Francis Murphy, like sex and alcohol, so the Bronx Boy
had to confront them as they came.

And they came. I remember getting terribly sick one night
and throwing up everything I had in me. One of the fellows I
was with was disgusted; he must have come from a different
background, he couldn't believe anyone could do that, not to
such extremes. I always did things by extremes, I was always
seeking attention. I guess I was badly drunk three or four times
when I was in the service, *badly* meaning loss of memory. The
worst was in Corpus Christi the night I drank a whole bottle of
tequila, which was over forty years ago; I still can't stand tequila,
I detest the very smell of it. I'm sure it's not the fault of the
maguey plant, an innocent thirsty cactus, let's just say that I
haven't forgotten.

Every eighth day we went to Howard Street, which was
supposed to be the place to go; to this day I don't know exactly
what Howard Street stood for, whether it harkened back to Al
Capone or was a sort of sin city but whatever it was that's where
we went. I remember gambling quarters at a table so there must
have been something illicit about it. One night I was talking to a
girl at a bar and suggested we take a walk to the beach so we
went there and after we sat on the sand she handed me her purse
and said: "I bet that's not the only bag you have on you." I was
flustered. I didn't know what to say. When she saw me like that
she immediately changed her manner and was very nice to me.
She wouldn't let me near her but she couldn't have been sweeter.
She really liked me and when we parted that night she said:
"Please come to see me. Next week. Please?" I said I would but I
didn't. I was eighteen years old and I didn't know up from down,
right from left, back from front; I wonder if all eighteen year
olds are as stupid, bewildered and unaware of reality as I was;
here was a human being who really wanted to speak to me, to
see me, to be with me, who looked up to me, and all I did was
fly airplanes eight days and then go in to a strange city and fill
up on beer because I had nothing to do and didn't know anyone,
so I spent fifteen boring, useless, wasted furloughs. I never kept
my date with her but one of the last times I went to Howard

Street I saw her and she saw me. She looked at me. Her face was terribly hurt and she had tears in her eyes. She said: "Why didn't you come? I waited." I probably had a lot of beer in me and blurted out something, an "I don't know why," or worse, an East Coast smart alec wisecrack. I have never seen her since and don't remember her countenance but I think of her whenever I think of my Glenview days, which I often do now as I get older. Life couldn't have been easy, a poor girl like that, going down to Howard Street every night and then to the beach with cadets and handing them her bag. I guess she was seventeen. Because of her I believe in eternity. A woman puts up with certain indignities, like talking to stupid drunken cadets, and if she will just hold the fort, if she will keep that inner spark—"Will you come to see me, please?"—one day she will see a vision that beatifies. I wish I had her chances. If you are reading this, dear lady wherever you are, I want to say I admire your memory and wish I had your chances. I apologize for being so rude.

Before I close I want to say something else about this autobiography. Recently I have come to admire the letters of Dietrich Bonhoeffer, who is to my mind the greatest figure of our unfortunate century. He is a special person who has been set aside, his memory is sacred, and when he says something I take it as gospel. Bonhoeffer said that we should all keep evil things to ourselves, we should not divulge them. That is part of our problem today, a cynical attitude towards violence, cheating, perversion, infidelity, slander, in a word, towards evil. Put anything in a book, movie, television program or advertisement; sadism, masochism, theft, brutality, anything, so long as it attracts audiences and sells the product. But I am not marketing a product, I am attempting to describe a life and eulogize a place, the Bronx, my beloved Bronx, our beloved Bronx to those who lived there, so I must say I am not putting down everything I remember in these pages; following Bonhoeffer, I am keeping some memories to myself. I may be an attention seeker, a Narcissus, irascible, abrasive, a loner, but at least I can boast I am not a cynic, and perhaps one day I shall sit on some Parnassus with my friend Bonhoeffer and the young lady I knew on the beach. If that happens my life will have been successful . . . there won't be any more Howard Streets.

I abandoned Chicago in November 1943.

14. Pre-Flight

Do you know what I did? Do you realize what I have done? I skipped Pre-Flight! In my enthusiasm for Glenview I gave the reader Pre-Pre-Flight, where we wore CCC uniforms, and Primary Training, but I forgot to do Chapel Hill, North Carolina. No one ever skipped from Pre-Pre-Flight to Primary, you had to do Pre-Flight first, naturally. Perhaps a diagram will help:

I. Pre-Pre-Flight	Hickory, NC	Winter-Spring 1943
II. Pre-Flight	Chapel Hill, NC	Spring-Summer 1943
III. Primary	Glenview, IL	Summer 1943
IV. Advanced	Corpus Christi, TX	Fall 1943-Spring 1944
V. Operational	Daytona Beach, FL	Summer 1944

(For Commisioned Officers).

I have described numbers I and III, now I must give II and IV, and then Operational.

I don't know why I am so anxious to recount Pre-Flight, perhaps it is just a tendency towards completeness. I remember my father's desk, the large green blotter perfectly centered, four inches of wood to the right of it, four inches to the left, the yellow pencils perfectly sharpened, all in a line, the letter opener, eraser, bottle of Waterman's Blue-Black Ink, fountain pen, little glass dish of paper clips, yellow pad, all balanced in perfect array, perfect symmetry. And I remember the cigar in the snow perfectly placed there and buried with reverence. I remember the one hour ablutions, clean white shirt and dark blue tie, polished shoes, vest, gold chain and watch, homburg, all in perfect order. I want this book to be like that, I want it to be perfect. And that's why I want to go back to number II, Pre-Flight. Of course I'd like to sandwich in Bronx Institutions once in a while because that's where my heart is; they keep coming back to me and I will write about them again if I can preserve the symmetry. I'll try, you can bet on that.

There's another way of saying all this. You might say that leaving out Pre-Flight is my unburied cigar.

Chapel Hill in the spring of 1943 was the most beautiful place you can imagine. I was assigned to Graham Hall, 203 Graham was the address I put on my letters, 24th Cadet Batallion, with most of the fellows I knew from Hickory and some others. Two of our leaders were southerners, one of whom was a good boxer. Although I remember his name I won't disclose it since I am not interested in identifying anyone and any resemblance to actual persons living or dead is purely coincidental.

The first days there we were dog tired having been up all night on a nineteenth century train from Atlanta, and they really stuck it to us. We ran in formation to the quartermaster's to get shoes, ran to get shots, ran to classrooms, ran to the chow hall, ran everywhere; we were up at five-thirty and ran it seemed until nine-thirty at night, beg your pardon, twenty-one thirty hours, when we hit the sack for eight hours. No one was awake at nine-thirty-one and no one stirred until reveille. I liked the routine. Mornings, half the batallion did athletics, mostly team athletics like soccer, football and basketball, the idea being that there are no lone eagles in aviation, only team mates; when you fly in the Pacific you have a wing mate whom you fly scissor patterns with against the more maneuverable though extremely vulnerable Zero; and you and your wing mate are part of a squadron which is part of a group. Individual sports were there too like parallel bars and boxing, and since I couldn't do fifteen chinups properly I was assigned to the weak squad, one of the biggest fellows in the battalion on the weak squad. My father had never emphasized athletics except as a spectator so I was unskilled. For some reason or other I wasn't the attention seeker at Chapel Hill I was at Primary and later on, I don't know why exactly, I liked it there I really did it was all so new. Maybe it works like this, maybe when you like something very much it absorbs you but when there are large temporal gaps or things arise you don't like you try to absorb them and go on seeking attention. I remember a movie about Toulouse Lautrec who was all right as long as he was painting, otherwise he drank so much he suffered hallucinations. Me? I was all right as long as I was running, running, running; running at something new and exciting, otherwise I was seeking attention. I also remember the meals we ate at Chapel Hill with eight or ten chops at a clip, piles of potatoes, vegetables, desserts, and then in the recess after lunch we'd go to the ice cream stand and eat a quart of vanilla ice cream. The Navy even bragged that the calories we ate were double those of the average person with no one gaining weight; if anything you lost it.

When we had athletics in the morning we had classwork in the afternoon. It was so hard to stay awake. The classrooms got frightfully hot and in classes like Recognition, where you turned off the lights for the slide projector, you could hardly keep your eyes open; everyone was snoozing at one time or another. Still, I liked Recognition. A plane's silhouette is flashed on the screen, that's a Zero, elliptical wing; another plane, Jap Betty, twin engine with such and such an empennage; that's a Spitfire, be careful, it looks like a Zero because of the elliptical wing. And I remember the destroyers; that's the Fletcher class, so many smokestacks and so many turrets in fore and aft position. It has been forty-four years since I saw those brief photos but their picture is clearer to me than the photos of this morning's newspaper.

We also had some Math for Navigation, triangular Math you might call it. You had the air speed and ground speed, air direction and ground direction and a wind vector. If you are flying at two hundred miles per hour with your nose pointed at thirty degrees and the wind is from 300 degrees at twenty miles per hour, just where are you going on the ground and how fast are you going to get there? In other words, if you fly two hours from Honolulu where are you going to end up in case you have to land, and will your carrier or island be there to receive you? The triangles looked something like this:

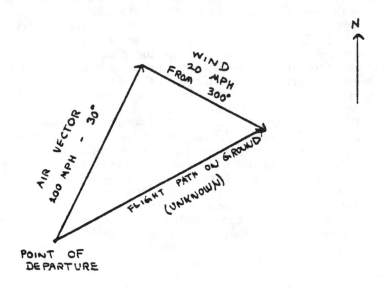

My diagram is rough indeed but I remember that the problems were simple, and given five minutes of instruction you could solve them easily.

I remember a couple of fellows flunked out of Pre-Flight not for moral or mental reasons but for physical deficiency. They discovered that one of them didn't have 20-20 eyesight; his name was Jimmy Connor. The morale was very high in the unit, everyone wanted to belong, so it was a tragedy for poor Jimmy to have to leave, it was a washout all right. I remember he was crying and couldn't speak to you. I wish we could revive this spirit in our country today.

I saw two celebrities at Chapel Hill and spoke to one of them for a minute. One day I was standing J.O.D. watch outside of Graham Hall when a tall, lanky cadet with the easiest stroll I have ever seen came walking by and said: "Hiya! Hiya doin'!" and a phrase or two more. It was Teddy Williams. He was very friendly, just a plain nice guy. I have often thought that Teddy was the greatest hitter of all time and that if he hadn't lost six years of his career—three in World War II, two in Korea and one the year he fractured his elbow in the All Star Game—he would have broken all the records, home runs, triples, doubles, runs and runs batted in. I imagine he has the highest slugging average ever; in any case he was the most graceful batter I have ever seen. He'd set up that cradle motion, that gentle rocking, left foot, right foot, left foot, and at that precise moment the ball would be over the plate and he'd swing, a true ballet. Sometimes I thought he looked like Cid just before he clobbered them.

The other celebrity was the chanteuse Helen O'Connell: "Those cool and limpid green eyes, a pool wherein my love lies . . . for happiness I find, for though they'll ever haunt me, all through my life they'll taunt me, Green eyes make my love come true!" Except for the ellipsis I still remember the words clearly although the meaning of *though, ever haunt* and *taunt* is not exactly clear. I still remember the words and that beautiful voice on Decca records, with the band, was it Jimmy or Tommy Dorsey I don't recall probably Jimmy, and one of the Eberle brothers, Ray or Bob, singing too. Helen O'Connell was sitting in a drug store having a soda with her beau the football player who was a legend around the Bronx since he played for Fordham College. Fordham had a good team in those days, one of the best, and when the Seven Blocks of Granite were there they had three scoreless ties with Pittsburgh, who had Marshall Goldberg, Cassiano and Stebbins, and Pittsburgh beat Notre Dame by five touchdowns. Teddy Williams and Helen O'Connell, those were heroic days!

Do I recall any more about Chapel Hill? I remember there was an Ivy League type, Waterford, a bit on the nasty side, and the southerner I mentioned before gave him a good boxing lesson though he himself was much smaller. But most of all Chapel Hill means this to me, Chapel Hill is youth, my youth. I was eighteen years old and my childhood was ending. Have you ever noticed how children don't live in the past or future but in the present? Adults will cling to the past or future; observe an adult when he is moving from a place he loves; he counts the days, the hours, the seconds, and the moment of departure tugs at his heart; he doesn't want to leave, he wants to stay, he has been happy and as he leaves he may be crying. Now observe a child who leaves the same place. He plays with his friends digging holes in the sand, hitting a ball, jumping rope until the very last minute and as the family station wagon pulls out he is laughing and bouncing and shouting goodbye, goodbye as if he were saying hello, and his friends are all laughing and yelling too. No past, no future, just the present, just joy. Mystics are like that too because they live in the present. Children are mystics and I was still a child at Chapel Hill; that's why the three months I spent there were a split second, a golden ray, a green pasture in my mind, like Teddy's swing, like Helen's green eyes. They will never change. Why? Because they are unchangeable. I was still a mystic at

Chapel Hill.

Perhaps that's why the good book says we should be like little children. Perhaps the evangelist had a vision of Chapel Hill. St. Paul saw the Bronx and I like to think he saw Chapel Hill too.

15. Advanced

To restore the order of this book: it's Pre-Pre-Flight, Pre-Flight and Advanced. I'm like that you know; I'm glad this chronological upset and restoration have taken place because they exemplify my most cherished habit, keeping the list. I must have a list. Every morning the Bronx Boy must fill out his items on a four by five inch piece of paper from a memo pad. I write *Thursday* let us say at the top of the sheet and then I write a series like this:

(1) Write *The Bronx Boy*
(2) Prepare Spanish 204
(3) Write the dean
(4) Get a haircut
(5) Wire for lamp
(6) Call E. Prentiss 963-1584
(7) Call Ted
(8) Student for Independent Reading
(9) Library: A. Lord, Salinas, Alan Seeger

I carry this list in my shirt pocket and keep referring to it all day and as I complete the items I scratch them off whereas on the reverse side I do the opposite, adding new items as they come up: Call the chairman, Get butter, Pick up Jane. My wife tells me I couldn't live without a list and that is true, she knows me best of all. So in this manuscript the words flow freely, there are no lists for them, but each morning as I finish my work I write down the next day's series at the foot of my yellow pad: Sun Pictures, Tin Foil Balls, Wagons (Con Ed), or, (1) Pre-Pre-Flight, (2) Pre-Flight, (3) Primary, (4) Advanced, (5) Operational. Given my scientific procedure I still don't know how number (2) got omitted and had to be placed in a later chapter, between (3) and (4), so I guess it must be chalked up to human inefficiency; no matter how hard you try to regulate everything and put every wheel and cog in its proper place, a human being is not a machine and will make mistakes. Or subconsciously the Pre-Flight violation of order may be the Bronx Boy's way of saying *non serviam* to regimentation.

Advanced Training: Corpus Christi, Texas; Vultee Vibrators; SNJ's; instruments, gunnery runs, dive bombing runs, navigational hops, six months of training and then we got our wings. We received our commissions too but that was the lesser part, it was the wings that counted. We were members of the elite, knights in pursuit of the Grail, bring on those Japs!

In Primary we had flown biplanes with 225 horsepower but in Advanced we were going to fly monoplanes, Vultees with 440 h.p. and heavier and faster Douglas SNJ's with 550. The Vultees were mainly used for getting us used to low wing monoplanes, for surveying the Texas land, where it was easy to get lost, and for instrument hops. The latter were fun. You went into a Link trainer for a while and learned the radio quadrants, N, S, O, A, like this:

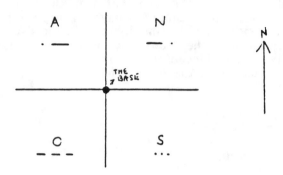

If you heard a Morse Code dih dah (• —), the letter A, you knew you were somewhere in the northwest quadrant so you started flying southeast on your compass; if you then started to pick up a dah, dah, dah (— — —), you knew you were in quadrant O and made an adjustment by flying east and slightly north; a dah, dit (— •), you knew you were in N; and if you heard dih, dih, dit (• • •), you were in S and had gone too far and had to turn back. In each situation you kept making alterations until you were directly over the base, where you heard no sound at all. All this was taught in a stationery Link ground trainer until the glorious day came when you took this knowledge up in a Vultee; you were in the back cockpit with the hood drawn so you couldn't see out and the instructor up front told you to fly the plane. The altimeter and ball-in-liquid level, resembling a carpenter's level, were all you needed to keep the plane aloft without spinning, but all of a sudden the instructor said: "Take me home!" Then the dah dit business over the radio began because you were thirty miles out in N quadrant somewhere and had to bring the airplane back to base without looking. It was fun.

Corpus was a Mexican town or I guess it was supposed to be because I only went there every eight days and had too much to drink. I had a bottle of tequila once and couldn't remember anything except my mouth was so dry I dreamt it was filled with a kind of cotton gelatin that I had to keep scraping off my tongue. It was awful and as I said before I can't stand tequila to this day. Corpus may have been Mexican but I saw nothing and might as well have had two blinders on the side of my eyes the way horses do, I saw nothing. At Christmas I was invited with a friend to a family's house for turkey dinner but they were not Hispanic so I learned nothing new. I vaguely remember the architecture, which resembled parts of Miami with Uncle Billy in 1939, and my host's telling me that the hottest chile of all was the chile peteen, a very small red pepper. He and his wife were very gracious but the Bronx Boy might as well have been in New Jersey. Two of the fellows in our outfit got venereal disease. One of them had a French name and my impression was he tried to create a French mystique about himself, French lovers and all that; today they would call him a macho but the word didn't exist in those days for an American so it was *Frenchy* with the venereal badge as a sign of his manliness. I remember I went to a dance and a girl tried to play another cadet and me off against each other but she didn't know who she was dealing with, not that it was an act of nobility on my part or anything of the sort, it's just that my father once said to me: "Never fight. Always walk away from a fight." So I did. She must have been one of those women who like to see men fight over them so I probably disappointed her, which is too bad for we might have become friends. But as I say I had blinders on, I wasn't making my own decisions since they had been made for me by my grandmother's Theology. Some people call this God's grace, to which I would answer yes and no.

Every night at Corpus we'd gather at a huge hall and have hamburgers and Jax beer from New Orleans, which was a joke on the airbase because it was a two per cent beverage made deliberately that way for Navy personnel. We'd drink bottle after bottle of it and eat three or four hamburgers and nothing ever happened. I remember that two straight nights at this canteen the clock read 9:50 and never changed because one morning a cadet named Kennedy went in, hitting a power line, and the electricity went out for forty-eight hours; those ciphers on the clock were his epitaph. There were more accidents at Advanced Training than Primary and more at Operational than Advanced, and I have since been told that more pilots were killed in the Jacksonville Command, Florida, than in the entire Pacific campaign against the Japanese. Cadet Kennedy's clock was a harbinger.

The most fun I had at Corpus was over Padre Island, where we did our dive bombing. We took our twenty pounders, climbed up to the prescribed altitude, turned the plane over and tried to drop our cargo on the targets painted into the flats below, which reminded me of two things, the slips, and the circles we shot at Glenview that were also a target. But it was more like a giant slip, a belly-moving, dropping, awesome slip. I can see how a pilot could be so fascinated he would take her right down to the ground or into a ship's smokestack. The day I went dive bombing one of the cooks got permission to ride along in the back seat and he was scared stiff. When we got back he thanked me more than once and must have thought that pilots were a particularly brave lot, which is not true; some are brave, some are not just as in any other walk of life. A plane is never dangerous until it

101

approaches the ground or another plane, and that day I was cautious. I didn't 'almost take her in', and I also missed my target.

One thing happened at Corpus that I particularly remember, anachronically you might say. One day an argument broke out in the mess hall between our cadet commander Honeybee and an enlisted man. Words flew back and forth and finally Honeybee bellowed: "I'm from Georgia." The enlisted man retorted: "And I'm from Michigan!" He was black. I would be misrepresenting this episode if I suggested it was typical, no, it was unique, but I suppose it's an indicator that the war, Our War for those of us born in the early twenties, was the watershed. Honeybee and his friend from Michigan were foretelling the events of the future.

I was commissioned at Corpus on April 3, 1944, Second Lt. James Ignatius Murphy, USMCR. Most people don't realize that Marine officers and men are Navy personnel so as a graduating cadet I chose the Marines because I thought it was a superior force; we were better than the others. I had been listening to propaganda. I didn't realize that some Marines are better and some are not and that it depends on the individual. I did meet two fine marines at Corpus just before I left for Operational Training in Florida, Lt. Colonel Lloyd and a young Major Vogel, who had been overseas in dive bombers and was awarded the Navy Cross. He was very kind to me and I can still remember him with his wife at a dance; I learned later that he was killed in a dive bombing accident, Stateside. It's curious: the clock will stop for you whether you're a cadet or an officer, at home or out there with the shrapnel because one day it comes and the uniform makes no difference. It's a different kind of dance.

My theme I say is memory. I put down persons, places and things as they come to mind. Things? No, not everything, bad language for example. I can't say I heard more of it in the Navy than elsewhere although I heard my share; it's a funny thing about bad language and ugly scenes, some authors seem to depend on them as if they were especially realistic, super-realism, openness, honesty. Do people talk that way? If so, put it down in the name of truth, record it. It's true that some people punctuate their sentences with fornication and excrement but most don't so why concentrate on these grotesque hyphenators? Besides, a writer is a gardener cultivating a small Versailles and even if he desires a bed of wild flowers he must keep them in order, that's it, order. This gardener must clip and edge and prune. Take a look at Nature; in the wild she can be beautiful as a distant majestic mountain or untended plain, an ocean swept by the wind, but go up close in your backyard and see the sunburnt grass, seeding dandelions and burdock and she's not beautiful at all but simply unkempt and even ugly. She needs caring for, so the gardener must weed the place out, removing the anomalous and replacing it with walks and grass and flowers, roses, above all roses. They are so beautiful. Yet they do have thorns. Roses are the gardener's novel, fragrant, colorful, sculpted, with needles underneath, and just as the gardener prepares manure to satisfy the rose so a novelist must employ scabrous language. In either case the ugly is subordinate.

The philosopher of Aesthetics should provide an exemplum and mine is the literature of Evelyn Waugh, master of English prose. In his novels I recall only one appearance of nitrogenous waste, in the war trilogy *Men at Arms*, where two high officers are talking in a London bar and one tells the other how his ministerial brother-in-law obtained for him the rank of general. "How awfully nice, he must be a good old boy!", the other says. To which the General replies: "Frankly, he's an awful shit." Such humor has very few peers.

I have divagated. I have strayed from the path. I was supposed to start Operational Training and here I have been discussing biffy humor. It's time to get down to work. I was going to stuff in one Bronx Institution here. "Choosing Up Sides," on the grounds that when you get an Institution you are getting me, James Ignatius Murphy, but I am going to defer it until the Appendix for fear of digression. If someone wants to check my judgment he can consult the Appendix here and now.

16. Operational

Daytona Beach in 1944 must have been the most beautiful place in the world. Río, Cancún, Acapulco, the Riviera, you can have them, I'll stick to Daytona; not today of course, not in 1984, it's honky tonk, but in 1944 it was beautiful and unspoiled like a young woman of eighteen. There is a saying in Spanish about *abriles*, Aprils, to indicate the halcyon days of youth and vitality; very well then, in 1944 Daytona had eighteen Aprils.

That's where I was stationed for Operational training, which was really advanced training for newly commissioned officers. Primary had 225 horsepower, Advanced 500, and Operational 1200 horses in F4F's, or 2000 horses in F6F's and F4U's. The pilots did everything the same except that the heavier planes had a higher stalling speed and smaller glide ratio. In other words, they came down faster.

But I want to describe the beach first. The base was three miles inland and from there a bus took us to Daytona and across the causeway to the beach, where the officers had a club. This was different from being a cadet since officers had every sixth day off instead of eight.

We had a squadron of eight Marines with a Navy instructor, a Senior Lieutenant who had seen action in the islands. He didn't fraternize with us although he didn't put a big gap between us either for the air corps was never like the old line where even gradations between sergeants and corporals could be meaningful. Things have changed since the war, but in 1942 over in the Army Air Corps they say the officers and men on the B-17's were all one, pilot down to gunner, all of the same age and all on a friendly basis. It was something like that in our squadron though not quite because our instructor, Lt. Strong, USN, was fifteen years older.

One day the eight of us bought a new garbage can, filled it with ice and beer, and brought it down to the beach where we set it on the sand with the lid on and went swimming. Then we came back and had beer and went swimming again. We kept this up all day, sticking the empty bottles upside down in the sand with the bottoms showing, so by the time the afternoon was over we had our turf on the beach fenced out, enough for a city lot. It was a great deal of fun. After the beach party we went into Daytona Beach and ordered two steaks apiece, which were two dollars in those days so you could eat all you wanted and we were singing and laughing and I'll never forget the good times we had at Daytona.

This brings to mind a subject I haven't discussed before, money. I had all the money I needed at Daytona, a hundred and fifty dollars a month base pay plus a hundred dollars in flight skins, two hundred and fifty total, me, the Bronx Boy, who had never really had any before. I always wanted to earn money when I was a boy (I remembered my Uncle Joe's concessions at the old Polo Grounds) but I never did. What I really wanted to do was work for Western Union and ride the bike in the olive uniform delivering messages, or work for Postal Telegraph and ride the bike and wear the blue uniform, and both uniforms had leather guards for the shins, but my mother wouldn't let me. I am sure it had something to do with class; in any case I didn't have part time jobs and the little money I had was given to me. But here in Daytona I had two hundred and fifty dollars a month, which would be two thousand now, but even so at the end of the month I was so broke I often had to borrow twenty or forty to tide me over to the first. Although there was some gambling it wasn't all that heavy so I must have spent it on beer and steak, a little whiskey but not much because I remembered the tequila, amusements and sending gifts back home. I had a girl at home and I sent her back a gold bracelet and I had an expensive wrist watch. So the money went.

Money. Someone asked Jane Austen: "What do you write about in your novels?", and she replied: "Love and money. What else is there?" In these paragraphs I am following half her recipe; I remembered the CHEAP sign on the dumbwaiter and I wasn't going to have any of that. I had no bank account, I spent all my money and I didn't send any home. A man on the train out of Daytona once said to me: "Buy Celanese stock, you can't go wrong," but I didn't. Sometimes I think I should have, can you imagine buying shares of Celanese in 1944, but I didn't and if I had that wouldn't have been me and this book is about me. How can you not be yourself?

Please don't misunderstand me. Today I wish I had a great deal of money drawing ten percent so I could give myself sabbaticals; I'd tell the dean every year: "I'm only teaching this fall semester, and no summer school either." Then I wouldn't have to deal with him and the rest of them nine months a year but I'd still have my students, who mean so much to me, and I could read all the books I've always wanted to and never gotten around to: Thucydides, Xenophon, Plotinus, the *Summa*, Gibbon, Guizot, Macaulay, Froude, the rest of Galdós' novels, the Civil War . . . I buy five or six books a month and I never get to read them. I'd also like to learn demotic Greek (I listen to my cassettes every day) and go to the Aegean and cruise the islands and mainland, Larissa, Melissochori . . . and I could do all that if I had money. Money gives you time, it gives you freedom, like the freedom I had at Daytona.

I met a girl in Daytona. Her name was Mavis Fume. I don't ordinarily describe people in these pages but I want to describe Mavis.

She was five feet five, dark complexioned, thin, with long jet black hair, the way girls used to wear their hair in the forties. I can't describe her clothing not because I don't want to but because I never noticed things like that in those days; if I visited someone's house for a few hours, five minutes after leaving I couldn't tell you whether the rug was red, yellow or blue, whether the windows had curtains or not, what the furniture was, I couldn't describe anything; I might not even be able to tell you whether there was a staircase going upstairs, let alone the color or shape. I simply didn't see the profile of things, I was a sort of ambulatory impressionist living in a world of quickly running black and white movies so I can't remember Mavis' clothing although I do know she was always neatly dressed and pretty and above all had an engaging laugh, which is the most important thing when a boy is nineteen, an open inferno with no direction, who doesn't know north from south, that a girl have a flattering laugh. When you do crazy things and sputter out your foolishness and get her to laugh it's the most flattering thing in the world. It makes you feel like King Kong, Beauty and the Beast. Come to think of it Mavis did have one dress that was kind of soft red like.

Mavis and I went to the beach every sixth day when I had off, and in the evenings we swam, sun bathed, talked, joked, ate steak, walked hand in hand, danced, drank beer at Llewellyn's on Broad Street, visited her house, and one day she, her parents and I took a car along Daytona Beach to the light house at New Smyrna. The sand was firmly packed, so much so that just before the war Sir Malcolm Campbell drove his car there at 230 miles per hour; after that he switched to the Utah Salt Flats, where he went over four hundred. Once we left the village the beach was deserted, there was no one, absolutely no one, and no superstructures until we got to the light house ten miles to the south where the four of us picnicked for an an hour and then returned to Daytona. I can vaguely remember her house on Vermont Street especially after sunset when everything was calm and peaceful and the scent of duke jasmine filled the air. Whenever I smell jasmine perfume or the aroma of flowers on a summer's evening I think of Mavis Fume and two happy months at Daytona Beach. The war wasn't hell to me, it was to the Europeans and one million American fighting men but not to me.

The day after the picnic Mavis told me her father had voted against Al Smith in 1928 but he was very sorry he had done so; he said he was wrong, she said, that Al was a much better man than Herbert Hoover. The statement will seem abrupt here but it wasn't abrupt in context, nothing was abrupt with Mavis although I was an attention-seeking person. I always liked being with her. So although the Al Smith statement came out of the blue it was no more forceful or less forceful than anything else she said even though she put some emphasis behind it. Mavis was emphasizing something.

Mavis and her parents were southerners. They came from Bluefield, West Virginia, which can be northern in a way, after all the state left Virginia during the Civil War, but she was definitely southern. I can still hear her say: "Well ah'll be a dog in the road!" She didn't say things like that often but when she did I found it cute and since we were friends I guess she was trying to please me.

One day we were strolling through Daytona when Mavis stopped in front of a furniture store. She looked at the display window and asked me if I liked the dining room set, the living room set, the chairs and tables and bed, "Do you like them?", she said. We talked about houses and furnishing houses and setting up a home; we must have stood there for forty-five minutes looking at the furniture. She was trying to tell me something, I didn't know what it was at the time for I was a big clown, an attention-seeking clown who didn't know anything, absolutely nothing, who didn't take heed of anything but himself. Mavis was trying to tell me something that rolled off me like water from oil cloth. I think I know what she was trying to say now because I matured about twelve years ago when I was fifty; now when I look back I descry many meanings I never saw before and realize what a boor I was, a social bumpkin, a clod, but this is only in retrospect; a fool doesn't know he's one, which is why he's a fool. We are all of us foolish but not fools because we are aware of our stupidity. I wish I had been more considerate to Mavis, I wish I had been kinder.

One night I was giving Mavis a good night kiss on her porch when she put her tongue in my mouth. It was a spontaneous act, a natural phenomenon without calculation, like an apple blossom or morning's dew, it just happened and that was that and nothing ensued. After all the apple blossom is terminated by a fall from the tree and the dew dries up with the morning sun, so Mavis kissed me that way and that was the end of that. I must have hurt her terribly. No particular reaction. Of course I say this now that I am mature, at the time I made no reflection.

I guess our days at Daytona were coming to an end and she sensed it whereas I the novocaine boy sensed nothing. As I look back I realize we only knew each other for two months, from early June to early August 1944, so the picnic, Al Smith remark, furniture, kiss and what I am about to say must have all come together within a week or two. Mavis got very serious one night. She was always smiling and joyous in my presence but this night she was serious; she told me that in her freshman year at college a boy gave her too much to drink and then took advantage of her and she wanted me to know that she said. She said she had a roommate who had the same experience and some of the other girls also. The oil cloth man again; a young girl's words, rain, tears on the oil cloth; she might as well have told me that snow is white or trees are green, a statement of fact that's all as if her confiding in me like that were a bland statement of fact. If someone told you trees are green what would be your reaction? You wouldn't have one, and neither did I the Bronx Boy, the glazed doughnut. I should have reacted, with every fiber of my being if I loved her and even negatively if I didn't, even a

107

defiance would have been better than my nothingness, the worst insult of all. Imagine a girl's respecting you so much as to tell you she's not a virgin and you stand there like a statue. What a fool! What a boorish, unfeeling, unthinking fool! A lump of coal! An oilcloth!

I remember the day I left Daytona for Quantico, Virginia. My train was leaving at noon. I hadn't seen Mavis for several days and try as I did I couldn't get a message through to her so around ten in the morning I took a cab to her house; she was there with her mother. I was very persuasive, an open inferno, so she rode with me to the station. I kissed her as the train came in, I kissed her and hugged her goodbye. I can still see her raven hair. She seemed bewildered. As the train eased out of the station I waved furiously, arms flailing like a windmill, the Bronx Boy attracting attention. But she just stood there. Rigid. I the statue had left a statue.

I have never seen Mavis since, and that was August 4, 1944, nor have I heard from her or about her. I told her once I had a girl back home and Mavis honored that. I had no tears in Daytona but I do now as I write; a few, not many (ever the stoical pruritus) trickle on the oil cloth. Mavis is one of my most beautiful memories, indeed I cherish the days I spent with her. Mavis in a way is a proof of God. There are supposed to be five proofs you know, from motion, design and intelligibility but the truth is that Mavis is the sixth. Experience tells me that years ago I saw Beauty, a celestial Idea residing in the mind of God. Girls are like that, they prove the existence of God, Mavis did.

I have been talking about Mavis Fume a long time now whereas my reason for going to Daytona was Operational Flight training; after this air base we were going to form squadrons and travel to the Pacific. Elliptical wing, a Zero! Twin engine, peculiar empennage, a Betty! Remember Pearl Harbor!

"Green Base, Green Base, this is Dog Fox 26, request permission to land. Over."

"Dog Fox 26, this is Green Base. Permission granted. Out."

"Green Base, Green Base, this is Dog Fox 40, request permission to land. Over."

"Dog Fox 40, this is Green Base. Permission denied. Beechcraft in traffic pattern. Circle base. Over."

"Green Base, Green Base, this is Dog Fox 40. Will circle base. Don't forget me, honey. Out."

I always liked radio discipline. It was fun. And I have often thought that someone could take all the Green, Blue and Red Bases and Dog Fox Forties, Daytona Fighter 40 and weld them into a poem because there's music there. A lyre. You weren't supposed to break discipline though, calling the BAM in the tower honey. DF 40 could get in trouble for that.

Of all the flying I have ever experienced the most fascinating was gunnery. One pilot took off fifteen minutes ahead of the others with the long silk sleeve attached to the plane, gradually ascended to five thousand feet and headed east from New Smyrna lighthouse while the rest of the squadron flew to New Smyrna and went to eight thousand feet, heading east out over the ocean in formation and staying off the sleeve plane's starboard wing; when they reached a position off the plane itself the leader tapped his head turning over the lead to the next in echelon, pressed the stick forward with left aileron and rudder and started an S dive towards the sleeve. The principle was the same as trap shooting, where you have to lead that clay pigeon, only this fifty caliber machine gun was going three hundred miles an hour and the target pigeon one fifty. Flying a collision course with the sleeve, the lead pilot pressed the trigger on the stick a few hundred yards out ducking at the last second under his target, and then he used his speed to climb on the port side where he formed a new echelon. The other pilots followed suit, regrouping at eight thousand feet off the port wing. This was the greatest sport, three dimensional teamwork, with an adversary you could shoot at and the only boundaries the ocean and sky. Each pilot had colored bullets that would leave a mark on the sleeve when they hit it, and after the squadron got back the chromatic count began: Blue bullets, 38; Green, 33; Red, 32; Orange, 25 . . . Blue had shot down thirty-eight Zeros. War was a great deal of fun.

I also remember Fitzgibbons. He was five foot six, soft spoken, pleasant, older; he was twenty-three whereas we were nineteen and would have finished his training a year before except for the ptomaine poisoning he contracted at a Corpus Christi picnic. Someone had served his battalion tainted meat and mayonnaise; two cadets died and Fitzie spent nine months in the hospital. He was my roommate.

One day we were coming back from gunnery runs and Fitzie had the lead. I was seventh in line so I was up there till the last and could see everything. Fitzie tapped his head before starting his descent, which he did gradually, turning, turning until he was a hundred feet in the air. Then something happened. The plane twisted and spun in, looking like a tootsie toy from my altitude, bounced and turned over, remaining on its back. It seemed harmless enough from five hundred feet, no fire, no smoke, no crushed parts as you see in the photos of automobile accidents, just a tootsie toy lying there flat on its back, all it had to be was turned right side up and the game could start over again and the playmates resume playing. When I got down, however, I was told that Fitzie was dead; strange, there wasn't a scratch on him, not a cut, nothing, but I was told the spinning plane broke his neck as he hit the ground. This was the first time anything like this happened to my squadron. Two weeks later Henson was to stall in from a hundred feet with the sleeve attached to his plane and get fifty stitches in his head, but the plane didn't spin breaking his neck. Things like this happened so frequently at Daytona that there was always some news at supper time but they never had much effect on you unless it was your squadron. The fellows you flew with. It's something like the neighborhood you live in where you don't like to see the next fellow get cancer, but it's nothing to having someone in your own family get it or you yourself, it's not the same. It's news but not visceral.

As Fitzie's roommate I was supposed to take him home. He had signed the papers making me his "In Case of Accident, Please Notify," and I was to take him home, but here was the Bronx Boy again, aloof, ingenuous, stupid, the oilcloth man. One of the flight instructors lived in St. Louis, Missouri, where Fitzie came from, and asked me if I minded if he took him home. I said yes he could, I didn't know how to say no, I said yes without reflection; if they had put any document before me, any, I probably would have signed it without reading. Don't speak up, don't talk, don't request, don't ask, respect the rights of others and give, even if you don't know what they're asking, give, it is better to give than to receive, run away from a fight. Jims, they're not worth fighting, keep away from me, Jims, as I keep away from everybody else, don't take Fitzie home if they ask, let the Lieutenant from Missouri do it, so I never took Fitzie home to meet his family and tell them what a wonderful person he was. To tell the truth, it's a good thing I didn't because if I had gone to his house I wouldn't have known what to say, I'd have been impervious to their grief. A statue. And I might have said something gauche, an East coast wisecrack trying to be smart.

What else? Oh yes, forty years after the war I visited Daytona and it was Dante all over again:

Nessun maggior dolore
che ricordarsi del tempo felice
nella miseria.

Well not exactly Dante, I'm getting dramatic. The misery doesn't apply to me nor the great sorrow because I have my wife and family but even so I found it doesn't pay to go back. There's some pain all right because you go back looking for the same and it isn't the same, it doesn't even exist any more.

When I went to Daytona in 1983 I didn't recognize one single solitary thing, not one. That beautiful beach is gone, victimized by small bars and unattractive hotels. I couldn't find Llewellyn's or Broad Street (had I imagined them, Mavis, are you my Dulcinea?), the place where the officer's club was, the base, which they told me was converted into the Daytona airport, an utterly glamorless place, not like the dramatic flight line I knew, the jasmine, steak house, Vermont Street, nothing. I had my family with me so the wrench was muted but nevertheless Daytona was gone, my Daytona, scene of deserted beaches and gunnery runs. I was supposed to go back six months after the war, February 14, 1946 it would have been; I had read about Gregory Boyington's Black Sheep Squadron and how they

110

promised to meet six months to the day after the war in a certain bar in San Diego and that's what I told her: "Llewellyn's, Mavis, six months after the war." But I purposely didn't go, I was married then, and I sometimes wonder if she went and waited, hoping to see a door open and a friendly face walk in. I hope not. I wasn't worth it. A statue. Anyway I hope life has been good to her for she deserved it and she's precious in memory. If you read this, Mavis, I have always thought of you, and . . .

17. The Church

I had my own accident four months later in North Carolina, which meant the end of the war for me; no more playing, no more playmates, no more shooting circles and gunnery runs. The fighting in the islands and Europe still meant nothing to me, I wasn't aware they existed, and Hitler, Hirohito, Stalin, the Russian Front, Tarawa, the Bulge were mere names that's all, they didn't exist. Why you might say I was a nominalist! The real things were beer, pipe tobacco, a broken leg and running to New York every chance I got to see my girl, and once we met halfway between New York and Rocky Mount, North Carolina, in Washington, D.C. That was the only reality. The leg took six months to heal and by that time it was June 1945, so it was over. My accident wasn't like Fritzie's, after all I'm here to tell it, it was more like Henson's except there were two front teeth out and a broken leg instead of fifty stitches. At one stage I went out to St. Alban's, Long Island for treatment at the Naval Hospital and you'd think I was John Basilone or Commando Kelly what with the compassionate looks I got on the subway train, the admiration, the stares for the hero with his shot up leg in a plaster cast. Naval wings, crutches, a plaster cast and a pipe in the mouth entraining for an invalids' hospital, a perfect Hollywood setting. Home is the hero, who could ask for anything more?

The truth is I was returning to Cherry Point one day when the engine conked. This was not Pre-Pre-flight, where you could glide a Piper Cub or Aeronca for a mile, or Primary, where you could slip an N3N or N2S into a field, but an F6F, a truly 'heavier than air' craft, so once you lost power she descended with a vengeance. Although I was not far from the landing strip I couldn't quite make it so I chose a bushy field alongside, with scrub resembling laurel. I didn't have to remember the instructions for a wheels-up landing, which had been drilled into me. I did just as I was supposed to, stalling her in at 68 m.p.h. when all of a sudden the plane leaped into the air and came down on its back. My mouth hit the gunsight but I was pulled right back; the shoulder straps saved me. The hood slammed shut so I couldn't get out. "Get me out, get me out," I started to yell like a suzerain ordering some vassal to do his job. There was no excruciating pain, no blood, I don't even think there was any fear, only a sort of anger. I was imperious. "Get me out!"

I must say they were very good about it. While I was coming down I had broken radio silence saying: "Red Base, Red Base, this is Charley Peter Twenty-Two. Forced Landing." The girl in the radio tower had objected to the landing, but then I yelled into the radio and turned it off. They were very good about it. I don't think I was in there thirty seconds when they had me out, which is the way it should be because you never know about

112

fire. And it was only when they got me out of the cockpit that I felt the pain; my left leg was broken. I could see from the faces of the corpsmen they didn't know what to expect, blood, gore, a shattered face, a dead body, and they were all frightened. I know I have often thought I'd like to be a policeman like my Uncle Bill except for the automobile accidents with families mashed to a pulp on holiday weekends, but as I say there was no blood, no gore or fractured skull, just two teeth gone and now a pain in my left leg. They took me to the hospital.

The next day the fellows came to see me. They were more—how shall I put it—respectful than usual though hardly somber; they smiled and joked a bit and then they left; after all, what are you going to say and you're not going to get somber. As long as they stayed at Cherry Point they came to see me, and I went to the BOQ for dinner as soon as I could.

About a month after the accident Lieutenant Colonel Quilly, Group Operational Officer, asked to see me so I met him in the hangar loft with two other officers investigating the accident. Colonel Quilly assured me the forced landing came from a lack of oil pressure which froze the engine, and there was no complaint against the pilot. I was glad to hear that, I said. Then he said: "Your landing was good, Murphy, wheels locked up, you came in fine. The trouble was you hit a tree stump hidden in the bushes, so we're having those stumps removed now." He said this with a quizzical look and friendly smile and I think he enjoyed the humor of the situation: you remove the stumps *after* the accident. But he was right. There was no sense bemoaning the past because all the indignation, righteousness and apologies weren't going to undo what happened. And the Bronx Boy took it that way too; you accept what happened, Primary, Daytona, Operational, Fitzie, Henson, the accident, it was over, done, gone, you can't undo the past. The Bronx philosopher, or statue, must move on.

Although I didn't realize it at the time, my military career and flying days were just about over. The leg took a long time to mend and when June 1945 came I was given utility hops. I flew one Major to the dental labs in Jacksonville, Florida; like me he had lost a couple of teeth. I never flew twin engine, so I never took more than one person up at a time, generally in an SNJ. When planes came out of overhaul they needed ten hours of breaking in before being returned to the flight line so I'd take them up for an hour or two, and once I had to fly some orders up to Anacostia, Washington. But for the most part I stayed around the base, had medical checkups, went to the movies, ate and drank at the O Club, gambled and went swimming in the Olympic pool. I also liked to drive jeeps around the base; people won't believe this but I learned to fly before I learned to drive because my father never owned a car and couldn't drive one himself. So shifting gears and buzzing about the station was fun.

The war was over. One day in mid-August a Marine Captain

113

came running into the flight room yelling: "A bomb! A bomb! They just dropped a bomb with twenty tons of TNT!" The secret had been kept by Intelligence because no one knew what he was talking about. There was a slight stir, but the Bronx Boy maintained his calm. So what? What of it? That's the attitude, stoical pruritus. Soon everyone would be going home.

THE CHURCH

I have neglected mentioning an important basis of Bronx civilization, the Roman Catholic Church. I spoke about All Saints and Rosadabrigid of course but these were run by religious orders, the regulars as they are called, whose only purpose was education. I didn't talk about the parishes and parish priests, the seculars, who influenced every area of society, medicine, motion pictures, law, theater, politics, even the calendar and vacations. Until the early thirties, when Mayor La Guardia beat Jimmy Walker at City Hall, St. Patrick's Cathedral was known as the Power House, furnishing energy to the five boroughs; there it stood at Fiftieth and Fifth raising its medieval spires to the sky.

Half the Bronx at least and perhaps two-thirds, the Murphys and Bacigalupis, had a mentality and tradition reaching back to the Council of Trent and beyond to the thirteenth century though I suspect it was more Tridentine than anything else. I think a few of the other citizens were medieval too, the Moscowitzes and Liebowitzes, Orthodox religious every moment of whose lives was prescribed by ritual. I am unable to write their story because I only know it superficially from the other side of University Avenue, Undy and Sedgwick, but perhaps my friend Segal will write it one day.

When I think of the Bronx I think of Cardinal Bellarmine and King Alphonso the Wise's *Seven Parts of the Roman Law* though we certainly had no one of Alphonso's stature. A Bronx Boy like me had a station in life, a stewardship, and he was expected to live up to it, the mode of living being more important than the station. A renowned surgeon or Supreme Court justice had the same dignity as a trolley car conductor, no more and no less, and although he may have been given more talents by God, like the man in the biblical story, he is essentially no better than the trolley man; he may have five talents and the conductor one, but on the Day of Judgment more will be expected of him and if he doesn't perform well his place in heaven will be far lower than his trolley peer's, and should he come empty-handed he may not see heaven and have to take up residence elsewhere. I do not write facetiously as I say this but am seriously recording a rule for life and frame of mind. There is of course much wisdom in this philosophy since it lends dignity to all human labor, and many of our doctors, lawyers, deans and chancellors could make use of it today. Professionals often forget they are supposed to serve their people rather than

114

take advantage of them; the primary goal of their art is something other than money. Properly received, the state in life is a wholesome doctrine.

Nevertheless it has its limitations. It has a certain pre-1789 and pre-Kierkegaardian character alien to the American experience, causing many Bronx Catholics pain. Overemphasized, state in life induces an other-worldliness belittling the achievements of this vale of tears. A trolley car conductor may be as good as a dean (I myself prefer the trolley car conductors) but he might also like to improve his stewardship and acquire some of the ease, comfort, freedom and education of a higher rank, and above all he might want these privileges for his children. Such aspiration is hardly sinful. If religious propaganda is bluntly presented, without nuance, the aspirations of the humble will be crushed since they are unlettered souls who cannot fend for themselves. A philosopher once said that the more a man understands the more he is, so perhaps a trolley car conductor should acquire more being through education, which will make him more like God. The Church should present its doctrine charitably, revealing to the faithful the great variety of human experience and then letting them choose for themselves; the Church must be the Great Revealer rather than the Great Dogmatist. Let a man choose his state in life no matter how high or low and then let him live up to it, and be he a beggar he will be everyone's equal and even their superior through humility.

I am not certain the Roman Catholic Church followed this doctrine in the Bronx 1930. Unlike the anti-Papists, I am not speaking of deliberate clerical malice but of human pride and stupidity, which are always with us. Take a group of immigrants, the Irish, give them absentee landlords, rackrent and the Great Hunger of 1848 and drive them in droves to a foreign soil where they are reluctantly welcome. Their only leadership is the Clergy, their only cement the Church, so they band together urging their rights, finally becoming clannish as people say; their leaders grow in power, stronger and stronger, until the cathedral becomes the Power House. William Butler Yeats called this condition 'priest-ridden', and I should agree, although you will always find an open fourth wall on your handball court in the United States of America. Nevertheless, I hold no admiration for anti-clericals from outside the fold. I am writing these thoughts because I want people to understand the Bronx Boy, James Ignatius Murphy, Jims, before he journeys to graduate school after the Second World War.

The clergy's misconstruction of state in life retarded the progress of Catholics in America and particularly of the Irish, who spoke English before their arrival. Considering the paucity of literature written by Irish Americans, this slow development is regrettable; after all, it was their cousins who gave birth to *Ulysses*.

Another prominent doctrine for every day living was the

occasions of sin, more specifically, "flee the proximate occasions of sin." The thought is thirteenth century and ultimately comes from Aristotle, who had distinguished between causes, conditions and occasions. In my original manuscript I have written two whole pages giving examples of these categories but I don't think I'll reproduce them now for fear of boring the reader, or worse, amusing him. Suffice it to say that the proximate occasions of sin are any person, place or thing apt to lead you into moral evil, and if they are at hand you must avoid them. In common parlance this is like saying "avoid bad company" or "stay away from that place, you always get into trouble there." The main feature of this doctrine was its stressing free will rather than the emphasis on environment and conditioning you see today. Bronx Boys were responsible for their acts and you were at all times aware you were responsible, so if you were apt to do wrong in certain circumstances you had jolly well better get out of there, flee them.

I have no trouble with this casuistry or with casuistry itself for that matter, even though the word has deplorable connotations. Every credo teaches that stealing is wrong but the question may well arise, is this particular act stealing? A judge can accept a birthday card but he cannot accept large sums of money. Where does he draw the line? Segal once told me the Talmud has a casuistic example in of all things a pickle barrel; if you are passing by, it may be all right to pluck a splinter off the barrel although it is prudent not to do so, but you cannot reach in and help yourself to a pickle. My Uncle Bill put it this way: "If you're ever a policeman, Jims, don't even take a cup of coffee then they can't say they gave you anything."

In the Bronx the Murphys were always aware of a state in life, the priestly state being the highest and the single state higher than the married, for as the good book says "let those who can take it." A few priests and nuns, a few bachelors and spinsters, and a host of married people in various walks of life all journeying towards the promised land, the communion of saints. The Murphys were also aware of free will and sin, at all times, and as I say there was little stress on environment; there were good acts and bad acts and people constantly had to exercise their will, embracing the good and fleeing the bad. I shall use the word *state* here in another sense; half the Bronx had this state of mind. The Catholic Bronx was a State of Mind.

I myself have no problem with these doctrines even today, when so many learned people seem intent on disassembling the house, encouraging disarray; when so many nuns and priests and former nuns and priests are more Catholic than the Pope and more liberal than the liberals, kooks you might call them and in some cases weirdos. I believe in free will, in fact I know there is free will since everyone asserts it by his actions if not by his words, and as every sophomore knows, actions speak louder than words; that explains why we all recognize hypocrites, who don't practice what they preach. Yes, I believe in free will but I would radically alter the perspective. Things get more hazy as I grow older; I can no longer categorize everything scientifically ninety-nine times a day and then start to label this act and that act and the other. Life isn't like that. The virtues must set in and take over, kindly habits disposing a Murphy to do the right thing.

Although I believe we exercise our will rather often, the thought has occurred to me that some people may get to exercise it only a few times in their life and perhaps even just once. I base this thought on experience. I did a stint with the Department of Welfare in 1949 and accompanied an applicant to his sister's apartment in Harlem. She was there with four small children, two, four, six and eight years of age, a man in a suit who seemed to be an arranger of some kind, and a giant happy-go-lucky drunken man who held an empty bottle in his hand, with another empty bottle on the floor. The giant was laughing and greeted me most amiably. He was stark naked. The arranger seemed annoyed and berated my client for coming there. I have thought: What will become of these children when they are fifteen? What example will they have had? They seem destined to sordidness by a will other than their own, to constant, habitual, degrading vice. And yet I am convinced that some time in their life, at least once, they will of their own volition perform a right action; they will help another human being more unfortunate than they, or perhaps simply let a victim go. They will do something good or not do something bad on their own account. And that is all that will be asked of them. But one cannot apply the laws of casuistry to them ninety-nine times a day.

Fleeing the occasion of sin certainly had one salutary effect, namely, the sense of scandal. This doctrine may have been overtaught by Brother Solomon and his Baltimore Catechism but it introduced the faithful to the rights of others; other persons have rights which Murphy must respect even if it makes him uncomfortable; he has no right to use other people as a means to an end because their dignity is such they are an end in themselves. And one should never set a bad example, especially before little children. It seems to me that modern advertising has lost this sense of *scandale* because it uses sex to sell beer. It has no right to do so.

There are so many doctrines I could write here, and perhaps I will return to put them down some day. Half the Bronx knew about poverty and poverty of spirit and sometimes confused the two. They also knew Aristotle's doctrine of hylomorphism although they didn't know they knew it and wouldn't have recognized the word if they saw it; the sacraments and many problems of ethics were systematically divided into matter and form, all of which leads me to ask a question. How much of the Catholic Religion is specifically Christian, the teachings of the Master, and how much is Greek? How many genuine articles of faith are there, religious truths to be known only by faith and not through reason? Offhand I can list only four with certitude: The Trinity, Creation, Incarnation, and Resurrection (Redemption). I can list two more that are articles of faith for me, the doctrine of Mary and efficacy of the sacraments, although these really come under the Incarnation. So perhaps there are just four. It seems to me that the existence of God Himself is a matter of faith for some, but of reason for a discerning philosopher. Abentofail seems to say so.

How much Catholic doctrine is really Greek, a philosophical couch prepared by pre-Christian pagans living in a state of unredeemed nature? How much is Greek? Is belief in the soul an article of faith? I have no objection to matter and form or matter and soul and the truth is I accept them, I am simply asking are they articles of faith or of Greek philosophy? Is it possible that some South Sea island tribe has a poetical explanation of human dignity surpassing that of the Greeks? Perhaps a loin-clothed tribesman observing the sun, sky, flowers, plants, insects, snakes and sea, above all the sea, has perceived some spiritual truth no Greek or Roman has ever seen. I say perhaps. I don't know because if he has made such a discovery he's analphabetic and has never written it down and his oral tradition will do me no good since I am no anthropologist.

In any case, I wonder how many articles of faith there really are. A half dozen I wager. But in the Bronx there must have been dozens ranging from indulgences to nine Fridays to Lent, created probably by canonical lawyers who resemble their secular brethren. The Bronx 1930 was orthodox beyond repair; we had spiritual curls behind our ears.

And in Lent we had a visible caftan, the ashes on the forehead, not above the hairline as they so discreetly place them today but dead center in the forehead an inch above the bridge of the nose, a great big smudge of black dirt. I believe this smudge was sincere and that the Christian was recalling the human state, remember man that thou art dust and unto dust thou shalt return; but I also believe that in many cases, my own for example, deep down within, in the subconscious, the Bronx Boys were telling the others, particularly the atheists and Protestants, left footers, that they were James Ignatius Murphy the Roman Catholic and that they had the inside track and didn't care who knew it cost what it may. Those ashes were dust and also defiance.

Ash Wednesday, prelude to Lent. I must speak of Lent, forty days of the year, one ninth of the calendar.

I don't recall anything like Mardi Gras in New York although some people might have gone to the movies that fat Tuesday, smoked several cigarettes and drunk a great deal of beer because that's what they were giving up for Lent. That was the important question: "What did you give up for Lent?" When you were a child you generally gave up candy or gum or going to the movies; when you were an adult you might give up the movies or beer or cigarettes. I knew one older French couple (the only French people I ever met in New York, there weren't any) who gave up smoking every year, and then at Lent's end, Holy Saturday at noon on the dot, they'd start smoking cigarettes again. That was quite a feat. Many people who gave up smoking didn't last all forty days. I remember Billy McCarthy at Rosadabrigid who was speaking to a friend in the cafeteria the first day of Lent:

"I gave up smoking, what did you give up?"

"Smoking. And beer too, if you give up smoking you have to give up beer."

The next day I saw them in the cafeteria again. Billy said:

"How long did you last?"

"Until five, just before supper. How long did you?"

"Beatcha. I lasted till six."

It wasn't easy to give up smoking, it never is. I remember Mark Twain's famous dictum: "It's easy to give up smoking, I've given it up a thousand times."

It wasn't always a question of giving something up. Some people would go to Mass and Holy Communion every day or to weekly novenas, stations of the cross or some other religious gathering. I once heard that doing something positive is the best of all, like performing the corporal works of mercy but I don't remember people doing that. The corporal works of mercy were feeding the hungry, clothing the naked and visiting the sick and those in prison. I used to have doctrines like this memorized but I don't anymore and I believe they were always seven in number; there seems to be so many things numbered seven, 7 capital sins, 7 corporal works of mercy, 7 spiritual works of mercy, 7 sacraments, 7 cardinal and theological virtues, that Jung might be right with his archetypes and Pythagoras with his numerology. We do indeed have a penchant for the number seven. I remember a lapsed Protestant once telling me that he admired the Mass very much because it had every single one of the archetypes, the only institution that does, and he disliked the ritual changes of the 1960's for that reason.

Then there were the indulgences, nine First Fridays, five Saturdays and also fish on Friday. Shades of Erasmus, the Christian scholar who four hundred years before had inveighed against indulgences and the emphasis on fish, which he claimed had commercial implications! There were indulgences for everything; if you blessed yourself with holy water you had sixty days remission of punishment for sins, that is, two months removed from the approaching temporal punishment of Purgatory. And other religious practices gave you plenary indulgences, for example, if you went to Mass and Communion nine straight First Fridays you were to receive full remission of punishment, complete removal of the time in Purgatory, which meant you went straight to heaven; and as I recall, the same reward was promised for five First Saturdays, which were set aside for the Virgin Mary. Most of these practices are gone now and the evening novenas and missions; the eating of fish on Fridays is gone too. Many of the post-Vatican II crowd are inclined to scoff at these former customs and seem to like change for change's sake but I wonder if all the innovations and transformations are for the better. At some universities today we have nine First Fridays running from September to May, which are conducted by different schools and colleges, the occasion being a late afternoon happy hour, in other words, booze instead of the sacraments. The professors gather every First Friday for a cocktail hour to flatter one another and to play up to a new dean. Some are lonely of course so in this sense the happy hour is wholesome as indeed all happy hours are, but why call it First Friday? I am convinced some *mauvais génie* has done this deliberately, some perverse descendant of the Enlightenment, an impish fool who gets his kicks by hocussing-pocussing religion; after all the expression *Hocus Pocus* comes from *Hoc est enim corpus meum.*

Erasmus may have been right when he opposed the rule on abstinence from meat, which may have had commercial overtones. In 1972 I met a very astute alumnus of Rosadabrigid who told me he had a prosperous fish business in Albany, but when he saw the findings of the Vatican Council he immediately got out and bought some bowling alleys. "The whole business is kerplunk," he said. And the truth is, in the Midwest the Arthur Treacher fish houses are empty; you never see anyone go in there, not like McDonald's and the others. The Long John Silver fish houses have folded too, or they start serving chicken.

On the other hand, I don't know, I can't see any harm in abstaining from meat on Fridays, a sort of minor sabbath. What harm will it do especially if you remove the mathematical addiction to indulgences? You can refrain from eating flesh as a religious recollection rather than a celestial accountancy, and you don't have to eat fish although you might, the principal custom being to refrain from meat. What's the harm? It seems to me every religion worthy of the name has some dietary law about things you eat and drink or conversely refrain from; after all the Eucharist itself is a paradoxical regimen of wheat and grapes. What's the harm? I wonder if these innovators are not throwing out the wisdom of the baby with the bath.

One thing I do know, I much prefer the Latin Mass. Were my wife to die or one of my children I'd want a High Mass, a *missa cantata* with the *Sanctus, Sanctus, Sanctus, Panis angelicus, Ave Maria,* and *Praeceptis salutaribus moniti* all sung by an Italian tenor like Joe Lazzeri, who sang at my nuptial Mass in 1946. I can picture the coffin moving down the aisle, and the candles, and smell the incense as Joe sings *Panis angelicus*; it brings tears to my eyes. And I am vain enough to think that that's what I'll have at my own funeral. It won't make any difference to me then of course because I'll be elsewhere but it makes a big difference to me now. What celestial music! I think of Luis de León's ode to the musician Francisco Salinas. Why shouldn't religious services be like that? Why shouldn't they be aesthetic? Why do they have to be drab? I have little sympathy for the relevancy crowd in the church and university, who want to give everything a social, practical purpose. Social engineers, that's all they are, that's not charity, they don't delight in anything.

In addition to Lent, First Fridays, novenas, missions and an ecclesiastical lexicon, we had a slew of holidays and it seemed some one was always getting off for a secular or religious fiesta, and there were also non-holidays that looked like holidays, call them social occasions. October 11 was Columbus Day; then there was Halloween (an occasion); November 1st - All Saints; November 2 - All Souls (occasion); November 2nd to 7th - Election Day; November 11 - Armistice Day; Thanksgiving; November 30th - St. Andrew's (beginning of Advent); December 8 - Immaculate Conception; Christmas; New Years; February 3 - St. Blaise (occasion); February 12 - Lincoln's Birthday; February 22 - Washington's Birthday; Ash Wednesday (occasion, a smudge on your forehead); March 17 - St. Patrick's Day Parade; Holy Thursday; Good Friday; Holy Saturday; Easter; May 30 - Memorial Day; that's quite a list for the school year and I have omitted a couple like Rosh Hashana and Yom Kippur back in the fall. The difference then was that holidays and special events were always on your mind and there was always one coming up and you thought about it and looked forward to it. I wonder if there wasn't a certain wisdom here and if the human animal isn't better off having a half a dozen holidays spread between early September and Christmas rather than having just one, as we do now. And they're not just days off, like celebrating July 4th on a Monday even though it falls on a Wednesday so you can have a three day weekend, they're events, celebrations with an aura about them - October 11th, the discovery of America, a day off; three weeks later, Election Day, have a bonfire! America is the best! One can't expect non-Catholics to celebrate December 8th but perhaps we could have other days: Nathan Hale's Day, Paul Revere's Day!, *Damn the torpedoes, Gridley, full speed ahead Day, Don't fire until you see the whites of their eyes Day!* And Armistice Day again! Why not? I'd suggest at least two days a month since we could all use more joyous time, our most precious possession. Time eludes all of us. Even millionaires don't have time.

The Irish and Italians in the Bronx lived in an ecclesiastical civilization they didn't understand. They could go way back, long before 1789, and feel at home. That's why when I read literature from the Middle Ages I feel an intimacy most scholars cannot know. I guess you might say I was priest-ridden and still am in a way because you don't just throw off something like that, it leaves an indelible impression. My wife wouldn't take a YMCA course twenty-five years ago because Father McGillicuddy told her not to; she'd go to the YMCA today all right but she is still quite a traditionalist. And so am I, the Bronx Boy who lived in an ecclesiastical society that perished in 1962.

1789-1962: it took a hundred and seventy-three years to revolutionize the Bronx, the most stupendous event in History. But I look back. I always look back. When I think of the Church at its best I think of a young girl in a white Communion dress holding a bouquet of flowers or a little boy in blue with a white band on his arm. We should all be like that. Always. We were meant to be like that. Children. And when I think of the Church at its worst I think of Brother Solomon with his strolling tiptoes and strap. After graduating from P.S. 11 I should have gone to Evander Childs.

18. After the War

Memory differs from the other faculties of body and soul. Recent practice makes an artist more adept than the practice of yesteryear; recent training makes an athlete more agile than the training of a decade ago; in a word, recent conditioning of body and mind is a virtue whereas the conditioning of youth is lost now; a man who has deteriorated through slovenly habits lives in a vicious state. But memory works the opposite way. A tricycle crash of fifty years ago, a small cut on the shin, a father's anguish, a mother's apple pie, a game of stickball or hide-and-seek are all of them clear as crystal whereas the events of this morning fade from memory. Occasionally a dramatic event, an automobile accident or friend's death, are well remembered but never so clearly remembered as the winter night you hitched on the University trolley coming home from Van Cortlandt Park your fingers numbed with cold as you said the Hail Mary a hundred times over praying the conductor would stop soon so you wouldn't fall off. Everyone has an experience like that when they're a child and never forgets it. Never ever as they say.

After the war I was twenty-two years old, an adult in body though not in mind and I did not mature until maybe I was fifty and certainly not before thirty-two. Thirty-two to fifty were my years of maturation, which may be average or better than average for all I know because I have since learned that some professors never mature. In my college today I know four senior professors who act five, six, ten and twelve years old respectively although their chronological age approaches mine. One argues and fights as if he had a pail in a sandbox; one is a spoiled little girl; one is clever, a bad little boy smoking behind the barn; and another practices all the deceits of a sullen teenager. All these fifty year old babies have one thing in common, an inability to deal with archaic imagery, to draw the line between present events and things that happened to them long ago as children. I began to draw this line between my thirty-second and fiftieth year and that's why I'm an adult now. I am very mature.

I remember my own history after the war very well though not so well as those sacred shrines P.S. 11 and Ringalevio. Were I to be graded by some mnemonic meter, a mnemonimeter, I would receive an A plus grade for 1924-1944, an A minus for the late forties and subsequent years, with the ciphers reducing to D and F for yesterday. I think part of it is caring. It matters little to me that some faculty committee sends me a copy of its fatuous minutes or the dean one of his ukases but I was really annoyed the day Timmy Shea displayed the cheesebox with the almost impossible holes for winning immies and frightened to death the day I was hiding from Vito in the cellar.

After the war I returned to Rosadabrigid to finish my program there. It hadn't changed, the same old ineptitude, except for the Irish priest who taught me Logic and one historian who later trained some very fine graduate students one of whom is famous today. I majored in History and at this time began to study Spanish on my own through a tutor, a Hills and Rivera primary grammar and the constant reading of easy texts. I also tried talking with a friend whose Spanish was about as subtle as mine: "Es menester que tú hables conmigo."..."It is necessary that you speak with me." *Es menester*: I must have sounded like Cicero trying to declaim in a foreign tongue; everyone knows what you mean and also knows you are frantically digging for words and juggling syntax like a funambulist in the linguistic circus. History led me to Spanish through the conquistadores because I was so fascinated by these men I wanted to know more about them, their language and country. If anyone needs some stimulation let him read Bernal Díaz's *True History of The Conquest* or a narrative of Jiménez de Quesada's expedition to El Dorado. There are also Prescott's great accounts, which I would rank alongside *Huckleberry Finn*.

After Rosadabrigid I enrolled at Mecca in Manhattan, the greatest collection of scholars of its day. They were all there, historians, poets, philosophers, economists, scientists, and with the GI Bill I could afford to study with any one of them as long as I wished: I could have gone to school from 1945 to 1955 if I wanted to, done nothing else and lived well. New York State also had War Veterans' Scholarships and the postage was still three cents and the subway cost a nickel. Surely this was an age surpassing the Medicis'.

I must single out one person at Mecca, my own mentor in Latin American History, Professor Feigenbaum. He had a slight European accent, imperceptible except for the *v*'s. He had been a newspaper correspondent during the Mexican Revolution and knew many figures of that era, I believe he was a friend of Cárdenas. He hiked through the Amazon two thousand miles with a mule and climbed the Andes to a town at 14,000 feet where he told us he could hardly breathe and here was an Indian walking briskly home playing a fife after working in a field all day, so the European will never conquer the Andes he said. I remember many anecdotes like this but above all I remember his philosophy of the little things, saying that they are the most important part of your life, your family, friends, games, a glass of wine, a walk in the country, a winter's afternoon. I have seen this philosophy expressed in Spanish writers like Azorín but I saw it incarnate in Professor Feigenbaum, a vital philosophy for all to live by. I could see it in his friendly smile, the way he puffed his pipe, his courtesy, his seriousness, his good humor, his rejection of grandiose schemes, his humility, the pride he took in the tractor on his farm, the farm itself which was like his father's farm he said, and the way he called weird theories out of Teachers' College crazy. A little word like that, no great philosophical discourse here, no circumlocution, no linguistic legerdemain or

British sublety although he knew several languages; weird educators were just what he said they were, crazy. I believe he went home at night and read Plato's *Republic*, which he mentioned once in class.

Professor Feigenbaum (the truth is that's what I always called him, not plain Feigenbaum the way mathematicians and non-traditionalists do) applied his philosophy of the little things to his vision of Mexico, which cost him the adherence of many scholars who otherwise respected him, and some of them I gathered did not like him. He argued that the real Mexico was not Mexico City with its modern urban civilization but the other Mexico of the Indian. Economists and government officials should keep this in mind when planning for the future and instead of trying to ape the United States and Europe with heavy industry and grand social schemes should encourage small local crafts and industries, the creation of small lakes stocked with fish, new sources of food such as the Brazilian tree whose fruit has the value of a potato, local roads, anything supporting the small towns and localities. In Mexico and elsewhere he was opposed to the growth of big government, preferring town to county, county to state and state to the national organization. I remember once he made a remark about one of our own states where some county sheriff had apparently said: "Who the hell does the governor think he is?" Professor Feigenbaum thought that the sheriff's ability to talk like that was wonderful. He held the same attitude towards Mexico: local rule wherever possible is best. I wonder if he wasn't right and if other scholars might not take pause and consider his attitude. Look at Mexico today, particularly its capital city, wouldn't it be better if this octopus which is strangling even itself were divested of so much political and economic power and if this power were redirected towards the provinces? I myself remember the Mexico City of 1955, beautiful, courteous, delightful, sunny, just like Professor Feigenbaum's smile, but I am told it is no longer so. In any case, he inspired confidence in his students and we all loved him. One last tribute to my master, a little remembrance of a small act: several Latin American students owed their careers to Feigenbaum, who tided them over when they had financial problems.

I spoke before of his guest seminar, an unusual collection of scholars and visitors. One week a Communist came from Argentina, the next week a Peronist, the next, two surviving members of the Braganza family in Brazil, then next an anthropologist from NYU, then a political refugee from Colombia and finally a Spanish missionary to Bolivia. The missionary was a delight. Feigenbaum introduced him and his topic and then the old man reached into his pocket and said: "One moment please, I would like to read my poem.", upon which he brought forth a bulky hand-written manuscript and read it to us for an hour and a half, about the condors coming

125

over the Andes and the fires in the mountains on St. John's Day, June 24th. Feigenbaum just sat there and smiled. This was Latin America. On another afternoon the young anthropologist from NYU had a huge scheme for reforming impoverished Puerto Rico, he was going to change the place from top to bottom, a radical solution. Professor Feigenbaum just sat there again and smiled, only this time he puffed his pipe and shook his head. It was his way of saying: "You're crazy."

I made a very good friend at Mecca. His name was Roberto. I haven't seen him in years but he will recognize the truth of Feigenbaum and how we all loved him. Feigenbaum died in 1967 . . . Adiós, maestro, may things go well with thee beyond Plato's cave.

What else can I say about Mecca? It was mainly Feigenbaum as far as I was concerned but I do remember this: it had an outstanding English and History department and when the professors there got together for a class they didn't call it 'interdepartmental' or 'interdisciplinary' as they do today but simply a university seminar. The current *inter* business is federal jargon issuing from Health, Education and Welfare, *inter* usually meaning antidepartmental and antidisciplinary. Those Mecca men were intellectuals who understood their own discipline and respected the discipline of others.

One thing used to cause me difficulty at Mecca, I guess it always has and always will. When I went to the library to the History stacks to study, one beautiful blonde from the main desk you passed by as you walked in used to come up and rearrange the books near my desk. She wore a strapless dress and reached up to the highest shelves she could find to move the books back and forth and she'd keep moving from left to right and up and down as she did so; she wiggled like this every time I went there. Another unusually beautiful girl who worked as a secretary at Mecca I'd see on the subway platform every night as I went home, and I used to see another buxom one at the 42nd Street Library between the entrance going up to Room 315 and the Chock Full O' Nuts on the opposite corner; as I came out of the library one evening I could see her coming out of Stern's department store across the way. Another girl I used to speak to asked me up to her room one night to help her with her philosophy. I still remember them all, the blonde hair, red lips, mode of walking, the . . . and I'd recognize each one of them if I saw them but somehow I managed to get by. I was married at the time.

I have to pay a tribute to Room 315, New York Public Library, 5th Avenue and 42nd Street, New York City or I'd be culpable of the kind of gross ingratitude leading to Dante's ninth circle. Many days I'd go there at 10 a.m. and take the elevator to the catalogue room on the third floor, which alone is bigger than most public libraries. I'd spend a half hour making out my request chits and bring them to the desk where the librarians checked them and sent them upstairs and then I'd go to Room 315 to watch the electric light board. My number would finally flash, 107 say, a visual impression having all the glory of winning the lottery. I had just won the lottery! I'd pick up my books, watch the small dumbwaiter as it went back up for more and walk down the long cathedral aisle to one of the desks where I'd deposit my books on the table, set them in front of me to right and left as a tiny fortress, staking out my terrain, assuring me of the retired life, and I'd go to work. I'd leave at 1:30 after the luncheon rush for the Chock Full O' Nuts for a hot dog, soup, cream cheese sandwich on whole wheat nut bread, whole wheat doughnuts and coffee, and I'd do the same again at 6:30 after studying all afternoon and ordering another stack of books to add to my fortress. That night I'd close 315 at 10:00 p.m. bringing my books back to the dumbwaiter, to return the following morning at 10:00. Once I did this every day for three weeks in a row after my first semester at Mecca and that may have been the most enjoyable intellectual experience of my life; I was studying the historiography of Argentina at the time, Sarmiento, Mitre, Vicente Fidel López, Roberto Levillier, the annual letters of the missionaries and the reception of the *Monumentum Germaniae Historiae* through the Neapolitan immigrant whose name escapes me now, Pedro something or other, and I can't possibly explain the joy I felt mastering this material, mastering it or so I thought. It must be nice to be a Pirenne, Ranke or Mommsen and spend your whole life, twelve hours a day and more, seven days a week, eating raisin nut bread and whole wheat doughnuts and studying just one subject, your own, until you become the Master. I got a taste of that during those three weeks. For a brief moment I was Master!

A true Master of course starts out running when he's six years old at full speed learning languages and history and philosophy, practicing every day the way basketball players do, always eager for the game, always getting in shape, and he keeps it up through lycée, Gymnasium and university and so on for the rest of his life; he doesn't really care about whole wheat doughnuts, haircuts, parties, dress, movies or anything else, just the subject he has wedded, she is his eternal bride and he her groom; where we ordinary students find time to study midst our commuting, working, eating, rearing of children, recreations and vacations, he does just the opposite, trying to find time to eat, comb his hair, brush his teeth, go to the bathroom and dress midst his life of study. But even so, I had my three weeks, I shall never forget them, and I recommend this to everyone: take some subject you dearly love, anything, the Civil War, Jehovah's Witnesses, family genealogy, golf, New Deal, Richelieu, Dicken's novels, Schopenhauer's mother's pushing him down the stairs, anything, and study it for three solid weeks at Room 315. You will love it! You are missing something in life if you don't.

I had a vocation to be one of the Great Scholars. I really did:

Don Marcelino Menéndez Pelayo, Don Ramón Menéndez Pidal, Don Dámaso Alonso and Don James Ignatius Murphy, the Quaternity. I really did. But even had I started when I was six Rosadabrigid would have put an end to it, Solomon too probably. I also had a vocation to be a great golfer, greater than Nicklaus. I had the physical equipment but I never played golf with my father. The Bronx Boy has not been a success.

After I got my Master's degree from Mecca in 1950 I got a teaching job at the School of Education in Seamus Orsini College, Brooklyn. I also started doctoral studies at New York Commerce, NYC, which so resembled its city of the same initials.

First of all a true historian, which I profess to be, must record the schism between all the universities and Education. I don't think I have ever heard a professor speak well of the School of Education, not even professors of Education, who seem to maintain a discreet silence. I believe the professional Educators had a venerable doctrine at one time, "Remember you are not teaching French, you are teaching children," which properly interpreted is existentialist; young children do not exist for Dondé's grammar, *la rue, le grandpère, les oiseaux*, listed in rueful patterns in a dark blue lifeless book, rather, French exists for the children; which is another way of saying that the sabbath exists for man, man does not exist for the sabbath. The Schools of Education, however, went too far, abandoned French and proceeded to specialize in teaching methodology for its own sake, juvenile psychology, the history of themselves and their own ruminations, an inbred philosophy of educational philosophy; they forgot that a French teacher must first know French for without it he has nothing to impart. In any case, all universities looked askance at their School of Education and felt apologetic about the mess there.

I myself taught at the Seamus Orsini School of Education for two years and came away pleasantly surprised. It was a peculiar place, better than Rosadabrigid in one way, in another way just as poor, not as renowned as Mecca certainly but possessed of a few good lay professors who gave it everything they had. I remember one girl passed the Foreign Officers's Examination of the Board of Examiners of the State Department with flying colors whereas I had flunked the same test at Rosadabrigid. She knew History when she answered those questions and I didn't.

Perhaps the student body was part of the key, enabling the school to do so much with so very little. It was about half Italian, half Irish with a few Poles and Germans thrown in, and another nationality or two, *another* being one Puerto Rican, one Yugoslav and one African black. I felt a certain comfort there and although it was Brooklyn provincial it was better than Rosadabrigid which was more brigid than rosa. I have been to Naples and sometimes think, whimsically I suppose, that they could solve the problems of Northern Ireland by bringing a half

128

million of those Irish to Naples and a half million Neapolitans to Belfast. That should calm things down. I love Naples; nobody cares there about smoking, jogging, jaywalking, traffic lights, war or pollution. Naples lives in the present. That's the trouble with those Irish, they're so damned serious, so deadly in earnest. The Israeli are the same; bring the Naples brigade to Jerusalem and we'd soon have peace in the Near East. Factory production would go down, the farms would wither, but we'd soon have peace and everyone could go swimming in the Mediterranean. Cervantes loved Italy. I love Italy too but above all Naples, which surpasses Florence and Rome.

Seamus taught me that a mixed student body, a social mongrel, is better than a thoroughbred. I forgot to mention the nuns and brothers there, who came as an amiable, dedicated bunch of students; they had true humility, the virtue I admire more than any other. Kelly and Segal had it, Professor Feigenbaum had it, and I didn't. I'm afraid I was unkind to many of the students at Seamus Orsini and although I regret it now thirty-five years later there's nothing I can do about it. That's the punishment for pride, the inability to recover; if you steal you can make restitution, if you lie you can untell the lie by speaking the truth, but when you're unkind to someone by your display of alleged superiority your hands are tied. The damage is done, the wrinkle is made and you are left with the memory.

The clergy at Seamus Orsini were an anomaly, but I think I can explain it now. They had no business running a university because they didn't know what a university was. Paradoxically, this ignorance may have been a certain strength; if you're going to have an institution, run it by someone who is a real pro or a real amateur but not an in-between. The professional of course will know what to do and providing he is right-intentioned will do it, and the amateur of good will may sense his insufficiency and get someone else to do the job for him; he will delegate his authority. The half-pro, half-amateur, the in-between like *homo administrans* at Rosadabrigid is a dangerous species for he thinks he's good at the job, which he isn't, and so he needs support but won't delegate authority because he doesn't think he needs assistance. Consequently he persists in his error. Were I an observer assigning grades, some stellar Abelard, I would send out the following report cards:

Mecca	Professional	A plus
New York Commerce	Professional	A minus
Rosadabrigid	Amateur-Professional	D to F
Seamus Orsini (The School of Education, mind)	Amateur	C plus to B minus

These grades only indicate intellectual performance and are not pointers to heaven. I know that Feigenbaum went to heaven because of his fine character, and I believe that some of the others from NYC, Rosa and Seamus joined him; about the others, I am not prepared to say. I hope I can join Professor Feigenbaum and the young girl from Howard Street, Chicago.

One of the professors at Seamus Orsini, Henry Roberts, was a devoted scholar of American History whose book had been reviewed not only in the scholarly journals but in the *New York Times* Sunday book section where it was very well received, an acknowledgment assuring its commercial success. I can see Henry now, steel moustache, eternal cigarette, friendly smile and willingness to talk about History. He was devoted to his students and it was his protegée who had done so well on the Foreign Service boards; it's funny, you couldn't speak of protegés for most of the students at Rosadabrigid and Seamus, since the professors didn't have any, but in Henry's case you could for he was there behind them, seeing them on to good graduate schools. And all this in a School of Education!

Another professor, Arturo Lynch, was my best friend, one of the three friends I have made in the teaching profession (one usually goes out of one's department to find a friend). Arty taught the nineteenth century English novel and once you got him started on Dickens, Meredith, Trollope and company there was no stopping him; sometimes we got delicatessen food on a Saturday and sat there for hours talking about the novel; his other love, Shakespeare; Moratín and García Lorca, the translated Spaniards you might say, for in spite of his Hispanic name Arty didn't know Spanish. He was very patient with me; I was a cut-up in those days, seeking a great deal of attention. At Seamus Orsini I'd sometimes stand on the desk in class to get an idea across, the idea being mainly *me*.

There were a few others, Vinnie, Tom, and another Tom, a nice bunch of fellows, undistinguished by scholastic achievement but possessed of common sense. Perhaps this was what gave Seamus its sobriety, permitting me to grade it C plus or even B; the students there were a humble Brooklyn crowd who really learned some Mathematics, French, English, and History, above all from Henry Roberts and Arty Lynch. The tone these men set kept the abuses of Education from running rampant as they did in so many Teachers' Colleges, so that the students had a rather good preparation in a discipline and not just the Educational union card. Education couldn't run to extremes.

The clergy at Seamus Orsini seemed to be a decent sort though their intellectual horizons were severely limited. One was haughty but you'll find that in any crowd of human beings, and one was stupid but you'll find that too. Another tried to teach his students humility by deliberately giving straight A scholars a C grade, as if such lack of humility on his part were going to teach this admirable virtue to the young people in his charge. He reminded me of O'Strich at All Saints. But all in all they seemed all right, which leads me to some reflections on ecclesiastical education. *All right* is not enough, it is not good enough in a university. The Catholic Church has paid a heavy toll for ignoring the example of Cardinal Newman, or better said its Catholic faithful have paid the toll. Over a hundred years ago this gentle scholar and true prince advised the Irish bishops not to compete with Oxford but to join it; don't set up your own universities he told them but try to send your students to the great English schools, perhaps establishing a college there, but no, they would not listen to him who knew more on the subject than all of them combined. I remember reading that after Tract 90, when Newman went to Rome, Keble made the remark: "Who is going to teach Newman Latin?" He knew more Latin than the *vaticani*.

The results of Irish contumacy have been disastrous. Look at the map of America, fifty states with a score of Catholic colleges and universities in each state, a thousand institutions, the Rosadabrigids of this world run by immigrants' sons who are intellectual hyphenates. There is nothing wrong with being an immigrant, a blue collar worker, a first generation white collar man or a hyphenate but certainly such people don't know how to run a university. It takes a couple of generations for that and even if you know what you're doing you can't afford to establish a thousand institutions, only a dozen perhaps in the major cities; even that is asking a lot but at least it has a sense of proportion. Universities are not part of the pastorate, and a classroom lecture is not a Sunday sermon; you may not agree with Erasmus and Bruno but you can't just denounce them; so if you honestly think one is a fence sitter and the other a gnostic you will have to read their books patiently, exercising textual control of the imagination, and if you do this don't be surprised if you modify your thesis, you never can be sure what you are going to find. Universities don't pronounce, they investigate.

The bishops didn't listen to Newman and American Catholics have paid the price. I knew some Physics majors at Rosa who went on to Mecca for their Ph.D. and found themselves so poorly prepared they had to return to Rosa for their advanced degree, but there was a difference now; their father's generation didn't know how bad things really were in Catholic colleges but now they knew that Rosa's degrees were inferior. These physicists would never stay there, never send their children there, never return there for alumni gatherings and never feel a tender regard for their alma mater but go off to Texas in computer industries. And who knows how many young students, so zealously protected by the bishops, left the fold because of that zealous protection? Long live the intellect! Long live Cardinal John Henry Newman!

Don't get me wrong. Don't misunderstand. One criticizes the thing one loves. Mecca too was not without stain; I remember a renowned professor there speaking lightly of Newman whom he looked upon as some sort of bagatelle, but the words of this pedant carried no weight with me; this well known Meccaite, this left-footer, hadn't exercised control of his viscera and you might call him a non-sectarian O'Strich. But I don't think of him when I think of that great university in Manhattan, I think of my beloved maestro Feigenbaum. That's the goal, all professors should strive to be like him, and that's why I call university administrators crazy.

I started out well at Seamus Orsini and perhaps I can say the students liked my classes, no, they did like my classes for a while. The academic hour began at 4:10 p.m. and ended at 6:00, but some days they stayed until 7:00 or 8:00 as I told them about the Inca Garcilaso de la Vega and Pizarro in Peru, or Bismarck and Cavour unifying their countries in the nineteenth century (as you can see, the professors had to cover every field at Seamus). I told them anecdotes I knew about the Indies, which I merely repeated from my Mecca classes, and every night I'd spend long hours at home reading about Mazzini and Garibaldi to make Cavour more palatable, and they seemed to appreciate my efforts. But as time went on I began to wear thin, I had so much history to teach, so I started introducing extraneous material from the Spanish courses I was taking at New York Commerce, which could be interesting at times though not germane. Lots of professors did that at Rosa and Seamus to pad out their courses, and I was no different. The students' interest started to wane and they didn't stay after class any more; I began to stand on tables during my lectures, tell jokes, shout my words, and finally I began to think that people were looking at me, staring at me and even saying things about me. I began to chew bubble gum in public and blow bubbles on the train from the Bronx to Brooklyn and I ate lollipops at times. I thought people were looking at me because I had a peculiar gesture of some kind. All this continued for a year and it kept getting worse no matter how much I studied, which was morning, noon, and night seven days a week, until one day an incident happened, a small insignificant incident to others but it wasn't insignificant to me. It's so embarrassing I don't want to describe it here. I won't describe it even though it leaves a gap in this autobiography. Perhaps I can explain it this way; objectively it was nothing, a bagatelle, but subjectively it meant the world to me. I was extremely unhappy. People were looking at me. It affected my work and I treated some students shabbily. I clowned even more.

As I say, this went on for more than a year when one day I was walking on Fordham Road and the Concourse, and near Poe Park I bumped into my friend Bobbie O'Brien whom I hadn't seen since Rosa so we walked west over Fordham to Unie, up to Kingsbridge and west past the Veterans' Hospital and north again on Unie. I have never met a more gentle person than Bobbie or anyone who knows more History, not the kind you learn in school but the kind you read when you were in grammar school, high school and college and went to the public library every week for and took out hundreds of books over the years and read every one of them; Charlemagne, Gonzalo de Córdova, Richelieu, Louis, the Roses, Disraeli, Parnell, Bismarck, Talleyrand, Caesar Borgia, the American Constitution, Civil War, you name it, Bobbie had read it in histories and biographies; he even knew people like Hastings, Lord Grey and Castlereagh. Much of my history I know from him, especially events like the Great Armada, one of the few historical questions he had studied formally, under Mattingly. I remember his many lessons, which were given as friendly chats rather than lessons although that was their effect on me.

I knew Bobbie from grade school as well as college, so he confided in me; he had had a problem and been to a psychiatrist; he described his meetings with his doctor over a period of months and how one day he was sitting in the park at Botanical Gardens, alone, when all of a sudden it all came gushing out, all the anguish and fear he had known since childhood. He told me the name of his malady, which I shall not write here since I am not interested in titillation or satisfaction of curiosity, suffice it to say that Bobbie O'Brien had been sick, he sought help, now he was well. That's all. So I told him about my problem, superficially of course never calling a spade a spade, and he gave me the name of Dr. Thomas Nicholas Megna. "Jims," he said, "why don't you go see him?" I can never thank Bobbie enough for his suggestion.

19. Dr. Megna

No. I can never thank Bobbie enough. It has made all the difference. I'm still somewhat gun shy but I don't think people are looking at me any more and I don't crave their attention. I no longer stand on tables. I often prefer to be alone but that's different, it's the deep seated preference of an older man rather than a craving, and it doesn't incapacitate me socially. I can live very nicely with it and more than that it gives me all the time I need for reading and writing, this autobiography for example. I wake up every morning at six and write ten to twelve big yellow pages for three hours and once I've done that the rest of the day is successful, it cannot fail to be a success once that's done, it simply can't. Some days are better than others of course because I get a great deal of things done, I mean a lot of things, but every day is productive. It's not a bad way to live and after I write each morning I make brown rice or Wheatena with cream and honey, wash and dress, clear up the mail, read Cervantes perhaps, a novel by Mary Renault or another book I happen to be reading, and prepare a lesson:

En el primer verso del *Poema de mío Cid*,
fíjense ustedes en el pleonasmo.

The pleonasm—life is a pleonasm. You do the same things every day until one day the job is finally done, the ultimate day not the penultimate, for 'nobody dies on the eve' as they say in Spanish. Sensible human beings are pleonastic rhetoricians periodically making the rounds whereas the nonsensical ones are lesser lights running to and fro in pursuit of pleasure, power, fame, fortune, whatever the fickle siren places before their eyes.

I remember the first day I went to see Dr. Thomas Nicholas Megna in that tall building on 57th Street. It was one in the afternoon. I took the elevator to the ninth floor; his secretary was there and other people were in evidence in the other offices on the floor. I later surmised that Dr. Megna was never alone during a first visit in case the new patient was dangerous. Who knows, I might have been the Bronx strangler! I surmised this because all subsequent appointments were at six in the evening, when the building was absolutely vacant.

Dr. Megna had a very pleasant manner. He was dressed casually in a sweater and tie and he made me feel at home, his moustache and blue eyes reminding me of Henry Roberts at Seamus Orsini. I have later learned from sartorial wisdom that sweaters indicate friendliness as opposed to a suit's businesslike formality. The doctor's manner was open, respectful but open; without saying a word he was being friendly.

He seemed easy going, never raising his voice or showing shock or surprise when I told him I thought people were staring at me and why. I shall not say *why* here, it is too embarrassing to be written in the pages of a book that is not a privileged communication but he didn't seem embarrassed by what I said, only interested, as if it were an important fact and it was a fact in my mind all right though not in external reality.

Dr. Megna made an appointment for a week later, and then a week later, and they were weekly for three months or so when they became bimonthly and then finally monthly until a year later they petered out. He never broke them off exactly, there just came a day when I didn't go around to see him any more, there was no need to go, an unconscious decision had been made that was mine. As I look back I realize it took a fine artist to achieve this gradual rupture.

He gave me the ink blot tests and one day showed me pictures asking me what they suggested to me; one of them was obvious, a nocturnal lady with her foot up on a stool, rolling down her stockings in a room of questionable decoration. Her face had that . . . special look. I recall that I fibbed a little when I answered that one for I thought of a woman I knew in the Bronx and wouldn't name her but my omission didn't seem to affect the cure of Dr. Megna. The conversations kept on, an hour a night once a week every week.

I particularly remember one night when he dressed differently. He had on a white shirt and tie and when he assumed a certain attitude or made a certain gesture he left me speechless, I couldn't talk. I realized he was telling me something, that the white shirt was my father's shirt or he himself was my father and that's why I couldn't speak. The anomaly began to dawn on me, the hidden labyrinth of the mind. The problem with me wasn't my mother, whom I didn't like, but my father whom I longed for so ardently and was dying to be with; all that showing off, the antics, the standing on a table in class, the bubble gum, even a ridiculous looking moustache I wore for several weeks at Seamus was an attempt to attract his attention even though he was dead. I'd do anything to bring notice on me. This explained the big white shoes I wore with the thick red gum soles, a subtle transformation of the white shirt, for to wear white shirts constantly would be too obvious. The tricky, deceitful, pitiless human mind would do nothing so patent.

Dr. Megna told me one thing that may have been true though I realize now it was probably his way of teaching. He told me the color pink had a terrible negative effect on him, he couldn't stand pink he said, and he attributed this dislike to a neighbor, a nasty woman who used to hang pink clothes on her line, pink blouses, pink slacks, pink tablecloths, pink towels, and so he couldn't stand pink, he never wore it and wouldn't allow it in the house. As I say, the story might not have been true, he could have made it up for my benefit to show the importance of chroma, but it might have been true and above all the meaning was clear to the patient, which is all a psychoanalyst is supposed to do, convey meaning to a foggy mind. This chromatic session lasted a full hour, which I look upon as the most important hour of my life. I stopped worrying you might say about white shirts. I wear a lot of colored shirts now though I still wear white if I feel like it, I haven't gone to the other extreme.

A thought has occurred to me just now, thirty years after my sessions with Dr. Megna. Pink is a girl's color, pink underwear, and he didn't like pink; maybe he was thinking of the nine o'clock Mass when he brought up that color with the boys on the right and girls on the left or the, so to speak, "Nine o'clock boys only schools"; thus the pink in his story would be as white as white for me and part of an even more profound chromatic scheme. I can't say. Much as I admire the man I don't think he was that keen. But he may have been.

Incidentally I have a pink shirt now, which may be another way of sitting on the left side of the movies.

One day towards the end of our sessions I taught Dr. Megna something and I'm glad I did because he really seemed to enjoy what I said; I could see his eyes light up and so I made his work worthwhile. His fees were extremely low, fifteen dollars I think, so I certainly hadn't repaid him on that score. But one day I did make the payment; I said:

"You know, it seems to me you doctors teach in a way no one else does. I teach Spanish to students who know nothing about the subject, but you are teaching someone who is the world's leading authority on the subject, himself. It must be nice to be a psychoanalyst." He was very pleased. I had paid the debt.

Much as I loved Professor Feigenbaum and am still his student, I owed as much to Dr. Megna. It's peculiar isn't it how the little things, a chat with Bobbie O'Brien and a trip to 57th Street, can change your life. When I speak of Dr. Megna to my wife now I call him Tom—Tom said this and Tom said that—but I never called him Tom to his face. It was always Doctor and my hat's off to him.

I believe very deeply in psychoanalysis and praise it on occasion to my friends and family. I know that some people poo poo it, a couple of my own sons do, but I don't, I always defend it because I have been there. It's like No Man's Land in 1914. I HAVE BEEN THERE, and just as the French and German soldiers had more in common with each other than with their own folks back home so I have more in common with those who know because they have been there, or better said been out there in the trenches. You speak a different language when you've been out there. I know that Freud has come under fire and that other doctors have offered estimable therapies, Viktor Frankl for example with his logos, and I will not gainsay such a reputable man, but if Freud discovered the iceberg of the mind with all that frozen stuff underneath, then he's my man. Long live Sigmund Freud! My hat's off to him. I too believe in psychoanalysis.

There may be a paradox here. If you are an Irish Bronx Boy with your life replete with meaning you scarcely need a logos but Freud's psychoanalysis to get rid of the excessive baggage that burdens, whereas if you are a Bronx Unitarian, a pilgrim for whom God is 'To Whom It May Concern', you have insufficient baggage and stand woefully in need of Frankl's logotherapy. Jansenists! Go to the atheist Freud! Unitarians! Go to the spiritual Frankl! There two therapies are really complementary. Perhaps for our limited minds, *logos* requires atheism to be understood.

I must speak now about my father, who was as innocent and pure as a man can be and nevertheless by his omissions did great harm. I shall have to define a few terms, but first a parable may help:

A man is driving down a foggy road, his mind fixed on what little he can see ahead. He is careful, orderly, lawful and observant of all the rules yet in his anxiety to get to his destination he runs over a little child he does not see on the shoulder. He does not know he has done so and continues on his journey.

He has torn a body without being guilty, he is still as innocent and pure as the driven snow. He is like the mother who gives her child the wrong medicine and wanting to cure her baby worsens the disease. The man and the mother are the cause, however innocent, of a terrible tragedy. To use an ancient terminology, they are materially though not formally guilty. Innocently they have done great harm.

That is why I say the most important event of my life happened forty years before I was born, when my grandfather was killed in the firehouse leaving my infant father in the hands of a Victorian Female Theologian. Who knows what she taught him? What she omitted? My white shirts, which meant so much to me, were a bagatelle compared to his experience: after all it was he who dying said: "I'm so glad, Kate, I couldn't take any more." So I know he was the cause of my . . . foolishness, let us call it that, foolishness, which alienated so many students at Seamus Orsini and still alienates some colleagues today. I can still be irascible. But though I know my father is the cause, I still resent the memory of my mother rather than his. The truth is she must have been the stalwart one, the brave one, the loyal trooper, Beau Geste holding the fort, and we would have all perished without her, but even so I resent her. I am not proud of this attitude, indeed I am wrong to feel that way, but I must record it as a fact if this is to be a true history.

My story of my father leads me to speculate on the divine. Why did it all have to happen? Why did it have to turn out this way? If my grandfather hadn't died in 1882 my father would have gone on to CCNY and the law, where he would have been a federal judge. He was more intelligent than most, his diligence was proverbial, and Judge McElroy, who ran the judicial end of the Democratic Party of those days, really liked him even though he was only a court clerk with a night time high school education. O'Shaughnessy and O'Reilly, who were federal judges, were less able than he and less conscientious. Had my father reached such a high station he would have seen through the veneer of Rosadabridgid's education and sent me on to Yale instead and to Europe for foreign languages; he did everything he could with the little he had and if he had had more he would have given it all to me, I know he would, he was like that. Money was never a question with him, he never mentioned it, his own mother having done so all his early life. And had I gone to Yale I might have written the two novels I was destined to, the one about the man and the boy descending the Hudson River on a raft, stopping at Hudson, Poughkeepsie, Newburg and Yonkers, meeting many people on the way, like the one-armed veteran who swam from Albany to New York City every year and perhaps seeing some enchanters at Tarrytown over the Tappan Zee where the long bridge is now. It might have been the great novel of American literature, about the Hudson, which surpasses the Mississippi, and had I gone to Yale instead of Rosa I might have written my other novel *The St. Patrick's Day Parade 1958*, when I bumped into Donald McGinty and we went to O'Neill's bar on 3rd Avenue and met Hippolyte Kelly who cut his hand on the glass and gave us the manuscript of his life just before he went to the hospital. *The St. Patrick's Day Parade* is really the autobiography of Hippy rather than a novel, a true chronicle of Washington Heights and New York in the old days when things were so much better; I might have published these books had I not gone to Rosa and had my father been well and I a real student of letters, but no it didn't happen that way; my grandfather died in 1882 leaving a baby boy in the hands of the Female Theologian. Some cynic will argue that this is the old "because of the nail the shoe was lost, because of the shoe the horse was lost, because of the horse the message was lost, because of the message the battle was lost, because of the battle the war was lost," but isn't all that true? Isn't life like that? Doesn't cancer strike, disrupting an otherwise prosperous family? Doesn't a small vial of spirits cause an accident, killing a family? Doesn't a quarrel over an inheritance do the same, people not talking to one another for the rest of their lives, like my dear Uncle Billy and beloved Uncle Joe? Over what? Over nothing. Of course I would have written my novels, there can be no doubt about it. Doubt is beyond peradventure, I would have been famous.

Why does Providence work like this? Why is a father taken from a one year old child, when he needs him most? Why is a father a cripple, like mine? I don't know. Herman Wouk says that in religious argument there is a classical argument *for* and a classical argument *against*. *For*: the argument is based on design;

138

given an intelligible universe, with orderly spheres, there must be an Intelligence behind it. It cannot happen from chance, which is unintelligible. Ergo, God exists. *Against*: if there is A Good Agent, how can he permit so much evil? Wars, famine, disease, a dead father? He can't. Ergo, God does not exist.

So an absent father would be a classical argument *against*. That may be so but I have never found it that way, I still believe in Providence though not as I have said in the accoutrements. I still believe. There is a mystery here. Perhaps if grandfathers did not die out of season and fathers were not cripples and sons not miserable louts like me, we would all be Federal Judges and William Shakespeares. Imagine a world ascending higher and higher on to perfection with everyone a Pascal, Shakespeare, Cervantes, Goethe, Dante, Plato, James Ignatius Murphy the novelist, there'd be no stopping. It might be unbearable, paradoxically it might be unbearable. Such hubris. Dear God, the lad courting our little Mary isn't a boy on the basketball team, he's a Federal Judge! Junior's friend isn't a stamp collector, he's Blaise Pascal anguishing over the cosmos! It might be worse than what we have now, it just might.

As I see it, the question of my grandfather, whose death has caused so much grief for three generations, proves in a way the doctrine of original sin. I don't like the doctrine and I don't like those who do, but I believe that something is originally wrong with mankind. It's not merely that I'm off the track or you're off the track or Brother Solomon is too, a virtue has been lost, originally, and even if we are good men like Dr. Megna and Professor Feigenbaum it is still lost. Who knows what Professor Feigenbaum's story was, what was missing in his life through no fault of his own? Or Dr. Megna's story, what was wanting to him? Something is lacking in everyone's life, my dead grandfather to my father, my crippled father to me, and I, I assure you, a fractured being to my wife and children. Everyone has a gap somewhere and that gap I call original. You can call it what you like but the truth is everyone has it so it has to be original, something that's wrong with the whole bloody species. Why Providence allows it I can't say for sure, and please remember I am arguing for the fact of its existence not for its desirability. I only know that if James Ignatius Murphy had been in on the Big Bang our atoms would be quite different.

Amen.

20. Instituta Bronxoniensa

I shall play hookey for a moment and disrupt my narrative with a Bronx institution but in a way I'm not on a hook because the Bronx is a part of me and talking about it is not disruption. As I grow older I think of it more and more, P.S. 11, the candy store, heggies, Ringalevio, Botchie, and so it belongs everywhere in a chronicle whose theme is memory. During the last twenty years I have found that a new event happens to me, then shift to memory, another event, memory, yet another event, memory, and so on, memory punctuating a major part of every day and generally meaning the Bronx.

I shall talk about Super, one of the most important men who ever lived, so much depended on the nature of Super. If Super was nice your life was a lot sweeter and if Super was not nice then life could be very difficult at times. I remember four Supers in particular but I never remember them smiling; only Jimmy, who was not a good Super.

Super is the shortened form of Superintendent just as we say phone for telephone or auto for automobile. Super was also called janitor although Super was used far more frequently than janitor since it had two syllables rather than three and contained an aura of mystery. We were more apt to say Mr. Nedsen our Super than Mr. Nedsen our janitor.

Mr. Nedsen was the Super at 1235. He was a short, stocky, powerful looking man with dark rings under his eyes and when he scowled you took notice. He never hit me or touched me or even came near to me, come to think of it he never did, but I was scared stiff of Mr. Nedsen. He really could scowl. He never spoke much he just looked at you, and our baseball-against-the-wall game depended so much on him because if he came up out of the cellar he chased you. He never ran or anything, he always walked slowly, deliberately, but he came over to the point where you and your friends had been hitting the ball. So you all fled. He never opened his mouth but his very appearance said louder than any words could say: "Get out of here or I'll strangle you, so help me Hannah with this cloth in this hand I'll strangle the living breath out of you." He always had that cloth in his hand, and the brass railings in the vestibule of 1235, the brass frames surrounding the name plates and the brass mail boxes inside were the cleanest I have ever seen except for Comfort Station. Come to think of it, the man who cared for Comfort Station looked a lot like Mr. Nedsen, the same size, same clothes and everything except for those dark rings under the eyes and the scowl. I guess if you were going to be a Super the first thing the landlord looked for was a man with a good cleaning rag and scowl because after the apartment house was cleaned the scowl kept the kids away. If the candidate for the job didn't have the dark look he must have applied to the city and worked for Comfort Station.

Mr. Nedsen lived in the cellar, which consisted of four main parts, his apartment, the passageways, dumbwaiters and a large storage room fenced off by floor-to-ceiling wooden pickets. Oh yes, I forgot, there was a fifth part, the boiler room where the ash barrels were kept, but I barely remember the place and was afraid to go in there, that scowl kept me away. I realize now that our Super's gloomy face had certain priorities and was a monosyllable for: "If you kids go into the boiler room I'll skin you alive; if you dirty up the brass or the vestibule I'll boil you in oil; baseball-against-the-wall, all right, once in a while but not too often and don't litter up the place; diamond ball in the street I'll tolerate as long as you don't hit the windows and be sure to hit the ball towards The House of All Nations across the street not towards 1235, and remember, don't give me any trouble." There are eighty-seven words in this message of Super, all of them telegraphed in one facial gesture, a scowl. Today someone would write a doctoral dissertation on semiotics or semiology or whatever they call it telling about signs and how people convey messages by gestures and clothing but that's a lot of nonsense. Mr. Nedsen had very little education; that gloomy face came naturally, the way a baseball player smiles when he hits a home run. It was part of the job. Now that I look back, Mr. Nedsen was probably the best Super in the Bronx which means the best Super in the United States of America, the best in the world. Our apartment was always spotless, the dumbwaiter always came every morning on the minute, the ashes were put out, the house was warm, but even so I can still see him leaning on the big black cannon-like cast iron railings guarding the staircase to the cellar. I can still see THE SCOWL.

Super had a son, Cliff, who liked Shirley Schapiro over in the candy store. They were ten years older than I so I really didn't know what it was all about but whenever he could he was over in the candy store. When you're six or eight and they're sixteen the candy store is where you both go but it isn't the same place exactly; I hardly ever spoke to Shirley although I remember her putting on lipstick, singing: "Siboney, that's the tune that they croon way down Havana Way, Siboney, that's the tune that they croon at the café," and dancing around the newstand shaking her hips. Shirley had prominent rhythmic hips.

Another Super was Mr. Zipps up at 1261. He was another scowler and if you think Mr. Nedsen could put a face on you should have seen Mr. Zipps. I rarely ever went up there except to call on Big Phelan, I was really afraid of Mr. Zipps. Somehow we knew that with our Super we could get away with baseball-against-the-wall once in awhile if we hit towards The House Of All Nations but with Mr. Zipps we knew we couldn't, it was better to stay away. He kept the place nice but even so I didn't like going there. Big Phelan used to tease Mr. Zipps' son Shrimpy all the time and one day he carried it to such an extreme that Shrimpy lost control and picked up a knife and chased Phelan

141

down the block. Rumor had it that Mr. Zipps gave Shrimpy the knife and told him "the next time he teases you, kill him," but I don't know, bad as he was I don't think he would have said a thing like that. We didn't have that kind in the Bronx, only good people, some gloomy faces maybe but good people.

I sometimes think I didn't like 1261 for another reason; it was on the corner where three principal streets merged, Ogden, Unie and Boscobel; there were cobblestones on Boscobel and the point on 1261 wasn't very good, and some of the cabbies used the corner as a taxi stand. I don't know, I may be right, you couldn't play a good game of baseball-against-the-wall with cobblestones and a poor point but then again I may be rationalizing and we stayed away because of Super.

The House Of All Nations at 1220 had the most unusual Super I ever remember, Jimmy, Jimmy what, I don't know because I'm not sure he had a last name and he was always smiling. Can you imagine that, a Super who smiled? He's the only one who ever did and he wasn't married like the others, he had no family. Jimmy was very dark so the rumor was he was a Turk but I'm not certain because no one ever ascertained his nationality. He had an accent of some kind but since there were no linguists on Unie I shall have to speculate. My guess is he came from some unusual place like Diego Suárez or Portuguese Goa, I'll opt for somewhere in the middle of the Indian Ocean, and that instead of having two or three ancestries like most of us Jimmy probably had thirty-two or sixty-four depending on how far back you want to go, ancestors from all the continents. He was much younger than most Supers, he was always smiling and used to like to talk to us. So we didn't stay away. The result was we were always playing around The House Of All Nations, especially baseball-against-the-wall; the area around the point was all chalked up, the sidewalks were chalked and the entrance way wasn't very clean. 1220 had a dirty look and I don't remember any brass railings. All in all I would say that Jimmy was a very fine person who was loved by all but he wasn't a good Super. You had to have a mean face if you wanted to be a Super and Jimmy had no scowl.

The last Super I remember was 1245, where Winnie Hodner lived. He was one of three brothers all of them tall and thin with a kind of inbred look or if not inbred, lean; their cheeks were hollow and they even walked lean. I remember their mother, whom they resembled, but I don't remember their father who rarely came out because he was working all the time. I can particularly see Winnie and his brothers leaning on the black iron railings leading to the cellar; 1235, 1239 and 1245 had all been built by Mr. Voss and Mr. Manangelli who apparently liked these metal frames. We rarely played in front of 1245 and I don't know why because the Hodners weren't exceptionally mean-faced, if anything they had a vacant stare; Winnie was our age, the points at 1245 were good, just like 1235's but even so we never played there. Perhaps we felt the presence of Scarface Finn the cop who had his apartment there with his horrible reputation but he wasn't around most of the time. I don't know why for sure but I do know that Winnie's family was quiet and reserved and like them Winnie kept to himself. He didn't play much. I also know he was killed during the war: there were three killed on our block, Winnie Hodner, Richard McGuire and Billy Smalling. Kelly was badly wounded. My own military career was a farce. Be that as it may I will remove my hat once more to Winnie the Super's son, who was killed in the Second World War. The Bronx was built on Supers.

21. State East

And now back to my narrative although I must confess I find it difficult to leave the Bronx. The *New Yorker* recently had a humorous map showing the streets of Manhattan on the East Coast constituting half the United States, with a few inches for the Plains and Rockies and California to the West, and another inch for the Pacific and Hawaii. And people have drawn similar maps for Texas. These geographic distortions come under poetic license and hyperbole of course, but even so their humor seems excessive. Now such a map for the Bronx makes sense, The Grand Concourse, University Avenue, Undercliff, Sedgwick, The Harlem River, Mississippi, Grand Canyon and Pacific, The Grand Concourse representing the hub of the nation. Why the South Bronx is even called The Hub and is there for all to see.

I left Seamus Orsini in 1956 for a teaching post at State East in Connecticut and I blush to think of my first classes where I taught a Spanish that was far beyond my comprehension for I had been trained primarily in History. I knew the present and imperfect subjunctive all right and could snap out neat answers like : "You form the imperfect subjunctive by taking the third person preterite plural, removing the *-ron* ending and substituting for it the *-ra* or *-se* endings, the latter having fallen into desuetude in America." What a pedantic way of speaking! But at the time I didn't know there was a future subjunctive also "fallen into desuetude" on both sides of the Atlantic so when we had a Cervantes passage with the verb *saliere* I was at a loss for explanation. The Bronx Boy couldn't handle it. I also didn't realize that the entire Spanish language had a peculiar tendency toward the dative case as in "I put to myself the hat," "He stole to me the money" and all those funny-to-the-English-ear constructions, which have grammatical names like Dative of Interest, Dative of Separation and Ethical Dative. I didn't recognize the pleonastic *no* in Máximo Manso's biography when he says: "I used to cry every night until my mother didn't come"; a student raised his hand on that one only to be met by silence. It was very embarrassing. There must be a whole decade of State East students from Connecticut, New York, New Jersey and Pennsylvania going about the New England and Middle Atlantic States misinforming people about Spanish because Dilbert Murphy had a conked out engine and hit a linguistic tree stump. I was simply in a field with too much shrubbery.

What else can I say about my days at State East? Oh yes, my first year I took the bus every morning to Jerome Avenue, the Lexie down to Grand Central and the New Haven to New Kent, Connecticut where I walked to State's campus. I taught Spanish for three straight hours and then reversed the New Haven, Grand Central, Lexie etcetera ride back to the Bronx where I worked on my Ph.D. dissertation; and two nights a week I went to New

York Commerce for classes and library work, and one of those nights I'd go to the theater after graduate school. I saw *Dial M For Murder, Picnic, Tea and Sympathy, Teahouse Of The August Moon, The Caine Mutiny Court Martial* and all those plays for $1.80; I'd go to the balcony, observe the seats below, spot an empty one (third row left, fourth seat in!) and go there for the second and third acts. I saw the very best plays from the very best seats for a dollar eighty. I know the plays of those days very well (I never get to go now) and I came to the conclusion they didn't have the spectacle, lyricism and theme of Lope de Vega's. Please don't get me wrong, I liked the plays very much and wish I could spend a year going to Times Square again some time; I can still visualize Joseph Cotton and Scott McKay in *Sabrina Fair*, John Kerr and Deborah Kerr in *Tea And Sympathy*, Jackie Coogan in *King of Hearts*, Mary Martin as Peter Pan, Laurence Olivier as Archie, and I loved every minute of this theater, but I noticed that the spectacle was frequently contrived, obviously brought in for audience relief and as for lyrics there weren't any; even Eugene O'Neil's fog people had to quote Baudelaire and Swinburne in *Long Day's Journey Into Night* when they wanted to lyricize their meaning. The night I saw *Long Day's* I was in the front row as close to Frederick March as I am to this yellow pad I am writing on and was fascinated by his performance. I also liked Florence Elridge's Virgin Mary speech declaimed under the influence of opium and Jason Robard's wastrel son but when I heard a song it was Baudelaire and Swinburne O'Neil was quoting. Lope would have composed ten songs for every play. Today as I write these lines and recall the theater nights I loved so well I can see that center stage has moved from Times Square to television's Masterpiece Theater.

In those days New York Commerce was as prominent in my life as State East because I was leading a triangular existence between my home in the Bronx, New Kent, Connecticut and NYC in lower Manhattan, a vital *ménage à trois* you might say consisting of wife and family, the dative case and Cervantes. I have two special memories of NYC, *The Lay Of The Cid* and Professor Francis Johnson:

With his eyes so strongly crying
. . .
Do not come to Burgos, Cid,
we cannot speak with you,
for speaking, King Alfonso says
he will pluck the eyes from the face.
. . .
The Cid and Jimena, one are,
like flesh and finger nail.
. . .
With his elbow dripping blood
he surveyed the Moslem scene . . .

The graphic art of the lay of the Cid, the vivid pictures; thirteen weeks, three hundred verses a week, we went through the poem line by line. The exile from Burgos, Raquel and Vidas, Martín Antolínez, the Count of Barcelona, the outrage midst the oak trees, the loyal Avengalvón, the series of glowing pictures lives on. My own favorite scene is Peter the Mute's challenge to the pusillanimous Fernán García, Prince of Carrion:

Tongue without hands, how dare you speak?

And the ensuing battle where cowardly ribs stick out of cowardly rib cages. I shall never forget my Cid.

My other memory is Professor Johnson. He was different from Feigenbaum although he had the same fine character, honest, true, devoted to his students. He spoke three languages fluently without an alien accent and I have never heard a more sonorous voice in English or in Spanish; he could have been a radio announcer. He knew ballet and music and edited a magazine; he was a great raconteur, I still remember his jokes and stories. But what I liked most about him was his ease of manner with us for after class we'd all go to Bruno's in the Village where he'd always order spaghetti *marinara*. He was always friendly, patient and kind and yet he always kept our respect; there was no thought of fraternization, he was the maestro and we were his students. I guess if you compared him to Professor Feigenbaum you'd have to say Feigenbaum was the more rugged type who would climb the Andes for History whereas Johnson was more the connoisseur who would journey to Florence for Art; that's the best way I can describe it. The greatest tribute I can pay my maestro is this: when I eat out I generally go to Italian restaurants and when I get there I order spaghetti *marinara*.

I spent seven years at State East, long enough to know the students. They were still segregated with the boys on one side of the river and the girls on the other in a State college of a different name, but that's not what I'm specifically talking about. What I mean is the difference between the boys who came from the New York City area and the boys who came from more rural places like upstate New York and countryside Connecticut. The latter were more easy going, calm and I would say peaceful. They had their problems as we all do but on the whole the tempo of their life was slower. They were placid. I have a hunch that their achievement scores, in the jargon of professional educators, were lower than the big city boys', and if my hunch is correct this lower station was compensated for by enviable emotional stability. The New York City boys seemed quicker, more on the go, more motivated . . . and also more agitated; they lacked that pervasive calm. Perhaps a social rule will emerge here, something like:

Live on the ox cart, be happy;
Live on the train, have success,

success precluding happiness. Were I a paremiologist I could create a superior rhyme but the law seems clear; country living is peaceful and undistinguished, city living successful and full of strife. I am talking of course of appearances for who knows what lay behind each student's countenance? I do know this though, and here I speak with certitude, that I myself am a living proof of the urban strife and ox cart tranquility law. Here in the 1980's, thirty years after leaving New York, I still hasten through STOP signs and yellow lights whereas my fellow mid-westerners stop for every sign and even jam on their brakes at the thought of yellow, and I'll walk across an intersection against a red light whereas they will wait for green even in a cold driving rain.

I was on a subway escalator once over on 55th Street and 3rd Avenue deep in the bowels of the earth with two friends, one a Venezuelan. We were going to a Hofbrau for beer and I started running up the moving stairway two steps at a time and got to the top twenty seconds before they did. When the Venezuelan finally arrived he said to me: "What did you do that for? What's an escalator for?", and he was right of course because an escalator moves so you don't have to. But he didn't understand. When you're a New Yorker you have to get there first, you just have to, it's not a matter of choice you have to, you can't wait for the yellow light. I loved the students at State East, they were a great bunch of _____, I was going to say 'a great bunch of guys', but that wouldn't be me I never called them guys. They were good people. The faculty was another cup of tea.

Here I must record a painful observation. At State East I met a professor, a Bronx Boy who was trying not to be. He came from the West Bronx the same as me but when writing his address on an envelope he'd put New York 57 instead of Bronx 57; the five digit zip code didn't exist at that time only two digit ones and 57 would get your letter there whether you wrote the Bronx or New York; 1235 University Avenue, New York 57 would do the job but why not put Bronx 57 and proclaim to the world: "This is me the Bronx Boy and I'm proud of it." I think he was ashamed of the Bronx as if it were an inferior culture and he was always so sweet and refined and liked to lord his French elegance over Spanish vulgarity. The Spanish were so gross, so coarse, the Inquisition, bull fights, revolutions all the time and yes you do have Cervantes but what else is there, all those cute inconsequential Latin American stories and Ricardo Palma the Peruvian dago, and Galdós who ever heard of Galdós, *Doña Perfecta* is a veritable source of risibility. Now French is different, take Emma Bovary, Swann, Gide, how can you think

147

of Galdós in the same breath, and the 18th century, such reason, such culture, such perfection, they were so refined. He never spoke of the Bronx, never, and if you started to mention it to him he'd cut it short somehow, change the subject or leave the scene. He was ashamed of that fair land. I never hated him, I never even disliked him but I know he hated me, I was still far too brusque since these were my Dr. Megna days. The cure was only beginning and I represented something he was anxious to forget, he wanted no part of it, he had been to the Ivy League and was different now, refined, superior, he had studied French. Me? I'll take Tommy Kelly, Milton Segal and Joey Bacigalupi any day of the week. They were better educated than he. From this experience I have devised a rule for life: Bronx boys should never go to Harvard.

I must describe the other faculty at State East, who were like the Bronx in a way. Two of them reminded me of Segal and two of Botchie but no one reminded me of Kelly; I was the only Kelly you might say. There was a difference though. One of those like Segal was not only a fine fellow he was a polished gentleman and I believe the most popular language professor on campus both amongst the students and faculty. He didn't talk much but had a certain wisdom about him that made talking unnecessary; that's the best way I can put it, he was one of those people who just don't have to talk. The other professor resembling Segal was the opposite of the first; he was always out protesting against something, injustice, the atom bomb, racial strife, public school discipline, something, abstract or concrete it made no difference he had to be out there marching; once I saw him leading a unit of pacifists down Washington Highway towards Queenstown. He always had a broad smile on his face and there he was waving his placard: DOWN WITH THE ATOM BOMB!, and although I wasn't about to do anything like that and wasn't cut of the same cloth he was the closest person I had to a friend at State East. I don't make friends easily and this was right after my sessions with Dr. Megna so I had no friends but he was my only half friend. He invited me to his house once to show me the garden he took so much pride in, and while we were visiting, our wives hit it off very well and so did our boys. When he came to my house I noticed that the realistic crucifix on the wall caused him discomfort so I put it in the bedroom where he wouldn't see it. I'm not one to hide my beliefs under a stone just to please some fools not worth pleasing but this wasn't like that, there's no sense flagellating someone with something they don't believe in or mentioning the rope in the hanged man's house; besides he was a New Yorker and knew what I was anyway. To boil it down, I liked Morty. He was gauche all right and some people considered him to be a fool always marching like that but he was honest and straightforward and I liked him. We were poles apart ideologically and I have never had sentimental feelings towards the Soviet Union and left wingers (I believe in a strong defense, the only way to assure peace) but even so I liked him. He had courage.

Of the two professors who looked like my friend Bacigalupi one was a replica of Joey, the nicest fellow you'd ever want to meet. After my first year at State he used to drive me up the Merritt Parkway in his big blue Chrysler and I can still picture the scene one winter morning when a van threw slush all over our windshield and we couldn't see anything for five seconds; sixty miles an hour, eighty-eight feet a second, four hundred and forty feet during that time span, and we had an opaque windshield. A moment later Aldo looked at me and I could read his eyes: "We nearly bought it," they were saying. He never asked for money although I insisted on paying for some of the gas (I have always remembered the dumbwaiter CHEAP sign), and he always had his *New York Times* and *Daily News* for different aspects of the day's events, ranging from PRESIDENT ASKS FOR SUMMIT MEETING to HE THREW HER OUT THE WINDOW BUT SAYS HE STILL LOVES HER with the accompanying photo of a black and blued blonde. That sums him up, you could talk to Aldo about anything and he would listen. Yes, Aldo reminded me of the Bronx and Joey Bacigalupi.

Of the other one, the less said the better for I don't propose to scandalize the reader and will not reveal his name. I could write an essay "The Compleat Rascal" on him similar to that essay on the compleat angler in my high school *Literature and Life* textbook only it wouldn't be an essay but a document listing academic crimes. He was so unlike Aldo and Joey, which brings to mind a grave thought. Sometimes you'll hear someone say: "People from such and such a country are not very nice" and you'll be inclined to agree because you've had a couple of bad experiences; but you no sooner give voice to the thought "I don't like those people" than the next day you meet one of them who is so kind and gentle and gracious that you kick yourself for harboring such a thought let alone express it. Absolutely the nicest. The opposite holds true too; you no sooner say "Oh isn't everyone from that country so nice, I just love that country" when you meet a consummate rascal from there, a man so wrapped up in a lie he can't distinguish the truth any more. So there it is, Joey Bacigalupi and Aldo Montefiore, my two dear friends, and the other "pistolero", a succinct portrait of human nature.

Of the other faculty, three were immigrants whom I found aloof or perhaps I was the aloof one since these were my days of psychiatry. One spoke several languages and seemed to be hyphenate in all of them including his own though this may have been an affectation; another was a giant European who also struck you as slightly affected though not so much as the erstwhile Bronx 57 boy; and a third I'd see in church at times, up in the loft, he may have been a bit shy. These Europeans either looked down on Americans or pretended to do so or

149

considered themselves superior to certain naive Americans like James Ignatius Murphy the Bronx Boy who used to smoke loosies, drink seltzer and play stickball. When I told the third European after Mass one Sunday that I liked St. Patrick's Cathedral because it was peaceful, dark and secluded he informed me that its darkness stemmed from Manichaeanism whereas the churches in his country encouraged the light. Now I mean really! There may even be some truth in what he said because after all Brother Solomon was a disciple of Mani but who is going to be so patronizing as to word the truth like that? Spelled out his words mean: "You naive American, you Bronx Boy, you Yank, your country is so young and ingenuous that the things you cherish are really faults, lacunae in your historical memory, whereas we in our ancient wisdom perceive these truths, having witnessed the cry of the Manichee two millennia ago and so my venerable country encourages the light." In truth his whole statement had nothing to do with religion or Mani; the five foot European gentleman and connoisseur was telling the six foot American cowboy that he was better. Isn't that the basis of all human argument? Doesn't it all boil down to this?: the stories I learned at my grandma's knee are better than your grandma's stories and I am better than you are.

I met one foreigner at East who was a bigot, the 1960 version of I-wouldn't-vote-for-Al-Smith.

I have reserved two professors for the last because they exemplify the one tradition of the university that is both its life's blood and terminal disease; I refer of course to tenure. Some academicians have created a mystique about tenure and I recall the cartoon in the *New Yorker* where a professorial scientist is looking through a mammoth telescope and remarking: "I wonder how the galaxy has coped with tenure."

Some will side with Voltaire's "I disagree categorically with what you say but will defend to the death your right to say it" and agree that this is the reason for tenure but I look upon that high sounding apothegm as theatrics. There's too much Walter Mitty in it, too much of the boy in the cartoon disdaining the blindfold as the firing squad raises its rifles. Can anyone imagine a State University administrator defending anybody to the death or even to a tiny scratch? No, in 1986 *homo administrans* is not like that, he would simply go out for more federal money and squash any candidate for tenure who stood in his way.

The basis of tenure is much more simple. A community of a million people has set aside a university with a Mathematics department of twenty professors and an English department of thirty. Everyone in the community knows some Math and speaks some English but only twenty faculty members are professional mathematicians and thirty others scholars of English literature. If they are to educate their students properly they can't be taking orders from the governor, mayor, State Legislature, ethnic leaders, religious leaders, labor unions, HEW moles, feminists or other extramural political corporations and above all they cannot be taking orders from amateur deans whose monarchical appetites are legendary. Twenty professors know more Mathematics than an entire city of a million people and must teach mathematical truth rather than respond to popular whim and the peculiar needs of the day; although they are hopelessly outnumbered by non-professionals they are not overwhelmed through tenure. This freedom from political concern is the heart of the university; the intellect is the soul.

If the above argument holds for Mathematics, how much more will it hold for History, Philosophy and Literature? Occasionally some freak will come along and abuse the system saying: "I love the Vietcong, I hope they will kill Americans," knowing tenure will protect his abnormal psychology, but he is a peripheral histrion. And after all every society has its sideshows.

Tenure can also be a disease, a malicious inseparable accident. A couple of tenured professors can kill a department and its discipline for forty years by being either jealous, resentful non-scholars promoting no one they consider a threat, or scholars who think that they alone will carry the torch of their science; the latter see themselves as Sainte Beuve or Ranke and know in their hubristic labor that additional scholarship were superfluous; they sit on the lid these lid-sitters so that no young scholar will be tenured. This is what happened at State East in the 1960's, when dozens of young professors started out with aspirations and never acquired tenure because of two counterfeiters. I was one in a dozen, an unhatched egg you might say owing to a pair of lid-sitters. Morty and Aldo would have put us through I know they would have but the lid men prevented them and that's why I went out to State West where I got a fifty percent raise in pay. State West was a revelation.

22. State West

My narrative is incomplete. I know it. Who is my wife? Who are my children? How old are they? Where did they go to school? Where are they now? What are they doing? That's what people want to know; after all this is my autobiography and if there's one thing people are going to read about it's your family. So why don't I include them here?

I have made several oblique references to my wife, sons and daughters, perhaps not so much to my daughters but if this is so it's the old nine o'clock Mass syndrome with the boys to the right and girls to the left, the All Saints-Rosadabrigid Boys Club where the males attend one school and the females another. I really make no preference and mean no offense, certainly not to my wife and daughters whom I love as much as my sons but when I think of days gone by I think primarily of Uncle Joe, Uncle Billy, cigar smoke, football games, Tommy Kelly, Milton Segal, Joey Bacigalupi and the lads on the right. I'm a rightist. I can't help it. It's habit.

But why don't I write about my family? If I do, what am I going to say? Take my children for instance, am I going to say I prefer number one to two, two to three, three to four, four to five, and so on, or that two, four, six and eight are more able than one, three, five and seven or have less athletic ability? Am I going to praise some over the others or withdraw praise or say that so and so is successful, talented, likeable and earning big bucks, as they say, but these are his flaws: pride, avarice, lust, envy, gluttony, anger and sloth? A more skilled linguistic surgeon might do this, writing volume after volume of penetrating psychological portraiture but I, I am afraid, am unequal to the task. I don't have the talent and even if I did I don't think I could get myself to sit down hour after hour day after day dissecting the character of each of my offspring: "When she was an adolescent she was a bit irascible and had a whine in her voice, for example the time she . . .", or, "He was very self-centered then but he's gotten over that and is always helping his friends now, for example . . ."; the examples multiplying to anecdote upon anecdote. To write like this would be fun in a way and certainly a worthwhile project aesthetically and historically but I don't have the motivation to do it, and, that's it, I'm not moved to do it and if you are not moved, driven really, then anything you write will not be worthwhile. Besides, there are ethical considerations. I don't think I have the right to lay bare the characters of living human beings even if they are or just because they are my relatives. I don't have the right. Besides everyone knows that adolescents are irascible and self-centered; after all that's what the word adolescent means, irascible and self-centered. So why labor the obvious? Perhaps that's the reason Graham Greene called his life's story *A Sort Of*

Life and told his readers nothing about his parents. He couldn't. He just couldn't.

If these thoughts are true of my children, how much more are they true of my wife? We are very close. It pained me before to write about Adrienne, Mavis, and the girl on Howard Street because when you're married you're supposed to live within your family and even your memory is supposed to live there and only there, but if I followed that stricture too closely I'd have nothing to say in these pages.

The Spanish language has a refrain to be applied here:

The married woman,
four walls and a broken leg.

You might say the same of a married man; I have seen the four walls of my house and will tell little of what goes on inside. It's not my way. It's private. Outside my home I'll tell a great deal though not everything for even there you must consider privacy.

There are also artistic considerations. When you write about your own family you are going to write eulogies and we all know what pitfalls lie there. I grant you there are exceptions. Francis Darwin's descriptions of his father Charles show him as a kind man and 'the best father who ever lived.' Francis had a very high opinion of his father and lavished praise on him but even so his story is palatable because it is well told; I have taught the biography he wrote in an honors class and know the students like it. They like Charles Darwin and also his father, Francis's grandfather, who was also 'the finest of fathers'. I know that I was envious when I read these pages and wish that someone could say that about me but they can't, not without prevarication.

I will make a simple statement about my family. When you see the joy in my children especially in the girls (remember, I am a segregationist) you see a living portrait of my wife, and when you see their somberness especially in the boys you see a portrait of James Ignatius Murphy, Jims, *summa cum laude* student of Dr. Thomas Nicholas Megna, M.D. In this sense I don't have to write about the younger Murhpys, you already know them.

* * *

And so I left State East for State West, a thousand miles away. I would have never gotten tenure back east and the west offered opportunity; Horace Greeley was right, go west young man go west. I know many New Yorkers teaching now in California, Arizona, New Mexico, Texas, Louisiana, Indiana, Illinois and the other states of the Midwest who will attest to the truth of Greeley's dictum; they are not renegades who despise their homeland for they still admire the five boroughs as they knew them back in the 1930's but they know that living today is better out west, it really is. You can take my word for it. Should you entertain any doubts just go to all the universities where the sun sets and ask for the New Yorkers. They'll tell you.

I must make a few comparisons now and then describe a tragedy. I must also tell you about the American citizens from beyond the Hudson, a thousand miles away. Perhaps I should begin with these Americans.

When I went to State West almost twenty-five years ago I was struck by several phenomena. The people there spoke English with a strange accent; although they were of German and East European stock they displayed a peculiar Irish brogue when pronouncing words like "O.K." and "Don't you know." I distinctly remember the announcer at the ball park saying "O.K. O.K." They also said "Thank you much"; I had never heard that courtesy before without the superlative *very*, "Thank you very much," so it sounded funny to me. Another expression they often use is "Can I go with?", which sounds to me like a direct translation from some septentrional barbarian. There were other differences too like "Let's suck a beer once," so a trained linguist would have had a field day. One torpid habit of Midwesterners definitely proves the verbal superiority of the Bronx; Midwesterners are absolutely ignorant of the contrary to fact subjunctive and subjunctive of conjecture and particularly don't know the non-indicative mood of *have*. I shall never forget the first time I heard an educator say: "If I would have enough money, I would go with," and, "If I would be you, I would have summer school." This syntax becomes distressful as one approaches an anterior preterite like: "If he had seen the monster he would not have been so brave," a phrase evoking in the Midwest several *would have seens* and *would have beens*. Mary Shelley would have written: "Had he seen the monster he had not been so brave." I wonder what the Midwesterner would do with that one. And if you go to parse a sentence such as "If he had had the money he would have gone," you are in for a hopelessly confusing dialogue, the *had had* being extremely provocative. Of course had James Ignatius Murphy had tenure at State East he had not come West.

The Midwest is naive vis à vis the East and I find this candor refreshing. I remember going to class and uttering a remark I thought was humorous only to find the students taking it down in their notes. On another occasion I said something in all seriousness expecting them to digest it and found that they were laughing. We were not on the same wave length, the Bronx Boy, the Ichabod Crane of the Midwest, and his charges. Above all I remember a point of Spanish sentence structure I was showing to the class, explaining that a feminine noun requires a feminine adjective and a masculine noun a masculine adjective but when the two are combined the masculine takes precedence and the plural adjective will be masculine. I made an attempt at humor:

154

The masculine always takes precedence,
but only in grammar.

A week later a student wrote on her examination paper:

The masculine always takes precedence,
but only in grammar.

As I look back perhaps I am the one who was naive.
I have a theory concerning this wit and ingenuousness. On
the other side of the pond, let us call them the thithers, you have
Gallic wit and English understatement, like Prime Minister
MacMillan's words when Krushchev banged his shoe on the desk
in the United Nations: "May I have a translation please?" This
humor does well in England. On this side of the pond, the East
Coast hithers have endeavored to imitate Gallic acuteness and
English aplomb; we are all familiar with the distinct humorless
frigidity of Ivy League schools, where some professors attempt to
be what they aren't. Out of this Anglo-Gallic hybrid proceeds a
smart alec, wisecracking East Coast wit where you frequently say
what you don't mean. Devastating irony. You overstate, you
understate, you beat around the bush but you don't give a
thought precisely. You display your wit and by implication your
intellectual and cultural superiority; I know that I myself have
been culpable. But I have been in the Midwest so long I am
slipping. In 1980 I went to a wedding reception on the North
Shore of Long Island and got talking to a fellow whom I found
very interesting. I liked what he was saying so I asked him a
question. He looked at me surprised and said: "I was only
kidding"; his friendly smile seemed to add: "I thought you knew
that." He was a nice fellow, it was I who was out of step. I had
been away too long and didn't understand.

Of course what I have said about the East Coast does not
apply to the Bronx, where people are always straightforward,
direct, sincere and, I suppose, naive. You call a spade a spade in
the Bronx, I never heard anyone call it anything else. Only
honest words like:
"Bofangoo, Kelly."
"Up yours, Segal."
And now we come to my profession, the university. The
great universities of the East are private corporations, Harvard,
Yale, Columbia, Princeton, Pennsylvania and in the South, Duke.
The state universities there are Johnnie-come-lately's built up
quickly by post-World War II obsessed state legislatures and
Health, Education and Welfare agents, and we all know what that
means. State East was such a university. But west of the Ohio the
opposite rule obtains, the great institutions being Berkeley,
Madison, Ann Arbor and Urbana, state universities opened after
the Civil War; and the private schools out West are just so so.
There are exceptions like Stanford and Chicago but they appear

as unnatural shrubbery, abruptly placed there by a millionaire.

The three universities I have taught at have been Seamus Orsini, State East and State West. Seamus I have already judged; the bishops in the old country had made a mistake by not listening to John Henry Newman and when their philosophy was transported to America the children of immigrants paid a price for their foolishness; there were a few rays of light at Seamus, lay professors like Henry Roberts and Arty Lynch.

But now I want to go over to the non-sectarian side to compare State East with West, and here a tragedy is in the looming. Although secularists may argue it's too early to tell, the omens are clearly inauspicious:

When shall we three meet again?
In thunder, lightning or in rain
When the hurly-burly's done
When the battle's lost and won . . .

Although the battle is being lost I profoundly believe in Hope and think it may still be turned. If only a great satirist would come our way, an American Swift, he alone might rout the enemy. I have sometimes thought we have our own Swift in Mr. Tom Wolfe but he seems to have missed his vocation, he of the magnificent titles, *The Electric Kool Aid Acid Test, Mau-Mauing The Flak Catchers* and *Kandy-kolored Tangerine Flake Streamline Baby*. These are fine, admirable studies all of them but they have a certain penultimate air. Where is Mr. Wolfe's masterpiece? Why hasn't he written his *Health Ed Welfare Outreach Waltz and Resource Person Feedback Tango*? Tom Wolfe has been called to judge the universities but unlike Paul of Tarsus before Damascus he has not responded.

State West was a revelation. I started there in 1964 when it was still the Great State West of tradition and it was so superior to State East and Seamus I could scarcely believe my experience. The dean was a real dean, gentleman and scholar, not like the punchinellos you see today. His attitude was always academic and was summed up in these words to the departments: "Ladies and Gentlemen, what is your pleasure?" He understood that outside his own field he was an amateur and consequently a follower instead of a leader, that the departments came first, the college second and the university last, and that academic life consists of the faculty and students gathered around the disciplines; the departments not only house every scholar from the youngest freshman to the oldest professor they also house Philosophy, History, Mathematics, Physics and Literature. Dean James Baumann never tried to pressure the faculty into something they did not want but took the lead from them and tried to be of aid.

In 1965 he named me chairman. I couldn't believe it. I had no ambition and less aptitude. Except for the students, I preferred to stay away from people rather than play the accommodator; I only wanted to read and write and teach and for me the most fun was in the writing, a solitary occupation. Nevertheless he made me chairman with the request: "Jim, go out and recruit the two best Hispanists you can find. We want them for our graduate and undergraduate programs." That was all. There were no directions, no quotas, no guidelines, no benchmarks, just get the best candidates you can, and so I tried. There were so many openings and so few candidates it was tough recruiting in those days, and the two men I brought whom the dean liked accepted positions elsewhere; a third used the offer we tendered him to boost his rank and salary back home. I could never go through an act like that myself, but many professors performed it so it wasn't frowned upon in spite of the annoyance; matching offers was received like a mild sunburn in summer; suffer it for the moment and get on with the next item of business. A year later I managed to land two candidates so the department's future was secure.

Believe it or not, State West had good faculty committees, and I express amazement here because I am thinking of the pusillanimous committees we have today. There was no Committee on Committees as there were back at East and the committees I served on were refreshingly sober. I traveled to the State Capital once a month for a meeting of the Executive Committee Of The Humanities, whose chairman was truly a pro. Courteous, discreet, diligent, he conducted a two hour session that was a joy to attend; we took up questions affecting our interests one by one, and as a buffer between the deans and departments we also passed on new appointments and promotion to tenure. We went over every candidate's publications, letters of reference and, to the extent that we could, his teaching record. The chairman's attitude was always professional and so was that of the other faculty except for the occasional promotion where someone was blocking another man's advancement out of personal grudge; you'll always find pettiness, even on a fine committee like that, but certainly not in our chairman, Dr. John Waters. He was James Baumann's peer and my hat's off to both of them. They were State West at its best. I hadn't realized my last sentence was going to rhyme when I wrote it but I think I'll let it stand since it makes a good slogan and an extremely accurate historical observation: 1960—STATE WEST AT ITS BEST. Although it was not obvious to the faculty's eye, the seeds of decay had already been planted. But more of this later.

The students at State West were of poor to fair academic background, which was the principal difference between her and the Ivy League. The men who taught in both schools (lest some acrimonious Phaia brandish her tusks and insist on *persons* instead of *men*, the faculty was male in those days) were competent and capable of fine instruction, but the student bodies differed. At Yale and the others your roommate was a valedictorian, a 4.0, a pianist, a debating champion, an award-winning Thespian, the son of a diplomat, a polyglot or an All State Quarterback playing intramural instead of varsity ball, whereas at State West your classmates were the offspring of tool and die makers, intelligent, talented, fairly well-off but devoid of academic tradition. At Yale students had direction before they got there and educated one another; at State West the education had to come from above. The West professors had an added obligation in 1960 and observed it. Do they observe it today?

The curriculum at State was as good as you might expect: fourteen credits in foreign languages and literature, twelve in the humanities, twelve in the social sciences, twelve in the natural sciences and then a major. English and Mathematics were also required. I personally don't care for the phrase *social sciences*, which smacks of Comte, but at State these words were largely an administrative convenience; the courses in Economics and Anthropology were very good. Concerning the requirements, I always told my classes to go beyond them and take Ancient and Medieval History, Ancient Philosophy, Ancient Art History, Greek and Latin, the farther back the better. I wanted them to resist the sin of present-mindedness.

I repeat that State was a great university in those days and even called itself The Great State University West in its official documents. The Business and Engineering schools were small, and health, education, welfare, feedback, outreach and interdisciplinary studies were still beyond the horizon. State West was such an epiphany I was filled with Baroque amazement. Compared to East it was a lion!

And now it behooves me to relate a tragedy. I must answer the call. A comediographer in spirit, an optimist who sees sunlight in the rain, I must nevertheless don the buskin for not to do so would be a lie, which I dare not commit since I have insisted on writing my life's true story. Everything I write here is true.

It all began in 1957 while I was at East, seven years before my transfer to West. The Soviet Communists launched Sputnik that year and the United States Congress retaliated launching the National Defense Education Act, the NDEA as it was known, the promise of things to come, one quarter of a billion dollars for strengthening America in the face of atheistic lunar aggression. I remember at East we had a special meeting of all the faculties, and even segregation had to capitulate so that the men and women from the two separate but equal campuses could assemble in solemn convocation. There were a quarter of a billion bongo bucks floating around out there, two hundred and fifty million Yankee semolians and what were we going to do about it? That's what the president of East wanted to know and so did the provosts, deans and chancellors. What were we going to do? One young French woman who taught her native language at the girls' college of East looked at me and exclaimed with that wonderful Gallic *r*: "God help theese countrrrreeee!" She was so right.

158

Nobody seemed to know it then but that young girl from a foreign land had more wisdom than all the braying deans and chancellors, the United States Congress and other buffoons legislating for Academia put together. A quarter of a billion macro bongos dumped everywhere as the honey wagon dumps its cargo in a cornfield, providing more fertility, greater growth and aroma.

God help theese countrrrreeee! The damage was done, the tragedy was to start, the university Oedipus gouging out his eyes and wandering the breadth of the land looking for he knew not what, looking for feedback.

Languages were hit especially hard. At first they seemed to prosper since they were a unique missile aimed at the heart of godless Soviet Communism and we language teachers were the one true Internationale beating the devils at their own game, sending our Spanish-speaking, Russian-speaking, Chinese-speaking, multilingual agents throughout the world with their audio-visual electronic approach, benchmarks, guideline interfacing thrust to preach the joys of democracy and cleverly chat with foreign potentates in their own tongue, thus winning them over to our side. The gift of tongues! Glossolalia! Babel destroyed! Two hundred and fifty million greenback mazoolas spread by health, education, welfare, dean and chancellor honey wagon boys so that Junior and his sister might fluently say: "Das ist ein Buch."

The first federal ukase called for language laboratories. The dollars were there for all to savor democratically without regard to race, creed, color or national origin providing you had a language laboratory, a modest place for students to visit and listen to cultivated tones declaiming sounds of different idioms: *la rue, le grandpère . . . ganaría, ganarías ganaría . . .* watch that Castilian *r*. In 1957 nobody had a language laboratory except Princeton with its old disks and gramophones, but Princeton didn't have a genuine laboratory, a paneled clinic with equipment putting human speech on a scientific par with Physics and Chemistry, with experiments you could see with your own eyes and touch with your own hands. Languages were as palpable as Bunsen Burners and could restrain Soviet forces until our Physicists could launch us beyond Sputnik to the moon. Languages were to hold the fort. As a result of these demonstrable truths three thousand language majors got three thousand dollars to go to college and three thousand high school teachers got summer pay for retreading at a workshop and didn't have to paint houses in July and August to round out their pay. The other two hundred and thirty-two million went to the electronics industry.

Two hundred and thirty-two million bongos for consoles, tapes, recorders, speakers, microphones, wires, soon to be obsolete and in need of replacement. The language journals devoted their advertisements to electronic input, showing a loving, attractive, well-dressed thirty-five year old woman instructing her high school students in a lovely setting. *Das ist ein Buch.* A quarter of a billion. One crackerjack university president had all his campuses fly grant requests to Washington within two weeks of the NDEA announcement, a month before other institutions had submitted their applications. Everyone agreed he was an academic genius. The new era had begun.

I realize that my style has changed as I talk about the NDEA and the universities. Hitherto I have tried to be what I am, the Bronx Boy, neither a great God-seeker nor sort-of-lifer but somewhere in between, an earnest Bronx Boy doing the best he can with his limitations, with an occasional sally into humor or at least a sincere attempt in that direction. But now my style has changed as if a different voice were speaking, a judgmental, one-sided, exacerbated, without humor sobersides. I can only plead that the reason for this alteration is a change in myself and when a person changes, his style changes too; still if it gets the message across I'll stay with it for then it's true, unpleasantly true and waspish but true and that's what this autobiography is all about, a true history. I wouldn't write it down if it wasn't true.

When I went to State West in 1964 it was recruiting well in History, Philosophy, Economics, Physics and the other disciplines; the new professors had all published solid books and articles in their fields, and I learned from a friend in the East that three of our mathematicians were very well known in his profession. I know that a lot of ink has been spilled over publish-or-perish and that many publications were better not written in the first place, but a good article, even one small article, will reveal a scholar's insight and his ability to put it in writing. If you have read Willis' short article on the Lazarillo as a triptych or Russell's arguments concerning *Don Quixote* as a funny book you will know what I mean. Read eight or ten pages and you can say: "This fellow knows what he's talking about, he has obviously read the literature in his field. Let's hire him." It's a question of quality, which State West earnestly pursued in the early nineteen-sixties. But the New Order was gaining momentum and the tragedy gathered steam in 1968 when Health, Education and Welfare sent out leading strings for puppets and puppeteers under the name of guidelines. Leading strings became guidelines; federal money, feedback; politicos, adjunct professors; people-on-dole-helping-HEW-agents-spend-their-grants, resource persons; jerry-built programs, interdisciplinary studies; ethnic ingrab, outreach; even a venerable word like *intern* became a resource person person, a new human object for spending federal money. The new art was language couching. Never call a spade a spade.

My best friend at West said to me one day: "You know, Jims, the higher the grant the more worthless." His name happened to be Professor Diamond so let us call it Diamond's Law: "The higher the grant the more worthless." His wisdom is unassailable. Consider my field for example; a young Spanish professor gets an American Philosophical Society grant for $2,000 to tide him over the summer so he doesn't have to teach and can concentrate on lyrical poetry. Fine. He gets a Guggenheim for $10,000 to add a semester to his sabbatical. Excellent. He can study, write or just read books and the extra money may send him to Europe. But from here on in Diamond's Law applies. Suppose he gets $200,000 for "Outreaching Spanish Wisdom to the Community," or $300,000 for "Bringing the Community To Spanish," or half a million, five hundred thou as they say, for "Solving the Problems Of The Underprivileged Community" with an appropriate acronym, SPOUC. What does this mean? It means the higher the grant the more worthless. Everyone knows the bloke can't reform the Community, the ubiety of Spanish Wisdom or the relation between the two, including the bloke himself. The grant's a phony. He has no true constituency in the Community, he's not an alderman, and most of all he doesn't care about the underprivileged or anyone else for that matter for if he did he would have joined Good Will, United Way and the Salvation Army or at least become a social worker. All he cares about is the grant. The money's the object, commonly called feedback, not the students or wisdom but the grant itself, Alexander Hamilton on the ten dollar bill, Andy Jackson on the twenty and whoever it is on the thousand.

He knows this. Everybody knows it, the dean, the chancellor, the entire administration. The grant carries a carrot known as overhead by which the administrators levy a charge of 50% on the grant's take for their rooms, typewriters, secretaries, electricity, heating oil and physical plant, which they're stuck with anyway grant or no grant. The federal government pays these charges in return for ultimate control. Fifty percent of five hundred thou for SPOUC is two hundred and fifty thousand dollars, how do you like them apples? The chancellor does and orchestrates the farce.

Where are the James Baumanns of this world? Where are they? They have disappeared. Dean Baumann realized he was an amateur in every field but his own so he never tried to lead his faculty but took the lead from them: "Ladies and Gentlemen, what is your pleasure? Go out and find the Renaissance and Baroque scholars you want; I will make a few discreet administrative checks, calling old friends on other campuses to ask about their academic citizenship and if they prove to be good colleagues I'll appoint them. When they arrive get together and tell me what you need and I'll try to support your programs. I promise to administer and not set policy for your department."

That was James Baumann, who respected his faculty and was respected by them. I have never met a more esteemed man on any campus, Rosa, Mecca, Seamus, NYC, State East, State West, Ivy, anywhere.

The new breed of administrators do things differently; instead of respecting their faculty they issue guidelines, frequently called benchmarks. The History Department may have a medievalist *providing* he ignore Diamond's Law and pretend to be an expert in urban affairs, getting grants for municipal improvement. Philosophy may have an Aristotelian IF he also has feedback and outreach; English a Milton scholar IF he has resource persons and community thrust; French, someone on Molière IF he has language tables for interfacing in the cafeteria; IF meaning that these professors are prepared to do everything but profess their discipline, the ostensible reason for their appointment. Above all, they must despise Diamond's Law.

When I teach my students to write term papers I tell them they should always clothe their ideas with examples: "Give two or three ideas," I tell them, "and an illustration or anecdote supporting them." I must now add an example to my own precept to show the ravages of Health, Education, and Welfare on my university.

When I first went to State West I worked with Petey Gibson, who had arrived two years before me. He was such a fine Golden Age scholar that old Stevens at Pennsylvania once said to me: "What is Gibson doing these days?" Stevens was ready to have Gibson replace him when he retired. But Petey went to work for HEW and ignoring Diamond's infallibility he piled up a series of outreaching grants, obtained travel money for the deans and stocked the library with thousands of dollars of social engineering books that no one reads today. Unappreciated, unrewarded, tired of ingrates, he terminated his teaching career elsewhere, on a secondary campus. Petey Gibson was no fool. Deep down within he knew he had sold out. He died a bitter man.

Roland Binde is another example, the very opposite of Gibson. Rollie had a way with people that the Spanish call *don de gentes*. Tall, handsome, personable, he could sell an Eskimo a snowball, which is just what he did at State West by selling himself to the administration. It so happened that Rollie couldn't spell; when I read his application I noticed he inserted accent marks incorrectly at the rate of twenty-three to a page; he wrote *hablándo, cása, nosótros* and omitted the mark on *arbol.* I really liked Roland very much and preferred him as a person to all my other colleagues; Roland as Rollie was O.K. but as a professor in a university he was another cup of tea, a disaster who once argued that the Guaraní were not really Indians. Some of the professors laughed at him. He was a big, amiable, tail-wagging Teddy Bear, a Rollie Pollie in a House of Intellect who never should have been appointed to a tenure track position, but the dean wanted him for his grantmanship and community-soothing political ability. The dean pushed him through. I remember I spoke to him the day he left us when his contract wasn't renewed; he had tears in his eyes.

And therein lies the tragedy. The administration no longer respects the faculty at State West and the faculty no longer respects the administration. As a matter of fact, they despise each other.

Modern educators like to speak of evaluations instead of grades, the faculty evaluating the students and the students evaluating a given professor's class at term's end. I shall use this peculiar application of *evaluate* for the closing paragraphs of my autobiography and attempt to evaluate Rosa and Seamus vis à vis States East and West, the sectarian in face of the secular. I have spoken poorly of Rosadabrigid and will sum up my argument now looking for ultimate causation; and I have spoken both well and poorly of State West, having witnessed its decline. Here again I shall seek causation, which seems pertinent in my autobiography since my entire adult life has been devoted to higher education; speaking of universities I speak of myself for I know no other world. Very well then, Rosa and West, here is my evaluation.

Outwardly the arguments in favor of Rosadabrigid were good and the physical appearance extremely good for here was a fine religious university, Catholic, on an attractive campus, run by men who had sacrificed their lives for their faith. The curriculum was fine on paper also: Latin, French, Mathematics, English, Physics and Philosophy were at the center, a course of studies most professionals would give their eye teeth for to restore to their campus today. Religion was there too, which if it be taken as Theology is an ancient discipline gracing any academic diploma.

The campus was beautiful, the architecture in good taste, the professors and seniors wore gowns; there were Latin awards for excellence and there was social sobriety owing to the dedication of the clergy, who always remained on campus, and to the large number of dayhops who went home at night to the stability of their families. Rosadabrigid had a lot in its favor.

Nevertheless something was fundamentally wrong to make it such an academic mockery. The bigot without thinking will scream "Religion! Get the priests out of there!", but that kind of scolding is too proximate; it is too immediate, too particular whereas I am looking for a more universal reason. I want to satisfy the intellect rather than the emotions, which seems to be an appropriate desire when discussing the failure of Catholic universities.

All institutions have an end which they must fulfill if they hope to achieve excellence; they have a primary purpose. When you go to a hospital you expect to find priorities such as these: Emergency Operating Room, Operating Room, Internal Medicine, Heart, Eyes, Ear, Throat, X-Ray, Anesthesia, Pharmacy. An expert might rearrange my order somewhat, introducing various subtleties, but even the most unschooled layman knows you go to a hospital for medical assistance, working from the high to the low, from hideous accidental wounds down to band aid scratches. A hospital may have a delightful tea room (where I live now it happens to serve the best lunches in town), a beautiful gift and card shop and a fine newspaper stand, which will attract visitors and become a conversation piece, but if the medical facilities are wanting it will be a poor hospital.

The same argument holds for any other institution. In a restaurant we want good food, although it may add music and even theater; in the theater we look for good plays and acting though it may provide an attractive wine bar; and in a super market we expect good meat and produce though it may pipe good music and sell inexpensive encyclopedias. Every institution will be judged by the achievement of its primary end rather than the added benefits no matter how splendid they may be.

A university should gather its faculty and students around the disciplines. Since the departments house the professors and disciplines and the students go there for their classes the university should always place the departments first: Philosophy, History, Mathematics, Physics, Literary Criticism and the others: these and their students are the primary goal, everything must be done to support them. But at Rosa it wasn't like that. There was on campus a vague substance, a haze, a mist called Religion permeating everything, the trees, the grass, the buildings, the gym, the clergy, the faculty, students and curriculum; somehow it was felt that as long as Religion was there all the other phenomena lacked ultimate significance; call this haze a sentimental unworldliness perhaps, a dulcet feeling of worldly disdain. But Mathematics unfortunately is of the world and must be studied here and now in time and space in a university, and when a student enters a Math class he ceases to be Catholic, Hindu, Atheist, old man, young boy, beautiful girl, fat or thin or anything else and becomes an empty page before the depths of the discipline. To put it in Rosa's Scholastic terms, a mathematician *qua* mathematician is precisely that, a student of Mathematics and not a novice of Religion. The same is true of the other disciplines and when these are not respected the Religious haze becomes a miasma.

Where does this argument lead us? I must say again that Newman was right and his adversaries within his church wrong. Instead of sprinkling Rosadabrigids all over the landscape the bishops should have tried establishing a modest college here and there within the great universities of this country. St. Michael's at Toronto will serve as an example. Yes, Newman was right. What I have said of Rosa may also be said of Seamus. I love the students and faculty there, who were far kinder to me than I to them, and I cherish their memory, Henry Roberts, Arty Lynch and the others—all American citizens should have their character. Still, you could barely see the real Seamus through the haze. The Brooklyn religious order should revert to charity and turn the school over to laymen, for Seamus Orsini priests don't know the nature of a university, whose primary goal is Philosophy.

And now I come to State West, which I shall evaluate rather

than East, for in judging any institution we should look to its best performance. Only the cynic looks at the worst and West was better than East.

When I journied out to State in 1964 there was extremely little haze; oh you'll always have some mystification where human beings are concerned, but of this misfortune State had the minimum. The students were as humble as those at Rosa and Seamus and naively came to class seeking an education. They were not disappointed. They took History, English, a foreign language and Mathematics. They had fine distributional credits in the Humanities, Natural Sciences and subjects like Economics; they also concentrated on their major. State West was bringing the students to the faculty and disciplines to afford them an education.

The changes became visible in 1968 when State so to speak created fine lunch rooms and gift shops, abandoning its primary medicine. The administration declared it an Urban Program University, UPU (an Oopoo as we say in the profession) and instituted all kinds of courses in Pollution, Traffic Control, Criminal Justice, Community Development, Minority Studies, Relevant Political Science and similar dynamos of the new era. It got rid of foreign language and Mathematics requirements and watered down English to high school level achievement. It created diverting courses in Physics and Chemistry. Finally it came up with a diploma called GUC, A General University Committee degree where a student could take a hundred and twenty credits in anything he desired, from Accounting to Urban Outreach. West became ethnic with Asian Studies, Italian Studies, Chicano Studies, Irish Studies, Black Studies, Indian Studies, Minority Studies, so it often had dual partnerships or adversaries, depending on the political climate; an Italian Department and Italian Studies, a Spanish Department and Chicano input. The women got into the act with Women's Studies, a female instructor of Chemistry constituting fifty percent of Women's Studies and a male Hispanist being fifty percent if he taught the feminine prose of Saint Teresa of Avila. The health outfit grew with courses in wellness and self-being awareness and the Center of Citizens' Concern (the new CCC) encouraged courses in parenting, grandparenting, and cousining. Business Outreach, Social Engineering and Nursing assumed their positions in center stage, pushing Arts and Humanities to the periphery. The Great State University West adopted a new lexicon of benchmarks, guidelines, interfacing, thrust, marketability, feedback, resource persons, spokespersons, subcultures, outreach, input, output and a score of other linguistic beauties which became the order of the day shunting aside the Queen's English. Courses became interdepartmental and interdisciplinary, euphemisms for antidepartmental and antidisciplinary, and deans and chancellors took charge telling the departments whom to recruit and how to recruit them. The administration lost its respect for the faculty

165

and adopted the motto: *Ad pulchritudinem tria requiruntur: civitas, utilitas, cupiditas.*

State West, this admirable academy I joined in 1964 when James Baumann was dean, became a miasma campus as bad or worse than Rosa, a tragic alteration. The clergy at Rosadabrigid were immigrants' sons who though unquestionably at sea were often honestly mistaken; they didn't know what a university was and had no business running one. They distorted the university hoping to advance the common good.

The administration at State has betrayed its intellectual traditions by creating a novel secular haze, but State West is different from Rosa. The deans and professors are not the offspring of immigrants with their hyphenated mentality; they have seen a paradigm in the old State University of their student days or in the Ivy League and have doctorates from the best universities. They know what is going on and they allow it. They are aware. Are they timorous? Fence-sitting? Cynical? Greedy? Do they thirst for political power? The dispassionate observer will have to seek the answer to these questions but whatever it might be he will find that just as Rosa graduates resent what Rosa did to them and refuse to attend alumni reunions, so State graduates will resent State West and its barnacle courses. Whereas the priests of the 1930's were ignorant, today's secular administrators are pusillanimous.

But fair is fair. No matter how little admiration I have for chancellors and deans, I have less for the faculty. The tragedy originates with them. If just one honest to goodness department, Philosophy, History, English, my own Spanish, will get up in public and say *non serviam*, giving its reasons for this posture, the fools upstairs will be unable to respond: *Ad pulchritudinem tria requiruntur: integritas, consonantia, claritas.*

Fifty years ago another tragedy occurred in central Europe. It has been blamed on everyone and everything touched by it, the aristocrats, bankers, industrialists, Versailles Treaty, American diplomacy, French isolation, the people, the Pope, Nietzsche, Luther, Depression, Neville Chamberlain; it has even been blamed on the victims themselves with the charge they did little to arrest it. It is my turn now to give my theory, the new historiography of James Ignatius Murphy. The J.I.M. School. Revisionism. I will blame it on the professors. You can't tell me that the professors with their doctoral degrees in so many subjects didn't know what was going on, they knew all right you can't tell me they didn't know. They must have known for if they didn't there is no epistemology and nobody knows anything. And what did the professors do? They sat on a fence with their benchmarks, guidelines, feedback, thrust, subcultures, and summer grants to attend to, and outreaching improvement, which must have all sounded wonderful in a foreign language given to polysyllables. The guidelines carried subsidies, what else are guidelines for? So the faculty did nothing. They might have spoken up. Could they have prevented the tragedy? Who knows, perhaps not. But they did nothing. The tragedy must be blamed on them.

A change of scene, of time, of proportion—similar conditions appear at State. The faculty alone knows what is really going on. The legislature doesn't know; they are pitiful amateurs applying the same politics to the university they apply to the construction of highways, what's in it for me? Although their action is contemptible they are outside contempt because of their ignorance; in spite of what the law says you can't blame a man for what he doesn't know. And we can't blame the public either, after all they are the victims; oh it's convenient to blame the victims just as it was to blame them a half century ago but the Bronx Boy halts at doing so. I just know it isn't fair. What can the public do and the students do, they who know least of all?

But the faculty knows, they are flour from another sack. The real faculty know, not the heddy gablers and marketability boys but the real ones who have devoted their lives to study. They really know, and what do they do? They elect faculty committees to follow the guidelines of those who disdain the university as an academy, guidelines of Health, Education and Welfare agents, of braying deans and chancellors.

I love Rosa, I still do, with all her faults I love her. And Seamus, those immigrants, I love them too, and Henry and Arturo; I can even abide the Education. And Mecca and NYC, how can I forget Professor Feigenbaum and his philosophy of the little things and Francis Johnson? They are part of me, I love them too. Even State East I love, Morty, Aldo and the students, who were a decent bunch, maybe I'll get back some day. And State West, Dean Joseph Baumann and the students, such fine people; I consider them all my family, I love them too. They are my universities and this is my country, the United States of America, they mean everything to me. But I have fears, great fears as I contemplate the tragedy. Can't the professors do something? They alone have the power. God help theese Countrrrreeee! I know now why my thoughts dwell only on the Bronx, P.S. 11, sun pictures, cheesebox, G-8 and his battle aces and Schapiro's candy store. The great is truly diminutive. And so I have hope. I have hope, but with the universities engaging in lies, God help theese countrrrreeee!

James Ignatius Murphy
The Bronx Boy
June 1, 1984

(A Note To Myself: Next week I leave for the Navy. I'll have to show this to Arturo.)

23. Scholarly Note

[1]The Bronx Boy's knowledge of theologians is not limited to musings concerning his father's childhood. In 1902 Father Luis Coloma wrote the following advice to the sixteen year old Alfonso XIII, whose father, Alfonso XII, died before he was born, just as my grandfather died when my own father was one year old:
(From Luis Coloma, *Spiritual Exercises For His Majesty King Alfonso XIII Before His Coronation*, in *Obras completas* (Madrid: Ed. Razón y Fe, 1960), p. 997) - "Third Point. We already know that the end of man on earth is to love and serve God, faithfully keeping the Commandments, in order to save his soul in this way. That is to say: that if man fulfills his end faithfully keeping the Commandments of God's law, he will save his soul. But, if he doesn't keep them and guard them?. . . What will happen?. . . Well, it will happen that instead of saving his soul, he will lose it . . . And does Your Majesty know what it is to lose your soul?. . . Well, to lose your soul is to lose God and to fall into the most horrible misfortune for eternity . . . And does your Majesty know what eternity is?. . . Neither Your Majesty knows it nor do I; nor can anyone properly fathom this awesome idea. One can, however, gather some notion of it through several examples and comparisons. Does Your Majesty remember the beach at San Sebastian? Do you remember that semicircle of sand flat which appears on the Concha when the tide goes out? Can anyone count the number of little grains of sand that are on that beach?. . . Impossible. Very well then: let Your Majesty imagine that a poor little ant takes from that beach a little grain of sand and walking at its own pace it carries it to Madrid and deposits it in Retiro Park . . . And he returns again to the beach and takes another little grain of sand and carries it to Madrid . . . And he returns again, and then again . . . How many years would that poor little ant need to move that whole beach from San Sebastian to the Retiro in Madrid:. . . I won't say hundreds of years, but thousands and thousands of centuries would not be enough. Would the years, the centuries be so many, so many that when the little ant finished his task, eternity would also be finished?. . . No, when the little ant finally gets through with his task, one couldn't even say that eternity had yet begun; because eternity never ends; and that immense passage of time would not remove from it even a solitary second . . . Well, imagine something else now; imagine that when the little ant begins its journey from San Sebastian to Madrid Your Majesty begins to suffer a headache or toothache. Imagine also that at the same time they take away from Your Majesty your mother, the person you love the most, and that with this pain of body and sorrow of soul Your Majesty begins to contemplate, all alone and without solace, the travels of the little ant, hoping that when it

finishes its task Your Majesty will see your mother again and will stop suffering . . . And when it finishes the task they tell you it will now have to transport the beach of Zarauz, and later that of Guetaria, then that of Zumaya, and later the entire world to another hemisphere . . . And even then you have done no more than to begin your suffering?. . . Can anyone think of anything more horrible? Then let Your Majesty, who is a mathematician, raise all this to the infinite power, and the infinite horror that will result, that—that is what it means to lose your soul."

Father Coloma wrote these words in the year 1902. Thirty-five years later the Bronx Boy heard this same advice from Brother Solomon of All Saints, only the imagery was wingèd, still diminutive but wingèd: "A little bird comes to the planet once every *billion* years and takes away one little drop of water from the ocean or one little grain of sand from the beach. Even so, when the entire globe will have disappeared, eternity and hell will have just begun. If you commit a mortal sin you will go to hell." This sanguine doctrine is called Jansenism, which both Coloma the Spaniard and the Irish seminarians got from the French. All good culture, dress, cuisine, bons mots, and fine little diminutives, little ants and little birds and little grains of sand, come from France.

My gratitude!

—James Ignatius Murphy

* * *

Before he left for Roosevelt Roads, James Ignatius Murphy insisted that this scholarly note to Chapter 4 (see page 24, line 11) be included in his autobiography. He must have spoken the following words to me a dozen times: "I'm not asking you to edit that note, Arturo, it's going to go in just as it is. You see, it's the key to the whole story. When I was a boy I used to think of the mud flats at Compo Beach, Connecticut, and how the little bird would come once every billion years to take one grain of that black soil away and how long it would take for one of the flats to disappear, and then all the flats, and finally the beach itself and all the water in Long Island Sound, at the rate of one drop of water every billion years. And then I'd think of the whole Atlantic Ocean, how long that'd take, and then I wondered how the little bird would manage the lots in the Bronx since they were pure rock. And all that time in hell. Mine was a unique biography. No, Arturo, it has to go in or my autobiography will be false, and I'm bent on telling the truth."

In compliance with Jim's wishes I have included this scholarly note with no changes although I have my reservations: I wonder if any man's mind can be so graphic as to picture a little bird's removing a grain of this planet once every billion years.

—Arturo Lynch

24. More Sentimental Verses

In my prologue I indicated that James Ignatius Murphy wrote two sets of sentimental verses about the Bronx and that I would include the second set in a later chapter. These verses follow those of chapter 6.

—Arturo Lynch

More Sentimental Verses of James Ignatius Murphy,
Dedicated To His Friends, Joey Bacigalupi,
Milton Segal And Tommy Kelly

I thought I saw old High Cash Clothes
and Courtyard Singer too,
boys picking up tin foil balls
as we were wont to do
once we took sun pictures, Jim,
holding them to the sky,
but no it was illusion
that caught my eager eye.
Shadow, G-8, Lone Eagle's plane
where are they, are they fled?
Stickball, punch ball, king of the hill,
Cheesebox, ten cent maltèd?
Where are the snows of yesteryear
that made our Flexies glide?
I've wandered to the Highbridge, Jim,
and felt the pang inside.
All these things were good, dear Jim,
yea scum bags, manure balls,
And God they say is good too, Jim,
who listens to our calls,
So good will never ever die,
one day we'll meet again
where the O car meets the Unie
and I'll see Adrienne . . .

I've wandered to the West Bronx, Jim,
I went to see the store
where Botchie bought the Halvah,
the store . . . forever more!

25. Instituta Bronxoniensa

In the original manuscript my friend Jim Murphy described more than a hundred customs he called *Instituta Bronxoniensa*. Since some of them of them were repetitions I have reduced them to eighty-four entries, contained in the present chapter. Although several of the instituta appear in Chapters 6 and 20, I list their names here so that readers will have a ready reference to Bronx tradition.

—Arturo Lynch

ASSOCIATION

I never heard of touch football in the Bronx for we always called it Association. Two to five played on a side, on University Avenue between Merriam and the bridge. There was no blocking or rushing the passer, and if the passer stood behind the goal line he could take all day. It's a wonder he didn't complete every pass except that the playing field, which was the width of the street, was narrow. Although there were very few automobiles occasionally a receiver would wreck himself against a parked car as he caught the ball, much like a tight-end today.

BAKERIES

There were three bakeries, Jewish, French and Cushman. The rolls at the Jewish bakery were the best ever made, especially when spread with Land O' Lakes butter. The Murphys ate them every Sunday morning after Mass, and I mean every. The Murphys didn't buy the Jewish cake, which seemed coarse, but perhaps the Segals did. For the best coffee cake ever made, there was a French bakery on Ogden Avenue opposite the Ogden Theater. I can still see the small, thin, sharp-featured woman with the brown beret and cigarette in her mouth who did the baking. The cake had many raisins and was cooked all through with butter and had none of that curry-like repugnant almond paste you see today. Thirty-five cents. I hope to get a recipe like that some day, master the art of cooking and bake a French coffee cake every Sunday morning, the day we always enjoyed it. Rolls and coffee cake on Sunday. The rest of the week might be given over to Cushmans: pound cakes, lemon flavored cakes, lady fingers and other gossamer flour; thirty-three cents and you had yourself a table cake. Since the Murphys were wont to eat rice pudding, tapioca pudding, bread pudding, chocolate pudding and custard almost every night in the week, Cushman's was a once or twice a week affair. Once in a great while we bought a birthday cake even though it was no one's birthday.

BARBER SHOP

A store owned by an Italian. The City of New York issued

licenses only to Italians. Adult haircuts were thirty-five cents, children's were a quarter, lollipop thrown in. Mr. Perucini and his assistant Tony were models of decorum, always polite, always courteous, always neat and clean. They were nice to me, I always liked to go there.

BASEBALL-AGAINST-THE-WALL

An adaptation of baseball, and we didn't need a big ten acre field to play it in. All we needed was an apartment house and two to six friends to play it, possibly eight, but no more. Go to New York and visit the venerable Bronx. Apartment houses there didn't have their bricks running right down to the ground; rather, a first floor apartment will have its window sills seven feet above the ground, then beneath them brick will run to two feet six inches or two feet nine inches above the ground, where a horizontal dado runs from one side of the building's face to the other, a groove and excrescence, sometimes rounded, sometimes pointed at 120° or 135°. An architect once told me that strictly speaking this excrescence is called a cornice not a dado, but we never heard either word in the Bronx; in our more human wisdom we simply called it the point. That rounded or pointed cement line, running two inches out from the bricks, was the most important part of any apartment building. Strike a rubber ball against it (after 1945 a Spaulding) and you will see it fly through the air as if ejected by a Louisville slugger. A fly to the street was a single, to the center street a double, to the far sidewalk a triple and to the wall on the other side of the street's canyon, a home run. I haven't seen this game in forty years, whereas I see the Yankees play three nights a week on TV, and I can tell you this, baseball-against-the-wall is a superior spectacle. I have seen them all and I can tell you this: my own favorite was Ted Williams but not even he could match Joey Bacigalupi for emotion when he played baseball-against-the-wall. I saw Williams go three for five once down at the Stadium, but one day Botchie went six for six, every one a home run twenty feet up on the House Of All Nations. I hope these pages will be Joey's shrine.

BLACK AND WHITE

Has nothing to do with scotch whiskey or racial discrimination. It's the name of a chocolate soda with vanilla ice cream they don't know how to make outside the Bronx. The soda jerk (Benny in Irving's drug store showed me one day) must put three squirts of chocolate syrup and three of cream in a large Coca Cola glass, then run the seltzer two thirds up the sides stirring it as it goes, after which he introduces two large balls of Breyer's vanilla ice cream with the vanilla beans whose specks you can see in them. Then he must cover the ice cream with a spoon, convex side up, protecting it from the seltzer he finally adds to fill the glass. Then he stirs again. If you say black and white outside the Bronx they think you may be a bigot and don't know how to take you, and after you explain and they make you a soda they leave out the cream and destroy the ice cream itself by pouring seltzer directly on it. They don't even know what a soda is outside the Bronx, they even call them phosphates as if they were a medicine or something.

BLT
    A bacon, lettuce and tomato sandwich served in Irving's drug store, Highbridge, The Bronx, to the teachers from P.S. 11. "Hold the mayo" means please put on no mayonnaise. My teacher Miss Friedman always ate BLT's hold the mayo. When I was in the fourth grade I had a crush on Miss Friedman but she didn't know it.

BOX BALL
    There were lesser games related to stickball, subgenres rather like dialects before a language. One of these was boxball, for which I have made a drawing:

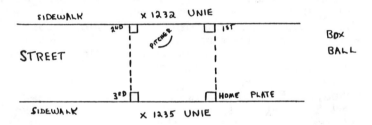

University Avenue was only thirty-five feet wide in the 1200 block so you weren't supposed to hit flies. The pitcher threw the ball in on a bounce and you hit it with your fist or open hand; if you hit a fly and it was caught it was out and if it sailed over everyone's head it was still out. You were supposed to hit a grounder and after that the rules were the same as the paradigm, stickball. For boxball you needed three men on a side or four if you have a catcher, and all this on a city street sandwiched between the canyon walls of apartment houses. Such inventiveness! Things were better in the old days, there can be no doubt about it.

BRONX HOME NEWS
    The Bronx had its own newspaper, which I often saw in bundles but never read. It didn't flourish over in our neighborhood except in 1263 but it seemed to do better over near Walton and the Concourse, where the swells lived. I vaguely wanted to be a *Bronx Homes News* delivery boy but not nearly so much as a *Saturday Evening Post* boy or a Western Union messenger in uniform.

CANDY STORE

I have devoted most of Chapter 6 to Schapiro's Candy Store, beyond peradventure of a doubt the most important of *Instituta Bronxoniensa.* But one year, 1937, Mr. Joel came from Austria and opened a home made candy store on Merriam, top of the hill. Home made hard candies and chocolates, which were delicious and expensive, fifty cents a pound. Although not every neighborhood was privileged to have a Mr. Joel, his appearance will demonstrate the importance of small enterprise, the creation of the little man, a Bronx institution.

CARDS

Sun pictures, stick for stick ball, tin foil ball, cheesebox, rubber ball, the other important object in the Bronx was your pack of cards, not spades, hearts, diamonds and clubs but cards, the real cards composed by the Gowdy Gum Company of Boston, Massachusetts, seat of American culture.

Going back, back, back, the farthest I can recall, I see cowboy cards of post office size with Hoot Gibson, Ken Maynard, Tom Mix and other legends. My own favorite was Ken Maynard, with that big white hat. He was a fine looking man. I saw him in person once and also Hoot Gibson because in the 1930's cowboys made the rounds of the Catskill Mountain movie theaters and we were staying in Stamford, New York not far from Oneonta. I saw those real cowboys.

The next set of cards were the Indians, Gowdy Gum size. The cowboys had been sepia like the Rotogravure section in the New York Times but these were brightly colored with deep blue sky, red and white beads, bronze skin and lots of feathers, white with black stripes on them. Most Indians just sat there serenely, majestically, a full bust; a few were in action shooting bows and arrows. Noble adversaries for the cowboys. And there were some other pictures too, movie stars, presidents with caramel instead of gum cards and some military scenes. They tried new ideas once in a while just as magazines and TV programs do today but by and large it was cowboys and Indians. But it wasn't that you had the cards so much that counted, it was what you *did* with them; they were your bat, your tennis racket, your lacrosse stick, your swagger stick, your sword; they were *you*, yourself, an extension of power and of being; they implied ontological perfection. The more cards you won the more you were.

The main thing about cards was that you and your friends played for them, an action demanding skill, courage and daring. It has never occurred to me before until now, as I write, fifty years later, but when you played cards you were engaged in an adventure. It was a question of honor.

One day, Segal, Botchie and I went down Ogden to P.S. 11, next door to Liebowitz's candy store, where the deep doorway was; it provided protection from the wind, which couldn't gust there. Botchie said to Segal: "Wanna play?"

"Sure. You first."

Botchie was righty and held his pack in his left hand; he took one card in his right, held it at full arm's length to his knee and flipped it toward the ground. The picture side was up: Heads. He flipped another card and another until he had twelve heads on the ground. Then he tried another: Tails. "That's enough. Match them, twelve heads and a tail."

Segal was righty too. He moved over a couple of feet from Botchie's pile and started flipping, seven heads, and then he hit a tail; he was lucky Botchie had missed on his last card. Then he flipped five more heads and picked up both piles. His pack was bigger now.

We played for half an hour taking turns at not playing until the school bell rang. I won ten cards that day and as I said before it did something to you. It was a great accomplishment.

There was one boy at P.S. 11 none of us wanted to play with, Jensen. Jensen could flip fifty heads in a row or fifty tails, as he saw fit, and who wants to go up against that?

Another version of Gowdy Gum Company cards was "Off The Wall" and here a picture would be worth a thousand words but I can't draw that well; if I ever have this autobiography published I will ask some artist to make me one. In Off The Wall the object wasn't to match heads and tails but to cover another card and the booty was yours; even if you covered a card by a sixteenth of an inch the pile was yours.

The first player held a card against the wall five feet above the ground and let it ride. It started to do revolutions and spun itself to the ground a few feet away. The second player held his card in the same spot and let it ride hoping to cover the first card, but for some reason, the pressure of hand, gust of wind, dulled edges of the card, Act of God, it didn't cover the first one. Then the first player went again trying to cover either of the first two cards, it made no difference which, and this went on alternately until someone covered a card and picked them all up. This game held special joy when there were gusts of wind because you never knew where the card would go, and since it could be played with three or more no one knew who the winner was going to be. The mysterious, the unknown, adventure, gambling; now that I think of it, gambling is a natural instinct, inherent to the constitution of the human being, and its more wholesome varieties should be encouraged. Like cards off the wall. Perhaps the world would be a better place if adults collected Indian cards from the Gowdy Gum Company of Boston, Massachusetts, home of American culture, and held them against the wall instead of going to the casinos in Nevada.

Again, some poet should write a sonnet glossing the line:

Indian cards and cowboys, I salute you.

Or he could write a narrative poem about something dramatic,

175

like the time Tommy Kelly flipped a hundred cards against Bacigalupi.

CHECKERS

Not the table board variety but the real kind you shot into small chalked squares on the sidewalk. I was never as good at checkers as I was at immies so I rarely played them. There were two kinds of checkers, the wooden, which survived better shooting over the rough cement, and the clay. I always preferred the clay as they were works of art with their black and red protruding crowns. The real clay checkers must be museum pieces by now, rivaling the sculptures of Cellini, for they have yielded the field to insipid, light weight plastic counterfeits. You shot from square to square and whoever got home first got the other Bronx boy's checker. You were allowed to hit the opponent's shooter to deviate its course.

CHEESEBOX

Philadelphia Cream Cheese, two and a half by three inches, in half inch thick silver blue packets, side by side, twenty-four bricks to a box, of cheesebox! Oh noble pine from the slopes of the Rockies, torn by wind and rain and sleet and snow, baked in the suns of high summer, thou borest the elements for fifteen lustra to fulfill thy exalted mission, till the cutters came to slice thee in slabs for Philadelphia cheesebox. They took thee, they sawed thee, they cut thee, they morticed thee into cheesebox. They packed thee, they shipped thee, they sent thee to Gristedes, to 1227 Ogden, round the corner from candy store. Wretches, scabs, they sold thy silver packets and cast thee, empty and abandoned now, into the ash can twixt Gristedes and Otto's delly. Thou wert bound for destruction in some nameless inferno when Timmy Shea passed by, he of artistic disposition. He saw thee, he coveted thee, he gathered thee and took thee to his home, tucked in the forests of Undy, and admired thee, noble beauty! He took his culper and engraved three small apertures in thy frontispiece, neath the P, D and A of PHILADELPHIA, revealing thy inner beauty. He carried thee up the steps to Unie and placed thee in the streets of Unie near a curb, the apertures facing the eye, and pronounced the stirring words: "Three for one." Kelly came, Bacigalupi came, Segal came, I came, Phelan and Smealy; the Bronx Knights gathered to admire thy noble beauty. Segal said: "Four for one," but Shea stood his ground and said: "three." The knights demurred but Kelly's eyes narrowed and he answered: "All right, three." He looked to the right, he looked to the left, he went to the center of the road. He reached into his pocket and took out a small glass sphere, his favorite shooter! Blue and white it was, in a marble cake swirl, it had won him many a tourney; he took aim. And all the while, oh cheesebox, thou stoodst there surveying the scene. The shooter came, towards thy entrails it came, faster and faster, but it struck the wood between the apertures and bounced off to the curb. Shea picked it up but Kelly barked: "Not my shooter, Shea, here's a purie." Shea scowled and frowned, but, smaller than Kelly, he simply said: "No puries, I won't take puries, only steelies, shooters and immies."

"All right, take this," and Kelly handed him a bright yellow marble. Shea was satisfied. Kelly looked to the right, he looked to the left and returned to the middle of the road. He shot again, and again, and again and again, he lost five in a row, then sank one, winning back three, then another, he was ahead now by an immie, then he shot again and lost more than he won. Finally he said: "Up yours, Shea, the holes are too small." And all the while thou stoods there, Cheesebox, as the Bronx knights litigated the size of thy apertures, but thou stoodst serene, above the heat of battle. Shea returned to Undy with thirty marbles; only nine had passed thy piney portals.

Oh Cheesebox, I am a woodworker! I have planed and crosscut, ripped and jointed, sanded and routed cherry, walnut, maple, oak and cedar; I have made tables, lamps, hutches, chairs but never in my days of wood have I seen any texture, any form, any craftmanship to match thy noble beauty! Cheesebox of yore I salute thee! Noble Cheesebox! Yesteryear Cheesebox, I love thee!"

Just as Ringalevio had many derivatives like hide and seek and cops and robbers, so Cheesebox had its vassals, one of them, immies in the street. I used to play it with Segal. I threw my shooter along the curb (there were hardly any autos then), very far, and then he threw his. The first one to strike the other's shooter won an immie. The same arguments arose over shooters, steelies and puries, and neither Segal nor I would take those ersatz composition immies, usually green, that some malevolent mind had manufactured out of sawdust; they were made in Usa, Japan. As we went down Unie towards the Unie hill, leading to the 44th precinct, we picked up Camels, Luckies, Old Gold and Chesterfield packages for our tin foil balls (q.v.), but Tarreyton was the best of all.

We also played in the dirt, the same marble games played elsewhere, even out west in Ohio, with a square etched in the dirt or hole dug in the ground. Although these games were fun and I admired the dexterity of many shooters they were not specifically of the *genus bronxoniense* so I shan't take any pains. In any case, they can't stand up to Cheesebox

CHESTNUTS

Or horse chestnuts. I never heard the term buckeye or Ohio buckeye until I was well past graduate school; they were simply called chestnuts and everyone understood you couldn't eat them. The only ones you could eat were the thin drab brown not pretty real chestnuts at John Manangelli's vegetable store which my mother bought for Thanksgiving stuffing though she complained they were too much work and usually used bread instead. My friend Henry Diamond tells me he used to string chestnuts together but I don't remember that. I cherish the memory of chestnuts and every September I pick them up across campus and in the surrounding neighborhood, they are so beautiful. Can you imagine what your furniture would be like if your tables and chairs looked like chestnuts as they come out of the shell. Simply beautiful. Nature's polish and dye are superior. As for eating chestnuts, you could get the thin edible ones only in front of the 42nd Street Library.

CHOOSING UP SIDES

When you have a half dozen or dozen Bronx knights waiting to take up arms in stick ball, punch ball or street hockey it is necessary to pair them off with military equilibrium, so you choose up sides. Two leaders step forth, usually Kelly and Phelan, who were the biggest, and Kelly says: "Odds or evens?" Phelan replies: "Evens." They both put their right hand behind their backs and Kelly says "One, two, three," upon which they whip out their right arm, one or two fingers extended. Both have their index and middle finger out, the thumb holding back the other two fingers: 2 plus 2 is 4, evens, Phelan has won the first round. "One, two, three," says Kelly: His hand shows an index finger, Phelan's an index and middle finger: 1 plus 2 is 3, odds, Kelly has won the second round. This goes on until one of them has won three rounds (like the basketball playoffs today, three out of five), and that one gets first pick. Kelly has won; he surveys the field of candidates: "I'll take Bacigalupi." . . ."Kowalski.". . ."Segal.". . ."Murphy.". . ."Schwarz.". . . "Seavey.". . . Botchie is the oldest and most athletic of the Bronx knights so he goes first, Seavey the youngest and smallest so he goes last. Then Botchie, Segal and Schwarz line up behind Kelly, and Kowalski, Murphy and Seavey behind Phelan to do battle on the stickball field. The game starts, and then . . ."Cheese it, the cops." I'd like to join a law firm called Kelly, Segal, Murphy, Kowalski, and Schwarz some day to bring the cops to justice for breaking up our stickball game. Police brutality. "Cheese it the cops,". . . down the sewer and cellars we go.

There was a variation of choosing up sides finger extension I must explain to complete this historical picture. Three, four or five Bronx knights want to play the game of kick-the-can, where only one person will be *it*, so it's not a question of choosing up two sides but of isolating one knight to be *it*. The knights gather in a ring; then the leader cries: "One, two, three," and all extend their fingers and the odd man is it; if there are three 2's and a 1, say, the 1 finger is *it* (or three 1's and a 2). If there is no odd man, the leader keeps saying "one, two, three" and the knights extend their fingers until someone is odd and *it*. As I say the knights form a circle as they do this, and the motion of their arms and chant of "one, two, three" forms a memorable choreography.

There was another way of Choosing Up Sides although this was only used for baseball and stickball. The two leaders of the potential teams stepped forth while the gang gathered round and one of them tossed the bat in the air, the other grabbing it at the middle as it descended. The second leader then grasped the bat just above the first's hand, and the two of them did this alternately, holding the bat tightly, until there was only an inch or two at the top. The last to go had to hold the bat gingerly with the tips of his fingers and revolve it around his head three times. If the bat fell out of his hand his adversary won and got first pick of the players but if it didn't he won and had first pick. The Bronx knights were usually chosen in the same order: Botchie, Kowalski, Segal, Murphy, Schwarz, Seavey, from the sluggers down to the peewees.

Just as gasoline in a sense is the most important part of an automobile, which cannot run without it, so Choosing Up Sides was the most important of all Bronx Institutions for without it there could be no Association, Stick Ball, Punch Ball or all the others.

COMFORT STATION

People today don't know what Comfort Station is, they have never heard the word, they do not know its refinement. Comfort Stations don't exist anymore but they did in the Bronx when I was a boy.

The majestic George Washington Bridge ran from 172nd Street in the Bronx, at the junction of Unie and Boscobel, to 181st Street in Manhattan at Amsterdam Avenue. Why the streets don't jibe, Manhattan being nine blocks off, I don't know, only historians can account for Manhattan's discrepancy; I do know, however, as we all did, that they don't jibe. The Manhattan end of the bridge had a great deal to offer, a White Tower hamburger place, the A trolley, a firehouse and warehouse for storage with that nice peculiar odor you sensed as you passed by, but the Bronx had even more, the Bronx had Comfort Station. As you walked east on the south side of the bridge towards the Bronx you saw it about sixty feet from the end of the bridge and you always walked into it, a large cream brick building two stories high, though you only used the ground floor. There was a large reception hall and two large benches with Church pew backs on either side; it was like being in Church don't you know. To the left it said LADIES, to the right GENTLEMEN and as you went in you saw how everything was spotless. I have been in sterilized laboratories, operating rooms, clinics and the homes of finicky perfectionists but I have never seen a place as clean, so very clean as Comfort Station. Those brass rails looked like gold always, at any time of the day, any day of the week; the drinking bowl like new ceramic and its crystalline water a celestial ambrosia; the copper tubes as though fashioned by Cellini, the floors, Italian marble, and the urinals, fountains from

179

Granada! Surely theses were not vessels to carry off disposal but intricate vertical aqueducts of geometric design, the flowing water creating cynesthetic beauty; intricate, yet simple, symmetrical. As I contemplate Comfort Station I see the great sweep of the Renaissance, in Florence, Toledo and beyond the Pyrenees. I am reminded of Garcilaso's eclogues, Cellini's salt cellar and the court of Francis I.

In Comfort Station I always saw a man in blue work clothes, five feet nine, quiet, cloth in hand, going about his business. Caring for Comfort Station. I didn't know who he was, I didn't even know his name. He had no plate on the door, no shingle, no recognition. Sir, I write these words to immortalize your deeds. Your were an artisan and gentleman, architect of Bronx culture. I salute you. Amen.

COURTYARD SINGER

This ancient bard appears in Chapter 6. He is a cousin of High Cash Clothes (q.v.).

CUBAN CIGAR ROLLERS

Another small enterprise, like Mr. Joel's Austrian sweet shop (this wasn't really a candy store because it didn't sell Gowdy Gum and newspapers). These Cuban gentlemen sat in a small store window two doors from the Ogden Avenue Theater and rolled tobacco leaves on open-faced wooden blocks with cigar forms carved in recess. They never talked or looked anywhere but only at the plates. I learned from Professor Feigenbaum at Mecca that in Tampa these rollers had the *lector*, a young scholar who would read to them as they worked, the novels of Cervantes, plays of Lope and lyrics of Garcilaso de la Vega, and that all cigar workers could recite from memory classical Spanish literature. Thus though of humble mien they possessed a broader culture than most professors today.

I don't want to misrepresent. Mr. Joel and the Cubans were ephemera whom I saw only in the late thirties, but they put in their appearance and deserve their place in this true history. "Variety is the source of beauty," and they gave variety. That's why the Bronx was so beautiful.

DELLY

The affectionate diminutive of Delicatessen Store, of which there were only two, the Jewish and the German. The City of New York issued licenses only to Germans and Jews, no others need apply. For James Ignatius Murphy a Jewish delly was a place you ate at after you got to high school but not before, and a German delly was a place you went to to take things home on Sunday after Mass but not on weekdays. A corned beef or pastrami sandwich at the delly on Jewish rye with a barrel pickle is the tastiest dish in the world, but as I say, that came later; in high school you usually went there for French fries and ketchup!

delicious!; or one of those long pure beef hot dogs resting on the steel plate. Years later in Mexico City I saw a Jewish delly in the Zona Rosa and asked the proprietor why he didn't have hot dogs in the window. He was an easy going nice guy but his wife wasn't; she was like Maggie in Bringing Up Father; she got annoyed, muttered something, and her facial gesture seemed to say: "Because frankfurters in the window are for canaille like you, that's why." What a snob! But she was wrong. Those fifteen cent wieners were right out of the top drawer, as good in their way as Nedicks and that's the highest compliment I can pay them.

The German delly was different. It wasn't a restaurant with hot dogs and open celery seltzer taps but a grocery store existing in memory as a long narrow row of shelves behind the store clerk, a long row of shelves behind you the customer, facing him, and a large porcelain and glass showcase in between; a deep narrow store smelling of gastronomical delight. There was potato salad, macaroni salad, shrimp salad, ham, Virginia ham, rye, pumpernickel, pickles, strange looking things no Murphy ever ate, head cheese, pigs' knuckles, all of them neatly arranged in spotless rows by a perfectionist. The German delly is no more; first of all, no perfectionists remain in the Bronx (there are no more awnings in the Bronx), and in the Midwest where I live now they don't know how to arrange things. That's it, to run a delly you have to be a special arranger, like a venerable composer of music. You have to orchestrate, it's a great art. That goes for Jewish dellys too. Anymore outside the Bronx they don't know how to run a delly.

DRUG STORE
When my cousin Nancy got a piece of dust in her eye in 1932 she went to Irving's drug store on the corner and said "Irving, I have something in my eye." He said: "All right, we'll take it out." He got a chair and put it in the middle of the tile floor (all drug stores have tile floors, it's not a drug store if it doesn't have a tile floor and the tile must be 3/4 inch, according to regulations), sat Nancy on it, rolled back the lid with a matchstick and touched the inner lid with a gauze. There was a black speck on it. Then Irving said: "How's that?," and had Benny and Larry give her a glass of water. "Fine, Irving," and that was that. In 1979 my daughter went to a doctor to have a speck of dust removed from her eye and after he did that he wrote on the Blue Cross Form: $42.00—Operation. The trouble with our country today is it has lost its Bronx values. Anymore doctors and lawyers are atheists.

DUMBWAITER
See Chapter V.

181

EGG CREAM

Although mentioned in one of the chapters, it deserves a special entry. Egg cream is the poor man's chocolate soda, the three center, made in a small Coca Cola glass with two shots of chocolate instead of three, one shot of cream, no ice cream, and seltzer to the rim rapidly stirred. Egg cream is lyrical and should be included in Roget's thesaurus of rhyme: dream, gleam, esteem, egg cream.

FLEXIBLE FLYER

In the winter no one had a sleigh or sled, they had Flexible Flyer, a brand name become name like kleenex for tissue paper and xerox for duplicator. I can still see the eagle wings painted on the center slat I lay on. Bronxites were famous for their apocopation and always called it Flexy. "It's snowing, get your Flexy."

HARP AND EAGLE

A Johnny-come-lately, coming into existence in March of 1933. For a Harp and Eagle bar and grill the New York Commissioner of Licenses issued permits only to citizens of Irish descent, refusing them to Jews and Italians. This was clearly a question of "Only Irish Need Apply" so the outraged American Civil Liberties Union righteously took the case to a federal court, where Judges Rabinowitz, Civita Vecchia and O'Shaughnessy ruled against the plaintiff declaring the Harp and Eagle license to be clearly constitutional; in a separate opinion Civita Vecchia said the ACLU complainers were eggheads. The Supreme Court of the United States of America upheld their decision.

HEGGIES

If you saw some tin foil or an immie in the street and the other guy saw it too and went to pick it up, you yelled "Heggies!" and if you did that before he got his hand on it he had to give you heggies, halfies; it was half yours. This made for occasional altercations since it was a judgment call, as they say in professional football today, although we never called it that. We never heard such a term.

HIDE AND SEEK

Or Hide 'N Seek. See Chapter 6, under Ringalevio Caw Caw Caw.

HIGH CASH CLOTHES

High Cash Clothes! Just as we call a blacksmith Smith, a wheelwright Wright and a tailor by his trade's name, so we called him High Cash Clothes, Mr. High Cash Clothes, Lower East Side version of the Meistersinger. He came every now and then with his ancient cry: High Cash Clothes!

I was sitting in the kitchen one day at noon finishing my

scrambled eggs before going to Schapiro's and P.S. 11 when I heard the song, twice I heard it, I don't think he ever sang it more than twice: High Cash Clothes! High Ca-a-sh Clo-o-thes! I wish I were a Tschaikovsky to record the music here, the timbre, but although I'm not I could sing it if I had to, with no prompting; perhaps I ought to do that, sing it on a tape recorder for posterity. I wouldn't be exactly the same; the truth is I'm not a bad singer but I couldn't put the love in it he had when he sang HIGH CASH CLOTHES. Like the Meistersinger he was an artist although his repertoire was considerably shorter; as a matter of fact it consisted of three words.

I heard him in the kitchen and looked at my mother. I didn't say anything but my eyes conveyed the message, "Can I?". No, she said, you can't, and that was the end of that. When you belong to a certain class there are certain things you don't do, you don't take old clothes and sell them to Mr. High Cash Clothes for fifty cents, that sum being his rendition of 'high cash'. You don't do that, you give them to the Salvation Army, which had their college up there off Tremont and Unie. Imagine taking one of your father's dark blue suits, an Upstairs garment, a Roman toga, and selling it, vest, jacket and trousers to some vagabond, probably a hyphenate, from the Lower East Side. No, give it to the Salvation Army. That's the better way.

So I never got to know Mr. High Cash Clothes the way I knew Courtyard Singer, our Meistersinger, though I wanted to. I used to see him a couple of times a month coming down Unie toward Highbridge, and where he went from there I don't know. He had a peculiar walk, a sort of sauntering, leisurely but not all that leisurely, like a boat drifting a little in the wind. He was a hard working man, and after he patched up the suits I guess he got five dollars for them. Maybe three. That was the 1930's.

I only got to speak to High Cash Clothes once, after the war, up around 1865 Unie near Burnside Avenue. He was strolling on the Acqueduct near Dr. Jacoby's house; he stopped, took off his hat and wiped his brow. He asked me how I was and I said fine and asked him how he was and he said not too good, things weren't any good now business was bad. I really liked him, more than that, I loved him. He was friendly and nice and he had humility, the real humility, not the kind you see today all blown up in the universities. I am so sorry I only spoke to him once because I would have liked him to be my friend. A real nice fellow. He looked like Rodney Dangerfield without all that foolishness and vulgarity, or I should say Rodney looks like him, for High Cash Clothes is a paradigm. He's gone now, he's really gone, he'll never return, like Meistersinger, the Golden Age; and as I write these lines my eyes fill with tears. The Bronx. Oh vanished Arcadia!

There were other citizens like Courtyard Singer and High Cash Clothes, but I didn't know them very well and won't dwell on them here. I guess you could call them the ambulating vendors, who were so common in the nineteenth century. There was the knife sharpener with his abrasive wheel who visited us about as often as High Cash Clothes, and he'd sharpen the knives right out in the street, the sparks flying. It was fun to watch the sparks. Once in a while you saw the elite of the sharpeners; he had a wheel mounted on the back of a small truck. There was the ice man who came until the ice boxes went out at 1245, that would be the year 1931 or so, and he was fun to watch with the shoulder pads and ice tongs, pincers I guess you would call them. Once, only once, I saw an organ grinder with a monkey on his shoulder; you can imagine how well that went over! The *Saturday Evening Post* man had lots of kids vending his magazines at five cents a copy, and if they sold enough they not only got commissions, they received pen knives as prizes. I wanted to be a *Saturday Evening Post* agent but my mother would have none of it, vendors belonging to an inferior profession; the same went for selling the *Bronx Home News*. There were shoe shine boys who made the rounds, especially in front of Irving's drug store on Sunday mornings, where the older crowd got their shoes polished and cleaned and pitched pennies against the red brick wall. And there were the horses and wagons either collecting junk or purveying vegetables. If you were an ice man, junk man or moving greengrocer you were an Italian. My mother never bought from them, she always bought from the stores. Sedentary Sicilians were all right, it was permissible to shop with them but not with the nomads.

The Bronx was alive then. People played in the streets, worked in the streets, walked about in the streets, they lived in the streets, like Naples and Mexico today. Anymore it's dead now. Like a giant coffin.

HORSE MANURE BALLS

Not just horse manure but horse manure balls. All the laundry wagons, milk wagons, junk wagons and occasional vegetable wagons were pulled by horses with canvas nose oat bags to chew from and as they ate the oats the horses passed them through their system to the street in the form of horse manure balls. It was fun to watch the sparrows flit from ball to ball lunching on the oats before the street cleaner came with his broom and shovel to sweep them up. Naturally everyone stayed away from horse manure balls except Jackie Smealy who used them when he lost his temper and pitched them at Big Phelan, who was teasing him. After that everyone had great respect for Jackie.

I DECLARE WAR

Perhaps the most ingenious game of all was I Declare War, for we Bronx knights who played it in the 1930's could not have had more than a decade to devise it, WAR being the fratricidal strife of 1918. It is one thing to fight a crusade, an armed effort combating the swastika and hammer and sickle, it is quite another for European nations to slaughter the flower of the next generation. Such carnage is never in season.

One day we played War. Segal drew a six foot chalk circle in front of 1225, at the bottom of the Merriam hill, with a tiny circle at the center and spokes radiating out to the circumference, carving the circle into pie sections. In each section he wrote a country's name: France, United States, England, Germany, Italy, Canada, Austria, Russia, Turkey. Then Botchie put a rubber ball in the center. The playing area looked like this:

The black dot at the center is the ball.

Everybody wanted to be the United States of America, nobody wanted to be Germany, and other nations were accepted reluctantly although Canada was the best of them and England was clearly preferable to Austria. Consequently the players had to choose up countries, it being understood that everyone was more or less allied against Germany. This particular day Phelan won and chose the United States, I was second and chose the next best country, Canada, and Smealy was last and had to take Germany. We all stood at the edge of the circle with one foot inside the pie slice of our country's name; we waited, then Phelan cried: "I declare war on . . .(dramatic pause and suspense). . . GERMANY!" Everyone started to run except the victim of aggression, Smealy, who picked up the ball and yelled: STOP! Everyone froze in his tracks and then turned around. Smealy eyed the nearest player, Kelly, took aim and fired the ball at him. He hit Kelly so we all returned to the circle, where Smealy had the right to declare war; had he missed him, it would have been Kelly's turn. No one ever declared war on the United States of America. P.S. 11 had done its job well:

I regret that I have but one life
to lose for my country.
Don't fire till you see the whites of their eyes.

I pledge allegiance to the flag of
the United States of America and to
the Republic for which it stands
         . . .

185

There were only patriots in the Bronx 1930.

Before I proceed, I DECLARE WAR reminds me of something. The rubber ball was so much a part of our lives that Bronx life was inconceivable without it. We were always bouncing it, throwing it, hitting it or simply tossing it to ourselves, catching it, or carrying it on our way to school, and I remember it bulging from our corduroy knickers pants pocket. Bronx knights, Kelly, Segal, Bacigalupi even used it in victory after a game for there were no cash prizes, bonuses, free agent increments, only good clean ball. When we lost at baseball-against-the-wall, for example, we had to stand at the point, head down with our behinds in the air, and the victor had the right to stand on the sidewalk across the street and throw the ball as hard as he could at the exposed dignity. Someone should write an Ode To The Rubber Ball. The Bronx stood on a rubber ball.

IMMIES

The popular name for marbles, the small glass spheres young boys shoot in games. They are listed here for linguistic reasons lest non-Bronx readers misunderstand them in the text (see the entry in the present glossary called CHEESEBOX). Heggies, Immies, Loosies, Two For Flinchin' and similar terms constitute a Bronx Rosetta Stone.

JAWBREAKERS

Also known as All Day Suckers. An extremely hard global candy an inch and a half in diameter taking several days to suck away. The quarter inch core is composed of foreign matter, like gum or tootsie roll chocolate. Authentic jawbreakers change colors as they diminish in size and can be stored in water overnight without melting.

JUMP ROPE

As I explained in my autobiography, I am a segregationist, boys on the right and girls on the left and ne'er the twain shall meet, and I never played potsy unless none of the boys were around and my cousin Nancy asked me to; you wouldn't want the others to see you playing potsy. So the present entry is an attempt at integration and describes not the games I played but the jump rope I observed of Nancy M., Jeannie D., Peggy S., Mickie W., Betty D., Chicky S. and the other girls all of whose surnames I could give if I wanted to, every one of them. I always liked Peggy, and Betty was very nice to me; they always had a smile. So I'll tell you about jump rope.

"A my name is Agnes, my father's name is Albert, my mother's name's Alberta, we come from Alabama, we're going to Arkansas. B my name is . . ."

"You're out, Mary Jane, you're not supposed to say Albert-Alberta. It's the same name."

"No I'm not, there's an Alberta in my class, Alberta Shatkin. It's a real name."

"B my name is Bonnie, my husband's name is Bobbie, we come from Birmingham, we're going to Bilgo."

"There's no such place as Bilgo, you're out. Give me my rope."

"There is."

"There isn't."

They jumped rope as they chanted their onomastic codes, and if they didn't miss a jump or a verse, as in Bilgo (if they couldn't think of a word they made one up, they never left a space blank), they won, meaning they had the right to keep on jumping and the others had to turn. Sometimes the girls sang other verses too:

I had a little brother and his name was Tiny Tim
I put him in the bath tub to learn him how to swim
He drank up all the water he ate up all the soap
He died the next morning with a bubble in his throat
In came the doctor in came the nurse
In came the lady with the big fat purse
Out went the doctor out went the nurse
Out went the lady with the big fat purse.

All this chanting to a jumping rope that went faster and faster, the rope handlers hoping the jumper would miss so they could have their turn. Adiós, Peggy. Adiós, Betty. I never saw you after the war.

KICK-ME-HARD

Kick-Me-Hard appeared every year at Halloween. Kelly, Segal and Bacigalupi went to the 5 and 10 and bought a box of chalk which though it resembled the chalk at P.S. 11 was cheaper and consequently softer and disappeared more rapidly as they used it. Sometimes Kelly, Segal and Bacigalupi were known to swipe chalk from P.S. 11. Then at Halloween they went around marking the sidewalk squares Kick-Me-Hard, especially the smaller slate squares near the open lots. If another Bronx citizen walked along and stepped in that square everyone had the right to kick him, with the result that in late October citizens were zig-zagging and hopping all over the Bronx, stepping in one square and avoiding the other.

Akin to Kick-Me-Hard was CHALKED SLAT FROM AN ORANGE CRATE. Jackie Smealy one October got blue and yellow chalk for his orange crate slats and between these and horse manure balls (q.v.) he was very much to be feared. This soft chalk was also used for drawing the bases and baselines of stickball, punch ball, diamond ball, box ball and checkers; potsy for the girls, I Declare War and writing *I Love You* or *Genie Loves Mary*. As I revise my thoughts I feel that after Schapiro's candy store chalk was the most important institution in the Bronx since all the others depended on it, and I am thinking of writing an essay "On A Piece Of Chalk."

At Halloween my friends also took their mother's silk stocking, filled the foot with flour, tied a knot at the ankle and swatted your back with it, like a medieval mace.

You never saw chalk in front of 1235 Unie. Even Kelly was afraid of our super's frown.

KICK-THE-CAN

A worthy cognate of Ringalevio Caw Caw Caw. See Chapter 6.

KING OF THE HILL

The park under the real Washington Bridge over the Harlem was very steep, a cliff almost, and there on the hill we played King Of The Hill. One of the knights, usually it was Big Jim Phelan, got on top of the hill and the others tried to rush him and tear him down, and as he fell one of the crowd would run to the top and yell "King Of The Hill." Then we had to rush him. It was a great deal of fun, I mean a lot of fun, the kind of free-for-all that's so important when you're twelve years old.

LEAF CIGARETTES

In the fall Bronx citizens took one of their mother's brown paper bags, brought it to the lots, tore it roughly into six inch squares, got dried brown maple leaves, crumpled them into bits, placed this autumnal tobacco on the paper and rolled them into cigarettes; in want of a glue joint they used abundant saliva to hold the ensemble together. Then they lit up. Although I don't smoke now I used to smoke and I know from experience that the body and aroma of maple leaf cigarettes surpasses everything that Camels, Luckies, Chesterfields, Old Golds and the Schulte Cigar Stores had to offer. They were real Havanas which nobody thought to write on: "Surgeon General Has Determined That Maple Leaf Cigarettes Are Dangerous To Your Health." When you're twelve years old using such quality leaf tobacco nothing is dangerous to your health.

LENDING LIBRARY

On Ogden Avenue about half-way to the movie was Lending Library, a card shop with racks of books you could rent for five cents a day or twenty-five cents a week. They were best sellers and detective stories. You could get books free at the Public Library but some people preferred Lending Library; they seemed to be cigarette smoking women in their thirties and forties, secretaries, home from a day's work wanting to while away an evening or perhaps even get through an evening and not wanting to walk a mile to the Public Library down by Judge Smith's hill. A convenient book shop. Irving's drug store for cigarettes and soda and three doors down to Lending Library. Television has destroyed the Ogden Theater and Lending Library. Things were better in the old days; everybody knows that.

LOLLIPOP
The correct term for circular hard candy on a stick. Foreigners sometimes speak of suckers, a familiar barbarism in the Midwest, but every Bronx citizen knows the correct term is lollipop. Lollipops came in four flavors, cherry, lime, lemon and orange, in the order of their popularity. Madame Fanny Farmer introduced a licorice brand, but this upstart never flourished being strange to the quintessence of lollipop; the quintessential lollipop, moreover, had a thin stick made of wood rather than the insubstantial rolled paper plastics you see today.

LOOSIES
These loose cigarettes have been discussed under Bronx Institutions and Candy Store, but they are so important a part of Bronx culture they must be repeated here. For one cent you could smoke a Camel, Lucky, Old Gold or Chesterfield, and unlike the cigarettes today loosies weren't bad for your health. Segal smoked Camels and if a pack wasn't opened he asked Schapiro to open one, which he'd do sometimes and sometimes he wouldn't. Botchie didn't smoke and always took a seltzer. Sometimes Schapiro would open Wings and sometimes I'd ask for them. Wings were longer, not as good, but longer. You got more for your money.

LOTS
Referred to as "The Lots." The Bronx is the finest piece of real estate in the world, so much so that Manhattan with its Wall Street, Night Clubs, Garment Industry and other enterprises anxiously built bridges over to the Bronx in order to be connected to its grandeur. Some people speak of meadows in the Bronx and hills and woods but the truth is the Bronx is one vast rock from East to West and North to South, two hundred square miles of solid ancient rock; just one lapidary monument out of geology, more formidable than Gibraltar, greater than the Moncayo. You could stick a skyscraper five thousand feet tall in the Bronx and you wouldn't need a foundation, only a basement to connect it to the sewer and water pipes below, no deep pilings, the rock does it all. And so the Bronx had block after block of the most massive buildings in the world, well constructed, firm structures no earthquakes could ever budge. Every fifth block, where the crags resisted drilling or the Great Depression brought construction to a halt, was a large empty lot. The one on University Avenue was four hundred feet long running three hundred feet over to Merriam Avenue, one hundred and twenty thousand square feet or three acres; and the lot opposite near the High Bridge itself and running down to

Undercliff was larger, with rock caves and *the woods*. There was another lot down Ogden near P.S. 11 and yet another near the 44th Police Precinct Station.

You cooked your mickies (q.v.) in the lots, burned your Christmas trees there or sometimes went there just to build a fire. There were rumors in *the woods*, however, of Pee Wee's Gang and you had to be careful. Pee Wee was very small and ten years older than we and he had a way of spitting a saliva bead through his center teeth and holding a cigarette in the corner of his mouth that was scary. One day I was standing in front of 1235 and one of Pee Wee's Gang, Ralph, came by and said: "Hey, kid, I need a match." I ran upstairs to the kitchen, got three wood stick matches and brought them down. He struck a match on the cement (it's a good thing for him Super didn't see him), lit up, tilted his head and blew smoke in the air. He puckered up his face and said: "Thanks, kid." Then he sauntered off cupping the butt in his hand. He seemed all right, he didn't hurt me. I saw Pee Wee once, on the landing of the steps down below 1225 Unie leading to Undie, and I heard him say: "I hate my old man."

In *the woods* was a deep crater ten by ten, with some boards and rugs over it. They say Pee Wee's Gang dug it and it was their hideaway. This was in the early thirties, before 1935. I have never heard of Pee Wee since. I hope he's all right.

MALTEDS

An important dietary phenomenon, they were ten cents. "I want a three glass maltèd, Mr. Schapiro, and don't put in the frozen milk. It puffs up too much." Somehow malteds were always chocolate, I don't recall any vanilla or strawberry malteds, maybe strawberry once in awhile.

MICKIES

Roast mickies, potatoes you cooked in the lots in fires made of orange crates; on the way home from P.S. 11 you stopped at the stores for your orange crates. Sometimes you got branches from a tree or wood from other boxes to use for the fire but such lumber was not essentially pure. For a true mickie you needed potatoes and the slats and ends from orange crates (q.v.).

MOVIES

Good movie houses had a Greek soda fountain next door; you could tell a good theater by the store at its side. The Ogden Theater had a Greek soda parlor, so did the Loew's Paradise up at Fordham Road, and the Park Plaza at Unie and Tremont. The Loew's 175th in Manhattan had one too; all the Loew's had one, that's how you could tell they were a good theater. The RKO's had them too but not always, they were just a cut below the Loew's, high class but not quite that high. The Greek soda fountains had the best black and whites (q.v.) of all, better than

Schraft's, better even than Irving's, but they were terribly expensive and cost a quarter; and their candy was the same way, expensive, the kind you weigh out and slip into a bag with a silver scoop. You never bought Good 'N Plenty, Lousy Heads or Bubble Gum at the Greek's; if you bought anything it would be special caramels, some with nuts in them, or dark chocolate covered filberts or orange slices, although to tell the truth if you said filberts in those days Kelly, Segal, and Bacigalupi wouldn't know what you were talking about and neither would I. Sometimes though you had an extra dime and went to the Greek's, and that French author was right about those little cakes; if you blindfolded me today, spun me around and took me to several places all over town and then to a fountain like that, the moment I walked in the door I'd say: "The Greek's." I could smell it. Besides, there was the glass cover on the tables and the ice cream parlor chairs. I didn't go there often but I loved the Greek's.

I haven't said much about the movies, have I? The movies are the greatest force in the advance of civilization, greater by far than Gutenberg's press. After all, Gutenberg's invention was for some whereas the movies are for all; not everybody reads but everybody in the Bronx went to the movies, the adults on Tuesday nights to get their free dishes and on Thursdays to play SCREENO, and then they stopped going on the weekends, turning the theater over to Kelly, Segal, Botchie and me. No adults went on weekends except a few who had to be there to take you in; there had to be some adults to take you in, otherwise you weren't allowed. After that you went to the children's section where the lady dressed like a nurse was sitting. Some elegant theaters like the Park Plaza, the Parky, up on Tremont Avenue had a man with an organ which rose up out of a pit and we sang songs between the features. The Parky's organist was Lou Bonda. I forget the name of the man at the Loew's 175th, no, it was Oscar.

NEDICKS AND WHITE TOWER

The Nedicks hot dog is the only thoroughbred descendant of yesteryear's Coney Island Chicken. Although two of these poultries made a nourishing, satisfying meal they required a special gravy for palatability, namely, Nedick's orange drink in which you could see the fibers of the inner orange and the rind floating around. For fifteen cents Bronx citizens had a meal that only Thanksgiving turkey can be compared to.

White Tower was a more expensive beef version of Nedicks; whereas Nedicks' comestibles a la carte cost fifteen cents, White Tower's were twenty-five cents, for two Salisbury Steaks on buns and a cup of savory coffee. The coffee they serve today is but a thin, pale imitation of White Tower's Colombian best.

Do you know, I have made a grave omission in this lexicon, I have left out Automat? How could I leave out Automat?

Perhaps because I was young in 1930 and only the swells could afford to visit Automat. I went once with my Uncle Joe, who gave me a handful of nickels and it was fun clicking the machines and getting creamed spinach, spaghetti, baked beans and rolls. I looked through the little windows, saw creamed spinach, put in the nickel and opened the little door: click! It was fun. I was a swell in the Bronx.

NOMENCLATURE

Bronx nomenclature. I guess you could call these games because they were in a way; Bronx knights were always playing. I have already explained Heggies (q.v.). If you were walking along and another guy waved his hand in your face and you flinched, he said "Two for flinchin' " and socked your bicep two times, and if you hadn't flinched you said "seven and a half for lyin' " and socked his bicep seven times and twisted his ear. Then he told you were lyin' and tried to do the same to you, and once again there were altercations. Sometimes a whole gang were socking one another on the arm. But the most memorable name is yet to come.

One Sunday Kelly, Segal, Botchie and I decided to go to Loew's 175th to the movies and we took the route over Highbridge (the bridge is boarded up now, you can't get in or out of the Bronx). When we got to the middle we started to throw our stones into the water to watch the splash. A coal barge was going up the river to the yards at 172nd Street, Bronx side, under the Washington Bridge, below Undy and Sedgwick, and we watched the tug edging it to its berth. Just then the sewers let out from Manhattan and we watched the coffee and cream water push a path fifty feet out into the river. There were things floating in this new stream, hunks of excrement, grunt mud, and some white objects like rubber balloons, maybe ten inches long. I had never seen them before. "What's that?", I said to Kelly, who was like our leader, sort of, he knew a great deal. Kelly simply said: "Scum bags." Bronx nomenclature. Scientific accuracy. In later years we often walked over Highbridge and reserved our best stones for scumbags.

They say there's a poet who writes odes to simple things, to an artichoke, to a beet, to an onion:

Oh onion, luminous balloon!

and that's the new idea of poetry they say; anything can be the object of your lyre. I am wondering if there is a bard somewhere, a grandson of my Highbridge perhaps, who is disposed to write a simple poem:

ODE TO A SCUMBAG

Oh scumbag, luminous balloon!

192

ORANGE CRATE

Expert cabinet makers talk of mahogany, cherry, maple, oak, walnut and cedar, but every Bronx boy knows that the most distinguished wood is orange crate. He needed it to cook mickies, to make roller skate boards (q.v.), to make chalk-the-back sticks at Halloween, to fashion clappers and to construct a certain kind of cardboard shooting gun. He might even use it to store things in at home. I haven't explained the clappers so I'll explain them now. They were two thin sticks six inches long and an inch wide, sanded smooth, which Bronx citizens held between their index finger and middle finger and ring finger of the same hand and then created a clapping, snapping sound with the hand's rapid movement. These orange crate castanets demanded great skill.

I shall also explain the wooden gun made from the end pieces of the box, where the wood was thicker. Bronx citizens removed the rectangle from one end of the box, took out the thin center piece and then cut off a corner, leaving four inches on one side of the corner and seven inches on the other. This pistol shaped object was made serviceable by cutting two notches at the juncture of barrel and handle (where the cocking arm is on a cap pistol) for the passage of a double rubber band; then a nail was driven in at the mouth of the barrel, a thick rubber band was placed around it, the two rubber ribbons running the length of the barrel to the notch, which held the band tightly in place. A 3/4 inch square of cardboard was placed on the shaft with one rubber ribbon below the cardboard and one above, and when the upward pressure of the citizen's thumb released the band from the notch, the cardboard bullet went flying towards its target. Some pistoleros developed an uncanny accuracy, especially when aiming their gun at the seat of another citizen's pants. Here is a picture:

Most important of all, this pistol must be made of orange crate, no other substance will do. The only wood as select as orange crate is cheesebox (q.v), but cheesebox is too small to make a pistol; one could, however, resort to it for clappers.

PITCHING PENNIES

To pitch pennies in front of Irving's drug store on Sunday morning you had to be an adult of nineteen and wear a fedora and suit jacket after Mass. So I never played except by invitation with Denny a couple of times and Big Phelan, but I watched

Mickie and Hughie, Bob and the others pitch pennies against the red brick of Irving's wall just beneath the large plate glass window with the medicine signs. They were very good at it and could sometimes get a leaner, which was a penny resting against the wall. You couldn't beat a leaner, all you could hope for was a tie. You had to shoot all the way from the curb across Irving's wide sidewalk. When we tried it we were lucky to get it a foot from the wall. That was 1934; Denny, Big Phelan and I were ten years old.

POSTAL TELEGRAPH
I always wanted to be a Postal Telegraph Delivery Boy when I grew up. They had blue uniforms, a garrison hat, leather leg guards, their own bicycle and an important job delivering messages around the city. And they say they made big money. Clarence Mackey owned Postal Telegraph, and my Uncle Billy told me he didn't want his daughter to marry Irving Berlin, who made his money writing songs on Tin Pan Alley. Sometimes I wonder why because Irving Berlin was famous, but then if you had a Navy of blue uniforms working for you maybe you wouldn't want your daughter marrying Irving Berlin either. Postal Telegraph went under in the thirties and Uncle Billy told me that Irving Berlin had to bail out his father-in-law, which was nice of him; still it's a pity he had to be bailed out. Those blue uniforms gave you a sense of peace and security, and courtesy. The Bronx 1930: things were better then, anymore you don't see such courtesy.

PUNCHBALL
There were lesser games related to stickball, subgenres, rather like dialects before a language. There was punchball, played on the same chalk field in the street as stickball, only we used our fist to propel the ball rather than an old broomstick. After the war they used the word *Spaulding* to name the ball, which was pink, but before the war I don't recall Bronxites using the word, and the ball was apt to be white or pink. This phenomenon shows once again that the Second World War is the Watershed Of History: until 1941, *ball*—The War—after 1945, *Spaulding*.

PUTTY BLOWERS
We called them putty blowers and sometimes bean shooters, a ten inch cylindrical piece of sheet metal with a three-eighth inch gauge and wooden mouthpiece. Anthropologists will call them blowpipes. We filled our mouths with small white beans and blew them one at a time at the other guy; we had nice wars in the lots (q.v.) with putty blowers. If you only had one bean in your mouth you could blow it harder with greater accuracy, but this single-shot, reloading method left you exposed to someone's Gatling machine gun fire; so you compromised, three or four

beans at a time, a BAR man rather than a rifleman or machine gunner. Anymore you don't see putty blowers. Distinguished legislators have outlawed them because they can hurt people they say, but then distinguished legislators never shot at Kelly, Bacigalupi and Segal in the lots. Distinguished legislators don't know what fun is, they never have fun. When you ran out of beans you used paper spitballs.

RADIO
Denny went home every night at 5 p.m. to hear Buck Rogers and Jack Armstrong The All American Boy; I didn't because I wasn't allowed. We only had radio on Sunday nights, 6 to 9, Fred Allen, Jack Benny, Fibber McGee and Molly, Major Bowes, George Burns and Gracie Allen, Charlie McCarthy, and I remember hearing a broadcast from Europe once in awhile, someone screaming into the loudspeaker. But that's all I heard. Joe Penna wanna buy a duck was on a weekday night, so I never got to hear him, but I used to hear the All Saints Boys discuss him. It is important to note that Radio was a fairly renowned Bronx institution, after the movies, Schapiro's papers and G-8 And His Battle Aces. The most important program was Jack Armstrong The All American Boy.

RAILROAD TRAIN
Important in the West Bronx because it ran along the Harlem River and stopped at Highbridge. We used to go down to the river to marvel at the steam engines there, vital monsters with energy bursting out their wheels, and clouds of vapor. No other machine seems so dynamic and strong. Down near the station was a factory where we used to gather clay for baking trays and dishes in our orange crate fires in the lots. Besides us only Fordham Road near Roger's Department Store had trains, so we were the two privileged areas of the Bronx. Vehicles today seem so lifeless compared to our iron dragons.

RINGALEVIO
The paradigmatic form of hide and seek, attributed to an ancient Bronxite, Ringo Levy. See Chapter 6.

ROLLER SKATES
We didn't have these fancy plastic jobs they have now; the wheels were made of hollow metal and when one of them wore through we had to take it off and replace it with another, an exercise demanding mechanical skill. We used to skate in the streets, which were so much smoother than the rough sometimes lightly pebbled sidewalks, though sometimes we'd find an extremely smooth, expensive sidewalk that was the best skating of all except you had to avoid the cracks, you had to raise your foot quickly every time you came to a crack. We played street hockey with roller skates, which was the best fun of all, and

after playing a couple of hours your feet felt funny when you took your skates off and walked on them, like floating in the air. Something like the astronauts. Roller skates were also used for Skate Wagons (q.v.).

SALOOGEY
In the Middle West they call this KEEP AWAY though you must admit SALOOGEY sounds better. Five or six boys are playing with a ball, tossing it around when all of a sudden one yells Saloogey! and they toss it to one another except for one boy who is *it*; prosaically put, they try to keep it away from him. If he succeeds in intercepting it he becomes a tosser and the one who last threw it is *it*, the victim now of Saloogey!

SALVATION ARMY
West Bronx citizens from High Bridge to Fordham Road knew the Salvation Army, who probably traveled as far east as the Concourse, I can't be sure of that boundary, but for me the dividing line in everything was the Grand Concourse, there was nothing east of the Concourse, that was it. My world: High Bridge to Fordham, Harlem River to Concourse, the most historic site in History. The Salvation Army had a college at Tremont Avenue and Loring Place near Unie and every Saturday night they came marching out with their band, down Unie to the Washington Bridge and over the Harlem River to Manhattan. I remember seeing them over at 181st Street just west of St. Nicholas Avenue in front of Wertheimer's and the Automat playing to beat the band and drawn in a circle. I loved the Salvation Army and still do, preferring it to St. Vincent DePaul, Good Will and all the others. Every Saturday night a beautiful girl came to our house selling the *War Cry*, which I bought and never read, and my mother would invite her in—sometimes there were two or three of them—for coffee. She would come in and talk for five minutes radiating joy, the real joy, the kind you see when kids are diving in a swimming pool or a fellow and his girl display when they take a stroll to the Hall of Fame on a May Sunday afternoon, or the joy I had when Uncle Billy took me shooting the .22 at the 77th Division range; not the ersatz joy. The Salvation Army girl was the most beautiful girl I have ever seen, with that blue bonnet and ribbon, was it red, it strikes me as red, tied under her chin. And the most joyous. I was ten years old.
It's funny about my mother and the Salvation Army. Here she made the wise choice of sending me to P.S. 11, then at the sacrifice of paying tuition the unwise choice of sending me to All Saints, where I learned religious intolerance although she was herself tolerant in that area, not class tolerant of course because delivery boys were delivery boys, persons who belonged downstairs, but religiously open to all. And except for 1928 my father never mentioned religion, politics, ideology or anything of

196

that nature; so here I was an All Saints Jansenist going to that insular institution from Monday to Friday and then admiring the Salvation Army on Saturday night. I suppose you could call this change of perspective American.

Now I can picture some wag of a critic, one of those—*ists*, formalist, structuralist, Marxist, semiologist, deconstructionist or some other, saying: "Irony; Jims in an ironist, he's spoofing the Salvation Army, he's talking tongue in cheek, that girl with the bonnet is Major Barbara." But the truth is I'm not spoofing, I'm really not, and I don't need some pedant of a critic to tell me how I'm writing. The proof is that I never saw the Salvation Army girl's Joy in Brother Solomon—in some of the other brothers, yes, Reilly had it—but not in Solomon. Nor do I descry it in the formalists, structuralists, Marxists, semiologists, deconstructionists or other—*ists*.

SAND BOX

I am not referring to playground sandboxes which we had of course: "Sonny, stop throwing sand in Sheila's eyes. Mommy told you." So Sonny keeps throwing sand in Sheila's eyes.

No, the sand box I speak of was under Comfort Station, on the hill, a large green wooden box with a lid for getting at the sand they used on the streets and trolley tracks in winter. When we discovered it we had fun there. Sometimes we'd get inside the box and the others got on the lid and if they stayed too long the one inside might be crying. I remember crying once; it's fun to get in a coffin but it wasn't fun to stay there.

SATURDAY EVENING POST

I seem to have a lot of S's on my list, some of which are admittedly small institutions, small but memorable. After all, you might say that a B entry like BUBBLE GUM is also of little consequence, but every time I see a certain Big League baseball player blowing bubbles at third base I think of P.S. 11 and the Gowdy Gum Company of Boston; to a Bronx boy these images are formidable. They loom large. Anyway, on Friday afternoons the *Saturday Evening Post* man came to Unie to park his car opposite Irving's drug store. Then his salesmen appeared, Botchie, Segal, Kelly, Denny, Big Phelan, Smealy to pick up their magazines and distribute them. Five cents a piece, and they got a penny from every copy, but more than that they could build up points for copies sold and earn the prizes pictured in the *Saturday Evening Post* man's catalogue. Denny got a beautiful pen knife after a couple of months and the others got prizes too. I wasn't one of the salesmen for the same reason I wasn't a Postal Telegraph boy: *she wouldn't let me.* Someone will say: "You're pouting; fifty years later and you're still pouting." Maybe so, but I think everybody's father should take him out and say: "You be a Saturday Evening Post boy!" Or, "You ride for Western Union!"

I never realized until years later the fine character of this magazine. P.G. Wodehouse wrote for the *Saturday Evening Post* and I never knew it, and those Norman Rockwell paintings are classics now, American Goyas. The most lamentable effect of television is the disappearance of the Saturday Evening Post. And of those prizes.

SCHOOLYARD
They call baseball the All American Sport but they should say All American minus the Bronx where the sport is Schoolyard Basketball; indeed this entry in my dictionary might be titled Schoolyard Basketball. Two Bronx citizens show up at P.S. 104 on a Saturday morning at seven. The twenty foot anchor fence is locked so they climb over it, the only proper way to enter the court for Schoolyard Basketball. They shoot fouls and play one on one; two more show up, and two more. They play half court. "You fouled, Botchie . . ." "Up yours, Kelly . . ." They play till nine-thirty, which is breakfast time, so they leave two players to hold the court and go over to the candy store to break their fast with two Pepsies (twelve full ounces that's a lot) and a loosie (q.v.). Denny pours Planters Peanuts into his Pepsie because he needs vitamins for the big game after breakfast when ten athletes will show up and play full court. In the eighteenth century Jovellanos wrote that entertainments and diversions are necessary in a well-ordered society, which explains why the Bronx was such a well-ordered society; there were no juvenile delinquents in the old days because of Schoolyard basketball. If big cities today built more schoolyards with twenty foot fences for climbing over and gave out good breakfast and basketballs they would cut the crime rate. It's surprising what two Pepsies and a loosie will do for you after a workout in the yard. Los Angeles could be like the Bronx in the golden days when the ships were made of wood and the men were made of iron, not the other way around the way it is now. Oh happy days! Oh Bronx!

SCOUTS
I refer to the Boy Scouts of America, BSA, Troop 205, which met in the Methodist church on Featherbed Lane. I have always liked that appellation, Featherbed Lane, surely the most beautifully named though most modest street in the world (it's all burned out now, gutted with fire, there are no more awnings). I have sometimes thought that Shakespeare shopped at a place called Featherbed Lane or even coined the word for it's worthy of his genius, Featherbed Lane.
At the Boy Scouts we used to play Johnny-Ride-The-Pony. In one squad a scout stood facing out, his back to the wall, while the others bent over towards him forming a train; then the other squad came running as hard as they could, one by one, leaping on the train, hoping to crush it in. If the train of upturned behinds held, it was the other squad's turn to form it; if not,

they had to stay there and get run at again.

The best of all were the hikes over to the Palisades. Roy Brown used to take us over the two Washington Bridges to New Jersey, and then north. It's all built up now. The summer of the year Errol Flynn played Robin Hood we went to Ten Mile River Camp in the Catskills, where we all cut good stout staves from the trees. For two weeks we got out our cudgels to give blows and parries, just like Robin, Little John, Friar Tuck and the other merry yeomen. I looked for dogs to catch arrows in their teeth but there weren't any. It was a lot of fun.

SCUM BAGS
    A Bronx decoration. See the article titled Nomenclature.

SELTZER
    The joke is that a new apartment house has bathrooms with three faucets, hot water, cold water and seltzer, or if it's Segal's house, celery seltzer; in any case, you couldn't quench your thirst in the Bronx without seltzer. Plain water wouldn't do; the fine air, Harlem brine, dust and exercise were such that thirst could only be satisfied with sparkling water. This was particularly true after Saturday morning in the school yard at P.S. 104; in all my born days I never saw Schapiro serve water.
    There was another kind of seltzer besides Schapiro's tap brand that came in quart bottles with a trigger at the top. The truck came once a week to leave a case of twelve bottles at the apartments of the predilect, of which I was not one because my mother didn't believe in this fine Bronx institution, seltzer.

SERIALS
    Saturday afternoon meant movies at the Parkie, corner of Unie and Tremont, with Lou Bonda on the organ and the dots on the screen jumping from word to word to tell you what to sing, Pathé News, Selected Short Subjects, two movies and the serials. Selected Short Subjects were mainly cartoons although once in a while you'd get a March of Time or something that was supposed to educate you. But most important of all were the serials, which ran for fifteen weeks and at the end of each episode someone was falling off a cliff or out a window, or being run over or lethally shot at—TO BE CONTINUED NEXT WEEK—which meant you had to go back next week to find out what happened. Everybody went back. And next week they played one minute of the last reel over again only this time something intervened to frustrate the obvious death of the previous week; somebody caught the lad before he fell from the cliff, or his clothes got caught on a bush, holding him until his friends could get there to pull him to safety. I particularly remember two serials, one about an underground city, the other about a killer aviator who always delivered his fatal message by a model airplane with a dart nose. The seemingly nice fellow was the killer aviator and in the last

frame of each reel he was always there talking to someone when the evil message came with the dart airplane and stuck in the wall, so he appeared to be innocent. It seems he would hold the model airplane behind his back, launch it surreptitiously and it would boomerang, turning around one hundred and eighty degrees and fix itself into a door. The threatening message was in the empennage. In the final episode the killer aviator had someone in his sights and was all set to press the trigger on the stick when the really good fellow flew up behind him, set his machine guns blazing and shot him from the sky. It was very exciting.

Occasionally you will hear derogatory remarks about serials—melodramas, pot boilers, thumpers, Grade B's they are apt to call them—but such criticism has no warrant. Dickens, Trollope, Meredith all wrote serial novels, a few chapters every month, and they are no Grade B'ers, and so did Balzac in France, Galdós in Spain, and all the others; indeed, the Spaniards call them "novels by delivery," a little bit being delivered every month. So no matter what the Aristarchians may say, I'll stick with *David Copperfield* and the serial movies about the killer aviator who delivered his threats by a model balsa wood plane.

SHOEMAKER

Mr. Bacigalupi, Joey's father, was a shoemaker. I have heard pedants say that Bronx shoemakers were really cobblers, that shoemakers make shoes while cobblers repair them, but Bronx citizens used the word shoemaker and if someone mentioned the word cobbler to Kelly, Segal, Phelan, and me we wouldn't have known what he meant. Once again the New York Commissioner of Licenses had a peculiar law and once again the American Civil Liberties Union took him to court and once again they were defeated by the nine justices in Washington: To be a shoemaker you had to be an Italian, no others need apply. In the Bronx the movie theater soda parlor had to be owned by Costopoulos, the candy store by Schapiro and the shoemaker's by Bacigalupi. And why shouldn't the law be that way? If Costopoulos serves better candy and soda, why give the store to Kochenmeister or Kozinski? It doesn't make sense. That is why the American Civil Liberties Union are called eggheads; they have no common sense. Mr. Bacigalupi always stood in the window of his store carving pieces of leather and running the shoes on the abrasive disks and brushes spinning from his machine. I always liked to go to his store to pick up the shoes; the smell of polish and shoemaker's glue was wonderful and whenever I smell something like that I return immediately in mind to the Bronx, the block on Unie between Merriam and the real George Washington Bridge, near Ogden, Boscobel and Undie overlooking the Harlem, where the words thine and mine didn't exist and damsels strolled the streets at night unharmed and unmolested, and citizens drew their sustenance from the Gowdy

Gum Company of Boston whose comestibles cost a penny. Things were better in the old days, they really were. I speak from experience, the only authentic authority. Bacigalupi's polish and shoe glue. *Petites madeleines.*

SHOESHINE BOY
One of the finest schools for young citizens was Shoeshine Boy, where a young man could verse himself in the free enterprise system of the United States of America. The historiography of Horatio Alger has preserved this institution for posterity but I never read Horatio Alger, I never even heard of him, and neither did Kelly, Segal or Bacigalupi. But we didn't have to read him, we *saw* him with our own eyes. Shoeshine Boy came to Irving's drug store on Sunday morning and stayed until two or three, shining up shoes for a nickel. I remember the older penny-pitching crowd seemed to enjoy pushing their fedoras back a little and raising their foot for the pedal on the box of Shoeshine Boy, upon which the latter would take out his brush and bottle of liquid and clean up the shoe; then he'd wax it, run the cloth over it, run the big dry brush and the cloth again and finally snap the rag with a flourish to signal he had finished. Then Hughie, Mickie, Big O'Brien and the others would push their fedoras back a little more, remove their foot and put the other one there for the same treatment. No journeyman, no guildsman, no master, no artisan, no philosopher ever professed a finer craft than Shoeshine Boy, who took such pride in his creation.
I wanted to be Shoeshine Boy. I remember once I got a couple of crates, not orange crate but peach crate, which was thicker, and made a shoebox. I wanted to go to the Five and Ten over on 181st Street and St. Nicholas Avenue to buy the brushes and everything; why the shoe polish only cost a dime and so did the black and brown bottles of liquid dye. The brushes cost more but you could have bought the whole caboodle for less than a dollar, which you could make back easily the first Sunday. But she wouldn't give me the money, it was a question of class. Shoeshine Boy, Postal Telegraph, Western Union and *Saturday Evening Post* agents were delivery boys and James Ignatius Murphy was not going to be a Downstairs delivery boy. The Murphys were different; leaving their ancestral home in 1848 they got off the boat decades before the others. If I had been Shoeshine Boy I could have bought storm boots in Thom McAn's Window, which laced up to your knee and had the pen knife and secret knife pocket on the side. Two Sundays shining shoes and they were mine.

SKATE WAGON BOXES
They are as vivid to me as cheesebox, tin foil balls and sun pictures; they were keen, real keen, better than any of the unsubstantial plastic creations you see today. All you needed was

a metal skate, a three and a half foot two-by-four board and orange crate (q.v.). You unscrewed the skate into two parts and nailed one of the plates with two wheels on it to one end of the two-by-four and the other plate and wheels to the other end; then you set the wheels on the ground and nailed orange crate to one end of the top side. Oh yes, I forgot, you needed a couple of slats for handle bars, just like the ones on the Harley Davidsons. Some Bronx citizens painted their skate boxes and put streamers, reflectors and names on them, and some even put lights on them but this was for show, the real elements being a skate divided in two, a two-by-four, orange crate and handle bars. I can still see them coming down Merriam Hill, six or eight in echelon like G-8 and his Battle Aces and the Lone Eagle. No Alexander, no Arthur, no Roland ever knew companions such as these. Napoleon's legions would have been dismayed! No one could have stood up to those knights in echelon coming down the hill on Skate Wagon Boxes, Caesar's Romans, Hannibal's elephants, Assyrian chariot, no one! Bronx knights of yore! The olden days! The golden days! I salute you! They don't know what it was like, this pasty faced nation today. Oh Bronx, Oh Bronx, I salute you!

SLING SHOT
There weren't many of these, but a few. You went to the woods to cut a small fork from a tree, peeled it, whittled it, notched both tops of the Y and fastened a big rubber band in the notches. Then you could shoot pebbles and the beans you had for putty blower (q.v.). They sold some artificial metal sling shots for awhile, the price three cents, but these were never as good as the natural ones so they disappeared. I imagine they have been outlawed. Everything good has been outlawed today, firecrackers, putty blowers, sling shots, sirens, musical car horns, spotlights, everything. Things aren't what they used to be.

STICKBALL
Our lives were formed by games, the candy store and games, and we had so many of them, so imaginative, so beautiful, so intelligently devised that I find children nowadays dull and boring.
Of all the games, stickball was king. The monarch. One strike and you're out. I remember one day Kelly was pitching. The rubber ball took a bounce half way to the chalked square plate, came up waist high and as it crossed over the plate took a wicked curve away from the batter, Bacigalupi. He swung and missed: "Take your finger out of the ball, Kelly, you prick. Pitch it over."
"Bofangoo, Botchie, you're out."
The argument went on for five minutes over Kelly's finger in the ball, as illegal a stratagem as a spitter in baseball, and finally it was resolved when someone yelled "cheese it, the cops." The old bag up in apartment 31 at 1215 had called the

44th precinct again and the squad car was rounding Boscobel and Unie, from Undy. Bacigalupi threw the stick down the sewer and everyone headed for the cellar at 1231, the best of all the cellars. While one sportsman hid there in the storage room, the others headed for the backyard fences leading to 1239, 1235, 1225 and out of 1225 to the steps down to Undy. The cops came and went and then the sportsmen emerged from their holes. They got another stick to pry up the iron sewer plate and held Segal by the ankles while he was lowered into the sewer to retrieve the bat; when O'Reilly was there he went in because he was smaller and easier to hold. Then the game began again, home plate chalked in the middle of the street, 1st base next to 1235, 2nd base in the middle toward 1225, 3rd base next to 1232, with a half moon for the pitcher's box. Cynics have derided this ancient sport and the aristocrats who played it, but they might remember that Leo Durocher was looking for Willie Mays one day because he wanted him down at the Polo Grounds. This is the same Willie Mays who batted .342 and had six hundred home runs against the pros. He couldn't find him. His million dollar king of swat and star fielder was down in Harlem playing stickball. Willie knew which was the monarch and which the pale reflection; stickball first, then baseball. Oh Kelly, Bacigalupi, Segal! Where are you now? You deserve your Hall of Fame, like Willie, Gehrig, Ruth. It is my ardent hope you find it in these pages.

STICK BALL OFF THE WALL

Which you played when you only had two, three or four Bronx knights to go with. It was simple. Kelly chalked a strike zone box on the wall, waist to chest high, and a plate on the ground in front of it where the batter stood. Kelly pitched into the zone, calling balls and strikes. If the batter missed the ball or didn't swing, the ball bounced off the wall and returned to the pitcher, so you didn't need a catcher; if the batter connected there were rules for singles, doubles, triples and homers, depending on the size of the playing field. One day Kelly pitched and called "Strike."

"It was a ball. It was a mile out!"

"Bofangoo, Segal."

"Up yours, Kelly."

Usually you had to go to the P.S. 11 school yard to play Stickball Off The Wall. Can you imagine Super (q.v.) at 1235 permitting you to pitch or slam a ball against the side of his building with all those windows sitting there? Not in a million years. His scowl would take care of that.

STINK BOMBS

They were made of old film and paper. One day Botchie and I went to the alley next to the Ogden Theater and found strips of film in ash cans. We brought them to the lots on Unie, wrapped them in newspaper, twisted the ends, lit them and when they started to flare stamped on them, an action resulting in clouds of celluloid smoke. A stink bomb! I have seen older boys light a bomb, stamp on it, throw it into a store and then hold the door handle so the owner couldn't open it. The store soon filled with smoke. I can honestly say that Botchie and I never threw one into a store, perhaps because his father owned one, but we might have. Some did and some didn't but everyone knew about STINK BOMBS.

STORM BOOTS.
Mentioned in Shoeshine Boy (q.v.). They were neat, they were keen. Thom McAn had them for $3.33 in black or brown leather, all sizes reaching up to your knees, with the pen knife and secret pocket. I always wanted them and still do in a way, I often think of them. But I was supposed to have had rickets and needed orthopedic shoes, and besides only certain classes wore them. Murphys didn't wear them.

SUN PICTURES
How could I forget sun pictures? They were so much fun I fail to see how they can have died out, it doesn't make sense. Kids today don't know what they are missing, which is just as well perhaps for if they knew they might despair:

Oh sun pictures, glorious sun pictures,
laminations of days of yore,
creations of Bronx Michaelangelos,
tis certes we'll see you no more?

Similar to Michaelangelo's paint, brush and easel, the artist had three tools. First, a cardboard holder, three inches by five, with four small brackets in the corners similar to the ones philatelists use for mounting precious stamps. Then there was a piece of white developing paper slightly less than three by five, to fit into the brackets, and finally a film, a negative to be fitted over the developing paper and into the brackets also. The paper was less sensitive than the paper Kodak uses for developing snapshots but sensitive nevertheless to the light seeping through the film. You mounted the whole assembly in a dark area and stood facing the sun for two to three minutes; that was the art, the timing of the true artists. If your timing was short, the picture was underdeveloped, and too long, the paper turned a dark purple; but if you were on target you had a beautiful portrait of Our Gang, Tom Mix or Jean Harlow. What other art can compare with this, what other art is so natural, where the two artists are a human being and the sun, Apollo riding his chariot through the sky? Piano music comes from a human being and a bunch of wires; violin music, the same; paintings from a human being and oil; books from a human being and paper—they all have feet of clay, insubstantial prime matter. But sun pictures!

Sun pictures rise from a human being and God's own personification, the Sun, source of life! Sun pictures! Nature's pride!

The best place to take sun pictures was in the lots, just south of 1200 Unie. I remember once with Kelly, Segal and Bacigalupi, we went to Schapiro's and bought our sun picture packets in the yellow envelope for five cents. Then we went to the lots, prepared our art and looked west, across the sweep of the Harlem, our countenance and hands facing the mighty god. It was a summer's evening, a midsummer's dream. Oh Kelly, Segal, Bacigalupi, will I see you no more? Michaelangelos Buonabronxi! Will I see you no more?

SUPER

As important a figure in the Bronx polity as the king's sheriff in the medieval shire. See Chapter 20.

TAG

Tag is a common game, known to all civilizations, Egyptian, Greek, Etruscan, Roman, Renaissance, Baroque and Bronx, so I shall record it only briefly here. Ringalevio (q.v.) was a sort of tag I suppose, a Bronx version requiring the person who was it to apprehend his victim like a constable rather than just touch him, and he had to hold him until he yelled Ringalevio, Caw, Caw, Caw three times. I notice today that except for swimming pools kids don't play tag much, another sign of moral degeneration and America's need to restore the yeoman virtues of the Bronx, where citizens stood in presence of the good, the true and the beautiful every day.

THANKSGIVING

More properly called Anything-For-Thanksgiving, the greatest day of the Bronx year, as great as Christmas even and in some ways better. At Christmas you got good gifts, the best of the year, surpassing those you received on your birthday, but the joy of Thanksgiving was you went out and got the gifts yourself; you earned them by the sweat of your brow; they were your own creation. From door to door you went begging, singing out "Anything-For-Thanksgiving" with iambic stress and an extra full note on the—*giv*. That chant was music and the people who answered the doorbell gave you money. Nowadays they go trick or treating at Halloween but any Bronx boy will tell you that we never did, we went Anything-For-Thanksgiving the last Thursday of November. The sun was always shining, the air was crisp, the faces were smiling, the turkey had a finer aroma; anyone who remembers will tell you that the people and customs were better then. I realize this is the second time I've brought up Thanksgiving but I want posterity to know how good we had it for it may help them in their despair. Some of us really enjoyed Arcadia, The Bronx, New York, United States of America, 1930.

THROW DOWN THE KEYS AND A TANGERINE

Frequently pronounced "Tro' down the keys and a tangerine." I heard it on the car radio thirty years ago: "Hey Ma, tro' down the keys and a tangerine," that's all I heard as I was tuning in, and I smiled. I knew. I could see the window.

Kelly and I lived in 1245 and 1235 Unie on the third floor, and Segal and Botchie lived on the second and fourth floors of The House Of All Nations. The three of them lived in front apartments facing on Unie, and I lived in the rear, facing down Undy.

"Hey, Ma, tro' down my ball! Hey Ma, hey Ma!" Kelly was yelling up at the third floor window of 1245. Suddenly the window opened and a hand reached out dropping a rubber sphere two and a half inches in diameter. Nothing appeared but the hand and the ball, an automatic reaction. Put a coin in a machine and out comes the candy bar selected; yell up at a window "Hey, Ma, tro' down my ball," and out comes the object selected.

"Hey, Ma, tro' down my keys and a nickel." Bacigalupi was standing before The House of All Nations. This was different, keys, food, rubber balls come out of the apartment machine automatically but nickels require a higher explanation. The head of Botchie's mother appeared: "What for, Joey?"

"I need it for the candy store."

Mrs. Bacigalupi disappeared and returned with the desired coin. "Don't spend it all on gum, Joey"; she threw the nickel to the sidewalk and disappeared.

The most important part of a Bronx apartment house after the point (see Baseball-Against-The-Wall) was the front window, where families could communicate with the citizens below. Many women had pillows they lay on the window sill in warm weather, which explains why Bronx windows are the same width as bed pillows, built that way to specification; and they would lean there for an hour or two, watching the action on Unie. Their offspring didn't have to yell Ma so loud. This fenestration of pillows became extremely significant after the war, when people bought more automobiles than the streets could hold and parking spaces were getting scarce, and on top of that drivers had to alternate curbs each night to satisfy the exigencies of the Department of Sanitation. Women would lean on their pillows for hours on end while their husbands sat in the cars below waiting for their signal to drive to an open space. I once explained this to a farm boy at State East, but he wouldn't believe me; he thought I was joking. I joked a lot at that time for I was just seeing Dr. Megna, but I wasn't joking, I really meant it. And I do now: our old stickball fields are nothing but a parking lot.

1618: The Defenestration of Prague. 1930: The Defenestration of Bronx. "Hey, Ma, tro' down the keys and a tangerine."

TIN FOIL BALLS

A most important institution, to be rated just after Sun

Pictures (q.v.). Anyone not initiated to this ancient custom would not understand the deep significance of these apparently prosaic words: tin foil balls.

Cigarettes then were not like they are now, dessicated, bloodless specters of their former selves, and they did not bear a sign saying they were injurious to your health. In those days a Camel was a Camel, a Lucky a Lucky, a Chesterfield a Chesterfield and an Old Gold an Old Gold, there were only four brands really, not hundreds of brands the way you see them today with long filters, short filters, cigar imitators, tips, fancy names, high tar, low tar and other prevarications. No, in those days a cigarette was a cigarette, good, clean, strong smoking, and you'd walk a mile for a Camel. And more than that the packaging was good too, good firm cellophane, bright paper, imaginative jackets, and within, wrapped around twenty cigarettes, strong airtight paper and a three by five piece of tin foil. Camels, Luckies, Chesterfields, Old Golds, all had good paper and good tin foil, both of which were separable, unlike the mode today where they cheapen everything, gluing thin paper to thin foil (it isn't even tin but an ersatz of some kind, a plastic innovation) so that you can't separate the two to make tin foil balls. There's nothing like real tin foil balls. In my opinion (which is a valuable one) only Sun Pictures may be superior, and even so it's a pretty even go.

One day Segal, Bacigalupi and I were playing immies in the street along Unie when Botchie saw it first, an Old Goldie. Someone had thrown it next to the curb, next to an automobile and you couldn't see it too well, but he saw it and made a dive for it. He took off the cellophane, then the jacket, and then he carefully peeled the tin foil off the inner paper it was attached to; you could always get it all off, but it was more fun to get all the foil off in one piece because then you could wrap it better. Botchie took a two inch silver ball out of his pocket and wrapped the foil around it. He let me hold it; it was nice and solid and heavy, like a lead ball, which meant he hadn't stuffed any paper or other foreign matter in it, or left any paper in it unpeeled from previous foils. This was a dandy.

We went down the Unie hill towards 168th Street, where it turns to the right down to the 44th precinct station on Sedgwick Avenue, and then I saw it, lying in the grass bordering the sidewalk, the most coveted one of all. A Herbert Tarreyton. I said before there were only four brands of cigarettes and that is true in the popular sense; you only saw people smoking four brands. My Aunt Mary for example smoked Old Golds and my Uncle Martin Chesterfields. The other brands that nobody smoked were Wings, long cheap things that Schapiro tried to pawn off on you when you were in high school and smoked loosies. There were Murads, Egyptian oval cigarettes in a fancy box with a pyramid on it and fancy tin foil that was so thin that it was unusable in tin foil balls, and I can honestly say I never saw anyone smoke one when I was a boy although I myself tried them once after the war. And there were mentholated Spuds, a precursor of the gimmicky cigarettes they sell today. And finally there were Herbert Tarreytons . . .

First of all, Tarreyton was an Englishman who wore striped pants and looked like Anthony Eden. His cigarettes had a firm cork tip, real cork, not a gaudy paper imitation. I didn't smoke at that time so I don't know how the tobacco tastes but I do know this: Herbert Tarreyton had far and away the best tin foil, you could even call it lead foil it was so thick and heavy, and it was worth three or four of the others. It really felt good wrapping it around your tin foil ball, and as I did so that afternoon I could see the envy written all over Segal and Botchie's faces. That was a memorable day, one of the greatest in my life.

It should be clear now why tin foil balls were such an important institution, and rumor had it that if you got your ball up to a few pounds, a five incher, you could sell it like gold and silver. It was an extremely valuable possession.

I once read a book about a man named Quixote, where the author argued that he was the greatest praiser of times past because everything was so wonderful then and the words *thine* and *mine* didn't exist and young ladies roamed the fields at night unmolested. Someone once suggested that I am like that, that I tend to praise the good old days because I can't stand the people I work with. There may be some truth in the latter statement but I don't think I'm just a praiser of times past, not at all, I am merely writing down the events from memory, as they are served up to me, Sun Pictures, P.S. 11, Tin Foil Balls, Stickball and the other institutions and writing them down. That's all. Look at the way I write. No fancy prose, no rhetoric, no embellishment. I am merely writing facts, historical facts, as they actually happened and these facts tell me this, I know it with certitude: Things were better in the Bronx in the 1930's. There can be no doubt about it.

TOPS

In the fall tops were on a par with Cheesebox, Tin Foil Balls, immies and checkers. You could spin them underhand or overhand, underhand was easier, and buy them for anywhere from three cents to more than a quarter; the three cent tops had a nail for a point, the better ones a ball bearing, and some were even manufactured with air ducts that whistled when they whirled. We used to spin tops to knock out the other guy's, and I remember people "walking" a top with a string, or on a string. When we spun our tops we tried to avoid coarse sidewalks, and sometimes we spun them on a movable surface like a board and then hop them over to another surface by flipping the board. Tops were fun indoors, where you could practice spinning them on the kitchen floor because kitchen linoleum is far and away the best surface for tops. I am a Bronx authority on the subject, and I ought to know.

TRAIN

Trains, not subway trains, weren't important in the Bronx unless you lived near one as we did over on University Avenue. We walked from Unie down to Undy down the park steps where we played king of the hill, to Sedgwick, across Sedgwick through Washington Park beneath the bridge, to the river. There was a big field there where the grass never grew, I never learned why, and a few times we played football. But we went down there mainly to see the trains and to stay away from the third rail; there was a rumor that if you touched the third rail you'd be thrown fifty feet in the air and die so we stayed away from it though we sometimes threw things at it to see if anything would happen. Sometimes we crossed the tracks to the river bank and watched the scum bags come out on the other side of the river. But most of all we watched the trains, big steam monsters, huffing and puffing as they got under way. High Bridge Station was only a long block away so many of the trains didn't go roaring through but were slowing down or starting up slowly. I have always preferred steam engines like the ones we knew in the Bronx when I was a boy to diesels. Diesels have no charm. Once, right after the war I took my Aunt Madge to the Highbridge Station to catch her train to Cleveland; somehow this was my last look, of her and Highbridge and the trains. They were all so beautiful, not like the airports you see today where everyone's in such a hurry rushing from one plastic bucket seat to another. Oh the trains! The steam engine! It's an objective fact: things were more beautiful in the old days.

TRIANGLE BALL

Another subgenre of Stickball. See the article on Boxball, above. The following illustration will help you understand Triangle Ball:

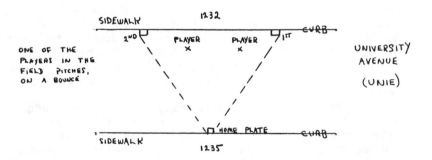

In Boxball you had three or four men on a side, in Triangle Ball only two.

209

TROLLEY CAR
I know I spoke about trolley cars before but I must list them here also. They deserve double mention, triple and quadruple and whatever comes after that. Ancient trireme, yacht, schooner, cart, wagon, bus, automobile, glider, airplane, man has never devised a more certain, safe and aesthetic mode of transportation. Even the steam engine comes after the trolley car. The Z, the U, the O, the W, the X, cars of certain destination, taking you to the Zoo and Yankee Stadium. I am an optimist. There is no Hades and no boat of Charon to cross it. Someday soon I shall ride you again, oh trolley car, we shall all ride you as we ascend the celestial Parnassus. Heaven rides on trolley cars.

TWO FOR FLINCHIN'
A major phase in Bronx NOMENCLATURE (q.v.).

VANNIE AND MACOMBS
I have seen many fine parks, in Cincinnati, Louisville, Milwaukee, Madrid, London, Mexico City, but I have never seen one to rival Van Cortlandt Park in my native Bronx, New York. And I have seen some fine buildings, Chapultepec Castle for instance, but they don't come near Joe Bogan's boat house where you rented a row boat in summer and went skating in winter. And Joe Bogan's hot dogs were almost as good as Nedick's. I need say no more.

For one thing, when I went to Vannie I had to take the U trolley all the way north to the end of the line, get off and walk past the golf course, as tough as Augusta they say, to Joe Bogan's, where the activities commenced. I have gone sleigh riding on that Vannie golf course and know that the hills were long and steep so they must have been monsters for the golfer.

Famous people went to Vannie; Leslie MacMitchell used to run there and I remember the day he came in first in Cross Country, two minutes ahead of the rest of the pack; he breathed deeply a couple of times and put on his sweat suit as if that was all there was to it. Some of the runners who came in five minutes after him were sick to their stomach. Leslie's 4:07 miles were world speed and he beat Cunningham, Fenske, Venske, Mangan, McCloskey and all of them. He ran for New York University at 183rd and Unie in the Bronx, which knew how to train its athletes: send them to Vannie.

Macombs Dam Park was different; instead of thousands of acres like Vannie, it was a few acres, just enough to make up a quarter mile track. Macombs Dam Park—we never had a nickname for it—was a stone's throw from the Yankee Stadium. It was fun going down there under the El tracks on Jerome Avenue, where I scored a point once for running fourth in the mile in a triangular meet featuring All Saints, St. Raphael and Cyprianus. In dual meets you needed fifteen points for a school letter but in triangular and county meets you only needed one, so I got mine. I ran a five thirty mile.

WAGONS, CON ED

The electric company was the Consolidated Edison Company, commonly known as Con Ed. Once a year repairs were made or new wires were introduced, so they'd come around, dig a six foot hole in the cement and set to work. When the job required several days they'd leave a red wagon in the street about the size of a delivery boy's only shaped like half a hexagon on top and with a far more substantial handle bar. Delivery boy's wagon was light and frail, swift and silent like a deer whereas Con Ed's was more like a water buffalo, locked so no one could get inside and more solid than a Brink's truck; its wheels were tougher though smaller than delivery boy's. Sometimes Con Ed would leave their red wagon for a month, so every day we had something to play on, the handle becoming a gymnastic bar. Electricians today drive around in flimsy vans, they don't have anything like the old wagons. My hat's off to Con Ed wagons, the Bronx 1930.

WAGONS, DELIVERY

The delivery boys had hand carts, six feet long, two feet nine inches across, eighteen inches deep, with large thin steel wheels and a nice broad handle. One of the delivery boys, Kochenmeister, was sixty years old. I always wanted to be a delivery boy; they marched their wagons proudly down Merriam Hill, stopped at the House Of All Nations, selected one of their boxes, heisted it to their shoulder and proceeded into the entrance and up the steps. One boy had the confident wholesome look of someone who knew what he was doing and when he came out of the apartment he lit his cigarette and blew smoke in the air. He was mature. I wanted to be like that, mature. But as usual, Murphys couldn't be delivery boys; they had to be something. Delivery boys were downstairs.

WESTERN UNION

Western Union boys had olive uniforms, like the Army's. They were real keen. See Postal Telegraph, above.

YANKEES

Any dictionary of Bronx idiom would have to list the New York Yankees with the understanding that *Yankees* included the old New York Giants of Polo Ground fame. Nowhere do I know of two super powers so obviously confronting each other as the New York Yankees on the Bronx side of the river and the New York Giants across the river at Coogan's bluff. In the World Series they met at the summit.

I remember seeing the Yankees when I was a young boy, Gehrig at first, push-em-up-a Tony Lazzeri at second, Frankie Crosetti at short, Red Rolfe at third, Bill Dickey catching, Red

211

Ruffing pitching or Lefty Gomez, and in center field the Sultan of Swat, the man who built the Yankee Stadium, Babe Ruth. I don't remember exactly who played left and right field in those days, maybe it was Twinkle Toes Selkirk, Tommy Henrich or Charley King Kong Keller, but whoever it was they were good. I remember Babe Ruth touching second base with his left foot every time he trotted in from the field, and it seems to me Frankie Crosetti always led off with a triple; he also pulled the hidden ball trick once on a runner and tagged him out off second. Although a pitcher Charlie Ruffing was a .300 lifetime batter whom they used to send in as a pinch hitter. Oh yes, I left out Ben Chapman, whom I saw hit an inside-the-park home run one time; try that one on for size, how do you like them apples?

Across the Harlem in the Polo Grounds Carl Hubbel was no slouch winning twenty-eight games in a row, and Gus Mancuso was an outstanding catcher. Mel Ott, who started in the majors at sixteen, had a way of pulling up that leg when he hit the ball out of the park, and Freddie Fitzsimmons used to face out towards second, away from the batter, kicking his leg just before he turned and pitched. I also liked Hal Schumacher. I mention the Yankees and Giants in one breath under the entry *Yankees* because many Bronx fans rooted for the Giants, for example Jimmy Hanrahan at All Saints did and he went to see many more games than the rest of us. Speaking of Jimmy Hanrahan reminds me of the betting pool at All Saints; the Bronx citizens there bet a nickel on six hits or more; they named three players who had to get six hits among them and then the bettor got paid five to one. That was during the late thirties and 1940, so everyone picked DiMaggio and all the players on the Brooklyn Dodgers, Duke Snyder, Dixie Walker, Pistol Pete Rieser, Pee Wee Reese, Babe Herman and Carl Furillo; one day Babe Herman went six for six and lots of the Bronx citizens cleaned up. Ted Williams was in there too for the Red Sox and he was always good for two for five providing they didn't walk him, but then he was one for two, which though .500 for the day didn't help you when you were looking for six hits. The odds were definitely stacked against you and yet I seemed to win sometimes.

I have never liked baseball since, not the way I liked it in those days. I could tell you everyone's average, was familiar with players like Paul and Lloyd Waner, Big Poison and Little Poison, and even knew how Hal Trotsky and Little Roy Weatherley were doing out on the Cleveland Indians. Bobby Feller was there too. Baseball meant a great deal to me; I don't know why, it doesn't any more, now I like football and basketball. Perhaps television has something to do with it, it has ruined the game. Baseball was meant to be played at 3:05 every afternoon with peanuts and hot dogs in the summer at the Yankee Stadium. Baseball was better in the old days. Ted Williams says that if they don't get back to that old 3:05 schedule there'll never be another .400 hitter because the man at bat can't be playing at night one day and noon the next, he needs the regularity.

YO YO

Yo Yo's weren't strictly a Bronx Institution but I remember one afternoon in the thirties some strange people came to University Avenue near 1261, probably Hong Kong people or Hawaiians, just before the *Saturday Evening Post* man came, so it must have been a Friday. They wore sleeveless sweaters with red, white and blue American emblems on them and they carried Yo Yo's. They were experts on the Yo Yo. I imagine now they were on an advertising campaign for a new discovery, the Yo Yo, but at the time I saw them as strange, different, a new variety. Variety: The Bronx was very beautiful. We had everything in the Bronx, from Turkish Supers (q.v.) to Yo Yos. Life was interesting then, not like it is now, plastic, monolithic, drab.

ZOO

I mentioned Zoo in Chapter 4 when I spoke of my father but I list it here since it deserves reiteration. It is common knowledge that the Bronx Zoo is the best zoo in the world with the greatest number and most vigorous of animals. It is even closed one day a week so that doctoral students of animal life can go there and in this sense resembles a library with outstanding primary sources. But I remember the bird house, lions, hippos, elephants, peanuts and chippies, above all the peanuts and chippies when my father took me to the zoo. That was 1930, the Bronx Boy 1930.

ADDENDUM

CAP PISTOLS

How could I have forgotten Cap Pistols? What a terrible omission! They were your main utensil from four to ten and consequently your main source of personal expression. You could buy them for a dime or a quarter, the latter sum purchasing a weapon of high quality, and you could even get them with pearl handles in leather holsters with a belt webbed for holding wooden bullets for two dollars or more, something your uncle might give you for Christmas. Usually you had a roll of fifty caps purchased for a nickel, but one year some Edison invented new caps for six shooters that looked like this:

THE CAP PAPER WAS ALWAYS RED.

The black dots in the illustration represent the six points of explosive powder and as you shot your caps the cap disk turned with the chamber of your new six shooter, putting a new source of energy before the hammer. You could count your shots, and after six of them you knew you had to pull out the burnt disk and insert a new one, which made shooting Indians a lot easier.

I learned something in 1980 that I never knew before. I was talking to an older female student one afternoon when her two little boys, 6 and 7 years old, came running up and pointed their cap pistols at me and yelled Bang! Bang! I had never realized it before: those cap pistols were phallic symbols and two little courageous manly boys were protecting their mommy by driving an old bull away. I admired their fortitude and since then rarely speak to older female students. I am afraid of being put to shame by a six year old man. You should always take such persons seriously.

26. Compline

I sing of the Bronx, I sing of golden days of yore, of Kelly, Bacigalupi and Segal, Denny, Big Phelan and Billy who died in the war; of the O and U and Z, swaying cars moving in rhythm; of P.S. 11, Mrs. Kavidson and Adrienne; Vannie, Macombs and the Harlem; the El, Menasha Skulnik signs; Sacred Heart Bazaar; Mary Janes, Loosies, Gowdy Gum cards; sun pictures, cheesebox and orange crate; tin foil balls, tops, horse manure balls; 'cheese it the cops', 'the parkie's coming'; Sedgwick and Unie, Undie and Concourse; anything-for-Thanksgiving and baseball-against-the-wall. I sing of the Bronx and I say: "I have seen the Elysian Fields, more than that I have lived there. I know. I speak not from faith but experience, I do not believe, *I know*. Mount Parnassus, Arcadia, Plato's sun, they are real. I have been there. Bacigalupi never lied to me nor I to him, how could we? What would we lie for? Kelly never stole from me nor I from him, what would we steal? You won immies, you didn't steal them. And Segal never gossiped about me nor I about him, what would we gossip about? His sun pictures were as beautiful as mine; the only talk I ever heard was of Jackie Smealy, the time he threw manure at Phelan, but that wasn't gossip, that was fear. Real fear. Everyone's afraid of horse manure balls. No, I have been there, I don't believe, I know. St. Paul says that hope and faith will pass away but never love, that love will always be there. And he's right because he must have seen it too, in a vision, the Bronx, Paul of Tarsus he saw the Bronx. You didn't have to believe, you saw it with your own eyes, candy store. You didn't have to hope, you knew the orange crates would be waiting, diamond ball, lots and mickies, they always were, you could take them for granted. Love was everywhere, we all loved cheesebox, stickball and P.S. 11, we all did, yes. I have seen the celestial plains. I have lived there, the Bronx 1930 when I was a boy, the Vanished Arcadia, you can take my word for it, we never lied in the Bronx.

That's why everything in this book is absolutely true, I wouldn't write it down if it wasn't. We never lied in the Bronx.

Amen.

Special Note On The Eve Of Going To Press

On September 1, 1986 Anna Murphy received a letter from the United States Department of State.

—Arturo Lynch
Ultimate Editor

About the Author

Gerard Flynn remembers the Bronx of O and X trolley cars, Saturday morning movie serials and Candy Store, Lou Gehrig and neighborhood stickball, Gowdy Gum Company cards and Ringalevio Caw Caw Caw. Educated in P.S. 11 on Ogden Avenue, he went on to a parochial high school, Fordham, Columbia and New York University, where he took a doctoral degree in Spanish. He has taught at four universities, the most recent being the University of Wisconsin-Milwaukee. When asked to describe his novel *The Bronx Boy*, he is fond of comparing it to Doctorow's Mt. Eden Avenue "from the other side of the street". The Bronx Boy is James Ignatius Murphy, Jims, who tells of his life in Highbridge on the west side from 1924 to 1940 and then describes his experiences in the Navy and Marine aviation. Jims also witnesses the decline of American universities.

Gerard Flynn lives with his family on a lake in Sheboygan County, thirty-five miles north of Milwaukee. Looking at the lake, he says, he can visualize the figures he knew more than fifty years ago: Bacigalupi, Segal, Kelly, Adrienne Kalm . . . Brother Solomon, Feigenbaum and Winnie, who died in the war.